The
REVENANT
of
THRAXTON HALL

ALSO BY VAUGHN ENTWISTLE

Angel of Highgate

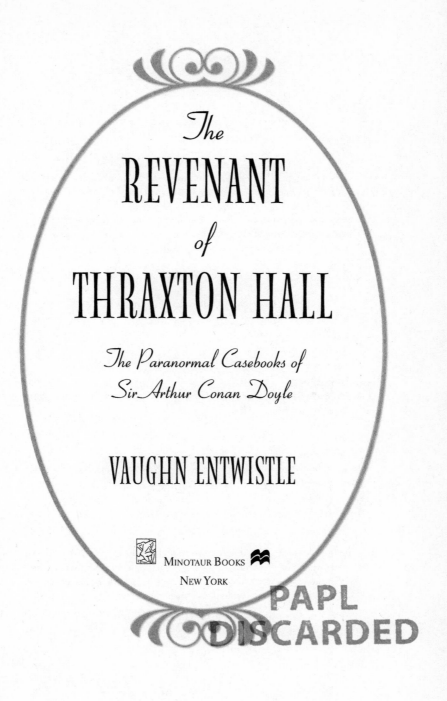

The

REVENANT

of

THRAXTON HALL

*The Paranormal Casebooks of
Sir Arthur Conan Doyle*

VAUGHN ENTWISTLE

MINOTAUR BOOKS

NEW YORK

THE REVENANT OF THRAXTON HALL. Copyright © 2014 by Vaughn Entwistle. All rights reserved. Printed in the United States of America. For information, address St. Martin's Press, 175 Fifth Avenue, New York, N.Y. 10010.

www.minotaurbooks.com

Design by Meryl Sussman Levavi

Illustrations by Laura Hartman Maestro

Library of Congress Cataloging-in-Publication Data
Entwistle, Vaughn.
    The Revenant of Thraxton Hall : the Paranormal Casebooks of Sir Arthur Conan Doyle / Vaughn Entwistle. — 1st ed.
        pages cm
    ISBN 978-1-250-03500-4 (hardcover)
    ISBN 978-1-250-03501-1 (e-book)
    1. Doyle, Arthur Conan, 1859–1930—Fiction.   2. London (England)—Fiction.
3. Mystery fiction.   I. Title.
    PR6105.N89R48 2014
    823'.92—dc23
                                                            2013032875

Minotaur books may be purchased for educational, business, or promotional use. For information on bulk purchases, please contact Macmillan Corporate and Premium Sales Department at 1-800-221-7945, extension 5442, or write specialmarkets@macmillan.com.

First Edition: March 2014

10 9 8 7 6 5 4 3 2 1

This book is dedicated to my wife, Shelley,

my inamorata now and forever. . .

CONTENTS

ACKNOWLEDGMENTS

First and foremost I have to thank my beloved wife, Shelley, for believing in me and encouraging my lifelong dream of becoming a novelist. For this and myriad other reasons, she continues to be the best part of my time on earth.

Thanks to my agent, Kimberley Cameron, of Kimberley Cameron and Associates. Kind, supportive, and immensely capable, Kimberley is a writer's dream agent.

Thanks to my posse of faithful readers: Cindy Thompson, Andrea Steckler, Nancy Coy, and Kristina Wright. I am lucky to have friends like these, who've diligently read most of everything I've written and have provided me with vital feedback.

I would also like to thank St. Martin's Press and my illustrious editors, executive editor Keith Kahla and his editorial assistant, Hannah Braaten, for their guidance and support through the publishing process.

Finally, I must acknowledge Sir Arthur Conan Doyle and Oscar Wilde, true literary giants whose genius has left an enduring legacy for readers and writers alike.

The

REVENANT

of

THRAXTON HALL

CHAPTER 1

A VOICE IN THE DARK

Sherlock Holmes is dead . . . and I have killed him.

The smartly dressed young Scotsman stared blindly through raindrops beading down the hansom cab window. Submerged in reverie, he did not notice that the cab had stopped. He did not see the limestone residences, nor their marble steps guarded by iron railings. All he heard, all he saw, were the misty wraiths of the world's greatest consulting detective and his arch-nemesis, Professor Moriarty, as they plummeted into a cataract of roaring waters, grappling in a final death-struggle.

A hatch in the ceiling above his head opened, and the driver of the hansom cab rained down a patter of gravelly syllables: "We're here, guv'nor."

The words jolted Arthur Conan Doyle into awareness. The seething vapors of the Reichenbach Falls evaporated and a London street materialized before him. He blinked, at a momentary loss. Where was he? Why had he taken a cab? Then he looked down at his lap and the torn envelope curling in the grip of his rain-dampened gloves.

A courier had delivered the letter that morning to his South Norwood home in the suburbs of London. He drew the cream-colored paper from its envelope and shook it open. The handwriting was elegant and unmistakably feminine. For a moment, Conan Doyle's soft brown eyes traced the loops and whorls of the penmanship.

Dear Dr. Doyle,

I crave an audience with the noted author of the Sherlock Holmes mysteries on a concern of the utmost gravity. This is a matter of mortal peril, and I believe that only an intellect such as yours can prevent a tragedy. Please visit me at number 42 _____ Crescent on Tuesday morning. Arrive no earlier than ten a.m.

Please help. I am a lady in desperate straits.

In place of a signature, the letter was signed with an elegant flourish.

An anonymous address.

A nameless summoner.

But as he tilted the page to the light, a phoenix watermark floated up from the fine stationery. Despite himself, he felt the stirrings of a coalescing mystery that would have intrigued his Sherlock Holmes.

A figure brushed past the cab window—he caught a vague, rain-blurred impression of a man in a hat, walking head down, a hand to his chin. No, holding something to his mouth—a cigarette or a pipe.

It was the briefest of glimpses. A momentary flash. And then it was gone.

The cab driver yanked a lever; the cab door flung open and Conan Doyle stepped down from the hansom. As he rummaged his pockets for loose change, a wraith of tobacco smoke swirled in the damp London air. His head snapped up as he caught a whiff. He threw a quick glance to his side, but saw only rain-puddled pavements and the endless parade of city traffic: black two- and four-wheelers drawn by plodding horses, their breath pluming in the damp air, hooves clop-clopping on the wet cobblestones.

The smoker had vanished.

He shook the image from his head and handed up two shillings to the driver. As he turned and took a step toward the glistening marble steps, it occurred to him to ask the cabbie to wait.

But too late—the driver whistled, shook the reins, and the cab rattled away.

Conan Doyle paused to peer up at the elegant, six-storey Mayfair home. But when he raised his head, an icy March rain needled his eyes. He dropped his gaze and, in a fashion surprisingly nimble for a big man, skipped up the rain-slick steps, anxious not to dampen his best top hat and coat.

The entrance of number 42 _____ Crescent featured a magnificent eight-paneled oak door painted a deep Venetian red. A large brass knocker provided the door's centerpiece—a phoenix rising from its nest of flames.

The exact double of the notepaper's watermark.

His gloved fingers grasped the knocker, raised it, and brought it sharply down upon its anvil with the percussive report of a pistol shot. He was about to knock a second time when the door flung inward, snatching the brass phoenix from his grasp.

A red-turbaned footman—a Sikh gentleman—swept the door aside as if he'd been lurking behind it.

Waiting.

Wordlessly, the servant drew Conan Doyle inside with a low bow and a beckoning wave of his white-gloved hand. The entrance hall, though opulent, was a gloomy snare of shadows. His breath fogged the air—it was colder inside than out. The footman took his hat and coat without a word, hung them upon a naked coat stand, and led the way to a closed set of double doors.

"Please to wait inside, sahib," he said in heavily accented English.

The servant bowed again and held the door open. Conan

Doyle stepped inside—and recoiled. The room was some kind of windowless antechamber, sparsely furnished with low couches and bookshelves. But further detail was hard to make out, as the room was even darker than the entrance hall. The only illumination came from the stuttering light of a single gas jet turned low.

"Just one moment!" Conan Doyle began to protest. "Am I to be cast into the darkness?"

Despite his complaints, the door was softly but firmly shut in his face.

"Wait! What? What is the meaning?" he yelled, and snatched at the door handle, which refused to turn.

Locked.

Outraged, he rattled the handle and banged a meaty fist on the door.

"See here you fool, you've locked me . . ." Conan Doyle fell silent as he tumbled to the truth: it was no accident.

In rising dudgeon, he strode across the room to the far door and seized the knob. But a firm yank revealed that it, too, was locked. The young doctor released a gasp of astonished umbrage and looked about. For several seconds he wrestled with the notion of seizing one of the end tables to use as a battering ram. But then the words of the letter ran through his head:

This is a matter of mortal peril, and I believe that only an intellect such as yours can prevent a tragedy.

Already half-convinced that he was being drawn into a web of charlatanism, Conan Doyle hitched up the legs of his trousers and dropped onto a cold leather couch, nostrils flaring as he gave a snort of indignation.

Minutes passed. Anger turned to curiosity as he idled, peering around the room. It became an interesting game, trying to fathom what was going on—the kind of game that Holmes—*NO! That part of my writing life is over. Holmes is dead and I am finally free to write the serious books I wish to write.*

In the room beyond, he heard a soft bump followed by the snick of a key turning in a lock. His eyes remained fixed upon the door, expecting it to open, but it remained closed.

"Doctor Doyle," a high, musical voice trilled from the other side. "If you would be so kind as to join me."

Conan Doyle sprang to his feet, dithered a moment, then strode to the door and flung it wide. To his surprise, the room beyond was even darker. The guttering gas jet behind him threw only a wan slab of light that sketchily illumined a hulking leather armchair. Everything else—the remainder of the room and its mysterious occupant—lay drowned in umbrous shadow.

My God! He thought. *It's a trap! I'm being kidnapped.* Conan Doyle owned a pistol, but seldom carried it.

Now he very much wished his service revolver was tucked into his waistcoat.

Every instinct told him not to enter the room. Undoubtedly, a gang of ruffians crouched in the shadows, waiting to spring upon him. But then the memory of the kohl-eyed servant conjured more exotic visions: a Thuggee assassin with his knotted silken kerchief, anxious to slip it around a white man's throat and snap his neck.

"Now see here!" Conan Doyle barked, hoping the steel in his voice would mask his rising fear. "I trust I have not been sent on a fool's errand. I am a busy man and have many pressing affairs—"

"Please, Doctor Doyle, forgive the unorthodox greeting. If you would kindly take a seat, I can explain."

Despite his fear, there was something about the voice, an earnestness that made him wish to linger, to find out more about its owner. He stiffened his posture and harrumphed noisily to show that he was not a man to be trifled with, then threw back his shoulders and strode into the room, his large hands balled into fists, ready to hurl a punch. When he stood before the armchair the voice spoke again: "Please, sir, be seated."

In the gloom, the chair proved lower than estimated, the drop farther, and he thumped into the cushion with a spine-jarring jolt, expelling air with an "oof!" The door, which he had left ajar, groaned slowly shut under its own weight and latched with a clunk. Darkness blindfolded his eyes. Shadows bound him to the chair. Arthur Conan Doyle found himself a prisoner of obsidian night.

Total.

Absolute.

He gripped the arms of the leather chair, feeling suddenly off-balance.

"I beg you, sir," the voice soothed. "Do not be alarmed. I—I owe you an explanation: the reason we must meet in darkness."

The leather arms creaked as he slackened his death grip.

"You are obviously at great pains to conceal your identity," Conan Doyle said, his mind racing ahead. The attempt at anonymity was pointless—it would be a simple matter to trace the owner of such a distinctive house.

"No," the woman said. "The reason is that I suffer—" Her voice grew taut. "I suffer from an affliction."

"An—an affliction?" Conan Doyle started at the loudness of his own voice. Hideous visions flashed before him. The woman must suffer from a disfiguring disease. "An affliction?" he repeated, affecting a neutral tone.

"Do not be concerned," she hurried to reassure. "It is not contagious. It is, rather, a disease carried through the bloodlines of my family. For me, every ray of sunlight is a needle dipped in arsenic. Even the wan glow of a lamp is a cloud of slow poison oozing through my skin."

For moments, Conan Doyle did not speak, his pulse quickening. As a doctor, he had heard talk of such an ailment: *porphyria*, a congenital disease. There was even a rumor that this malady touched the family of the royal personage.

Think, Arthur! he chided himself. *Think as your Holmes would do.*

By now the total darkness had become oppressive and a rising sense of vertigo told him that the chair and the floor beneath his feet were rotating slowly backward and to the left. The sensation was strengthened by the impression that the woman's voice seemed to be moving around the room, first left and now right and then, most disturbingly, floating up to where he imagined the ceiling to be.

He blinked, and his vision swarmed with ghosts. As a medical man and student of the eyes, he knew the specters were a natural phenomenon—the light-recepting cells on the surface of the retina firing spontaneously like mirrors bleeding light in a darkened room. Deprived of sight, Conan Doyle opened his other senses to sieve every possible clue. First, the voice. Female. Definitely. He had seen convincing fakes on the stages of the less-reputable music halls. And while strolling in the most dangerous parts of London, seeking physical sights and sounds and sensations for his mysteries, he had been solicited by lissome creatures who dressed in daring women's fashions but who possessed Adam's apples and husky voices.

No, he was certain. The voice sprang from feminine lips. But there was something about it, an uncanny aspect. His mind summoned the word from the shadows around him—ethereal.

"I understand you wish to protect the good name of your family," Conan Doyle said. "But might I at least know your first name?"

A momentary silence followed as the woman mulled his request. "Forgive me, but I wish to remain anonymous. However, should you find it in your power to assist me, I will reveal all."

He cleared his throat. "I am a writer, madam, a mere scribbler of tales. I do not know what I could possibly—"

"It is a case of murder," she said bluntly.

The words cradled on Conan Doyle's tongue languished and died. "Murder?" he repeated.

"Murder. Violent. Sudden." Her final words came out in a strangled voice. "And premeditated."

Conan Doyle cleared this throat. He had somehow known this was coming and dreaded it. "I am afraid I cannot help you, madam. I am no policeman. Nor am I a detective. However, I do have many contacts at Scotland Yard—"

"I have already spoken to the police," she interrupted, disdain icing her words. "As to the detectives at Scotland Yard, they were— I am afraid to say—unable to offer the least assistance."

"But as I said, I am no policeman."

"And yet you have created the world's most renowned detective?"

There was a time Conan Doyle would have been flattered by the compliment, but now he felt only irritation. "A trifling fiction, madam. It is a common misconception held by my readers. Sherlock Holmes is a mere phantasm of my imagination. A bit of whimsy. All my adventures, I am afraid, have taken place at my writing desk. All in my mind."

He did not bother to inform her that he had recently killed off the "world's most renowned detective." All of London would soon be buzzing with the news.

"And is the mind not the most dangerous battlefield of all?"

It was a penetrating observation and left him momentarily groping for a rejoinder.

"As I previously stated, madam, I am not with the police. If you believe a murder has taken place—"

"No, Mister Doyle," the woman hastened to explain. "That is my problem. I need you to solve a murder . . . that has not yet taken place."

Leather squeaked as he shifted in the armchair. He fought the giddy sensation that her voice had swooped above his head and that she now stood behind his chair, a hand hovering over one shoulder, ready to alight.

"I am sorry, I do not understand you."

"I will be murdered in two weeks' time."

"Has someone threatened your life? How can you possibly know—?"

"I am a spiritualist medium of some renown. I have moments of clairvoyance. Visions of events that have yet to happen. For the last year I have had the same premonition. The details loom sharper with time. In two weeks I will be murdered during a séance—shot twice in the chest."

The fiction writer in Conan Doyle immediately saw the logical flaw in such a story. "But if you can foresee the future, then surely you must see the face of your murderer?"

"Unfortunately, no. That is hidden from me. The room is lit only by candlelight and the faces of the sitters little more than smudges of light and shadow. There is, however, one face that is recognizable—the face of the sitter on the murderer's left hand. Until six months ago, I had no name to put to that face. But then I saw a photograph in *The Strand Magazine* of an esteemed author. It was your photograph: Doctor Arthur Conan Doyle, the true genius behind Sherlock Holmes. You are the man I see in my visions."

Moments passed before he found his voice. "Madam. Many people have dreams, visions—what you will. Most are silly, illogical, and only have a meaning we ascribe to them. Few truly foretell the future."

His words marched out into the darkness and tumbled over a cliff into silence.

When the woman spoke again, there was a hitch in her voice. "I believe these dreams, Doctor Doyle. I believe I will be murdered.

I also believe you are the only one who can prevent my death. Will you please help me?"

The voice seemed to be moving, gliding past his left shoulder. A faint breeze caressed his cheek. His nostrils pooled with the musk of perfume. He heard the swish of silken thighs brushing together, a sound that sprang prurient visions into his mind. He imagined a young woman, dressed in nothing more substantial than the diaphanous pantaloons of a harem girl. He found himself becoming aroused and wiped his sweaty palms on the arms of the chair, struggling to empty his mind of such thoughts.

He was a married man. A gentleman. A doctor.

"What do you say, Doctor Doyle?" He started as he felt warm breath lick the bowl of his ear. She must be standing next to him. Touchably close. "Will you help a young woman in distress?"

Something in her voice made him want to believe. Want to help. Want to save her.

But then he thought of his wife. Of the impropriety.

The year just passed had been the most turbulent in Conan Doyle's thirty-four years. His father, Charles Altamont Doyle, had finally died in a madhouse after a lifelong battle with melancholia and alcoholism. His beloved wife, Louise, had been diagnosed with galloping consumption and, despite the advances of modern medicine, her lungs were shredding to rags. He could not help this young woman for many of the same reasons he had killed off his most successful artistic creation, Sherlock Holmes, for Arthur Conan Doyle no longer believed in a world where a man—even a man with advanced powers such as a consulting detective or a medical doctor—could alter Fate.

"I—I am afraid I must decline," he stuttered. "But as I said, I personally know many of Scotland Yard's best—"

"Thank you for your time, Doctor Doyle," the woman interrupted, her voice cracking with disappointment. "You have been most kind."

"No, I beg you to reconsider. My offer is genuine. Inspector Harrison is a personal friend—"

"I will detain you no longer. Please forgive the imposition."

He felt a stir in the air currents and heard a soft bump and the rasp of a key turning in a lock.

He was left to grope his way out in the darkness.

Alone.

THE MOST HATED MAN IN LONDON

As the hansom cab turned onto Strand Street, Conan Doyle noticed that a crowd thronged the pavement outside the offices of *The Strand Magazine* and spilled out onto the road. For the past four years, *The Strand* had enjoyed an arrangement as exclusive publisher of the Sherlock Holmes stories, and the Baker Street detective had boosted circulation so that queues formed outside newsstands whenever a new story was published. In turn, the stories had made a wealthy man of their author.

But now, as the cab drew up, Conan Doyle noticed with surprise that many in the crowd clutched crudely drawn signs and wore black armbands. He quickly surmised that some major figure in British public life had died and assumed the worst: the death of the queen or the queen's consort—at the very least, the prime minister or a beloved national hero. On the last score, he was correct, albeit in a fashion he could not have foreseen.

He stepped down from the cab and handed up a coin. The driver snatched it and, impatient to be gone, lashed the horses' ears most cruelly. The two-wheeler lurched away like a cheap piece of stage scenery, suddenly revealing Conan Doyle to his audience. For a moment, the two regarded one another. His eyes scanned the crudely scrawled signs: BRING BACK HOLMES and SAVE OUR HERO. It was a touching display of public sympathy mourning the loss of a beloved fictional hero, and the doctor's eyes moistened. But then he noticed other signs that read: MURDERER!, BLACKGUARD!, and CONAN THE COWARD!

Mutual recognition happened at the same instant; the crowd roiled into a snake pit of hisses, boos, and angry, shaken fists.

Something arced high in the air—a hurled cabbage—and smacked Conan Doyle straight in the face, staggering him backward and toppling his hat. Stunned, he stooped to recover his topper as a second cabbage shattered greenly off his broad shoulder. He stood gaping in astonishment.

"Bloody swine!" shrieked a slatternly woman's voice.

"Murderin' Barsterd!" a coarse-bearded navvy brayed, and spat a gleaming oyster in his direction.

More invective followed, in an even more profane fashion. Worse yet, so did the rotted refuse of an entire barrow, flung by angry fists, all following a trajectory toward Conan Doyle's large head.

He raised both arms in a gesture of appeasement and summoned his best public speaking voice to quell the near riot.

"Good people. If I might speak a few words—"

A hand grabbed him by the collar of his overcoat and hauled him away, just in time to avoid another volley.

The hand belonged to a young redheaded fellow with a wisp of post-pubescent whiskers prickling his chin. The man, a boy really, probably five years shy of his twenties, wore a broad, news runner's cap pulled down over his large ears.

"Beggin' your pardon, Mister Doyle," he apologized as he struggled to drag the author's muscular bulk toward the front doors of *The Strand*, "but Mister Smith is in a right tizzy to see you." A shriveled tomato whizzed low overhead, narrowly missing both men. "But perhaps not as anxious as this bloody rabble!"

Still reeling, Conan Doyle allowed himself to be dragged inside. As they slammed the doors on the unruly mob, a vegetable avalanche drummed against the glass.

"Mister Smith is waitin', sir. We'd best go straight up."

Conan Doyle snatched his coat sleeve from the young man's grip, refusing to be manhandled any further. "Enough!" he barked. "I can see for myself the tenor of the situation." He agitatedly brushed shreds of cabbage and splattered tomato from his shoulders and coat sleeves. Feeling eyes upon him, he looked up. The normal hubbub of the office was silent. Pressmen, reporters, runners, every man-jack in the place was staring at him, their ink-smeared faces etched with the doomed resignation of passengers on board a sinking ocean liner—and he was the captain who had steered them onto the rocks.

* * *

"I see that I am the most hated man in London," Conan Doyle said as he entered the office of Herbert Greenhough Smith, *The Strand Magazine*'s senior editor.

Smith was barely visible behind collapsing heaps of mail stacked high on his desk. "H.G." was a man in his thirties with round glasses and a bushy moustache that challenged Conan Doyle's in its extravagance. He looked up with the bleary, bloodshot eyes of a man who has enjoyed little sleep in days.

"I think you underestimate public sentiment, Arthur. You would have been more popular had you beaten the prime minister to death with a puppy whilst he was speaking before a crowd of widows and orphans."

Conan Doyle ground his molars as he pondered the remark. He indicated the letter-strewn desktop with a distracted wave. "All this?"

"Hate mail," Smith answered flatly, crumpling a letter in his hand.

"Good Lord," Conan Doyle breathed, sinking into a chair. "All since publication of 'The Adventure of the Final Problem'?"

H.G. Smith sighed and shook his head. "No. This is just the morning post! We receive another sackful with every post. We've begun heating the offices with them."

Smith tossed the crumpled letter into an overflowing wastebasket and cast an accusative stare at Doyle. "We've stopped replying to the letters. We haven't the staff."

Conan Doyle cleared his throat and quietly said, "This shall pass, H.G., I promise you."

The editor slumped in the chair, his face tragic. "Will it, Arthur? On news of the death of Sherlock Holmes we received twenty thousand canceled subscriptions. Twenty thousand! *You* may survive the death of Sherlock Holmes; I'm not sure *The Strand* will."

"*The Strand Magazine* and I are in good accounts. Fear not. I shall not abandon you."

"But why, Arthur? Why kill Sherlock Holmes?"

"Why? Because the stories are mere conundrums. Always an impossible murder inside a locked room. Cryptic final words scrawled in the victim's own blood. Inscrutable ciphers. Clues scattered here and there among the paragraphs like scraps of rubbish snagged in a hedgerow. The grand reveal at the end. It's little more than a conjuring trick performed at a child's birthday party. It is turning my brain into porridge and my reputation into a mere scribbler of penny dreadfuls. I believe it's high time I left such unprofitable nonsense behind."

The senior editor choked on an ironic laugh. "Hardly unprofitable, Arthur. Holmes has made you a rich man." His eyes widened in alarm as a sudden thought struck him. "No! Please don't tell me you're entertaining wild notions of returning full-time to medicine?"

Conan Doyle bit the inside of his cheek and ruffled his moustache in irritation. Despite all his studies, his medical career had been a complete flop. It was a truth he did not care to admit to—even to himself. For years he had spent his days writing stories in his doctor's office, blissfully uninterrupted by the nuisance of patients.

"In all honesty, I am weary of the man," Conan Doyle grumbled. "Do you know I receive letters addressed to Sherlock Holmes asking for autographs? People confuse the puppet with the puppet master." He snorted and continued, "I am afraid that Sherlock Holmes is keeping me from greater things."

"I don't see what the problem is, Arthur. You're a fast writer. You can knock out a story in two weeks! Surely you can continue to write a story a month—or every other month—in between—"

"No. It's not just that. I feel he is sapping me, like a psychic vampire, draining me."

"I like that idea!" Smith said, suddenly energized. "Sherlock Holmes and the case of the psychic vampire! It has a ring—"

"No, H.G., stop! I am done with Holmes. Now and forever. I will not change my mind."

"But he's made *you*, Arthur. He's made *The Strand*." Smith's pleading tone had devolved to a whine.

"I have many more ideas besides Sherlock Holmes."

"I have no doubt of that, Arthur, but surely—"

Conan Doyle shook his head, threw back his shoulders, and hooked his thumbs behind the lapels of his overcoat. "Many ideas, my friend. Ideas that will soon make the public forget Sherlock Holmes. Ideas that will have a real impact on the world."

Both men flinched as the office window behind H.G. Smith exploded inward, showering glass upon them. A huge cobblestone dug fresh from the road bounced off the desk and caromed forward, straight at Conan Doyle's chest. But thanks to reflexes honed by years of playing cricket, he deftly caught it in his large hands.

Smith leapt to his feet. "My God!" he gasped. "Are these people insane? That could have killed either one of us!"

"Very easily," agreed Conan Doyle, hefting the weighty stone in his hand. "I'll say this, though: whoever threw this stone has a hell of an arm—he should be bowling for the England cricket team." He thumped the cobble onto the desk in front of him. "But I'm afraid it has served only to make my decision final and utterly irrevocable. The world has seen the last of Sherlock Holmes."

Both men suddenly noticed the scrap of paper tied to the cobble with a grubby length of twine. Conan Doyle snatched the paper free and peeled it open. His eyes scanned the note and a deeply sad smile formed beneath his walrus moustache.

"What does it say?" Smith demanded.

Conan Doyle held up the paper to show him. The message was short and to the point—a single word bleeding ominously through the paper in a scrawl of red ink:

Murderer.

CHAPTER 3

WILDE IN THE CITY

Although it was barely 3:00 P.M., the city was smothering beneath one of the dense, yellow, soot-choked fogs known as a "London particular." In the unnatural twilight, amber haloes trembled about the streetlamps as the hansom dropped Conan Doyle at the front door of the Savoy.

Inside, the restaurant bustled with warmth and life and light. The author was a frequent guest at the Savoy and his entrance typically caused no excitement. But tonight, as he scanned the tables looking for the person he was meeting, heads turned and flung cold, belligerent stares in his direction. A moment later he noticed, with unease, that many of the diners also wore black armbands.

Bad news had beaten him there.

Instinct told Conan Doyle to put his head down and keep walking, as a moving target was harder to hit. Then his glance happened to fall upon a lone figure sitting at a corner table: a small schoolboy hiding behind an obviously false moustache. But then the boy made eye contact and Conan Doyle recognized it was a false child with a real moustache: J.M. Barrie, playwright and close friend, with whom he had a dinner engagement. A year ago, Conan Doyle and Barrie had pooled their collective genius to collaborate on *Jane*

Annie, a comic opera commissioned by Richard D'Oyly Carte. The play had been a resounding catastrophe, jeered by audiences and pilloried by critics. After each excruciating performance, the friends had slunk away to salve their wounds with a whiskey or three. Thankfully, *Jane Annie* closed after only fifty performances—before either man suffered permanent liver damage.

As Conan Doyle squeezed through the tight sprawl of tables, the diminutive Barrie (who at scarcely five feet in height was often mistaken for a schoolboy) rose from his chair to greet him.

"J.M.," said Arthur, swallowing the smaller man's hand in his own fleshy grip.

"Arthur."

A waiter appeared and hovered as the two settled into their chairs. Conan Doyle noticed a half-drained tumbler of scotch in front of his friend.

"I am drinking the holy waters of Mother Scotland," Barrie said, rolling the r's in his rich brogue.

"I, too, am in dire need of baptism," Conan Doyle replied. He nodded to the waiter and said, "Same for me, Henry—and make it a triple snit."

Although both men were Scottish born, after living in England for most of his life Conan Doyle's Edinburgh accent had been polished to a soft burr.

"Ach!" Barrie said, eyebrows arching in surprise. "A triple snit this early? I take it you've had a bad day, Arthur?"

"A quite beastly day," Conan Doyle snarled, pausing as the waiter set down a scotch in front of him. He then added: "Extraordinarily bad!" He quaffed a mouthful of whiskey, shuddering as it burned down his throat, then wiped a napkin across his moustache and fixed Barrie with his intense brown gaze. "But let me tell you how it began, with an encounter the like of which would seem fantastical even in a tale of fiction—"

"Ah, here is London's most celebrated murderer!" The voice that interrupted him was loud, urbane, and utterly unforgettable. Conan Doyle looked up at a large man dressed in a bottle-green cloth overcoat heavily trimmed with fur. The coat was worn thrown about his shoulders like a cape and splayed open to reveal a lemon-yellow jacket with a white silk cravat. On his head he wore a black broad-brimmed hat pulled down rakishly over one eye.

Oscar Wilde—of course, who else would dress in such a fashion? He was accompanied by a slender young man who stood too close to Wilde's shoulder, the way a pilot fish rubs up against the flanks of a shark. The young man was tall and thin with slender wrists and high cheekbones. He wore his short blond hair curled and brilliantined. With extravagant eyelashes and features as delicate as a porcelain doll's, he was altogether too pretty to be a boy. He never looked directly at Conan Doyle or Barrie, but peered at them shyly from the corner of one eye. Conan Doyle shifted in his chair with growing discomfort. Rumors about Wilde flew on the wind these days, and this was obviously Oscar's latest "companion."

"Hello, Arthur," Wilde said, and then appeared to start and made a show of peering down at Barrie, as if he could not quite make him out. "Why, is that you down there J.M.?" he queried. "Ah yes, I see the moustache if not the man it's attached to. Honestly, J.M., if it were not for your enormous talent it would be so easy to miss you."

Wilde's closest friends were often the butt of his wit, but it was never with any malice.

"Ach, it would be hard to miss you, Oscar, in any crowd," the diminutive Scotsman retorted before dunking his moustache back into his whiskey.

"Really? I am told people miss me the moment I leave the room." Wilde punctuated his remark with a ridiculous, self-mocking smile and everyone chuckled. It was impossible to be in a bad mood when Oscar Wilde was present.

Wilde threw himself into an empty chair, shrugged the coat from his shoulders, and drew off his hat with a flourish, releasing his long chestnut curls. The young man pulled his chair closer to Wilde and perched delicately.

"And who is this, er, *friend*, of yours, Oscar?" J.M. asked in a tone so pointedly ironic it made Conan Doyle cringe.

"This is George . . ." Wilde said, and added in an exaggeratedly posh voice, ". . . also of the theater."

Wilde noticed the heavy glass tumblers of scotch set in front of each man. "Ah, good whiskey, the official drink of any wake. I take it we are lamenting the loss of the much-loved Sherlock Holmes. I shall join you in a glass to see the old man off, but then we must switch to champagne, as befitting any celebration."

The waiter brought a whiskey for Wilde, but nothing for his young companion. Wilde sipped his whisky and smiled joyously. "Mmmmmn!" he breathed, smacking his lips. "Could anything but whiskey slake a true Irishman's thirst?" He patted his young companion on the knee. "I'm afraid George here does not drink. Quite reprehensible isn't it? I've always said that an absence of vices is a vice in and of itself."

Wilde quaffed his whiskey in three deep gulps, then semaphored the waiter with a flourish of his handkerchief. Moments later, a huge magnum had been cracked and each man held a freshly charged champagne flute.

"What are we celebrating, Oscar?" Conan Doyle asked, wondering if Wilde had a new play opening that he had somehow failed to hear of.

"What are we celebrating?" Wilde repeated, flashing his long-toothed smile. "Surely my arrival is always a cause for celebration!"

As usual, Wilde's personality engulfed the table, preventing any chance of normal conversation. Conan Doyle studied Wilde's animated face as he launched into another witticism. *Lady Windermere's Fan* had been a resounding success the previous year, making him the wealthiest and most successful man of letters in London. But despite Wilde's beautiful wife and two children, his enthusiasm for the companionship of young men had lately become a virulent source of scorching gossip.

"I offer a toast," Wilde said, mildly slurring. "A toast to the ghost of Sherlock Holmes. May he watch over poor Arthur and keep him safe in his dotage."

"To Sherlock Holmes."

Champagne flutes chinked, everyone smiling and laughing as they imbibed. Everyone except Conan Doyle, who choked down a mouthful of chilled Dom Pérignon along with the last of his pride.

Suddenly, Wilde rose from the table, drew on his coat and hat, and then seized the champagne bucket and tucked it under one arm.

"And now Oscar Wilde must take his leave. Come along chaps. I have a four-wheeler waiting outside to convey us to our next destination."

"I'm afraid I have a train to catch, Oscar," Conan Doyle said. "My wife—"

"This is modern London, Arthur," Wilde scolded, "not the Scottish provinces. Here in the civilized world the trains run on time and after dark. I promise you will be in time to catch the ten thirty to South Norwood."

"But where are we going?" Barrie demanded.

"To witness the inexplicable," Wilde said. He paused for a moment to strike a theatrical pose, one hand clamped to his breast. "A mind-ripping spectacle that will leave you both confounded and astonished. I saw it for the first time last night and thought it quite miraculous. But miracles lack luster unless one has witnesses."

And with that, the Irish playwright swept away with his young shadow in tow. J.M. Barrie and Conan Doyle dallied a moment and then rose from the table and followed, hurrying to catch up, mere flotsam dragged along in Oscar Wilde's irresistible slipstream.

* * *

The carriage they rode in was new and luxuriously appointed— another of Wilde's mad extravagances. The bucket of chilled champagne was wedged between Wilde and the carriage door. He sat scrunched hip-to-hip with George, so close that their knees constantly brushed together. J.M. Barrie rolled his eyes at Conan Doyle, who cleared his throat and averted his gaze, peering out the window. He had assumed that the four-wheeler was heading north to the Royal Lyceum, where another in their circle of friends, Bram Stoker, was manager. Instead, he was surprised to find they were heading south, to one of the more disreputable districts of London.

"I must remonstrate with you, Arthur," Wilde said, tossing off his third glass. "You are poaching on my reputation as a scandalous man of letters. You give birth to the greatest hero of modern times and then you kill him off. Just like that. As if he were nothing. My God, Arthur, you are fearless, truly you are. Your audacity makes me dizzy." He grabbed the magnum and hoisted it dripping from the bucket. "And I find the best cure for dizziness is always more champagne."

Bubbly slopped and overflowed as Wilde attempted to replenish their glasses in a swaying carriage jouncing along cobbled streets cratered with potholes.

Minutes later, the four-wheeler deposited them outside the gaudily lit marquee of Gatti's-Under-the-Arches, a music hall literally built beneath the arches of Charing Cross railway station. By day the street was an odiferous mélange of butcher shops and fish stalls. By night, even with the shop fronts shut and the barrows and stalls stacked away, the lingering tang of fish heads and pig's trotters shivered in the air.

"We're late," Conan Doyle noted. "The performance has already begun."

"Nonsense," Wilde said. "Oscar Wilde is never late. It is everyone else who arrives too early. In fact, our timing is perfect—the queues are gone and the performance we have come to see will take the stage in a few minutes."

The large Irishman led the way, and the four of them swept past the ticket office without paying, unchallenged by the gray-haired codger in the booth, who merely pressed his face against the grille and called after, "A pleasure to see you again, Mister Wilde."

Wilde acknowledged him with an imperious wave. They passed through the doors and into the darkened music hall. As they took their seats in the front row, a comedian was being booed from the stage.

Conan Doyle leaned across and shouted over the bray of hoots and yells, "What are we here to see?"

"The inexplicable," Wilde answered cryptically.

The band struck up a blaring number to drown the booing and hissing. The comic scrambled to gather up his props and had barely fled the stage when a bevy of dancing girls burst into the footlights, kicking and prancing so that the tops of their short skirts flirted with the thighs of their stocking-clad legs.

Although Conan Doyle had heard of such lewd performances, he had never actually attended one, and found that, for once, rumor understated reality.

The women were all young and spritely, full of life. They whooped and shrieked as they danced. Conan Doyle found his heart thumping and his face burning. He dropped his gaze and focused on the edge of the stage. Wilde leaned over, squeezed his knee, and whispered: "You'll survive, Arthur. Just lie back, relax, and think of the empire."

J.M. Barrie muttered in a low voice, "I hear the dancers at the Moulin Rouge wear no undergarments at all."

"It is true," Wilde agreed. "I have been to the Moulin Rouge many times. Although . . ." He smiled a languorous smile. "The view from here almost rivals that of Paris. In fact, if you look hard enough, you can see Kent."

That was the final straw for Conan Doyle. He started to get up from his seat, but Wilde pulled him back down. "Stay, Arthur," Wilde chided. "This is precisely the kind of medicine the good doctor needs."

By now Conan Doyle could not take his eyes off the parade of young female flesh and squeezed the armrests of his chair with a crushing grip.

The girls danced off the stage to a chorus of bravos, yells, and the thunder of stamping feet.

There was a pause, and then the theater manager, announced by the off-stage emcee's disembodied voice as "Mister Henry Purvis, Esquire," stepped to the front of the stage. He was a worn-thin man in a worn-thin evening suit. Purvis had been the manager since the music hall opened, and if anything was in more need of a thorough tarting up than was his establishment.

The beam of a spotlight meandered across the boards until it found him. "Tonight, Ladies and Gentlemen," he announced in a *basso profundo* that was quite surprising, given his lean frame, "Gatti's has the rare pleasure to present not just a performer, but a unique individual who is one of the true wonders of the age. His name is Daniel Dunglas Hume, the greatest psychic medium in the world. Mister Hume's abilities have been studied by some of the best scientific minds of our time and have been found to be absolutely genuine."

As Purvis spoke, a number of painted backdrops lowered from the fly loft depicting Daniel Dunglas Hume performing feats of psychic wonder. One canvas was painted with the figure of a finely dressed man holding a skull in a Hamlet/Yorick pose, as if contemplating the mysteries of death. The other canvases illustrated a séance with a ghostly apparition of a woman's face appearing above Hume's head; a hand bell ringing inside a bell jar, while Hume stood several feet away, his fingers to his temples; and most dramatically, Hume levitating several feet into the air before a group of astonished spectators.

"Who is this chap?" Conan Doyle asked.

"One of your fellow Scotsmen," Wilde muttered. "But grew up in Connecticut. Speaks in an erudite Yankee accent with the odd Scots vowel sound tossed in to season the mulligan."

"Oh gawd, a conjurer," J.M. Barrie said in a dour voice. "I hate bloody conjurers!"

"Ladies and Gentleman," the theater manager's voice rose to a dramatic crescendo, "be prepared to be astonished. I give you, the wonder of the Americas. The wonder of London. The wonder of the world—Daniel Dunglas Hume!"

The spotlight swerved away from the emcee and focused upon a tall man who stepped from the wings. The crowd did not applaud, but seemed to be holding its collective breath. The band played a restless stir of cellos as the solitary figure strutted across the stage. He wore a full moustache, with no beard or cheek whiskers, and sported a fine head of hair with auburn curls that tickled the collar of his shirt and curled upon his noble brow. Hume was dressed in a black velvet jacket and serge gray trousers, a red jabot tied around his neck. In his right hand, he clutched a fine lace handkerchief, which added to his air of a dandy. His effect upon the female portion of the audience was apparent by the susurration of excited whispers and the way he drew their faces like needles to a lodestone. He stopped at the edge of the stage and bowed, his posture relaxed.

"Good evening, my British cousins." His accent was indeed mellifluously "Yankee." "My name is Daniel Dunglas Hume. Tonight, I shall perform—"

"Levitate!" an uncouth Cockney voice bawled from the cheap seats up in the gods. "Come on, Yank! Let's see ya fly!"

Hume's composure never wavered. He held up a hand, importuning silence and began again. "I shall perform a number of wonders, but I regret to say that I am somewhat fatigued, having only recently arrived in your fine country. Every performance is slightly different and is dependent upon the cooperation of the spirits." He smiled handsomely. "And what this tired old body can achieve."

"Levitate!" the cockney voice howled again. "Let's see ya lev—" There was a thud and a loud "ooooof" as someone took it upon himself to silence the heckler with a clenched fist driven between his shoulder blades.

Hume looked up and smiled, nodding in appreciation to his anonymous helper. "Tonight I shall—" He paused as something caught in his voice. The handkerchief flew up to cover his mouth as he coughed explosively. He seemed on the verge of a coughing fit, but visibly forced himself to relax. Having regained his composure, he pulled away the handkerchief and began again. "Teleportation . . . is the ability to move distant objects instantaneously through the power of the mind alone."

This set the crowd abuzz with excited murmuring.

"But first . . . first I must pause to recognize the presence of genius amongst us." He looked toward Conan Doyle and his companions. "Or, more correctly, the presence of three geniuses amongst us." He gestured and a spotlight lit them up. "Tonight, we are graced with the presence of three of London's greatest men of letters: Oscar Wilde, Arthur Conan Doyle, and J.M. Barrie. Gentleman, welcome."

The delighted audience burst into thunderous applause. Oscar Wilde leapt to his feet, bowed his head, and made a salaam gesture to the crowd. J.M. Barrie stood up from his seat, (which made remarkably little difference to his height) and acknowledged the applause with a polite nod. When Conan Doyle rose, the applause subsided noticeably and was mixed with a low grumbling and scattered boos—apparently the news about the demise of Sherlock Holmes had followed him there, like his own personal rain cloud. He ducked his head in a quick bow and sat down again.

Hume strode to the very edge of the stage. "For this demonstration, I shall require the assistance of a member of the audience."

A forest of hands went up. Hume pointed to a pretty young woman in the front row, a few seats from Conan Doyle.

"Young lady, do you have an object I could borrow, say a golden guinea?"

The young lady blushed and dropped her eyes bashfully, shaking her head.

"Obviously not a native of England," Conan Doyle muttered to his companions. "Anyone could see from the young lady's dress she's a shop girl, unlikely to be carrying a golden guinea in her purse."

"But I'm sure he's already got a guinea up his sleeve," Barrie whispered. "Ready to make the switch."

"Mister Hume, if I might be so bold," Wilde spoke up, rising from his seat. "I have an object the young lady might borrow."

The spotlight swung over to fix him in its beam. Wilde reached inside his jacket pocket and took out what at first appeared to be a large coin. He held it aloft so that it sparkled in the light. "While attending Trinity College in Dublin, I was awarded the Berkeley Gold Medal for Greek. It is one of my most treasured possessions and quite unique. You could not find its double anywhere in England." Wilde threw Barrie a sardonic glance. "Therefore, I think it will make a perfect substitution for a golden guinea, any of which—as my friend J.M. Barrie aptly commented to me—could be quickly substituted by a magician of mundane talent."

Hume smiled broadly. "An excellent observation, Mister Wilde, and I thank you—and Mister Barrie. Your gold medal will make an excellent substitute, and I promise it shall be safely returned to you."

Wilde handed the medal to Conan Doyle, who admired it for a moment, and then handed it on. The medal was passed along the front row until the young lady received it.

Hume continued. "Although I have never seen this medal, I presume it is embossed with something approximating heads or tails. Would you agree, madam?"

She looked it over. "Yessir." She spoke in a broad cockney accent. "It's got an 'orse on one side an' a castle on the other."

"Well observed," Hume said. "Now, young lady, when I give you the word, I want you to toss the medal and catch it on the back of your hand. I will attempt to discern whether it is heads or tails—castle or horse. Do you understand?"

The young woman nodded and smiled.

Hume stretched out his arm, the fingers of his hand extended. He lowered his head and appeared to concentrate. From the orchestra pit, a drum roll grumbled.

"On the count of three," he said. "One . . . two . . . three!"

The young lady tossed the heavy medal into the air. It glittered in the spotlight as it spun and she caught it on the back of her hand. On stage, Hume closed his fingers and snatched back his hand. "Now tell us," he said to the young lady, "is it heads or tails?"

The young lady lifted the hand trapping the medal and gawked with surprise.

Vanished.

She looked up at Hume with alarm. "It's gone, sir!" she cried, jumping to her feet. "It's gone. I dunno how, but it's gone!"

The crowd gasped.

Hume did not move, milking the moment. Then he slowly extended his arm, the fingers of his hand clenched in a trembling fist.

"It's in his hand," Barrie whispered. "I'll bet my life it's in his hand."

The entire audience leaned forward in its seats, craning to see, as Hume unfolded his fingers, one-by-one.

But the hand was empty.

Hume's arm fell slack. He threw a defeated look at Oscar Wilde. "Mister Wilde, I am greatly embarrassed to admit it, but I seem to have lost your prized medal."

For once, Oscar Wilde was speechless, his face stricken with a look of sick surprise.

Then Hume smacked a palm to his forehead, as if just realizing something. "Ah, I have found it." He smiled at the Irish playwright. "Mister Wilde, if you could check the inside pocket of your jacket."

Wilde fumbled in his inside pocket and drew out the Berkeley medal. A smile returned to his face as he rose from his seat and held the medal aloft to show the audience.

The audience burst into cheers. Hume took a modest bow.

But then the chants began: "Levitate . . . Levitate . . . Levitate . . ."

Hume raised both hands in an appeal to quiet the crowd, but his minor miracle had only made them hungrier for a big miracle: they wanted to see a man rise from the stage.

The shouts of "*Levitate . . . Levitate . . . Levitate . . .*" grew louder and masked the sound as Hume clamped the lace handkerchief to his face and his body was wracked with a coughing fit, his face visibly paling.

Conan Doyle turned to Wilde and had to shout to be heard. "The fellow's not well!"

On stage, Hume had managed to stifle his coughing attack. He wiped his mouth with the handkerchief and waved a hand to silence the crowd. When the hubbub finally abated, he spoke in a ragged voice. "Very well, then. I shall attempt the levitation."

The crowd roared with approval and burst once more into applause. Hume dropped his head, seeming to gather his energies. Silence fell as he raised both arms and lifted his gaze to the ceiling.

Moments passed. Nothing happened. A bead of sweat trickled from Hume's hairline and ran down his cheek.

And then, slowly, imperceptibly, he seemed to grow taller. A cascade of gasps rippled from the front to the back rows of the theater as empty space appeared between the stage and the soles of Hume's shoes. He rose slowly, hesitantly, into the air: a foot . . . two feet. When he reached three feet his ascent started to waver. His face was strained, running with sweat, a vein bulging on his forehead.

And then he began to sink. Slowly at first, and then he dropped the last foot to the stage, landing heavily. He forced a smile, dabbed at his sweating face with a handkerchief, and tried to make a showman-like flourish, but then his eyes rolled up into the back of his head as his legs buckled and he slumped to the boards.

Women screamed. The audience surged to its feet, as did Conan Doyle and his companions.

The manager, Mister Purvis, ran to the lip of the stage as several stagehands helped carry off Hume's limp body. "Not to worry," he flustered. "Mister Hume is simply tired from his travels. He will be topping the bill again tomorrow night, after he has had time to properly rest." Purvis waved a frantic hand at the orchestra, which sought to cover Hume's awkward departure with a cheerful blare of music.

J.M. Barrie leaned over and slapped a hand on Wilde's shoulder. "You were right, Oscar," he commented sardonically. "That was quite inexplicable."

THE GHOST OF SHERLOCK HOLMES

The Doyle family home in South Norwood was asleep when Conan Doyle let himself in with his key. He crept up the stairs and paused halfway, listening to the soft surf of light snores emanating from the bedrooms of his children. The peace was broken by a jagged, hacking cough, like broken glass shaken in a sack. He noticed that a light still glimmered beneath the door of his wife, Louise's, bedroom. He ascended the stairs and rapped softly at her door. A moment later, her wearied voice called from inside: "Come, Arthur, darling."

Conan Doyle creaked the door open and slid inside. The bedroom was dimly lit: a single lamp, turned low, pulsed softly on the bedside table.

"Hello, Touie."

His wife's face, pale and drawn, appeared above a clutch of bedclothes. She smiled wanly up at him. The bed creaked beneath his weight as he sat down and reached to stroke her cheek with the back of his hand. Her skin was cold and clammy.

"How are you, my darling wife?"

"Much as always." Her eyes searched his face. "So it's done then? The world knows?"

He nodded sagely. "The deed is done."

"You are upset, Arthur?"

He shook his head. "Pah, no!"

She reached an icy hand from beneath the sheets and squeezed his own. "You cannot hide your feelings from me, Arthur. I sense that your soul is in turmoil. The world is unhappy with you?"

Conan Doyle nodded, forcing a sardonic smile. "As you predicted."

"Are you mourning, too?"

"Me? No—not a jot! No, I feel the loosening of shackles. Now I may write what I please. Now I am free to create the works that will live on—" He caught himself. "The works that will make my name."

"Yes, Arthur. You will be famous the world over. You *are* famous. My husband, the famous writer!"

"Touie, I love you so much," he said, his voice tightening. He reached down and attempted a clumsy embrace.

He felt a small hand push back against his chest.

"No, Arthur!"

"Come now, Touie, might a husband not embrace his own wife?"

"*No!*"

Conan Doyle drew back.

"We cannot be close," his wife said. "We have agreed. You already risk too much coming in here so often."

"I don't care about the risk—"

"The children will need you," she interrupted, her voice steely. "You will be all they have after I . . ." Her voice evaporated, leaving the unspeakable truth hanging.

"We'll have no talk of that kind," he gently chided.

Louise Doyle paused a moment, and then spoke what was clearly on her mind. "Arthur, I understand a man's . . . appetites. I have loved you these many years and I know that you are a very physical

man. I would never hold it against you should you find the need
to . . . to avail yourself—"

"Touie, do not speak of this."

"Discreetly, of course. I know you would be discreet—"

"I made a vow to you, Touie, on the day we wed. I stand by that
vow."

"Yes, you love me. I never doubt your love. But you are still a man,
Arthur. A very handsome, vigorous man. I know you must long for
that . . . for that intimacy I am no longer able to give you."

Conan Doyle touched his wife's lips with two fingers and gently
shushed her. "May I bring you anything?"

She sank back into the pillows, resignation on her face. "Nothing. No." She paused. "Yes. A sleeping draught."

He nodded, choked down the sob in his throat with a forced
smile, and left the room.

The Scottish doctor retrieved his Gladstone bag from the entrance hall table and carried it into the kitchen. First he sifted
some white powder into a glass, added water and then a few drops
of laudanum. After a moment's consideration, he took down another glass and mixed one for himself, a small one. Conan Doyle
normally slept like a hibernating bear, but after the day's events his
thoughts were in turmoil. He downed his sleeping draught on the
spot, and then took the second in to his wife.

* * *

When Conan Doyle entered his ground floor study, a lamp had
been left burning on his writing desk as he had instructed his domestic staff. (One never knew when a bout of insomnia would turn
into a new character or short story idea.) He paused on the way to
his desk to touch some personal totems scattered about the room: a
battle-worn cricket bat with the script *Thunderer* painted on the
blade; a harpoon he kept as a souvenir of a youthful foray as ship's

doctor aboard a Greenland whaler; an African mask from a sweaty and miserable year on the Dark Continent.

He flopped in his chair and undid several buttons of his waistcoat. The whirlwind day had left him enervated, but his nerves were too inflamed for sleep. His scalp prickled and it gradually occurred to him that he was being watched. He looked up at the portrait hanging on the wall beside his desk. It was one of Sidney Paget's original drawings of Sherlock Holmes, commissioned for *The Strand Magazine.* In it, the hawk-nosed, gaunt-cheeked Holmes was drawing on a cigarette, peering suspiciously out at the viewer.

Conan Doyle had never particularly cared for the illustration. Feeling the sting of reprimand in that stare, he got up, lifted the portrait from its hook, and set it against the bookshelves out of his immediate line of sight.

Then he settled himself at his desk, snatched open a desk drawer, and took out his writing journal. Lying beneath the journal was his old service revolver. He lifted it from the drawer and hefted its steely mass in his hand. It had been many years since he'd last fired it. But even unloaded, the Webley .455 was a formidable weapon that exuded an aura of lethal potential. He set the pistol back into the drawer and pushed it shut.

He flipped open his writing journal, drew the fountain pen from his jacket pocket, and unscrewed it. For a moment the pen nib hovered over the blank expanse of paper, and then a quiver of excitement ran through him as he began to jot down ideas, lines of dialogue, a few rough sketches of a new character that had been fulminating in his mind for some time—a character called Brigadier Gerard. By the time he had filled the first page with his tidy blue handwriting, fatigue settled upon his shoulders like a lead apron. He blinked, rubbed his straining eyes, and turned up the wick of the desk lamp.

It was then he noticed a letter sitting in the middle of the desk blotter. Clearly one of the servants had placed it there for him to read. He could not imagine how he had failed to notice it sooner.

The stationery was of the finest quality, and he felt a slight sense of déjà vu as he picked it up and ran the blade of a letter opener beneath the flap. He drew out and unfolded a sheet of vellum. The paper was printed with a header: SOCIETY FOR PSYCHICAL RESEARCH.

> Dear Doctor Doyle,
>
> Your name has been proposed for membership of our newly formed Society for Psychical Research (SPR). Our organization has been founded to promote the scientific investigation of Spontaneous Phenomena such as hauntings, apparitions, mediumship, thought transference (or "telepathy"), and all forms of "psychic" manifestation. Our first meeting will take the form of a four-day retreat at Thraxton Hall in the County of Lancashire. In addition to some of Britain's most respected psychics, many leading scientific and learned persons of unimpeachable character will also be in attendance. As a man of independent thought, keen intelligence, and with a doctor's training, we should be honored to have you as a member.
>
> Yours respectfully,
>
> Henry Sidgwick.

Conan Doyle flushed with excitement. He had envisioned just such an organization himself: a body of sober, yet open-minded individuals dedicated to a rational, scientific study of the supernatural. Now it had happened. He raised the letter to read it one more time, but found that the neatly written sentences had transformed to meaningless gibberish. He blinked his tired eyes. For a moment, he went dizzy as electric ants scurried across the surface of his brain. He smelled smoke, cigarette smoke—he could even name the particular brand of tobacco—and looked up in alarm.

The study remained empty, but then he noticed a wraith of silver smoke curling in the air. Strangely, it seemed to come from the portrait of Sherlock Holmes leaning against the bookshelves. Had it somehow caught fire? The fire in the fireplace was not lit. How then?

More smoke jetted into the air as the surface of the portrait began to bulge. It stretched farther and farther, and then ripped open as the head and shoulders of a man emerged. Conan Doyle watched, slack-jawed, as Sherlock Holmes squeezed himself up from two into three dimensions and stepped from the canvas into the room.

"Wu-what? What the devil!" Conan Doyle stammered.

The Baker Street detective puffed at his cigarette, his steely eyes gazing back at his creator. "To answer the question you have not asked," Holmes said in his dry, ironic voice, "yes, I am real."

"This is impossible!" Conan Doyle hissed.

Holmes crossed to a leather armchair and sat down, never taking his eyes from Conan Doyle. "Once you have eliminated the impossible, whatever remains, *however improbable*, must be the truth."

"I wrote that," Conan Doyle said, indignation beginning to replace his fear. In fact, he was surprised at how unsurprised he was. "Just as I wrote you. You are nothing more than a phantasm of my brain. *That* is the truth!"

Sherlock Holmes seemed to reflect upon that for a moment. "Yes, you created me. And now I exist in the minds of thousands of readers. Tell me, Arthur, how many minds do *you* exist in?" He crossed his legs and brushed a fleck of ash from his trouser leg. "That summons you answered this morning, the one that bore a distinctive watermark."

"The phoenix?"

Holmes nodded. "Of course, you know that the phoenix is the heraldic symbol of a famous English family?"

Conan Doyle did not know that. He nervously combed his fingers through his short brown hair.

"The Thraxton family," Holmes said. "The meeting of the Society for Psychical Research will take place at Thraxton Hall in two weeks' time. At which time the current Lady Thraxton will be murdered. Shot twice in the chest at close range."

"At a séance," Conan Doyle breathed, finishing the thought. He looked up. "Then Hope Thraxton is the *medium of some renown* I have read of in the papers?"

"The game is afoot my boy," Holmes said. "The question is— are you ready? Will you take up this challenge? Or will you turn away, as a lesser man might?"

Conan Doyle shook his head. "No. This isn't real. None of it." He looked back at his writing desk for the letter. It had vanished. He gasped and threw a quick look back at Holmes. The leather armchair was empty, but retained a human-shaped dent.

Conan Doyle started awake. He was slumped over in his chair, the fountain pen in his limp hand trailing a blue smear across the page. He blinked. Rubbed his numb face. He had fallen asleep at his writing desk. Then he dimly remembered the soporific he had taken.

"Damnation!" he cried. The dream had seemed so real and he had slid into it imperceptibly. He scanned the desk and his eyes eagerly pounced upon the page of fresh writing in his notebook. He wanted to reread what he had written. But instead of amusing dialogue and apt character descriptions, he found only the same word scribbled over and over in his own handwriting:

Elementary.

Elementary.

Elementary.

When he turned the page, the *Elementarys* continued.

He slammed the notebook shut. There had been no letter. No spectral projection of Sherlock Holmes. It had all been a dream, an hallucination brought on by a soporific of his own concoction. He wobbled to his feet, gripping the armrests for support.

Nothing, he thought, *just a silly dream*. But as he made to leave the room he noticed the curling arabesques of cigarette smoke hovering near the ceiling.

The next morning, a letter from the *Society for Psychical Research* arrived in the first post.

THE BEST OF BOTH WORLDS

Conan Doyle awakened with the mysterious woman's words—*A medium of some renown*—echoing in his head. The phrase jogged loose the memory of a news cutting he had read somewhere. After an hour's search, he found the article in a recent issue of *The Strand Magazine*. Triumphant, he slipped the magazine into his leather portfolio and determined to read it on the train to London. He was heading back to the capital city with a specific mission in mind: he would return to number 42 _____ Crescent. Only this time he would be forearmed with something he lacked upon the first visitation—knowledge.

* * *

As he enjoyed the privacy of an empty carriage on the ten fifteen to Waterloo Station, Conan Doyle pulled out *The Strand Magazine* and paged through it until he came upon a headline: "Medium Communes with the Dead." Beneath the banner-black type was a photograph of a medium seated at a séance table holding the hands of two sitters on either side whose faces could not be seen. The medium was a young woman in a black silk dress. Her hair was pinned up and she wore a sheer black veil that shadowed her face.

The photograph had been taken without the benefit of flash powder, and the lengthy time exposure required in the dimly lit room had caused the image of the medium's face to be blurred by motion. It gave a rather uncanny effect: a main image and then a secondary ghost image—as if the camera had captured her soul leaving her body. Beneath the photo was a caption: *The medium Lady Hope Thraxton conducting a séance.*

He stared at the image for a long time. He had craved to see the young woman's face ever since his dark interview. But now, even though he possessed a photograph, her true likeness remained tantalizingly out of reach. The article's author, whose name he did not recognize as a regular *Strand* contributor, gave a rather breathless account of a séance he had attended at a "fashionable London address." No doubt this was the Mayfair residence Conan Doyle had recently visited. Here the medium supposedly contacted her spirit guide, providing a conduit that allowed direct communication with several relatives who had passed over to the other side. The author claimed to be an expert investigator into the supernatural who had unmasked many false mediums and charlatans, and who remained convinced that Lady Thraxton was the most gifted psychic he had ever encountered.

The train whistle blew, signaling the station ahead. Conan Doyle returned the magazine to his portfolio. Minutes later, he stepped from the echoing vault of Waterloo Station into the clamor of Waterloo Road: the clatter of carriage wheels on cobblestones, the cries of costermongers hawking "fresh fish" and "posies, a penny a bouquet," street urchins begging "spare a farthing for a poor young lad"—his mind so distracted he imagined he could hear his name being called: "Arthur! I say, Arthur!"

Then he noticed an inconspicuous black carriage pacing him with an extremely conspicuous Oscar Wilde hanging out the carriage window waving a white handkerchief. Conan Doyle stepped to the curbside as the carriage pulled up.

"Been calling your name for ages, old fellow," Wilde said. "Daydreaming about some new character, eh? Someone to replace the redoubtable Sherlock Holmes?"

"Something like that," he answered—it was easier to go along with the lie.

Conan Doyle informed Wilde that he had an errand to run in Mayfair and the Irish playwright insisted on giving him a ride. When the writer climbed inside, he found that Constance, Wilde's handsome wife, was seated opposite. Sitting beside her was a strikingly beautiful young woman. Conan Doyle plumped himself onto the leather cushion next to Wilde and hurriedly doffed his top hat in deference to both ladies.

"Hello, my dear Constance," Conan Doyle said. "You are looking lovely as ever."

"You are an inveterate flatterer, Arthur." Constance Wilde smiled and added, "That is why you are my favorite amongst Oscar's friends." She paused a moment before asking in a soft voice, "How is Touie?"

"She endures," Conan Doyle answered with a pained smile.

Constance Wilde reached forward and squeezed his hand. "Our thoughts are with her always . . . and with you, dear Arthur."

Conan Doyle nodded, but could not summon a reply as the words were lodged somewhere in his throat.

"You've met George, of course," Wilde said offhandedly. Despite the presence of two ladies, he had a cigarette dangling slackly between his large fingers and the carriage was fugged with smoke.

Conan Doyle peered at the young woman, fighting the urge to waft a hole through the curtain of silver smoke. She was a young, slim, ravishing beauty with long ringlets of ash blond hair cascading down about her shoulders—quite unforgettable. Conan Doyle was certain he had never before clapped eyes on her. "No. No, I don't think I've had the pleasure."

He leaned forward and grasped the young woman's hand, which was fine-boned and weightless as a bird pecking seed from his palm.

The carriage rumbled away with a jerk, and for the next five minutes Wilde filled the space with the sound of his own voice, gesturing grandly as he told a very funny story about something his youngest child had said that morning. Suddenly, he noticed something out the window and rapped at the carriage roof with his walking stick, saying, "Ah, here we are, ladies; Harrods awaits."

The carriage lurched to a halt, and Wilde threw open the door. Constance offered her hand once again to Conan Doyle. "So nice to see you, Arthur. Do give my love to Touie."

"Of course."

The ravishing young woman gathered her skirts and leaned forward, bringing her face close to Conan Doyle's. Her eyes met his for a moment and the drownable depth of their blueness snatched the breath from his lungs.

"Who was that exquisite creature?" Conan Doyle asked, watching the women disappear through the front doors of Harrods.

"You've already met. Come along, I know we imbibed a few glasses of champagne last night, but you were your usual sober self when we parted."

"Last night?" Conan Doyle repeated, realizing with a jolt why the young woman's face had seemed strangely familiar. "You mean, your companion, George? It was a young woman . . . dressed as a man!"

Wilde's large frame shook with laughter as he drew a silver cigarette case from his jacket pocket, flipped it open, and selected an opium-soaked cigarette, lighting it from the one already burning. "My friend goes by two names: George when he is a man. Georgina when she is a woman." He paused to lower the carriage window and toss away his unwanted cigarette. "Surely as a medical man you must have come across such cases."

Wilde said it with a coy smile upon his generous lips, and Conan Doyle could not tell if he was having his leg pulled. But after several moments, he could hold his silence no longer and asked, "So you mean George, or Georgina is . . . is . . ." He could hardly bring himself to say it. ". . . an hermaphrodite?"

"The best of both worlds, don't you think?" Oscar Wilde replied, tendrils of silver smoke wreathing about his brow like a Roman Emperor's laurel crown. He drew deeply and exhaled a nimbus of smoke out both nostrils. "Imagine the possibilities: male and female in one body. The mind boggles, does it not?"

Gears jammed in Conan Doyle's brain. He liked to think of himself as a man of the world. As a young buck he had mixed with some rough sorts: sailors, thieves, ivory smugglers, but Oscar Wilde still managed to shock his middle-class sensibilities to their quivering core.

"So," Wilde drawled, "what is this mysterious assignation in Mayfair that drags Arthur Conan Doyle from the domestic idylls of South Norwood into the 'cesspit of the Empire' at this hour?"

Conan Doyle related his meeting of the previous morning. Through it all, Oscar Wilde listened with such rapt attention he neglected to puff even once on his cigarette. "And all this happened in total darkness?" he asked when the tale had been told.

Conan Doyle nodded.

"And you never glimpsed the young lady's face?"

"Profound darkness—I could not see a hand in front of my face."

The Irishman's eyes flickered as he pondered deeply on Conan Doyle's tale. "Good Lord," he said, finally drawing deeply on the stub of his cigarette. "I am envious of you, Arthur, deeply envious. First your literary imagination runs rings around mine—"

"Oh, I hardly think that's true—"

"And now this. You have real adventures to tell. The greatest exploits of my day usually happen at the breakfast table and concern toast and the challenge of which flavor jam to choose. You must allow me to accompany you. I must meet this medium of some renown, if only to hear her voice in a darkened room."

For some reason, Conan Doyle did not want to share the experience with Wilde, but he could think of no reasonable excuse to deny him. So in the end he simply muttered, "As you wish, Oscar."

* * *

The carriage circulated number 42 _____ Crescent three times. After the third orbit, Wilde glowered at Conan Doyle and said with exasperation: "Arthur, there is only one number 42 _____ Crescent and we have passed it thricely."

"But that's not it," Conan Doyle insisted. "It doesn't look right."

"Looks right or not, I insist we stop." Wilde rapped on the carriage ceiling with the head of his walking stick. The carriage pulled up in front of the residence with the bright red door and the two men clambered out. As they walked up the front path, something struck Conan Doyle as wrong. And then, as his fingers grasped for the brass knocker, he realized what it was.

"It's gone!" he said.

Oscar Wilde pointed to the gold numbers above the door lintel with his walking stick. "Number 42, you said, and there we are."

"No, there was a door knocker—a brass phoenix. But look—"

Conan Doyle ran his gloved fingers over ugly scars where screws had been hastily wrenched from the wood. He scanned the door, puzzled. "No knocker," he pointed out, "and no door pull. How shall we knock?"

"Loudly," Oscar Wilde replied, and banged three times on the door with the base of his walking stick. He looked at his friend and stifled a snicker. "I feel rather like Black Rod opening Parliament."

Both men waited as the echoes of Wilde's blows reverberated through the house and died away.

Nothing.

The two exchanged glances. Conan Doyle nodded, and Wilde raised his walking stick and once more drove it hard into the door . . .

. . . which swung open and stood agape.

"Not latched properly," Conan Doyle observed. He looked at Wilde. "Should we be polite and leave?"

Wilde chuckled. "An open door is always an invitation. It would be impolite to ignore it."

The two men stepped into the gloomy entrance hall. All was marble and stillness. Conan Doyle shouted several "Halloos," but nothing stirred. "How very strange," he remarked. "No servants. No lights. No one at home and even the door knocker has been removed."

"An empty house," Wilde said, soaking in the palpable absence, "is like a body from which the soul has fled. It is a thing quite dead, is it not?"

The two shared a look and then Conan Doyle walked to the double doors and crashed through them. "This is where I waited."

The room was empty and unlit. Dust covers had been thrown over the furniture.

"Apparently the lady has left for her estate in the country," Wilde speculated.

"And taken the door knocker?"

"A valid observation," Wilde agreed. "That does seem like excessive overpacking."

"And who the devil are you two?"

Conan Doyle and Wilde started at the loud voice behind them. A well-dressed couple—man and woman—stood at the open door.

On the front walk behind them, a parade of servants waited, visibly sagging beneath armfuls of luggage.

Caught, well and truly. There was no point trying to lie.

"I am Arthur Conan Doyle."

The man's anger dissolved into disbelief. "Conan Doyle . . . of the Sherlock Holmes stories?"

Conan Doyle nodded. "Yes, sir, I have that honor."

The man gave a skeptical grunt and shifted his disbelieving glare to Wilde. "And I suppose you're going to tell me that you are Oscar Wilde?"

"Bravo!" Wilde bowed his head modestly. "I congratulate you on your perspicacity."

The man nearly choked on the impudence of Wilde's reply, but then his wife leaned over his shoulder and said, "I—I do believe they are who they say they are, dear. I have seen both gentlemen's photographs in the newspapers."

The man's mouth dropped open. "This cannot be," he said, suddenly unsure.

"And yet I remain convinced of it," Wilde responded. "My wife calls me Oscar and she has an unimpeachable memory." His face took on an interrogatory look. "But tell me, have you seen *Lady Windermere's Fan?*"

"Uh, yu-yes. Tu-twice," the man stammered.

"Wonderful!" Wilde said, smiling. "You display excellent taste." He drew out his silver cigarette case, took out a cigarette, and placed it between his full lips. "Might I trouble you for a light?"

The man hesitated and then reached into his coat and drew out a box of matches. He struck one and kindled Wilde's cigarette. The tall Irishman puffed several times, then threw the man a penetrating gaze and asked, "And who might you be, sir?"

The man looked a little baffled as he stammered, "I—I am the owner of this house. I live here."

"Ah yes, of course you do," Wilde said pleasantly, shaking the man's hand. "Arthur here was just saying how much he's been looking forward to meeting you." Wilde threw his friend an arch look. "Isn't that right, Arthur? Please explain to the gentleman why we are here."

Conan Doyle made a face as if he had just swallowed his own tongue. He threw Wilde a cutting look and pulled his features into a smile. "Why are we here? Well—" His mouth opened. His vocal chords strained. No sound came out.

There was a kerfuffle at the front door as a short and portly man shouldered his way past the waiting servants. He had protruding eyes and they rolled, showing the whites, as he entered in a great state of agitation, jowls quivering.

His eyes first affixed themselves upon the man and woman who claimed to be the owners of the house. "Mr. and Mrs. Jennings, I do most humbly apologize for my tardiness—impenetrable traffic on Hungerford Bridge and then I could not locate a cab."

"Yes, quite," said Mr. Jennings, with obvious irritation. He nodded in the direction of Conan Doyle and Oscar Wilde. "Perhaps you would be so good as to explain to these two, ahem, theatrical gentlemen as to who is the legal owner of this property?"

The bulbous eyes rolled onto the two friends, first taking in Wilde's broad frame and then settling upon Conan Doyle.

"I must apologize. I am Alfred Cheetham, Realtor. I handled the rental of this property."

"Rental?" Conan Doyle pounced. "And who was the former tenant?"

The man's face contorted in a sickly smile. "Sorry, sir, but I am not at liberty to divulge that information. Suffice it to say, it was a person of rank from a noble family that rented the property while Mr. and Mrs. Jennings were wintering in Tuscany."

Conan Doyle was dumbstruck. "But I was just here yesterday and they were still in residence."

"I, er, yes, the previous tenant earnestly communicated the need for a rapid removal—a family emergency of some kind."

"Rapid enough to require prying the knocker from the front door?"

The Realtor nodded, jowls quivering. "I woulda said they was doing a bunk, except everything was paid for up front and proper."

"Well, there you have it, Arthur," Wilde said. "We may never know the truth."

"Ah!" the estate agent said, reaching into an inner pocket. "Are you Doctor Doyle? Doctor Arthur Conan Doyle?"

The Scottish author affirmed that he was.

"The party in question, the former tenant of the house, believed you might stop by. I was instructed to personally deliver this letter into your hands."

Conan Doyle plucked the handsome bond envelope from the estate agent's sweaty grip. It was addressed simply: DOCTOR DOYLE. He opened it by tearing off one end of the envelope and shook the letter out.

All parties watched silently as Conan Doyle's eyes skimmed the blue swirl of handwriting. His expression seemed to change at one point. From the flicker of his eyes it was apparent that he was re-reading one particular line several times. Then he refolded the letter, returned it to its envelope, and secured it in an inner pocket of his overcoat. He looked up at Wilde and smiled. "Well, Oscar," he said with forced good humor. "I believe we have been sent on a wild goose chase."

He reached forward and shook the hands of the returning homeowners. "It's all clear now. A simple miscommunication. You have been very gracious. Oscar and I are so sorry to have bothered you."

* * *

"What did the letter say, Arthur?" Wilde asked as they were walking down the front path to the waiting carriage. "Was it from our mysterious medium?"

Conan Doyle gave a careless shrug and muttered, "No, it was nothing, Oscar. I am afraid it's all been a misunderstanding. I'm sorry to have involved you."

They climbed back into the carriage and set off across London. Oscar Wilde bided his time and then asked again as the carriage was crossing Piccadilly Circus, "Arthur, are you going to tell me what was in that letter? I watched your face as you read it. You have a positive genius for storytelling, but I'm afraid you could never make a living in the theater. What you read in that letter disturbed you greatly."

"It is nothing, Oscar. I think I've been the butt of an enormous practical joke."

"Really? How droll. I like a good joke, Arthur. Please share the hilarity." Wilde furrowed his brow in reprimand. "Read me the letter."

"No, my friend, it's really nothing—"

Oscar Wilde rapped three times on the carriage roof with his walking stick. "Stop here, Gibson," he shouted. The carriage ground to an immediate halt.

Conan Doyle snatched a look out the window. They had stopped right in the middle of Piccadilly Circus. "What? Why have we stopped?"

"Read the letter, Arthur."

Conan Doyle cast a glance out the window. Their carriage was blocking traffic. Cab drivers began to hoot and whistle. Two rough-looking laborers seated on a brewery wagon laden with barrels shook their meaty fists and began to curse at them in the vilest Billingsgate.

"Oscar!"

Wilde leaned back in his seat, drew a silver hip flask from his pocket, unscrewed the cap, and took a nip. Conan Doyle scented the smoky aroma of single malt. Wilde savored the mouthful, smacking his lips before saying, "I'm sorry, Arthur, but this carriage shall not move until you have read me that letter."

The roar of screams and imprecations from outside grew louder as the knot of traffic with Wilde's carriage at its center tightened around them.

"But Oscar—!" Conan Doyle pleaded, beginning to sweat.

"I have all the time in the world, Arthur." Wilde took another nip from his flask and leisurely screwed the cap back on. "From the brouhaha around us, it seems the rest of London does not."

Something thudded against the side of the carriage with a shattering crash—a hurled bottle.

"Very well, Oscar! Very well!"

Oscar Wilde suppressed a smirk and rapped on the ceiling with the head of his walking stick. "Drive on, Gibson!"

The carriage lurched forward. Wilde looked at his friend expectantly.

Conan Doyle swallowed his frown and unfolded the letter on his lap. "It's just nonsense, Oscar—"

"Read it!"

Conan Doyle cleared his throat and began:

Dear Doctor Doyle,

    I have had cause to reconsider my request to you. Please burn this and all letters you have thus far received from me. It is not myself I fear for—I believe in Fate and that nothing can change what has been foreordained. However, the other night I had a peculiarly vivid dream. I saw you in a coffin, your hands folded upon your chest. Your face was ghastly pale. Your chest did not rise and fall. You were dead. Quite dead—of that I am sure, for I sensed, even within the dream, that your soul had departed your body. I believe this is a vision of the near future and that further contact between us will cause you to suffer great harm. This is the reason I have quit my London home on such short notice. Thank you for your concern. Please keep me in your thoughts and prayers.

It was signed as before, with nothing more than a flourish of blue ink.

Conan Doyle fell silent after reading the letter. He folded the letter, slid it back into its envelope, and returned it to his inside jacket pocket, hands visibly shaking. The carriage trundled along streets thronged with traffic: omnibuses; ostler's wagons; barrows piled high with wilted flowers, stinking fish, blackening turnips.

All of London going about its daily business.

Neither man spoke for some time, and then Oscar Wilde said, "Of course, anyone who sends a letter and then begs the recipient to burn it means quite the opposite." He pondered a moment, tapping steepled fingers against his full lips, and then asked: "The letter had the same phoenix watermark? The Thraxton family crest?"

Conan Doyle nodded, with grim emphasis.

"Of course, you are still going to Thraxton Hall, aren't you, Arthur?"

Conan Doyle nodded again, and said, "Of course." He stared blindly out the window at a pair of working men brawling in the street outside a gin palace. Both men were staggering drunk and their wild, flailing punches did little real damage as they rolled in the gutter in a tangle of limbs.

"Of course," Wilde repeated. "And, of course, I shall be going with you."

THE JOURNEY TO SLATTENMERE

Two weeks later, Doctor Arthur Conan Doyle, accompanied by Oscar Wilde, thundered north in the first-class carriage of a steam train. Conan Doyle shuffled three letters in his lap: the original summons to number 42 _____ Crescent, the invitation from the Society for Psychical Research, and the most recent missive warning him of the psychic's vision of his death. He lifted the Thraxton letters to the light streaming in through the carriage window so that the watermark, a silver phoenix uncoiling from its nest of flame, floated up from the paper.

He looked up at a sharp snap and riffle of playing cards. In the seat opposite, Wilde absentmindedly shuffled a deck of cards. "Care for a game of cribbage?" he asked.

"We don't have a cribbage board."

By way of answer, Wilde reached over to one of his open bags and drew out a full-size cribbage board.

Conan Doyle's mouth fell open. He dreaded to think what Wilde did *not* have in all that luggage. "Not just now Oscar."

Wilde noticed the pages in Conan Doyle's lap. "Reading those letters again, Arthur? You're going to wear them to dust from the abrasion of your gaze."

"They're the only pieces to the puzzle we have. I'm perplexed."

"And I'm homesick," Wilde said, rising from his seat and tugging down a suitcase from the overhead rack. He opened the case, tossed inside the deck of cards, and then lifted out a fuchsia shirt with lace cuffs, holding it up to his neck and checking his reflection in the carriage window. "You're a doctor, Arthur. Is homesickness a malady one can die of?"

Conan Doyle harrumphed. "We're only two hours out of London, Oscar, and no, I don't believe homesickness has ever claimed a victim." He lowered the letters in his lap. "Speaking of victims, I am pondering how to save our lady medium. How does one prevent a death foretold?"

Wilde had pulled down a hatbox and was trying on a wide-awake hat with a yellow flower stuck in the brim. He scowled at his reflection in the carriage window and tossed the rejected head gear back into its box. "I would argue that the best way to avoid being shot is to arrange not to be in the same space as the bullet will occupy after the gun has been fired."

Conan Doyle chuckled. "Very metaphysical, Oscar." But then his eyes widened as the thought percolated in his brain. "Although, you may have struck upon something. If we stop the séance from happening, or somehow interrupt it, the premonition can never come to pass."

"Or it may still happen, in some hitherto unforeseen fashion—Fate and all that."

Conan Doyle shifted uneasily in his seat. The idea of Fate, a future that is somehow unavoidable, had crossed his mind many times in the last two weeks.

When he looked up, Wilde had taken down yet another hatbox and was trying on a straw boater.

"Did you really find it necessary to bring quite so much luggage?" Conan Doyle asked, eyeing the teetering stack of leather suitcases jammed in the overhead rack and piled on the empty seats around them—and that was merely the overflow—the bulk of Wilde's luggage had been consigned to the baggage car.

The Irishman paused and threw a pitying look at Conan Doyle's solitary suitcase, which occupied the seat next to the author.

"No doubt you have three tweed suits in that small case, Arthur—all identical. Stout, sensible clothing for the stout, sensible fellow you are. However, I am not like you. Though it pains me to admit the truth, I am somewhat corpulent these days. A man of my height and girth cannot wear tweed—it makes me look like a map of Scotland. If I am to appear at my best, I must dress in a fashion to suit the occasion, my mood, the lighting, the season—even the time of day. It has ever been a source of complication in my life." Wilde cast a second doubting glance at Conan Doyle's sad item of luggage, double-taking at the cricket bat fastened to the bag with a leather strap. "Why on earth did you bring a cricket bat, Arthur? I know you're inordinately fond of the game, but I hope you're not expecting the members of the Society for Psychical Research to break into two teams for an impromptu cricket match on the manor grounds."

Now it was Conan Doyle's turn to become defensive. "No. The bat is . . . it's a . . . good luck charm. I always keep it near. It helps me write."

Wilde raised his shaggy eyebrows as he looped an ivory silk cravat around his throat and drew it into a bow. "Then it is fortunate indeed that your preferred sport is not polo. There would not be room even in a first-class compartment for *my* baggage and *your* pony."

Conan Doyle began to mouth a question, but then thought better of it. However, a few moments later, he worked up the nerve to ask: "That acquaintance of yours. George—Georgina."

Wilde threw his friend a lascivious look and drawled suggestively: "Yeeeeeesss?"

"The other night you said—I mean . . . is *he?* I mean . . . is *she*—?"

"Is Georgina really an hermaphrodite?" Wilde said, preempting him. "Why do you ask, Arthur?" A wicked grin twitched the corners of his mouth. "Are you interested?"

"What? Oh, no! Good heavens, no!"

"Don't be shy, Arthur. Curiosity is a natural human emotion. If you like, I could put in a word for you."

Conan Doyle turned crimson. "I—I—I merely ask out of medical curiosity. As a doctor. Just. Professional. Purely. Professional."

"Of course," Wilde echoed, an impish smile on his large face. "*Professional* interest."

The Scotsman turned his flushed face to the carriage window, murmuring something inaudible.

Wilde finished dressing. He had changed into the attire of a country gentleman: black leather riding boots, voluminous jodhpurs, a scarlet felt jacket, and a long waxed coat designed to shed a tumultuous downpour. "There," he said turning to model his outfit for Conan Doyle, "do I not look the picture of a bucolic gent?"

Conan Doyle raised his eyes and took in Wilde's outlandish garb. "You are sure to leave a memorable impression upon the people of Slattenmere, Oscar. I have little doubt your visit will soon become a colorful anecdote of local history."

"Excellent!" Wilde beamed. "As it should be." He joggled his hips from side to side, a frown on his face. "It is rather stiff, however—and heavy. I hope it will not cause me to appear less than graceful, or plodding. I could not abide it if people thought Oscar Wilde was a plodder." He reached a decision. "I shall perambulate the train corridor to gauge the effect on our fellow passengers. Expect my return shortly."

And with that, Wilde flung open the carriage door and plunged into the swaying corridor. He banged the door shut behind him and lumbered in the direction of the second-class carriages.

Conan Doyle breathed a sigh of relief. Oscar Wilde was a dear friend, but he welcomed an interlude of silence for his own thoughts to foment. He carefully folded the letters and slipped them into the leather portfolio open on the seat next to him. Then he drew out a slim volume, bound in distressed leather, with a flap and an integral strap that wrapped around the book and was secured by a lock. Above the strap, CASEBOOK NO. 1 was embossed in gilt lettering. Conan Doyle dug beneath his collar and drew out a key on a ribbon. It turned in the lock and the journal sprang open. The first few pages were covered in Conan Doyle's neat handwriting—a description of his encounter with the mysterious medium in the darkened room, and all the subsequent events, including his trip with Wilde to the hastily abandoned residence in Mayfair, and his hallucinatory encounter with Sherlock Holmes. As he paged further, a short, squat envelope fell out. Conan Doyle picked up the letter and unfolded it. It was an answer to a query he had sent to a medical colleague—a specialist in rare diseases. He had written relating the symptoms the medium had described as her ailment. The response reaffirmed her claims:

Dear Dr. Doyle,

The symptoms of your patient correspond to a diagnosis of acute porphyria, an hereditary disease of the blood. Symptoms range from abdominal pain and acute sensitivity to sunlight (capable of causing blistering), to mental disturbances such as seizures, hallucinations, and paranoia. Unfortunately, there are no known therapies for the disease. If you require additional counseling, please don't hesitate to refer your patient to me for a more complete diagnosis.

Best Regards,

Dr. Henry Everton.

P.S. When is your next Sherlock Holmes story due out? Looking forward anxiously.

Conan Doyle refolded the letter and returned it to its envelope. He had purposely waited until Wilde was absent before reading it again, and now he found himself greatly agitated. Although he was physically fearless, given his family history the faintest whiff of madness terrified him. In fact, the characters, images, and stories that flowed in a unstoppable stream from his imagination often led him to fear what would happen were he to let slip the leashes of his own mind.

He closed the cover of the Casebook, snapped shut the lock securing the strap, and tucked it back into his portfolio. Then he turned his gaze to the window. Outside, the English midlands blurred past: an endless expanse of hedgerows and flat green fields dotted with red-and-white Hereford cattle grazing the lush grass.

Whoomph!

The carriage swayed heavily, everything went black, and Conan Doyle's ears popped as the train plunged into a tunnel. A tiny electric bulb glimmered bravely overhead, but was too feeble to push back the darkness. Out the windows, Conan Doyle caught only a vague impression of soot-blackened tunnel walls rushing past and his own dim reflection in the glass. But then he noticed there was something amiss with it. The figure in the reflection had his legs crossed and was smoking a cigarette. Conan Doyle blinked his eyes and looked again. It was not his reflection, but the image of Sherlock Holmes. The hawk-faced detective exhaled a lungful of smoke. As he drew the cigarette from his lips, he raised his hand in what might have been a mocking wave.

Whoooooooosh! The carriage swayed again as daylight burst in through the windows and the tunnel fell behind. At that moment, the carriage door bumped open and Oscar Wilde jostled in, muttering, "No, this simply shall not do. A poet must make an entrance looking like a poet." He yanked off the hat and sailed it across the carriage, then snatched loose the buttons of his coat. "Maybe you are right after all. Perhaps an adventure in the rural territories calls for tweed—" Wilde halted mid-sentence, catching the look on his friend's face. "Whatever's the matter, Arthur? You look like you've seen Jacob Marley's ghost!"

Conan Doyle pried his eyes from the window with difficulty. "Ah, er, no, just feeling a little homesick. Like you, Oscar."

Wilde pulled the shirt over his head and stood there bare-chested, his skin the color of putty, his ample podge spilling over the front of his trousers. "That has passed. I am no longer homesick. My moods are as mercurial as my wit. Indeed, I am looking forward to conquering the rustic dominions."

Conan Doyle shifted in his seat. Was he beginning to imagine things? And, more terrifyingly, given his family history, was he losing his mind? He had quite clearly seen the image of his consulting detective in the window glass. Either way, he was starting to believe that what his mother had said in her last letter was true: it was easy to kill Sherlock Holmes with the stroke of a pen. However, his ghost was proving considerably more difficult to lay.

CHAPTER 7

A DREAD AND UNWELCOMING VISTA

The station they arrived at was tiny: the waiting area a wrought-iron pergola scarcely large enough for two people to shelter beneath, the booking office a tiny wooden box with a glass ticket window. Even the platform was short—barely longer than the painted station sign that read SLATTENMERE.

Conan Doyle and Oscar Wilde debarked and stood on the platform surrounded by the heap of Wilde's luggage. Then the train, the station, and the world around them vanished as the railway engine released a cloud of steam with a *whhiiiiiisssssshhhh* like a punctured dragon. The cloud rose, swirled, dissipated, and the station reappeared as the train began to roll away.

Wilde took a deep breath in through his generously proportioned nose and coughed. "Ah," he fretted, "as I feared, the country air is overly oxygenated. I am quite giddy. Honestly, Arthur, how am I to breathe without a pound of London soot in my lungs?"

"You'll acclimatize, Oscar."

"Perhaps a cigarette to soothe the bronchioles," Wilde said, fumbling in a breast pocket for his silver cigarette case.

The train was chuffing into the distance when they heard the approaching clop-clop of hooves, and soon a pony and trap drew up on the platform. The driver was a broad-backed young man in a laborer's cloth cap, worn shirt, and braces. He looked down from his seat at the waiting Londoners and said, "Does tha' be the gents what are fer th'all?"

Wilde threw a nonplussed look at Conan Doyle, who nodded at the fellow and said, "Yes. That's right."

The young man leapt down from his cart and tugged the peak of his cap in respect. "Me name's Frank—Frank Carter. Carter be me name and carter be me trade." The young man paused, raised his head and made a show of scenting the air, then nodded toward the line of black clouds crowding the far horizon. "Oh, it's gunna rain, awreet. Tha' can smell inth'air."

Wilde threw a baffled look at his companion. He could speak five European languages fluently and translate Greek and Latin, but had no ear for English regional dialects. "What on earth did the fellow just yammer?" he whispered to Conan Doyle.

"He said it's going to rain. I think he's quite confident in his prediction."

Wilde bit his lip, his eyes wide with distress. "Oh, bother," he said. "I do hope my bags shan't get wet."

The young driver piled case after case into the back of the cart, turning and twisting each bag like puzzle pieces. Conan Doyle noted that the overloaded cart soon had a decidedly backward list, the cart stays threatening to hoist the small pony off its feet.

"Job's a good 'un," the cart driver said, patting the final bag as he slipped it into place like the capstone atop a pyramid. "We got 'em all, I reckon."

"Whatever do you mean—all?" Wilde asked. "That is just the baggage that carries my most immediate necessities." He pointed to the place thirty feet away where the rest of his baggage had been unloaded from the baggage car and stacked on the platform.

The carter's face fell. "Bloody hell!" he exclaimed. "No way can we fetch that lot." He pushed the cap back on his head and looked at Wilde. "It'll tek me a few trips, I reckon."

Wilde looked from the young man to Conan Doyle for interpretation. "Your extra baggage will be brought up to the Hall later, Oscar."

Wilde's face collapsed at the news. "We really are in the country, are we not? I fear my homesickness is returning." He clambered up onto the wagon and took his place on the seat. "Oh well. We are in the provinces. I suppose I'm expected to rough it."

With three large men and a cart overloaded with luggage, the small pony strained and trembled, unable to overcome the sheer inertia. The carter was obliged to jump down, put his shoulder to the back of the cart and heave with all his might to get things rolling, and then hop back up and snatch the reins from Conan Doyle.

The road outside the station turned instantly from cobblestone into a rutted dirt track cratered with potholes puddled with water. The cart swayed alarmingly as it jounced through them, Wilde's leather bags and portmanteaus creaking symphonically. After only twenty yards, the main road turned sharp left and passed straight through a farmyard. Geese honked and scattered. Chickens continued pecking obstinately, the cart wheels scything dangerously close. In the middle of the cobblestone yard a huddle of figures armed with glinting pitchforks assaulted a heap of straw—grimy children and rumpled farmhands, their patched clothes so stiffened with filth they could have stood up without their owners. As the cart rattled past, the farmhands gawped at the two well-dressed gentlemen as if they had descended from the moon. Wilde raised his straw boater to them and shouted: "You're all welcome to see my play when you come down to London. Tell them at the box office that Oscar Wilde grants you all the tickets you require." The farmworkers stared gormlessly after them as the cart turned out of the farmyard and rumbled along a lane bounded by tall hedgerows on either side.

Wilde took a deep, chest-expanding breath and let it out. "Ah, the country air is bracing if somewhat dungy. I must have my photograph taken posing in front of a hay wain wearing a rustic smock and a battered straw hat, a stalk of corn in my mouth."

"Really, Oscar?"

Wilde goggled his eyes in horror. "No, of course not. I should not allow myself even to be buried in such attire!"

The day brightened, and even though it was early April, the temperature rose to a comfortable degree, the air soft and balmy. They passed through a small wood glorious with birdsong and drunk with the scent of bluebells carpeting the forest floor. Gradually, the trees thinned and the wood fell behind as they passed through more farm fields, the lane ascending toward a crossroads where a dead and leafless tree crowded the verge, its gnarled roots clutching a faced stone slab inscribed with lettering worn blurred and indecipherable by centuries of rain.

"What does the writing on that stone say?" Conan Doyle asked the driver, pointing.

"*Gallows Way,*" the young man answered. "They used to hang criminals, witches, and other badduns from that very tree."

"I'm sure it draws tourists in droves," Wilde drily observed.

"It used to," Frank replied. "Five hundred or more folk would turn out for a good hangin'."

"Really?" Wilde said, eyes widening. "Five hundred people?" He turned to his friend and said, "Remind me to add a hanging scene to my next drawing room comedy."

As the cart passed the dead tree, a ragged-tailed crow dropped from its perch on the topmost branch and swooped low over their heads, cawing outrage as it flapped into the distance. The cart trundled onward to the crossroads where a hand-painted sign reading SLATTENMERE 1 MILE pointed straight ahead. A sign pointing at ninety degrees read Trough of Blackheath. The cart turned left without slowing.

"I thought we were going to Slattenmere?" Wilde asked.

Conan Doyle shook his head. "I consulted a map before we left London. Slattenmere is merely the largest town, after which the train station is named. We are heading for Thraxton Hall, which is somewhere up there." He pointed to a series of low green hills rising in the distance.

"Oh my!" Wilde said, biting his lip. "I have vertigo already."

"Those hills are just the beginning of the climb. There are even higher ones beyond. Better find your cloak. It's going to get chilly."

The pleasant farm fields soon fell behind. And then so did the trees and the hedgerows as they began to ascend into bleak moorland, treeless and carpeted with purple heather. The terrain became steeper and more spectacular, with waterfalls splashing into rocky pools and granite crags rising from green moorland that swooped into deep crevasses, their shadowy bottoms littered with the bleaching bones of sheep that had grazed too close and tumbled to their deaths.

"Forbidding and yet fabulous," Wilde said. He had produced a fur-lined cape from one of his voluminous suitcases and now huddled inside it, his long face framed by a wolf-fur hood. "It's like the Swiss Alps in miniature. I would not have guessed I was still in England."

They reached another, even steeper climb, which slowed the cart to a crawl and obliged the men to dismount and walk alongside. The wheezing pony slogged to the top of the final rise, where the carter yanked the reins to stop the cart and allow the beast to rest.

Conan Doyle and Wilde both marveled at the view. From this height, the road plunged downhill in a series of dizzying switchbacks into a small valley where a tree line grew along a riverbank—the sound of water tumbling over stones could be heard. In the distance stood the towering hulk of a great house.

"That must be Thraxton Hall!" Conan Doyle said, pointing.

"Aye, that be it, sir," the carter agreed, nodding.

"Looks rather dreary from here," Wilde remarked in a tone of deep disappointment.

Suddenly the ground shook with a low rumble—thunder.

The men looked back. The clouds were closer, steaming slowly toward them like black aerial dreadnoughts. A jagged flash of lightning forked at the base of one, and after a long pause, a rumbling crack of thunder drummed the hillsides.

Wilde grew ecstatic. "The storm is pursuing, Arthur! I feel positively Promethean." With a dramatic flourish, he threw open his cloak. "Perhaps I should bare my breast to the thunderstorm and dare it to strike!"

Unimpressed by such theatrics, the young driver turned his head and spat. "Nay, it's tekkin' its time. Won't be here for yonks."

Wilde leaned close and whispered in Conan Doyle's ear: "Translate, Arthur."

"Our young friend remarked that if self-immolation is truly your goal, you must be prepared for a long wait."

"Ah, never mind, then," Wilde said, frowning with disappointment.

After allowing the pony ten minutes to rest, the carter and his passengers clambered back onto the seat and set off down the hill, the cart tipping precariously at each switchback in the rutted road. At the base of the hill, the roadway crossed a sparkling ford. It was a mere trickle of ankle-deep water, but Conan Doyle noticed a muddy line on the larger boulders showing that the river could rise by several feet after a deluge.

The carter shook the reins and the pony and cart lumbered into the ford. As it reached the middle, one wheel struck a submerged

rock and the cart lurched to a halt. The young driver made a click-
ing noise with his mouth and the cart juddered forward. The wheel
struck the rock, slowly climbed . . . and then dropped over the other
side into a deep hole. The young carter swore under his breath. He
flicked the reins and geed the pony again, which leaned into the
harness, straining, but the cart would not budge.

Stuck fast.

Cussing under his breath, Frank Carter jumped down from
the seat and splashed around to the back of the cart to push. Conan
Doyle also jumped down, water instantly flooding his shoes and
soaking the hems of his trousers. He sloshed around to the far side
and grappled for a handhold. "Come along, Oscar," he chided. "All
hands to the wheel."

From his perch atop the wagon, Wilde looked down with an
abject expression. "These shoes cost me two guineas, Arthur. If
you two stout yeoman cannot free the cart, I suggest we send for
the Royal Navy."

"Two guineas for a pair of shoes?" Conan Doyle blurted. "Ridiculous!"

"Yes, I agree. I would have happily paid twice that amount. I
practically ran from the shop, thinking they had made a mistake in
their reckoning." Wilde raised a leg to show off his gleaming, ankle-
high boot. "Handmade on a wooden last modeled after my own foot.
Guaranteed against broken stitching, premature wear, loose soles,
toe scuffs, stains, and Acts of War. But sadly . . . everything *except*
submersion."

Conan Doyle rolled his eyes and gave the driver a nod. Together
they braced their shoulders against the rear of the cart and heaved,
straining until their leg muscles shook. Despite their trembling efforts, the cart merely rocked forward slightly and fell heavily back.

"I reckon she's stuck fast," the carter said. He removed his cap
and wiped his brow, fixing Conan Doyle with a disgruntled look.

"Too much weight with all the baggage. I'll have to walk back to th' farm and fetch a coupla shires to pull her out. Might tek me an hour to get back."

Wilde threw his friend a questioning look.

The Scottish doctor cleared his throat peevishly. "Our driver will have to go back to the farm and fetch a shire horse. It's going to take a while."

Conan Doyle peered into the distance. "The house isn't that far from here," he observed. "Looks like about two miles across the fields. I've walked farther than that after supper for a constitutional."

Wilde sniffed and drew the silver cigarette case from his pocket, scratched a match alight against the sole of his two-guinea shoe, and puffed a cigarette into life. "Very well," he announced. "Our rustic friend can go for help. You, Arthur, can carry on as the advance party to announce my imminent arrival. I shall remain here to guard the baggage train from attack by marauders."

Conan Doyle waded back to the wagon, unbuckled the cricket bat strapped to his luggage, and tucked it under one arm.

"Good heavens!" Wilde said, eyeing the bat. "I spoke in jest about the marauders." He looked around in alarm. "You don't think there are any, do you?"

"I shouldn't think so, Oscar." Conan Doyle waded from the ford and stood on the dirt road, stamping his feet to squelch the water from his shoes.

"Then why on earth are you taking a cricket bat?"

"Walking stick," Conan Doyle explained, leaning on it and walking up and down a few steps to demonstrate. "Plus, I can practice a few batting strokes along the way—limber up the muscles. Cricketing season starts in a few months. This year I plan to score a century."

Wilde was about to say something when he was interrupted by a long, drawn out rumbling like the collapse of a distant mountain range.

The carter looked up. "Storm's gettin' close," he said, eyeing an ominous black armada of thunderclouds cruising the western horizon. He turned his head and spat. "But tha never knows. Might miss us."

Another boom of thunder shook the world.

"Sounds like God's dark laughter," Wilde moaned. "An ominous portent!"

"Very well, then," Conan Doyle said. "I'm off. I'll let them know you'll be late."

And with that he strode off up the road. After a quarter mile he came across a stile and clambered over it into a rolling field. But after only a few minutes he was beginning to regret his decision to walk. The ground was soft and sodden, and he could scarcely take his eyes from his feet for the constant need to sidestep and dodge the many piles of sheep manure plopped across the field—though he had yet to see a living, bleating beast. He plunged into a deep ravine and scrambled up the other side, sweating through his tweed suit. His shoes were caked in mud and muck, but he was glad of the cricket bat, for having a prop saved him from many a fall. As he topped the grassy knoll, he paused to catch his wind and got his first good look at Thraxton Hall. Lit by a shaft of light bursting through dark clouds, it seemed charming: a grand manor in the old style, its limestone façade glowing warm against a backdrop of emerald trees that climbed the sloping hills beyond.

In the field before him were the sheep, a *baa*ing flock of a hundred or more that split apart and reformed behind him as he strode through their bleating masses. In contrast to the fat fluffy breeds of southern England, these were Lakeland sheep, thin and scrawny—sure-footed beasts that could brave blasting winds and bitter cold as they foraged the grassy hillsides.

Large limestone outcrops dotted the field. And then Conan Doyle noticed that what he had initially taken for cloud shadow was in fact a small coppice of rowan trees. His path to the house took him close by, and when he finally drew abreast he noticed a dark path leading into the coppice. Something about the gloomy path enticed him, and then he caught a glimpse of movement—a young girl in a bright blue dress. She was holding a rag doll clutched to her flat bosom, her large eyes watching him as she took a step backward and dissolved into the shadows.

Conan Doyle blinked, not entirely sure she wasn't a trick of the light. He changed course and walked toward the coppice, giving himself permission for a brief exploration. As he entered the path and rounded the first corner, he caught another glimpse of her. She was not a beggar's child. The dress was expensive, with bows and frilly pleats, but it was stained and dirty. Again it was just a glimpse—he snatched an impression of timid eyes and cheeks streaked with tears—before she darted away, out of sight beyond the curve of trees. He quickened his pace. The path wound in an inward-tightening spiral, so that he could never see more than ten feet ahead. It abruptly ended at a gloomy clearing. At its center stood an oval of rugged, chest-high boulders—a stone circle built by the ancient Britons. A shallow ditch encircled the stones, and around that was a raised mound, built from soil shoveled from the ditch. It was a site of great antiquity. Conan Doyle estimated it to be from a thousand years B.C.

He looked around. Listened. The woods were preternaturally still. The young girl had vanished. "Hello?" he called out. "Are you lost? Please come out. I promise I shan't hurt you."

Nothing stirred. He peered into the shadows. Had he really seen a girl? The trees of the coppice were packed tight, the lower limbs a mass of bare branches. A girl in such a flimsy dress would be torn to ribbons trying to penetrate the thicket. He felt foolish, certain he had been chasing a trick of the light.

With the cricket bat swinging at his side, he stalked the perimeter of the circle, and in the unnatural twilight of the clearing it was impossible not to sense the shades of ancient Britons, dead these many millennia, hovering close.

The rusty caw of a crow snapped his head up. A large black bird perched in the top of a nearby tree. From its ragged tail feathers, Conan Doyle recognized it as the same crow that had swooped over them at the gallows crossroads. The bird cawed again, and then dropped from the tree, swooping low, and pecked him on top of the head. He gave a shout of pain, and when he ran a hand through his hair, found that the beast had drawn blood. He heard a rustle of feathers and looked up to see the crow swooping again. But this time he was ready and swung the cricket bat, connecting solidly with the bird, which tumbled end over end and crashed in a splay of black wings. However, the crow was merely stunned and, after a moment, rolled onto its feet, and gave its wings a shake. The murderous black eyes glared at Conan Doyle before it sprang into the air and flapped away, cawing with rage.

Conan Doyle turned and strode out of the coppice, reemerging into slanting golden sunlight. From here, he could not see the house and set off in the rough direction. He reached another dry stone wall, and as he climbed over the stile, found to his surprise that Thraxton Hall was but a short walk away. By now the image of the young girl was written off as a mere hallucination and, energized by his victory over the crow, he set off at a military pace, jauntily swinging the cricket bat at his side, which, despite Wilde's skepticism, had served him well.

❦

CHAPTER 8

THRAXTON HALL

Thraxton Hall had seemed glorious from afar, but up close was a hideous Gothic Pile, hulking and gloomy, with a confusion of gables and a roofline porcupined with chimneys, many with brick-work zigzagged with cracks, broken chimney pots, and some in a partial state of collapse. The entire west wing was in an advanced state of disrepair, shedding scabrous chunks of its limestone façade. The building's many windows—all tightly shuttered—were tall and narrow and gave the impression of mouths that had been stoppered, mid-scream.

A number of ladders were leaned up here and there, and tiny figures spidered up and down them—workmen apparently repair-ing the shutters. The massive double doors of the house were reached by ascending a short flight of stone steps, the finials of which were a pair of carved stone phoenixes. The wind was blowing from the house and carried to him the tang of banked coal fires as well as a familiar whiff of Turkish tobacco, so that even from this distance, he could guess the identity of the cigarette-smoking figure loung-ing with his back against one of the phoenixes guarding the front entrance: Oscar Wilde. Somehow the cart had been freed and had beaten him to the house.

"Hello, Arthur," Wilde said as Conan Doyle trudged up, looking worn and red-faced. "I hope you enjoyed your stroll. Did the cricket bat come in handy? Did you knock one for six?"

"In a manner of speaking," Conan Doyle answered. He was tired, his feet were soaking wet, and he had no desire to launch into a long explanation. "I discovered a stone circle. Probably a thousand years old. Perhaps two."

"Let us hope our accommodations are not of similar antiquity," Wilde said, pursing his lips and jetting a silver stream of smoke into the air.

"What are those chaps up to?" Conan Doyle asked, nodding to the tiny figures teetering atop the ladders.

"Workmen fetched from the village to open the shutters. I've been watching them for twenty minutes."

Conan Doyle frowned in puzzlement. "Why don't they just open them from inside?"

"Because they've been screwed shut. Apparently the inside of Thraxton Hall hasn't seen the light of day in many years."

"How very odd."

"Yes," Wilde agreed. "I also thought it peculiar." He took a lazy drag on his cigarette. "But at least the rugs won't have faded."

Just then, Frank Carter emerged from the shadowy rectangle of the open front door and tripped down the steps toward them.

"That's the last of yer bags, sir," he said to Wilde, touching the peak of his cap. He was breathing hard after lugging Wilde's considerable ensemble of baggage, and obviously eager to be on his way, but Wilde arrested him with a raised hand.

"One moment, young Frank," he said. He pulled a coin purse from his pocket, produced two golden guineas, and held them out to the young man.

"But I've been paid already, sir," Frank said, eyes saucering at the largesse being offered to him.

"That's as may be," Wilde argued, "but you have saved my two-guinea shoes, and you need to be suitably rewarded." And with that he pressed the coins into the young man's calloused palm.

"But, sir. I can't take it. It's *too* much."

"You *will* take it, Frank, because you have earned it. You will take it but you must promise me one thing."

The young man gawped at him uncomprehendingly.

"You will save one of the guineas for your wedding day. With the other I expect you to treat yourself to a nightly pint in the pub at the end of your day's labors. I insist the money is to be spent purely on pleasure, such as only the young can fully enjoy."

Frank Carter's eyes misted as his large hand closed on the two coins. "Thank you, sir. I reckon I don't know what to say."

"Say nothing, and I shall expect similar stalwart service from you on the return journey. Now, be off with you before the pub shuts."

The young man was stunned by Wilde's act of kindness. "Yes, s-sir," he stammered, once again touching the peak of his cap. "Thank y-you very much, sir."

As young Frank drove the cart away, still beaming with his good fortune, Conan Doyle threw his friend a look of gentle reprimand and said, "That was ridiculously generous, Oscar."

"Yes, I know," Wilde agreed. "But I am a ridiculous man. How else am I to maintain such a reputation without acting so?"

A smile formed beneath Conan Doyle's walrus moustache. "Spot on," he said quietly.

A polite cough drew their attention to the top of the stone steps where a figure appeared in the darkened doorway: a tall, impossibly slim, hollow reed of a man dressed in the sober livery of a butler. His hair was shock-white, his face creased with years. He did not look at either of them directly, but stood at the threshold staring blankly into space as he announced in a creaky voice: "Gentleman, Thraxton Hall is waiting to receive you."

As the two ascended the stone steps, Conan Doyle noticed the servant's shockingly shabby appearance. The shoulders of his butler's jacket were sprinkled with dandruff. He had apparently brushed his thinning hair with a comb missing most of its teeth. His black jacket and trousers were stamped with dust prints. But as they climbed the final steps, Conan Doyle saw up close the man's eyes were milky white marbles set into the deathly pallor of his face. Wilde noticed them at the same moment. The two men exchanged a look, and Conan Doyle silently mouthed: *Blind*.

"Welcome to Thraxton Hall," the butler intoned. He must have guessed their proximity by the sound of their footsteps, because he stepped backward at the precise moment they reached the top of the stairs and bowed. "I am Mister Greaves, the butler."

They stepped into a marble entrance hall both vast and cavernous. The ceiling floated forty feet above their heads and the walls that soared up to support it were hung with giant portraits in elaborate gilt frames—the heirs of Thraxton, who stared somberly down at them. One particular painting immediately caught Conan Doyle's eye—the portrait of a lady in her closet, apparently attending to her makeup. The woman had a long mane of auburn hair that framed a face of great beauty. Given the fact that the portrait occupied pride of place in the entrance hall, he assumed it could only be a portrait of the mysterious Lady Thraxton, the "psychic medium of some renown."

To one side of the grand staircase, the servants of the house stood assembled in a line to greet them. In the dim light they resembled a collection of the rather less convincing effigies dragged from storage in a dusty corner of Madame Tussauds' waxworks: a pair of ancient footmen, a hirsute gardener, and four women: a flour-dusted cook, a willowy maid, a moon-faced scullery girl, and a forbidding-looking matronly woman whose long gray hair was swept up into a giant nest for some kind of roosting bird. Conan

Doyle scanned for the Sikh footman who had opened the door of the Mayfair home to him, but he was notably absent.

"Good Lord," Wilde murmured sotto voce, "the house is five hundred years old and retains its original staff." He took a final drag on his cigarette, dropped it to the polished floor, and crushed it out beneath the sole of his two-guinea shoe. The matron hurled him a Medusan stare, mouth puckering like a leather purse cinched tight. It was clear she did not appreciate guests using her Italian marble floor as an ashtray.

"I am Mrs. Kragan," she said in an Irish accent: not the lilting music of rural Ireland, but the harsh, guttural tones of Dublin. "I am head housekeeper. If you find anything not to your liking, you are to report it to me." It was an order, not an invitation. "Now Mister Greaves will show you to your rooms."

"Alfred . . . Tom," Mister Greaves called, "take the gentlemen's bags." The footmen shuffled forward until their shins collided with the luggage. From the way they groped at the pile, it became clear that, with the exception of the gardener, all the male domestics were as blind as Mister Greaves. When the footmen had gathered up two bags in each hand, the butler said, "If you would follow me please, gentlemen," then turned and limped away in his faltering gait.

"Follow him?" Wilde whispered. "The fellow cannot see where he is going. We could wind up walking off a balcony into thin air!"

As they reached the base of the grand staircase, Mister Greaves paused and indicated a long gallery to their left. "That is the portrait gallery. It leads to the ballroom and the west wing, which, I'm afraid, is in a state of disrepair and extremely dangerous. Guests are encouraged not to stray there."

They plodded up the staircase, which creaked, squeaked, and squealed with every step. As they neared the landing, the teetering structure shimmied violently beneath their feet, threatening imminent collapse and forcing both men to death-grip the banister.

"Do not be alarmed, gents," Mister Greaves said, never faltering in his plodding ascent, "the staircase has done that for the last twenty years."

Thankfully, they reached the second-floor landing safely, and turned right, following a long, open gallery.

Wilde's misgivings about Mister Greaves soon proved to be wrong. The two friends silently followed the cadaverous butler as he effortlessly navigated a maze of gloomy hallways. Along open landings. Up and down creaking stairways. The other servants, although burdened with luggage, shambled silently behind like shades of the dead condemned to wander the labyrinthine passageways of Thraxton Hall for eternity.

"I should explain why the house is so dark," Conan Doyle muttered to his companion. "Lady Thraxton has an ailment. A sensitivity to the light."

Wilde glanced at him. "Hence the reason for screwing down the shutters?"

"Precisely."

"And a staff of domestics," Conan Doyle continued, "most of whom lack sight, and therefore do not object to working in a house in perpetual darkness."

"I noticed that the corridors have a raised runner on each side." Wilde indicated with a nod.

"So that the blind servants may navigate by feel?" Conan Doyle speculated.

"Clever," Wilde agreed, "if somewhat grotesque."

* * *

As they reached the third floor, the workers atop the ladders were just cracking open the window shutters. Shades were unscrewed and flung back from the glass for the first time in decades, spilling in shafts of golden light swirling with galaxies of dust motes.

They turned a sharp left and trooped along a gloomy corridor until Mister Greaves stopped at an unmarked door. "This will be your room, Mister Wilde." He produced a key, groped the door with one hand and, finding the lock, turned the key in it.

"The room, sir," Wilde said, addressing the butler. "May I enquire, is it haunted?"

"Haunted?" the butler repeated, his frown deepening. "I'm afraid there are stories about nearly every room in this house."

"Excellent!" Wilde beamed. "I must always have an audience— even if it's a spectral one." He turned to Conan Doyle. "I shall be unpacking and choosing my wardrobe for the evening. I may be some time."

Having dropped off Wilde and a portion of his baggage, Mister Greaves continued on to the next room. They had gone barely twelve feet when Wilde's piercing scream made Conan Doyle turn and run back. When he dashed into the bedroom, Wilde was biting the back of his hand, a look of utter distraction on his face.

"Oscar!" he cried. "What is it?"

"This room . . ." Wilde said in a wretched voice, turning to his friend with an almost deranged look, ". . . is quite ghastly!"

Conan Doyle exhaled a heavy sigh. "You gave me quite a turn. I thought you'd seen something horrible."

"But I *have* seen something horrible—the bed, the rug, the furniture, the wallpaper . . . the wallpaper . . . ," he repeated, pointing to each in turn. "It is *all* horrible. Who on earth was their decorator, Hieronymus Bosch? I'm sorry Arthur, but I fear I must leave at once."

"But we've just arrived, Oscar!"

"I know, but this place is gloomy, dull, and unspeakably ugly. And you know how much I cannot abide ugliness in any form. I live for beauty. I must always be surrounded with pulchritude and the perfume of fresh-cut flowers, or I simply wither."

Conan Doyle swallowed his frustration and fought to keep his expression neutral. "I see. Very well. We shall arrange for you to leave in the morning."

Wilde clapped him on the shoulder. "You're a good friend, Arthur. Always understanding. But you must admit, I did get you this far."

"Yes," Conan Doyle muttered between clenched teeth. "However would I have managed without you?"

He left Wilde to fret about his accommodations and followed Mister Greaves along the corridor to the next room. The butler produced an enormous jailer's key and groped the door with his free hand. As he fitted the key into the lock, he paused a moment and turned his blank gaze toward Conan Doyle. "May I enquire, sir are you a sound sleeper?"

"Why, yes," Conan Doyle replied. "Very sound."

"And are you troubled by excessive dreaming?"

It was an odd question, but then everything about Thraxton Hall was odd. "No, not unusually so."

Something approximating a smile formed on the old man's face. "Then this room should serve your needs."

Mister Greaves entered, walked directly to a suitcase stand, and set the bag upon it. As he followed the butler into the room, Conan Doyle's mouth bittered with a film of must and mildew. Despite the fact that the windows had been left open in an attempt to air out the space, the room had the feeling of an ancient tomb that had only recently been broken into. Having deposited the suitcase, Mister Greaves shrugged a barely perceptible bow and ambled toward the door, his feet scuffing the worn rug.

"I say," Conan Doyle said, "do you have any idea when the other guests will be arriving?"

The tall butler paused and spoke without turning. "They are already here, save for one. A sherry reception is planned at three, followed by dinner in the formal dining room. I shall come to fetch you and Mister Wilde at the appropriate time. Anything else, sir?"

Conan Doyle shook his head, and then realized his mistake. "No . . . no thank you, Mister Greaves."

The butler bowed his head and shuffled toward the door.

"Oh, yes. Wait. One final thing."

The butler stopped and turned to face Conan Doyle, his aged face molded in an expression of infinite patience.

"Mister Greaves, might I inquire how long you have worked for the family?"

"I have served the Thraxton family since I was a boy, as my father before me."

"So you knew Lord Thraxton intimately?"

"Which Lord Thraxton sir? I have served under three. The youngest, Lord Alphonse Thraxton, left the house when he reached the age of majority. He fell into a crevasse whilst mountain climbing in Switzerland. The body was never recovered."

"Did he get along well with his father?"

A grimace tightened the net of wrinkles. "No, sir. There was no love lost betwixt the two. The elder blamed his son for his first wife's death—she died in childbirth."

"Ah, I see. Not a happy story."

A grimace tightened the net of wrinkles. "There are *no* happy stories in this house," the butler said matter-of-factly.

"So you are the longest served?"

"Yes, as you might imagine, sir. Mrs. Kragan has been with the family for thirty years. The next longest serving retainer is Toby, the gardener."

"I see."

"Will that be all, sir?"

"Indeed. Thank you, Mister Greaves."

The butler nodded and then turned and limped toward the door. But for the fact that he dragged one hand along the poor jamb as he left, it was impossible to tell that he lacked sight. When the door had closed on his tall frame, Conan Doyle looked around at the accommodations he had been given.

The room was situated on the front of the house, and the windows, now that the shutters had been pried open, looked out on the pleasant valley fields and the coppice with the stone circle. But even with three tall windows facing a southern aspect, the room seemed drenched in darkness. Almost everything was constructed from the same kind of wood: an aged walnut so dark it was almost obsidian—the wall paneling, the wardrobe, the armchairs, and the old-fashioned four-poster. Together they sponged up the light. Something made him look again at the wall paneling. It was all ornately carved: an immense, complex foliate design that did not repeat itself. It appeared like a forest of winding vines and oak boughs, three-dimensional. And then his eye began to resolve figures peering out from the vines as they crawled, clambered, or slithered through them. They were not human, although several had quasi-human features. Conan Doyle felt a moment of heart-stopping déjà vu when he realized he had seen something very similar before. His father had been a painter by profession and a drinker by predilection. During his brief periods of sobriety, before the drink irrevocably robbed him of his mind, Charles Altamont Doyle had made an income as an illustrator. He had continued to paint as part of his therapy in a mental institution. When these paintings were mailed to the family upon his death, Conan Doyle found them deeply disturbing and burned them in the fireplace. The paintings were filled with weird, elfish creatures; part-animal, part-human, as if his father's madness had been a lens that allowed his vision to pierce the veil of normal existence and glimpse a strange and unsettling world that lurked unseen around us.

Conan Doyle pulled his eyes away from the wall paneling with some difficulty. He was still clutching the rubber grip of *Thunderer*, his favorite cricket bat, and now he set it down beside the bed. He went to his suitcase and unfastened the leather straps. Upon release, the tightly compressed contents sprang up several inches. As Wilde had predicted, the suitcase contained three tweed suits; however, they were not precisely identical: one was oatmeal, one was beige, and one was muffin-colored. Conan Doyle lifted them out and set them aside. His hand rummaged beneath layers of socks and cotton drawers until it closed upon a small leather bag: a miniature version of his full-sized Gladstone; it contained a stethoscope, a suture kit, and a few vials of drugs. He set aside his sharply pressed suits and rummaged once again. This time he pulled out a bulky object trussed in a black cloth. He unwrapped it to reveal his trusty service revolver. He had hesitated about bringing it. But the medium's description of her murder—two bullets in the chest, fired at close range—meant that he was facing an armed adversary. Conan Doyle did not intend to enter the fray at a disadvantage. He regarded the Webley .455 for a moment, slipped his hand onto the grip, and hefted its weight. Then he rewrapped the pistol in its black cloth. He peered around the room, searching for potential hiding places, then stepped to the bed and slipped it beneath the mattress. It was perhaps an obvious place, but he suspected that the domestic staff of Thraxton Hall would not be changing the linens for a few days.

Finished with his unpacking for now, he dropped into a chair, kicked off his shoes, and peeled the wet socks from his feet. He got up wearily, crossed to the bed, swept aside the bed curtains, and lay down. The pillows were hard and lumpy. The sheets felt damp.

He looked up at the once-white four-poster canopy, which was sagging, yellowed with age, and holed in places—a dozen small shadows marked the corpses of moths that had eaten their final meal and died there. Then his eyes traced down the nearest of the four bedposts. It, too, was made of the same dark walnut as the wall paneling and was carved in the same gothic style: a menagerie of ghastly leering faces and hideous chimeras ripped from a nightmare. Nothing about the bed or the room was comfortable or seemed conducive to rest, but it had been a long day and he was exhausted. He closed his eyes for a moment, feeling a sense of vertigo as if he were sinking into the mattress. There was a clock somewhere in the room; he could hear its tick, tick, tick.

The metallic heartbeat of Time.

He thought to look for it, to see what the hour was, but could not bring himself to open his eyes or lift his head from the pillow. And then he heard the sound of weeping, as if from a long way away, and felt the heart-clutching sensation of being utterly suffused with despair. It was his last conscious thought before he slipped into a sleep so horribly deep it felt more like drowning.

He was awakened by the thunderous crash of the building falling down about him.

CHAPTER 9

THE SOCIETY FOR PSYCHICAL RESEARCH

Conan Doyle's eyes flew open. The canopy above glowed with a shivering, supernal light. The bed he lay upon shook violently as a Doom Crack roar rumbled on and on and on. Then the light seemed to be sucked back, like a retreating tide, out through the open windows. A moment later he heard the rain. It began as a gentle hiss that quickly rose to a pounding tumult. An icy gale gusted in through the open windows and whipped the long curtains into a frenzy. He rolled from the bed and rushed to wrestle the windows shut as icy raindrops spattered his face. Outside, day had turned to impenetrable night—the storm clouds he had seen earlier had finally tracked him to ground and a deluge was bouncing off the stone paths. It was only when he slammed the last window shut, muting the storm, that he noticed an insistent knocking at the bedroom door.

He opened it to find Oscar Wilde lurking outside. He had changed attire yet again: black velvet knickers and silk stockings with buckled shoes, a velvet waistcoat, white shirt, and a puce cravat. Pinned to his lapel was a sunflower he had carefully transported all the way from London, kept safe in a moist handkerchief. Atop his head he wore a tasseled red fez tilted at a jaunty angle.

"Arthur," he said, breezing into the room, "do you have a mirror in here? My room is fully appointed when it comes to mold, mildew, must, dust, rust, fungus, rising damp, and deathwatch beetle, but for some inexplicable reason it is completely devoid of mirrors. Can you fathom it? Oscar Wilde in a room without mirrors! The mind recoils. How is a gentleman to dress? How is he to shave?" Wilde's gaze ricocheted around the room and finally came to rest on Conan Doyle's face. "I see no mirror in here, either." His expression soured. "Am I in purgatory?"

Mister Greaves tottered into the room in time to overhear Wilde's comments. "I'm afraid, sir, there are no mirrors anywhere in the house."

"No mirrors?" Wilde said, a note of panic creeping into his voice. "Surely you jest?"

The aged head tremored a *no*. "The late Lord Thraxton had all the mirrors removed following the death of his wife."

"Removed?" Conan Doyle said. "Whatever for?"

"He said that mirrors encouraged vanity."

Wilde flinched, momentarily taken aback. "He says that as if it were a bad thing."

"I would be happy to shave you, sir," Mister Greaves said. "I am an excellent barber. I shaved Lord Thraxton every morning . . . before his, ah, unfortunate demise."

At the offer, Wilde clapped a hand reflexively to his throat, his eyes widening with horror. The fact that Mister Greaves was facing in quite the wrong direction as he spoke did nothing to engender confidence in the blind butler's dexterity with a razor.

"Please tell me Lord Thraxton did not die in a shaving-related accident."

The ghost of a smile haunted Mister Greaves' chapped lips. "You may rest easy on that point, sir. Lord Thraxton vanished while walking on the moors and was never seen again."

Wilde was unable to suppress a shudder. "Strangely, I remain unreassured."

Mister Greaves coughed dryly. "If you gentlemen are finished with your dress, the other guests are waiting in the parlor. I've been sent to fetch you."

"Come, Arthur," Wilde said. "If we leave now we shall be fashionably late. If we dally further, we will be boorishly tardy."

* * *

The two friends followed Mister Greaves' halting perambulation down flights of stairs and along shadowy corridors. They seemed to be taking a different route back downstairs. Conan Doyle tried to take notice of key features: the location of landings, staircases, marble busts, scowling portraits, and giant urns, so he could navigate the return journey, but the house was a shadowy maze, and he soon gave up. "I'm lost," he muttered. "I don't know how we shall ever find our way back to our rooms."

"I should have fetched a ball of twine," Wilde moaned. "Or left a trail of bread crumbs. I fear we may wander these hallways until our clothes wear to rags. Where exactly are we going?"

"To meet the other guests . . . in the parlor. Take note. We are solving a murder in reverse order: meeting the perpetrator *before* the murder is committed."

"What I am supposed to be looking for?"

"I have no idea," Conan Doyle admitted. "An individual of questionable character? A devious mind? A personality capable of murder?"

"You have just described most of my critics."

They reached the ground floor, where Mister Greaves eventually led them into a large formal room brightly lit by a pair of giant gasoliers suspended from the ceiling. A suit of armor, ominous and threatening, stood on guard to one side of a fireplace made of huge fieldstones. The room was furnished in a mismatch of armchairs, love seats, fainting couches, chaise longues, cane chairs, and sofas of varying styles and eras, dragged in from different rooms to provide adequate seating for the guests, ten in number, who stood in knots, making conversation. Heads turned as the pair entered. As usual, Wilde drew the most attention, thanks to his greater stature and outlandish style of dress. The enormous yellow sunflower pinned to his lapel helped a good deal.

"Ah, here is our famous author!" announced a man who broke from the clutch of guests he was chatting with and stepped forward to greet the two, his hand extended for a handshake. He was a man of advanced years with a mane of graying hair and a frizzy salt-and-pepper beard spilling down upon his chest. "You are Arthur Conan Doyle," the man said, vigorously pumping the author's arm. "I am very glad to meet you. I am Henry Sidgwick, current president of the Society." He turned to Wilde, his face lighting up with recognition "And you are Oscar Wilde, the playwright!"

"It is an honor, sir," Wilde said, bowing slightly as he shook Sidgwick's hand.

"It is an honor for *us!*"

"That is what I meant," Wilde added, setting the group atitter.

Sidgwick barked a laugh. "There's that famous wit I've heard so much about!"

"Yes, I have found that my reputation means I must always be witty. Should I fail to perform, I am instantly labeled as an aloof snob or a crashing boor."

The room laughed again, and the rest of the guests surged forward, suddenly energized to shake hands with the playwright whose fame in London society was exceeded only by his notoriety.

"I do hope I did no wrong in inviting my friend along," Conan Doyle put in quickly. "I know your original invitation was only to me, but Oscar is very much interested in the field of spiritualism."

"No!" Sidgwick gushed. "Not at all. Indeed, we are honored to receive the esteemed Mister Wilde as our guest!"

Conan Doyle hung back as Wilde greeted each person with relaxed grace and good humor. It was in just such social situations that Wilde shone, while Conan Doyle fidgeted, ill at ease at being the center of attention. Plus, it presented an opportunity to study the other guests. Many he recognized from their photographs in the newspapers: the scientist Sir William Crookes, a tall spectacled man of middle years with white hair, a pointed white beard, and elaborately waxed mustachios (and whose breath smelled of top-drawer scotch); Madame Zhozhovsky, the Russian mystic, a lady in her eighties, squat and stout as Victoria herself, with penetrating gray eyes set in a face like an unrisen soufflé. She hobbled about the room on a walking stick made from a staff of gnarled hawthorn, accompanied, bizarrely, by a small monkey perched on her shoulder. To Conan Doyle's great amusement, the monkey was wearing an embroidered waistcoat and had a tiny red fez perched atop its head.

As she stumped forward to greet them, Conan Doyle leaned close to his friend and whispered, "Oh, look, Oscar, someone who shares your dress sense."

Wilde quailed upon seeing the monkey. "Oh, Gawd!" he moaned. "How very regrettable."

The two men straightened as the stunted form shuffled up to them.

"You may call me, simply, *Madame*," the old lady said in a tremulous voice lacking the meagerest trace of a Russian accent. She presented them with her monkey. "And this is my familiar, *Mephistopheles*."

"How utterly . . . delightful," Wilde said, his expression suggesting quite the opposite. He extended his hand for a handshake, but then snatched it back as the monkey bared its fangs and hissed at him.

Henry Sidgwick introduced his wife, Eleanor, a mathematical genius in her own right and a handsome, if somewhat plainly dressed woman. Then a strange figure moved toward them: a man, several inches shorter than Conan Doyle, dressed in a white military uniform—a red sash slashing diagonally across a chest jangling with a dozen military medals and multicolored campaign ribbons, a pair of epaulettes like horse brushes balanced atop each shoulder. The man wore an officer's military cap with a shiny black brim. But, most disconcertingly, his face was hidden behind a three-quarter mask of white leather. Only his mouth was visible, surrounded by a moustache and fiery red chin beard worn short-cropped like a Russian Tsar. He marched stiffly up to them, clicked his heels together, and threw them a short bow.

"This is the Count," Henry Sidgwick hurried to explain, having seen the rather alarmed looks on their faces. "The mask is for a reason. The Count is traveling incognito." And then he added in a conspiratorial whisper: "To avoid any whiff of scandal at home."

"And where is home for the Count?" Wilde asked, offering his hand for a handshake.

"That you must excuse me," the Count answered in heavily accented English. "But to say I must not. In my country, I heff many enemies."

"Ah," said Wilde. "I find that a man cannot be too careful in his choice of enemies. I hope that we shall all be friends."

The mask swiveled as the Count focused his attention on Conan Doyle. "And you are the ingenious creator of Sherlock Holmes. These stories I read with enjoyment very much."

"Thank you," Conan Doyle answered quickly, anxious to move on to a different topic. The Scottish author shook the Count's hand. He wore white cotton gloves on his small hands, had a limp, effeminate grip, and smelled of floral hair oil.

Conan Doyle detested him at once.

"Tell me, Doctor Doyle, are you here to catch a murderer?" the Count asked.

Conan Doyle's mouth dropped open in surprise. But then the Count chuckled at what was apparently an attempt at humor and patted a shiny leather pistol holster strapped to his side. "I always carry a veapon. In my country, I am the constant target of assassins." He chuckled again, inexplicably. "I confess my English is not so good, but I look forward to practice my skills with two masters of the language." The Count clicked his heels again and snapped off another bow, then spun on his heel and marched back to his seat.

"Good Lord," Conan Doyle muttered to his companion. "What an extraordinary character!"

"I imagine he is wound up each morning with a large key in the middle of his back."

"Gentleman," an American voice announced from behind them. "It is a great pleasure to finally meet ya, face to face, so to speak."

They turned. Daniel Dunglas Hume stood before them. He was dressed in a long frock coat and an ivory shirt, a black bolo tie cinched about his neck. As before, he clutched a white lace handkerchief in one hand. He shook both their hands warmly, a smile on his handsome face. "I regret that you were there to witness my little attack of travel fatigue. I can assure you I am quite rested now. In fact, I have been asked by Mister Sidgwick to provide our members with a little sample of my abilities after dinner—the levitation."

"I am sure you will rise to the occasion," Wilde quipped, which caused all three of them to chuckle.

"Traveling is draining at the best of times," Conan Doyle said. "Should you find yourself feeling unwell, feel free to call upon me. Although I am better known these days for my scribbling, I am first and foremost a doctor and would be happy to extend my services should you require."

Hume smiled. "Why I thank ya, sir. That is most obliging. Y'all are most kind. Should I find the need, I shall avail myself of your services."

He was interrupted by the sound of bolts being shot. Mister Greaves cleared his throat to catch everyone's attention as he announced: "Lady Hope Thraxton."

Double doors swung open revealing a long corridor so gloomy it seemed like a shaft mined into a block of night. Conan Doyle presumed that, because of her porphyria, the windows on the part of the house Hope Thraxton resided in—her rooms and the corridor leading to them—remained tightly shuttered. They heard the approach of soft footsteps, and then a figure appeared: a slender woman, dressed in black, her face hidden behind a black veil. The room fell so quiet Conan Doyle could hear the rustle of her silk dress. She glided into sight but paused momentarily at the terminator between light and dark.

Conan Doyle felt his pulse quicken. He could not look away. The woman seemed to gather herself and then stepped into the light. As she entered the room, no one spoke. She advanced a few more steps, the veiled face scanning left and right.

Oscar Wilde leaned close to Conan Doyle's ear and whispered out the side of his mouth: "I feel like a worshiper in Ancient Greece, come to consult the Oracle of Delphi."

The Scottish author did not answer but continued to stare in rapt fascination. The woman brought her hands up to her veil but hesitated, torturing her audience a moment longer, and then merely smoothed the veil in place without lifting it.

Somehow, he had imagined an older woman. But it was clear Lady Thraxton had inherited the title at a surprisingly young age. Even through the veil, Conan Doyle could tell she was a young girl of barely more than twenty years . . . and very fetching.

"I welcome you all to my home," she said in a sonorous voice— the same musical voice he had heard in the darkened room. Her eyes fixed momentarily on Wilde, and her brows arched in surprised recognition. Then her gaze fell upon Conan Doyle and lingered meaningfully, and he felt his stomach somersault. She broke the gaze first and moved forward to offer her hand to Henry Sidgwick.

"No," Conan Doyle murmured to his friend, never taking his eyes from her Ladyship. "She is more than an oracle, she is the goddess incarnate."

"'Strewth!" Wilde said, throwing his friend an astonished look. "You are truly smitten, Arthur. You've lapsed from prose into poetry!"

Conan Doyle flushed and spluttered "Ah, no . . . no . . . I . . . no . . . not at all." He had no time to finish the thought as Sidgwick conducted Lady Thraxton to meet them.

"We have a surprise guest," Sidgwick said by way of introduction. "Mister Oscar Wilde, playwright and wit."

"Your Ladyship, I am entranced," Wilde breathed. And with his usual drama, he bowed and, taking the young lady's hand, lightly kissed her gloved knuckles. The Lady preened with clear delight at such a flamboyant display of gallantry.

Even through the veil, the exquisite almond curve of Hope Thraxton's eyes set the Scottish doctor's knees quivering. And then they were face-to-face as Sidgwick introduced them: "This, milady, is Doctor Arthur Conan Doyle, famed author of the Sherlock Holmes mysteries."

Hope Thraxton met his eyes squarely and extended her hand to Conan Doyle, who, cursing his own shyness, timidly gripped her hand for a moment and then relinquished it.

"I have read all your Holmes stories," she said, in her girl's voice. "I very much enjoyed them. I don't know how you think of such clever plots. I find them quite mystifying."

Conan Doyle bowed modestly. "I am flattered to hear it, your Ladyship." He had feared she would give away their prior meeting with a comment or a look, but when she moved on instantly, he felt crushed.

Further introductions were interrupted as the head housekeeper, Mrs. Kragan, appeared at the open door, her black eyes glinting like nail heads driven into wood. She cleared her throat and announced in an abrasive squawk, "Dinner is ready, milady."

Amid an excited smatter of conversation, the group drifted from the parlor into the hallway and then filed into a large dining room. This part of the house, if still irrefutably ugly, was opulent with gilt, gold leaf, and sterling, and spoke of the kind of wealth accumulated through generations. From the dining room's green leather walls, more of the Thraxton ancestors glowered down upon a long table set with fine china and three enormous silver candelabrums.

Conan Doyle and Wilde took two seats at one end of the table, and the Scotsman was disappointed to see that Hope Thraxton took her place at the head of the table, with the Count seated at her right and Sidgwick and his wife seated on her left. His neighbor was a young man in his mid-twenties. With an unruly mop of brown hair, a dense brown beard, and an intense dark-eyed gaze, he reminded Conan Doyle of a ratting terrier he had once owned as a young boy.

"I don't think we've been introduced," the Scottish doctor said jovially, extending his hand. "I am Arthur Conan Doyle."

The young man shook Conan Doyle's large hand with a clammy grip. At first the doctor surmised that his dinner companion had suffered a stroke, for the corner of his mouth was tilted awry. Soon, however, he would conclude that it was a permanent sneer the small man was quite unconscious of.

"Doyle?" the young man repeated in a nasal midlands accent. "That is an Irish surname, is it not?"

"I was born a Scots, but the family roots are in Ireland. Do you find a difficulty with that?"

The young man shook his head disinterestedly. "I confess I

really don't care." He seemed to remember his manners and volunteered, "I am Frank Podmore."

Wilde leaned across his friend to speak to the young man. "This is *the* Conan Doyle of the Sherlock Holmes stories."

Podmore's expression never wavered. "I'm afraid I do not know what you speak of."

Wilde slumped back in his seat, a hand clamped to his heart in a pantomime of shock. "Sherlock Holmes, the detective. You must have read the stories in *The Strand Magazine?*"

"Stories?" Podmore repeated, without the faintest gleam of recognition lighting his eyes. But then the penny dropped and his sneer deepened. "Ah, *fiction,*" he said in the tone of a man who has trodden in something nasty. "I am a scientist. I don't have time for stories about things that never happened. All my reading is devoted to bettering my mind."

Wilde and Conan Doyle shared a look. "Well," Wilde said. "I suspect that explains our predicament, Arthur. All our reading is apparently devoted to worsening our minds."

All eyes were suddenly drawn by a penetrating chinking sound that set everyone's teeth on edge. At the foot of the table, Henry Sidgwick had risen from his chair and was rapping his spoon against a wineglass. "I would be remiss if we began our dinner without expressing gratitude to our gracious host, Lady Thraxton, for opening her wonderful home to us for the first meeting of the Society for Psychical Research. I am sure this will be a week we shall all long remember." He raised his glass in a toast. "Please raise your glasses to Lady Thraxton."

Everyone stood, except for the Lady, who lowered her veiled head demurely. Her shyness struck Conan Doyle. *Please, dear lady, be at ease,* he thought. *You are among friends.*

Instantly, she raised her head and fixed him with a soft gaze that radiated gratitude.

Conan Doyle's heart tumbled. It seemed as though he had transmitted the thought and she had received it. He dropped his eyes to his wineglass. *What if she can read my thoughts? She is, after all, a medium.* He shifted his feet and plumbed his mind for an image of his wife, Touie, but found only the image of the young woman's exquisite, almond-shaped eyes.

"*To Lady Thraxton.*" The room responded, with Conan Doyle joining in a moment too late.

Lady Thraxton raised her head and said, "Thank you. Thank you all," in a small voice. Her nervous glance flitted from one person to the next, but when her look fell upon Conan Doyle, it lingered a moment longer before moving on.

"The Lady seems to be taking special notice of you, Arthur," Wilde muttered close to his ear.

"Yes. I'm sure it's about the letter and the, er, circumstances that brought us here."

Wilde mused a moment and said, "Hmmn, I think not. I have seen that look in a young woman's eye before, and I believe it concerns danger of a very different kind."

"Nonsense!" Conan Doyle blustered, trying to laugh it off. He lifted the champagne to his lips and took a sip, but found to his own surprise that his hand trembled and that his heart was softly pounding.

CHAPTER 10

THE LEVITATION

It was several hours later when the members of the Society for Psychical Research reassembled in the second floor music room: a generous space with a high ceiling of ornate plasterwork, a grand piano, and a fire roaring in the large stone hearth. By now it was fully dark outside the windows and the hammering rains had finally abated.

Most of the men smoked—Wilde seldom did not have a Turkish cigarette dangling between his thick fingers. The Count, enigmatic behind his mask, sat enthroned in a winged armchair, a large cigar clamped in his jaws. Even Conan Doyle puffed away at an after-dinner pipe. Several of the windows had been opened at the top and cracked at the bottom to allow smoke to escape and cool night air to enter. Daniel Dunglas Hume, one of the few non-smokers, had chosen a seat near the open window, so as he said, "to taste the sweetness of the fresh air." Lady Thraxton, veiled as before, had chosen a seat beside him.

Conan Doyle sat in a cane chair, while Oscar Wilde lounged next to him on a divan and, with his red fez, somehow managed to resemble a wealthy camel trader idling in a Moroccan hashish bar.

The gaslight in the room had been dimmed at the request of Lady Thraxton to "entice the spirits to draw near."

Sidgwick addressed the group with his back to the firelight, which kindled his wispy white hair and beard into a fiery corona. "At my special request, Mister Hume has agreed to attempt the levitation." He beckoned the American forward with a wave. "Mister Hume, if you would please join me."

Daniel Dunglas Hume rose from his window chair, strolled to the center of the room, and stood beside Sidgwick. "I shall endeavor to do my best," he said, tossing out a theatrical bow and a wave of his handkerchief. "Hopefully, my powers shall prove equal to the task this evenin'."

The sitting members clapped appreciatively. Conan Doyle noticed that Frank Podmore, lurking behind his sneer at the back of the room, did not. Lady Thraxton perched in a seat in the shifting light and shadow next to the fire. Though she never turned to look his way, a smile lingered on her lips and Conan Doyle sensed her attention constantly upon him. Then he felt the gaze of another—the Count. Though most of his face was hidden behind the mask, Conan Doyle caught the liquid gleam of one eye, and knew that the Count was staring straight at him.

Sidgwick clapped his hands together, beaming with enthusiasm. "And as we are here to perform a scientific study of paranormal phenomena, could I have two volunteers come forward to observe the levitation at close quarters?"

Conan Doyle was about to rise from his cane chair, but the Count was already on his feet, and then Sir William Crookes, who was sitting closer, juddered up from his armchair and shambled forward, together with Sidgwick forming an equilateral triangle about Hume.

"I shall now attempt the levitation," Hume boomed in a theatrical voice. "Ya'll should know, it is the most physically taxing of all my abilities. I believe it relies upon the alignment of the celestial spheres. Some evenings, it comes real easy. But on some occasions, I cannot manifest it."

A short, barked laugh made heads turn. Feigning innocence, Frank Podmore sat casually adjusting his cuffs, a sardonic smile smeared across his face.

Hume pressed the handkerchief to his mouth and cleared his throat, then dropped his head dramatically. "Please allow me a moment to prepare myself."

Conan Doyle heard Frank Podmore, sitting somewhere behind him, give a derisive snort and mutter a single word beneath his breath: "Charlatan."

Wilde also heard it, and flung Conan Doyle a disbelieving look. Dunglas Hume, standing another fifteen feet away, should not have been able to make it out, but he raised his head, opened his eyes, and stared straight at Podmore. For once the American's good humor deserted him, and he scorched the younger man with a look of pure hatred. But then he recomposed himself, closed his eyes, and dropped his head once more. Hume fell into a pattern of deep respiration, so that his sonorous breathing filled the room. He raised his arms like a pagan worshiping before an idol, his brows knitted in intense concentration.

The room held its breath. Members watched, rapt. A minute passed, but nothing happened. And then another. And another. After a full five minutes had elapsed, Sidgwick raised a hand to halt the proceeding. But then a tremor passed through Hume's body, his face convulsing with effort. A vein pulsed in his forehead.

He seemed to straighten his posture further, but then Conan Doyle noticed that his shoes no longer touched the carpet. A collective gasp rippled through the room as he ascended, slowly at first, and then faster, until he hovered fifteen feet above the floor, the crown of his head bobbing within inches of the plaster ceiling.

It was a miraculous sight. SPR members looked from one to the other, mouths agape.

But it was just the beginning. Hume lowered his arms until they were against his sides. His body began a slow backward rotation until he lay supine. Then he floated silently over Conan Doyle's and Wilde's heads until he reached the open window—the gap was barely two feet—and glided straight out into the night.

Cries of surprise and alarm filled the room as members leapt from their seats and rushed to the windows. Dimly illuminated by the light spilling from the music room windows, Hume floated twenty feet from the building, stopped, and rotated back into the vertical. His eyes remained shut the whole time. The music room was on the second floor and Hume hung suspended motionless forty feet above the stone flags of the courtyard. Then, after perhaps a minute, he rotated to a supine position and drifted back toward the house. He floated in through the far window and reached the middle of the room, where he revolved into the vertical, arms raised above his head, and floated gently to the floor. His feet touched down and he stood, once again, between the three observers.

No one spoke or made any sound. Finally, Hume lowered his arms, raised his head, and opened his eyes.

The members of the SPR burst into wild applause. Sidgwick leapt forward and seized Hume's hand, pumping it wildly and slapping him on the back. "Astounding, old chap," he said. "That was simply astounding."

Conan Doyle threw a look of amazement at Wilde, who returned it and applauded loudly, a cigarette drooping between his lips.

Sir William Crookes was shaking Hume's hand and rabbiting on about "the most amazing spectacle he had ever witnessed." None of the men congratulating the American psychic seemed to notice the man's demeanor. He was deathly pale and sweating profusely. The audience cried out as the American's knees buckled, and he would have fallen if Sidgwick and the other men had not held him up.

"I am sorry, gentlemen," Hume rasped. "The levitation is very draining." With their help he wobbled to his feet. "I'm afraid I must retire for the evening."

Frank Podmore jumped up from his chair and stalked from the room without a backward glance. On his way out, he brushed shoulders with Mrs. Kragan, the Irish housekeeper. She had been standing at the open door, silently watching throughout. Her eyes were wide and crazed, both hands covering her mouth. Conan Doyle noticed the rosary clutched in her hands and heard her mutter, "Tis the work of the devil. We shall all be damned for it!" Then the housekeeper turned and fled, as if fearing contamination by such ungodly doings.

The guests applauded as Daniel Dunglas Hume left the room moments later, assisted—virtually dragged out—by Mister Greaves and two of the other servants.

"Well, well," Wilde observed drily. "I should hate to be following that act!"

MADAME ZHOZHOVSKY

During the rumpus when Hume was carried from the parlor, Madame Zhozhovsky remained in her seat, stroking the monkey in her lap. When calm returned, she asked in a quavering voice for a chair to be set in the middle of the room, along with a low footstool on which to rest her sore foot. Then she levered her bulk from the sofa using the crooked black walking stick and stumped to the waiting chair with her pet monkey trailing on its leash. Before sitting, she faced the room, looking left and then right without smiling, and raised a hand in a seeking gesture, staring over the heads of her audience, as if her gray gaze were penetrating the veil separating this world from the next.

"I can tell the lady practices that gaze in the mirror," Wilde muttered, and Conan Doyle stifled a laugh in his handkerchief.

With a mystical look upon her face, she swept the uncanny gaze around the room like a searchlight before pitching her tremulous voice to its lowest register: "This is a dangerous house . . ." She allowed several seconds for that ominous pronouncement to sink in, and then added, ". . . and you are all in peril for your souls."

She shuffled backward to the chair and dropped heavily into it, then gingerly set her sore foot on the footstool and leaned on her stick, peering around. "Before this meeting proceeds, you need to know what dangers you face and how to defend your minds against psychic attack." She fell silent for a moment and then raised her stick and banged it on the floor, making everyone jump. "Thraxton Hall is one of the most haunted houses in England. Over the centuries, it has been the scene of much unhappiness. Sir Henry Thraxton, the first lord of the house, was murdered by a brother who coveted his wife. The second lord was sucked into a bog while stalking a wounded deer and drowned in full sight of all his retainers. There is also a ghostly child, a young girl in a blue dress: Annalette Thraxton, the youngest daughter of the second lord, thrown from an upstairs window by her crazed mother in a fit of madness, the poor child's brains dashed upon the rocky ground."

Conan Doyle straightened in his chair, thinking of the spectral girl he had glimpsed in the coppice of the stone circle. He was about to speak up, but Madame Zhozhovksy continued, "Whenever the blue girl is seen, death follows soon after."

Conan Doyle's stomach fluttered and he reigned in the words he was about to speak.

"But more recent times have seen their share of tragedy. Lady Florence Thraxton was found dead at the base of the grand staircase, her neck so badly broken her head was turned completely around—"

"That's not a ghost story," Wilde murmured to Conan Doyle, "that's a tale of shoddy carpentry. Fix the bally staircase, I say."

"And six short months later," Madame Zhozhovsky continued, apparently just getting into her stride, "Sir Edmund Thraxton, the last sitting lord, vanished whilst walking on the moors and was never seen again. But most famously, there is the *white lady*—"

"Ah!" Wilde said, louder than he intended. "There is *always* a white lady."

Every head turned to look. Wilde dropped his head and pretended to be picking fluff from his trousers.

"The white lady," Zhozhovsky began again, pulling her eyes away from the Irishman, "is reputedly Mariah Thraxton, the scorned wife of the third Lord Alfred Thraxton of the 1780s."

"And did she also die a violent death?" Conan Doyle spoke up.

Madam Zhozhovsky nodded, setting her multiple chins jiggling. "Murdered during a séance." A cruel smile congealed on the old lady's lips.

The news shocked Conan Doyle, who suddenly found his gaze locked with Hope Thraxton's startled violet eyes. He looked away with difficulty. "Do we know any more of the circumstances?"

"Yes, indeed, we do," Henry Sidgwick interrupted, clearly proud to show off his academic knowledge. "It's well documented, thanks to the trial of Lord Thraxton. He caught his wife performing a séance with her maid in the turret room in the western wing; he accused her of witchcraft, produced a brace of pistols, and shot her dead on the spot."

The room contracted with the collective catching of breath. Conan Doyle's gaze turned back to Hope Thraxton, who was staring down at the rug, her lips quivering.

"I presume Lord Thraxton was hanged for the crime?" Wilde spoke aloud.

"Oh no," Sidgwick countered in a cheerful voice. "Quite the opposite. At the court of inquiry, he was commended for his actions and all charges dropped." Sidgwick chuckled from somewhere inside the white vortex of beard. "This was, after all, during the height of the witch hunting craze."

"They would not allow her to be buried in consecrated ground," Hope Thraxton interjected. "And so she was buried at the crossroads just outside Slattenmere."

"Gallows Hill," Conan Doyle murmured to his companion. "The very crossroads we passed through just this morning."

"It is a very lonely place," Hope Thraxton continued, her gaze focused on something far in the past. "Even in the realm of the spirits, the centuries pass slowly. . . ."

Madame Zhozhovsky banged her stick on the floor to jerk everyone's attention back to her. "Mariah Thraxton did not die immediately but lived long enough to utter a curse against her husband and the house of Thraxton. Her husband followed her in death soon after. Thrown from his horse whilst riding to hounds, his spine was severed. Alfred writhed in screaming agony for a full week before death released him—the first victim of Mariah Thraxton's curse, a curse that lingers to this very day."

Wilde turned to Conan Doyle with a wide-eyed, mocking look and whispered, "Not very cheery is she?"

Madame Zhozhovsky overheard Wilde's flippant remark and lashed him a scorching look that curdled the air between them.

"This house is filled with ghosts, revenants, inchoate spirits, and what some call . . ." She added in a voice that set the syllables trembling, ". . . the *lower intelligences*."

Oscar Wilde's hand shot up. "I should know this, coming from the Emerald Isle—the land of spooks and banshees—but what exactly is a revenant?"

Madame Zhozhovsky shifted forward in her chair, leaning heavily on the walking stick. She thrust out a hand, her penetrating gaze once again seeming to pierce the veil between this world and the next. "A revenant is a ghost or a corpse that rises from its grave and walks among the living. Sometimes, when death is sudden, the soul is expelled violently from the body. Incorporeal, confused and frightened, it drifts in shock. It does not know it is dead, so it clings to the places it knew in life. In other cases, an unconfessed soul returns, animated by all the wickedness it did in life, to do harm to the living."

"If it's a ghost, how can it possibly do any harm?" It was Sir William Crookes, his speech slurred by 95 proof.

Madame Zhozhovsky pushed on the gnarled stick, straining to heave her bulk up from the chair. "All malevolent ghosts are a threat. Revenants are the most dangerous form of spirit. They appear as solid and human as you and I, but they are here to deceive the living. To lead them to death and ruination. The lower intelligences are fragments, broken pieces of the psyche absorbed by the stone and wood of a building. They are the residue of violent emotions: love, lust, fear, anger, rage. If you open yourself to them, if you allow yourself to be vulnerable, such strong emotions can enter you and poison your mind. A revenant cannot enter a house unless it is invited in. But malicious spirits are full of tricks and cunning. Amateurs who dabble in necromancy do so at the peril of their immortal souls."

While she had been talking, the monkey had scampered a circular path, winding the leash tight around her legs.

"You are all in terrible danger," Madame Zhozhovsky added. "All of you."

Conan Doyle happened to look down and saw the leather strap wrapped around the elderly lady's legs. He raised his hand and started to speak. "Madame—"

"All of you!" she said. "Fear for your souls. I can offer you a protective spell—"

"Madame," Conan Doyle said aloud. "If I might—"

"For the danger is near, Very near—" Madame Zhozhovsky tried to take a step forward and the leash cinched tight. She fell full length and somersaulted over the footstool, hitting the floor with a tremendous thump, horrifying the watching Society members and sending the monkey into a shrieking frenzy. Members leaped to their feet and rushed to assist, but the monkey hissed and flashed its fangs menacingly, keeping everyone at bay.

Wilde pushed back the red fez on his head and regarded Conan Doyle archly. "The deuce," he said. "I'll wager that is the first time her feet have been higher than her head in decades. This truly has been a diverting evening. First a floating American and then an acrobatic old lady with a monkey. I'm very happy now I didn't stay home."

CHAPTER 12

DARK ENCOUNTER

After the first SPR meeting adjourned for the evening, it took the two friends twenty minutes of wrong turns and backtracking before they finally located the third floor landing where their rooms were located. As they trudged along the hallway, each carried a glowing paraffin lamp (this older part of the house had never been plumbed for gas jets). Both men sagged with fatigue, and even Oscar Wilde's continuous narrative of the day's events had dried to dust. When he arrived at his room, Conan Doyle fumbled in his pockets and brought out his large key. It turned in the lock with a brassy clunk. But as he pushed the door open his eye was drawn to a folded sheet of paper lying on the rug.

A note.

He quickly deduced someone had slipped it under the door. Bending, he scooped it up, unfolded the paper with one hand, and held it close to the lamp glass. The note was short. A few brief sentences. He recognized instantly the feminine hand.

I knew you would come.

Conan Doyle's heart lurched at the words. The next line fired a jolt of excitement through him.

The ballroom. Midnight.

H

He tilted the paper to the light. A phoenix watermark floated up from the surface.

"Ah, one more thing, Arthur!"

His head snapped up. Wilde had not gone into his room after all and was sauntering toward him. Conan Doyle crumpled the note and jammed it into a jacket pocket, but his friend had already seen it.

"What was that note you were reading?"

"Note? Ah . . . nothing, nothing. Just . . . some ideas I was jotting down . . . for a story."

The Irishman cast an insinuating look at Conan Doyle's pocket and raised his bushy eyebrows; a supercilious smile twitched the corners of his mouth. "Ah, I see. Notes for a story. I think I know exactly what kind of story." He tapped the side of his ample nose with two fingers, throwing Conan Doyle a knowing wink. "Don't worry, shan't ask again."

Conan Doyle felt his face flush hot. Wilde turned toward his room, but then turned back again. "Ah yes, I was going to remind you that I'm leaving in the morning. If you hear a strange noise coming from my room, do not be alarmed. It will be me stripping the wallpaper from the walls. It is far too loud to permit any sleep."

* * *

Conan Doyle lay on the bed fully dressed, pocket watch laid on his chest, waiting for time to push the hands around to midnight. As he rested, the stuttering light of the paraffin lamp on the bedside table made the creatures watching from the wainscoting jerk and tremble. When the Witching Hour finally struck, he slid from the bed, pulled on his tweed jacket, and stole quietly from the room.

He had only a vague idea of where the ballroom was: in the

ruined west wing of the house that guests were encouraged to stay away from. He crept down the grand staircase to the first floor, stepping on the very edge of the treads to avoid creaks.

In the entrance hall, a single lamp had been left burning. Conan Doyle stood still for several long minutes, listening, but nothing stirred. Even the servants were abed at this hour. He liberated the lamp from the hallway table—the house would be unnavigably dark without it—and crept down a long gallery lined with portraits of dead Thraxtons, whose luminous eyes followed his progress. The portrait gallery terminated in a set of massive double doors. He gratefully noted that the key had been left in the lock and the handle turned freely in his hand. He stepped through into a large, dark, echoing space—the ballroom. Conan Doyle paused a moment, setting the lamp down at his feet to peer around.

Moonlight, milky and diffuse, flooded in through the tall windows. And then he noticed a glowing white figure standing at one of the windows, looking out.

The white lady, he thought, believing, for a heart-stopping moment, he was looking upon a specter, but then the woman turned from the window and looked straight at him.

It was no ghost. It was H—Lady Hope Thraxton.

Instead of her black lace dress, she wore a diaphanous white nightgown. Lit from behind by moonlight, it glowed translucent, revealing that she was quite naked beneath; he could see the contours of her body, the pert, small breasts, curvy hips, and shapely legs.

He reasoned she must not realize how exposed she was. He knew that, as a gentleman, he should protect her modesty by averting his gaze. But his heart was drumming and he could not tear his eyes away. Her face illuminated with happiness when she saw him. She broke free of the window and floated across the ballroom floor to meet him, as silent and light as a filament of smoke. The white nightgown, without the backlit moonlight, regained its opacity and became, once again, just a white nightgown.

Her long hair was unpinned for bed and fell in a cascade of auburn ringlets about her shoulders. She reached the glow of his paraffin lamp, and for the first time he saw her face unconcealed. He knew she was young, but without the veil he could see she was still a girl: a fetching beauty with pale skin, fine cheekbones and full lips, elegantly arched brows, and the most astonishing violet eyes. In the dim light, her pupils were madly dilated, and when he raised his lamp to splash light across her face, she winced and turned away as if in pain.

"So bright!" she cried.

He apologized and lowered the lamp. "I forgot . . . your condition."

"As you may have guessed, I must needs be a creature of the night."

"Yes. Of course—"

She dropped her head, looking discomfited, and he realized he was staring. He tried to allay any concerns she might have had about his motives. "I returned to your Mayfair residence the day after our meeting, but you had removed to Thraxton Hall."

"Yes." She kept her gaze on the floor. "I knew you would have a change of heart. That you would wish to help me. But then I had the new vision. The one in which I saw—" She stopped as if afraid to speak the words aloud. "You received my second letter?"

"Yes, I did."

"And still you came?"

"How could I stay away when a beautiful young woman's life was threatened?"

Her eyes gleamed liquid as she looked up at him with something more than mere gratitude. "You are very brave, but . . ." She trailed off, emotions rippling across her face. After a moment, she composed herself enough to ask, "Doctor Doyle, do you believe in Fate?"

He searched himself a moment, and then answered: "Honestly? I do not know. I became a doctor because I wanted to heal people. But my own wife is dying from consumption and I am powerless to save her." It was the first time he had admitted the truth—even to himself—and now he realized that his motives in coming to Thraxton Hall had not been entirely selfless. He was running away from a death he could not prevent.

She seemed to read his thoughts and touched a hand to his. "You do believe in Fate. You believe we cannot change our destinies."

He did not want to answer, lest she abandon hope. Instead he asked: "Have you had a subsequent vision?"

"Yes. Just last night."

"And was it the same as before?"

She nodded, her chin quivering. But then her eyes widened and she looked up into Conan Doyle's face. "No! It was not the same. I saw the séance room. Again I could not make out the faces of the sitters except for you and one other."

Conan Doyle's heart leapt in his chest. "Who? Who was the other sitter?"

Her eyes flashed. "He was seated on my left, holding my hand—"

"Yes?" Conan Doyle urged.

"It was your friend . . . Mister Wilde."

Conan Doyle took in the news, his mind racing. "And Oscar has never been in your dream before?"

She shook her head. "Never."

"Then, perhaps, the future has been altered. I am not entirely certain I believe in Fate. But I do believe in Free Will. I believe our actions can shape our destinies."

"But you just told me of your wife."

A flash of pain swept Conan Doyle's face. "Yes, it is true, I have been unable to cure her disease, but I believe my efforts have greatly prolonged her life."

"But her Fate is the same, nonetheless. I have suffered from my adversity to the light since I was a child. It killed my mother. I knew it would one day kill me. Even so, I had not expected to die so young. But if it is my Fate to be murdered in the next few days, then I must accept it."

Conan Doyle was struck by the maturity of the young woman. Her fearlessness. He did not speak for some time as his mind worked at the problem like restless fingers probing a knot reefed tight. Then the beginnings of a notion began to stir in his mind. "It may not be possible to overcome Fate, but we may be able to hoodwink it."

She smiled. "You are an irrepressible romantic, are you not, Mister Doyle?" She held out a slender hand to him. "The family history of the Thraxtons does not bode well for me." She slipped her tiny hand into his. "Come, I must show you what you are up against."

* * *

They left the ballroom by the far door and penetrated farther into the hall's west wing. Conan Doyle allowed himself to be led, one hand holding aloft the glowing lamp, the other lightly held in Hope Thraxton's cool grasp. If Thraxton Hall's east wing was ugly and eldritch, the west wing was something clawed from a nightmare. The space had been abandoned to decay: peeling wallpaper hung in curls from the walls, fallen plaster crunched underfoot, doorways swollen with damp hung ajar on twisted hinges. Most of the rooms were stripped bare, apart from, here and there, a rusted iron-clawed bathtub, a listing chair, a broken-backed table. And the deeper they went, the more ruthless the hand of entropy had been.

"When I was a child," Hope said, her voice light and lyrical, "I was forbidden to enter the west wing; my grandfather said it was too dangerous." She laughed. "So of course, I would sneak in to play with my friend."

"A friend?"

"Seamus, the son of the housekeeper. Of course, I was also forbidden from fraternizing with the domestic staff. I was nine years old; Seamus was fifteen."

Conan Doyle tried to sound casual as he asked, "And your play was completely innocent? Childhood games? Did he? I mean . . . were you—?"

"Interfered with?" She looked uneasy. "No. Or at least, I have no recollection."

"You played hide and seek?"

"Oh no!" she said, smiling impishly. "Even as children, we knew the reputation of the house. We would wander through the rooms, calling out to the ghosts to show themselves."

Conan Doyle stopped and studied her face. "And did you ever see anything?"

"Not at first. Not until we found . . . the special room." She read the interest on his face and smiled. "It is a place that resonates with ghosts."

They climbed a rickety stairway that rose steeply to a turret room. As they topped the landing, Conan Doyle froze. At the far end of the hall, a doorway hung slackly ajar and the glowing figure of a woman stood watching them. It raised an arm, and he suddenly realized that it was Hope Thraxton's image, reflected in a mirror, its silvering flaking loose and mottled with black patina so that it tore her reflection into ghostly ribbons.

"This is the room," she announced. "As children we called it the mirror maze."

Conan Doyle paused at the threshold. A vague sense of dread made him reluctant to enter, but she tightened her grip on his large hand and pulled him inside. When he raised the lamp and looked around, an astonished gasp ripped from him. The room was filled with mirrors—dozens and dozens of mirrors—an odd jumble of all types and sizes: cheval dressing mirrors in their pivoting frames, oval wall mirrors leant up against scabrous plaster walls. Mirrors pointing this way and that so they caught the glow of his lamp and juggled the light back and forth between them, their beveled edges refracting like prisms and flinging jagged shards of rainbow against the walls. He saw himself and the small woman beside him reflected from a dozen dizzying angles—even the back of his head.

"I loved mirrors even then," she said, abandoning his hand as she stepped forward to the large cheval mirror and gazed dreamily into its depths.

"After grandmother died, grandfather had all the mirrors in the house taken away. Although the fashion may seem quaint now, the tradition then was to cover the mirrors after someone died, lest the spirit of the departed see their own reflection. But grandfather's mania persisted. I was permitted only a small hand mirror for tying bows in my hair. Of course, I was a vain young girl, and when my grandfather caught me looking at myself he would grow angry and wag his finger and say, *Look long enough in the mirror and you will see the devil.* Of course, such a belief was a dangerous thrill to young people, so when Seamus and I found this room we spent hours gazing into the mirrors waiting for the devil to appear."

"And did you ever see him?"

She laughed softly. "No. But one day I did see my spirit guide. She was kind to me and after that I would steal away every day to come and talk to her. She was lonely . . ." Hope tilted her head dreamily. ". . . so very lonely."

Conan Doyle thought of the story Madame Zhozhovsky had related, of Mariah Thraxton's murder—in this very room—shot dead by her husband armed with a brace of pistols. "You are speaking of Mariah Thraxton?"

"Yes," Hope replied, her voice brittle as a handful of autumn leaves.

"Did Seamus see her, too?"

She shook her head. "I'm not sure. I was very young. And it was so long ago. But he told his mother what we were doing. And the next time we visited the mirror maze, Seamus stayed outside and locked me in."

"Why would he do such a thing?"

Hope Thraxton's lips tremored. Her vision seemed to retreat inward as her mind journeyed back to that day. "His mother told him to. I was locked in here for five days. I had no food. No water. I became weaker and weaker. When I finally hovered on the edge of death, I heard a voice calling to me. Though I had barely enough strength to move, I crawled to the mirror and looked in. The lady in the glass was young and fine and very beautiful. She was dressed in an antique style. I instantly recognized her. Her portrait hangs in the entrance hall."

"Mariah Thraxton?"

"Yes. It was she who taught me how to speak to spirits."

"And what of Seamus? Was he punished? What he did was unspeakably wicked."

"I cannot hate him. He thought he was doing right because his mother had poisoned his mind. She thought my affliction, and the affliction of my mother before me, was part of the curse upon this house. I crouched in this room for hours, which became days. Meanwhile my grandfather and the servants searched the woods and the fields for me, convinced I had run away, but I was in the house all the time."

"What happened? Did Seamus finally free you?"

She shook her head. "No. Mister Greaves broke open the door and found me lying on the floor. Close to death. But for him, I would have perished."

"Wait. You said Seamus's mother was the housekeeper? Is Mrs. Kragan the same housekeeper?"

She nodded. "My grandfather wanted to sack her. To cast her out. I begged him not to. In the end, after I wept many tears, he relented. But Seamus was banished forever and sent to live with relatives in Ireland."

"But why would you take her side after she nearly murdered you?"

"She was the closest I ever had to a mother. And a mother who hates you is better than no mother at all. Had my grandfather sacked her, she would likely have starved on the streets. Part of her is grateful to me for saving her, but the other part hates me for what happened to her son." She turned from the mirror and gazed at him levelly. "And that, Doctor Doyle, has ever thus been the story of Thraxton Hall. It is a house that teeters on a knife's edge between happiness and despair."

A loud, ominous banging interrupted them like some malevolent force hurling itself against the walls of the house, trying to break free. Startled, Conan Doyle looked about him—the booming seemed to be coming from all directions.

"The front door!" Lady Thraxton said, breathlessly. "Someone is knocking!"

"At this hour?"

Scarcely able to contain her agitation, she pushed Conan Doyle toward the door. "Hurry," she said. "Return to your room. We must not be seen together."

Conan Doyle snatched up the lamp and fled the room. He paused at the top of the stairs and looked back for Hope, but she had vanished. He tore himself away and bounded down the stairs and along the corridor. His footsteps echoed as he sprinted across the ruined ballroom, the paraffin lamp swinging wildly at his side, throwing the grotesque shadow of a giant striding across the walls. The maniacal pounding continued as he raced through the portrait gallery. He reached the entrance hall, where the knocking was deafening. He quickly set the lamp back on the entrance hall table and then froze as he saw a tall, thin figure shambling toward him.

Mister Greaves.

Conan Doyle tried to think of an excuse to explain his presence in the entrance hall at nearly one in the morning, but then he remembered that Mister Greaves was blind.

"Yes! Yes! I'm coming!" Greaves shouted as he ambled to the door. He had obviously dressed in haste. His jacket was misbuttoned. His collar was unattached at one side and dangling. He reached the door and groped along it until he came to the large iron bolt and shot it loose. As he fumbled with his key in the door lock, Conan Doyle crept past and began to tiptoe up the stairs.

"Good night, Doctor Doyle," Mister Greaves announced in a loud voice.

Conan Doyle froze and looked behind him. The aged butler had paused in his efforts to unlock the door. Despite Conan Doyle's stealth, Mister Greaves had sensed a presence—but how had he known who it was? The young doctor realized he was being given time to make good his escape and sprang up the stairs. He was climbing the second flight when he heard the front door open and footsteps entering the house. When he reached the third floor landing, he moved to the nearest window and looked out.

Illuminated by intermittent moonlight, rain fell in slanting shafts, needling the standing puddles on the forecourt. A carriage had drawn up at the front steps of the mansion. Its shape seemed vaguely familiar, and then Conan Doyle recognized it for what it was: a hearse. Seen obliquely through the rippling window glass, rain-blurred figures milled around the open front door. He heard voices, snatches of shouted conversation. A figure swept out of the front door and skipped lightly down the steps. A tall man—a gentleman by his dress—top hat, a rain cape swirling about his shoulders.

He strode quickly to the hearse, where two men were unloading something heavy: he watched them heave at a rectangular shape he first assumed was a large steamer trunk, but it looked uncannily like a coffin.

A hand touched him on the shoulder, and Conan Doyle started violently, spinning around. A shadowy figure stood before him. It took several long seconds before Conan Doyle identified Frank Podmore. He must have crept up silently.

"You gave me a start!" he said, his heart vaulting.

"Sorry," Podmore said in a tone that suggested the opposite. "I saw you standing there."

"I could not sleep."

"I never indulge in sleep."

"Never?" Conan Doyle asked skeptically.

"I have trained myself not to crave sleep. It is a waste of valuable time that is better spent advancing my mind." Podmore turned his face to the window, staring down at the figures in the courtyard below. In the darkness, his terrier eyes gleamed.

"Do you know who is arriving at this late hour?" Conan Doyle asked.

"Our final guest."

"Final guest?"

"Lord Philipp Webb."

"And who is Lord Webb?"

Podmore laughed mirthlessly. "Another charlatan, like all the rest." And with that he walked off into the shadows without bothering to say good night.

* * *

As Conan Doyle trudged the gloomy hallway to his room, the events of the night carouseled in his head. Struck by a sudden revelation, his steps slowed and he stumbled to a halt. He had been watching Hope Thraxton's reflection in the cheval mirror as the cacophonous knocking began, and she had spun around, startled by the din. But it seemed now, as he reviewed the action in his mind, as if the reflection in the mirror had lagged a moment behind. He recalled the double-image photograph of Hope Thraxton in *The Strand Magazine*. There were something elusive and other-worldly about her that even the laws of optics could not capture. And then a further thought occurred to him. Hope had harried him from the west wing, while she had stayed behind. How else could she return to her rooms, if not by the same route? As his hand closed on the cold brass doorknob, he dithered, fighting a strange compulsion to turn on his heel and retrace his steps back to the mirror maze, half-convinced he would find Hope Thraxton's image trapped behind the glass, a prisoner screaming to be set free.

A GUEST ARRIVES LATE

Conan Doyle lay awake for hours, his mind a whirling vortex. If Hope Thraxton's premonitory vision proved true, she would be murdered in just days—at the third scheduled séance. He tried to focus on her dilemma, but instead, his mind cascaded with images. Her lips. Her eyes. Her lithe young body, naked beneath the sheer nightgown. At last he sat up in bed, abandoning any hope of achieving sleep.

He retrieved his Casebook and unlocked it with the key he kept around his neck. His pen scratched quickly across the page as he wrote an account of his adventure in the derelict west wing. Because it was a private journal, Conan Doyle's descriptions of Hope were uninhibited. He found himself becoming aroused at the memory of her body glimpsed through the translucent nightgown. Although Conan Doyle was hardly an artist of his father's caliber, he liked to fill the journals with sketches to remind him of his experiences. Now he found himself sketching a likeness of Hope Thraxton. He worked at it for twenty minutes or so, then stopped to regard his handiwork.

It was a fair if not a great drawing, but it lacked something. And then he remembered—the birthmark in the shape of a waning

crescent moon that lurked in the crease of her smile. A few quick pen strokes and he added the peculiar birthmark shared by generations of Thraxton women.

His eyes flashed up from the Casebook as he smelled smoke. Tobacco. A familiar brand.

Sherlock Holmes sat in an armchair set against the far wall, legs crossed, the elbow of the arm holding his cigarette cupped in his hand.

"So," Holmes began. "What have you learned thus far?"

"Learned? I've just arrived. I have barely met the other guests."

The consulting detective's face soured in a vinegar smile. "You are not here to attend a soirée. You are here to prevent a murder. These people are not merely guests—you must view each one as a potential suspect. You must think as a murderer. Get inside his, or her, mind. What is the most salient point in a murder investigation?"

"I . . . well . . ." There seemed to be a barrier between Conan Doyle's tongue and his brain. "Whomever has the means—"

"Motive!" Holmes snarled, interrupting. "Motive is crucial! Anyone can find the means to murder another human being— especially if it involves something so rudimentary as firing a pistol at close range. All it will require is a concealed weapon and the advantage of darkness. No. You must determine who has a *motive* to kill Hope Thraxton."

"But I— It's too soon. I scarcely know these people, or their history."

"Precisely. So you must endeavor to find out. But frankly your judgment is already clouded by your infatuation with the young woman."

"Infatuation? I don't know what you're speaking of—"

Holmes silenced him with a contemptuous wave. "Your wife is at home, dying of consumption. How many times has she crossed your mind? Have you spent so much as a second thinking of her?"

Conan Doyle's mouth opened. He strained, but could think of no counter. Shamefaced, he dropped his head. "No," he admitted in a cowed voice.

Holmes drew upon his cigarette and exhaled a plume of silver smoke. "No, you have not. Lady Thraxton has described her dream. Yours was the first face she recognized. At this moment, I would consider you the primary suspect."

Conan Doyle bristled. "Me? That is preposterous! Why on earth would I murder Hope Thraxton? I have come to prevent harm to her."

The hawk-like visage fixed its creator with a needling gaze. "You are the primary suspect because jealousy—especially sexual jealousy—is the number-one reason why men murder women. You have been infatuated with this woman since that first meeting in the darkened room. Even before you knew what Hope Thraxton looked like, you have been mentally undressing her."

"That's—! That's—outrageous!" Conan Doyle spluttered. "Why am I having this conversation? It's ridiculous. You're a phantasm. You're not real!"

"Is it ridiculous?" Holmes leaned forward in his chair. "How clearly is your mind working? If I am a phantasm, then why are you conversing with me? And how is it you can even see me? After all, the room is in darkness." He nodded to the bedside table.

When Conan Doyle looked, he saw that the lamp was not lit, and yet he could clearly see everything in the room. When he looked back at the chair, it was empty. Sherlock Holmes had vanished.

He awoke with a start, clawing at the bedsheets. He had fallen asleep with the Casebook open on his chest and now it slid off and thumped to the carpet. The oil lamp had burned dry hours ago. The room was in darkness, but light limned the edges of the heavy curtains.

And he knew at once that he had overslept.

* * *

Breakfast was served in the conservatory, an airy glass structure with wrought-iron tables and desiccated ficus plants withering in giant urns. By the time Mister Greaves led Conan Doyle into the space, most of the other guests were already tucking into their breakfasts, and the chatter of conversation and the clatter of silverware on bone china were clamorous. Wilde sat alone at a small table in a far corner staring out the rain-streaked glass at the wet, sheep-dotted swells of grassy turf. He had pushed aside a breakfast plate scummed with the yellow remains of quail eggs. Wilde, now in his late thirties, was accumulating weight with every year. Despite the fact that he had obviously breakfasted well, he was attacking a scone with a knife.

"You look like death," he observed as Conan Doyle flopped into the chair opposite.

The Scotsman looked at his friend with eyes that were bloodshot and dark-circled. "I did not sleep well."

"I slept marvelously," Wilde said, buttering a scone with his usual aplomb and then lavishing it with a dollop of clotted cream topped with a blob of rhubarb jam. "I shall be departing as soon as I've finished packing. As I came down to breakfast I noticed a carriage waiting outside."

"Let us hope that carriage is not here for you, Oscar."

"Why ever not?" Wilde mumbled, sinking his bovine teeth into the scone.

"Because it is a hearse."

Wilde choked, spitting scone crumbs. He wiped cream from his mouth on a linen napkin and threw his friend a horrified look. "Egad! Tell me you jest."

Conan Doyle described the strange event he had witnessed the night before: the arrival of the final guest in a most unconventional means of transport.

"The deuce you say!" Wilde said after hearing the story. "How macabre! Whatever can that be about? I almost wish I were staying for the denouement."

A servant set down a plate with a full English breakfast before Conan Doyle—fried bacon, fried eggs, fried mushrooms, fried tomato, a thick slice of fried bread, and several rotund sausages still sizzling and suppurating fat. "I am indeed sorry that you won't be here to find out, Oscar," Conan Doyle said as he peppered his eggs.

But then the fierce-eyed Mrs. Kragan appeared and hovered over them, her claw-like hands knitted tightly at her bosom, her lined face set in its perpetual scowl of disapproval. "I am sorry to inform you, Master Wilde, but with all the rain we've had overnight the river is up and the ford is impassable."

Wilde's face fell at the news. "Are you saying that I shan't be able to leave today?"

The gray head shook in a parody of regret. "No one shall be able to come or go. We are quite cut off."

Wilde began to open his mouth, but the housekeeper guessed what he was about to ask and preempted his question. "For several days at least."

To this pronouncement, the greatest wit in the world could only answer with a grunt of exasperation.

"Are you feeling well, Oscar?" Conan Doyle asked as he knifed off a chunk of sausage and forked it into his mouth. "You look like death." He chuckled around the mouthful of hot sausage as he chewed. "Looks like you'll be here for the denouement after all."

CHAPTER 14

MESMERIZED

The members of the SPR were slowly drifting into the parlor. Many stood in knots, conversing. A few clustered about a table laid out with a punch bowl and glasses. A card table had been set up at the back of the room at which Madame Zhozhovsky sat like a small fat spider reading the palms of anyone gullible enough to fall into her web.

"Palm reading!" Wilde exclaimed as he and Conan Doyle entered the room. "How amusing. I have often thought of hiring a gypsy palm reader for one of my soirées."

The two friends hovered close, eavesdropping on the proceedings. The Scottish doctor was open-minded about most aspects of the paranormal, but he put little faith in determining a man's Fate based upon the wrinkles on his palms. Still, he was interested enough to listen in as Madame Zhozhovsky had managed to catch hold of the cynical Frank Podmore and presently had his hand pinned to the table. Her head was bowed as she studied his life line, so that she could not see the look of utter disdain he was lashing her with. "Your love line is interesting," Zhozhovsky said, tracing his palm with a finger knobby and twisted with arthritis. "See how it breaks here? I see a great loss."

Podmore recoiled as if he had touched something hot. He attempted to snatch his arm away, but the old lady held on to his hand with a firm grip and forced it back down onto the tabletop.

She studied Podmore's palm a second time. "You have a short life line." The penetrating gray eyes looked up into Podmore's face. "Fear water," she said, her tone ominous. "You will die by drowning."

Podmore snickered as he extricated his hand from hers. "Unlikely. I am an excellent swimmer."

The old lady's expression never wavered. "Palmistry is an ancient wisdom, proven over millennia. You will die by *drowning*."

Podmore's sneer quivered and collapsed.

Oscar Wilde was standing at Conan Doyle's shoulder, watching intently. "Oh, I love this sort of thing, don't you?" he gushed. "I've had my palm read before. Many times. They always predict a long and happy life."

Frank Podmore got up and slunk away, and Wilde lunged forward to occupy the vacated seat. "Do me next, Madame!" he urged.

Madame Zhozhovsky cradled Wilde's large hand in hers and traced a finger along his palm. "Your love line breaks most interestingly." Her eyes swept up to meet his. "Much confusion here, I fear."

Wilde's eyes widened slightly. The eagerness evaporated from his face. "And what of my life line?" he asked with sudden trepidation.

She dropped her gaze, her eyes metronoming across Wilde's fleshy palm. A brief look of distress swept her features and she sat up straight, pushing his hand away. "That I cannot read," she said dismissively.

"No, you did see something," Wilde pleaded. "Please . . . you must tell me."

She sighed and held out her hand. He placed his large hand, palm up, in hers. Once again, her pudgy finger traced his life line. After a musing silence, she said, "You will not live a long life."

Shock and alarm rippled across Wilde's face. "But it will be a happy life, no?"

"Who can say?" she mused, pushing his hand away. "It is not an exact science."

Wilde wobbled to his feet and stumbled back to join Conan Doyle, deeply shaken.

Madame Zhozhovsky's gray graze swept the room and captured Conan Doyle's eye. "Doctor Doyle, would you like to know your future?"

"Just going for some refreshments," Conan Doyle answered, abandoning his friend while he arrowed toward the punch bowl. With his consumptive wife hovering on the brink of death, he had no interest in finding out about his future. He was reaching for the silver punch ladle when a female hand reached at the same moment, and their hands clashed.

"Oh, do excuse me!"

Conan Doyle looked up into the smiling face of Eleanor Sidgwick. He estimated her age to be about the same as his own, early thirties—at least twenty years her husband's junior. She was a handsome, woman, if somewhat plain, with brown eyes and brown hair parted in the middle and scraped back into a tight bun—the very picture of an academic. She was looking straight into Conan Doyle's eyes and drew her hand away slowly.

"May I pour you some punch, Mrs. Sidgwick?"

"How gallant! Eleanor—please call me Eleanor—and yes, that would be lovely."

Conan Doyle ladled fruit punch into her crystal glass, and then filled his own. He turned to walk back to where Wilde was waiting and found that Mrs. Sidgwick was blocking his path and looking up at him expectantly.

"Er, I am sitting with my friend, Mister Wilde. Would you care to join—"

"Oh yes!" she leapt in. "That would be most accommodating!"

As they approached, Wilde rose from his seat and bowed. "Mrs. Sidgwick," he said, and taking her free hand, kissed her knuckles.

"Oh!" she said, flushing. And then again, her voice a girlish flutter: "Oh!"

Conan Doyle held her chair until she sat and looked at both men with the bright eyes of a young girl who has just been invited to her first party.

"I must say," she gushed. "I am very thrilled to sit with two men of such fame." She threw a furtive glance across the room to where her husband, Henry Sidgwick, was holding court with Sir William Crookes and then turned her attention back to them. "It is so refreshing to converse with two giants of the arts. My husband never stops speaking of science and mathematics."

"Oh, I hardly think I'd describe us as giants," Conan Doyle said.

"Never argue with a lady, Arthur. Especially when she is correct." Wilde smiled and bowed his head in homage. "The mantle of *giant* rests comfortably upon my shoulders."

She moved forward in her chair, so that her knee was touching Conan Doyle's, and whispered conspiratorially: "How are you gentlemen finding our little group of eccentrics?" He moved his leg away, but she shifted forward again, regaining contact.

"Stimulating," Wilde said. "And Mister Hume's demonstration of levitation exhausts my list of superlatives."

"Indeed, Mister Hume is the brightest star of our gathering. And so handsome and at ease, as only our American cousins can be."

"Yes," Conan Doyle agreed. "But tell me, why is it that Frank Podmore seems, how shall I say—"

"Somewhat acerbic?"

Conan Doyle nodded.

Eleanor Sidgwick made a move to touch her hair as she scanned for anyone close enough to eavesdrop. "Of course, I don't like to gossip."

"Neither do we listen to gossip," Conan Doyle assured her.

"Arthur speaks for himself," Wilde said, laying his large hand atop hers. "Where gossip is concerned, I am a hummingbird and it is the nectar upon which I feed. Dear lady, do continue."

Despite Wilde's encouragement, Mrs. Sidgwick's face betrayed her reluctance. "I will say no more than there is bad blood between Frank Podmore and Mister Hume . . . and between the Society in general."

"But why?" Conan Doyle questioned. "I understand Podmore is a scientist."

Eleanor Sidgwick tittered. "Frank calls himself a scientist. In truth he is a clerk in the post office. Oh, I suppose it is true that he did attend university and has a very keen mind."

"Then why is he so scornful of Hume?"

She paused before answering, obviously choosing her words carefully. "Frank has experienced a number of *disappointments* in the spiritualist world. Especially where Mister Hume is concerned. Frank wrote a book called *Phantasms of the Living*, which described a number of sessions that verified Mister Hume's abilities under strict scientific conditions. But a short time afterward, Frank turned on Mister Hume, claiming that he had faked many of his feats and duped his sitters. I believe, however, it may have been Mister Hume's character flaws that colored Frank's opinion."

"Character flaws?" Wilde repeated, leaning forward in his seat. "Do go on. I never tire of hearing of other people's flaws, especially as I have none of my own."

"No . . . I really should say no more," she said, fanning herself with a folded program. "It is all gossip and rumor."

Wilde stroked the back of her hand and adopted a fawning expression. "Dear lady, must I plead?"

She giggled, and as Wilde had given her permission, took a deep breath and began: "Well, it appears that Mister Hume is something of a cad—especially where ladies are involved."

"Delicious," Wilde purred. "If I had wings, I would be buzzing now."

"Mister Hume traveled the continent for a number of years, and always as a guest of wealthy patrons. Whilst in Paris, he was summoned to the Tuileries to perform a séance for Napoleon III. He also performed for Queen Sophia of the Netherlands. I understand she was quite smitten with his powers." And then she added in a hugely incriminating voice: "*All* of them."

"Well, I can't say I'd fault him for using his gifts," Conan Doyle argued, oblivious to the innuendo.

"But don't you see? Mister Hume has no income, but lives at the expense of others: royalty, aristocrats—and especially ladies of means. The biggest scandal involves one Mrs. Lyons, a wealthy widow."

"A wealthy widow!" Wilde said. "How titillating. I have a penchant for stories that involve wealthy widows."

"Mrs. Lyons adopted Hume as her son."

"As her son?" Conan Doyle said, incredulous. "How old was Hume at the time? How old was Mrs. Lyons?"

"The age difference was but a few years. You can imagine the scandal, especially when the widow gave Mister Hume sixty thousand pounds, it is said in an attempt to gain introduction to high society. When Hume failed to live up to his promise, the lady brought suit in the courts for the return of her money. The case was decided against Hume, and Mrs. Lyon's money was returned. Of course, Mister Hume's reputation was pilloried in the press and left Frank Podmore totally disillusioned with his onetime hero."

At that precise moment, Daniel Dunglas Hume strode into the room and struck a theatrical pose, back arched, chest thrust out, thumbs hooked behind his lapels. Compared to the ashen-faced man who had been carried from the room the previous evening, he seemed completely rejuvenated. Spotting the punch bowl, he crossed the room with the strutting gait of a barnyard rooster.

"Please excuse me," she suddenly announced. "I am very thirsty."

As Hume was pouring himself a glass of punch, Mrs. Sidgwick rushed over and nearly collided with him. Conan Doyle and Wilde watched as the two exchanged pleasantries and then Mrs. Sidgwick held up her glass as Hume filled it for her with the punch ladle. They moved to a nearby love seat and sat down together. Hume said something and smiled, at which she stroked his arm playfully and simpered.

"Dear me," Wilde said. "It rather looks as if we've been cuckolded—despite the fact that we are giants."

Conan Doyle grunted. "It seems Mrs. Sidgwick is seeking male company other than her husband. She acted as if she did not receive a kiss on the hand very often."

"From the look of her aged husband," Wilde noted, "I'd say her lips are even more lonely."

* * *

When the grandfather clock in the corner chimed the hour, Lady Thraxton arrived in a whisper of black veils. Conan Doyle's shoulders slumped as he watched the Count draw up a chair for the Lady and then drag a chair for himself close by. Taking the Lady's arrival as his cue, Henry Sidgwick clapped his hands for attention and called together the Tuesday meeting of the Society for Psychical Research.

"This morning," Sidgwick began, "Mister Frank Podmore will provide us with a lecture on *Animal Magnetism*." Sidgwick waved for Podmore to come forward from his seat.

"I'll be interested to hear this," Conan Doyle whispered to Wilde.

Podmore took Sidgwick's place at the center of the room. His eyes swept the audience with impatient disapproval as he waited for stray knots of conversation to shrivel up. Then he cleared his throat and launched into his lecture. "Today, I shall be speaking about a paper I wrote last year—"

A knock at the parlor door interrupted him. Mister Greaves shuffled in and bowed his head as he announced, "Lord Philipp Webb."

A tall man in a black suit entered. He was fastidiously groomed, his short, glossy black hair parted in the middle and pomaded in place. His large nose was anchored to his face by a modest black moustache with waxed and curled ends. The nose had a prominent bump, which provided a convenient ledge for a pair of pince-nez, from which dangled a black ribbon. His black pinstripe suit showed impeccable tailoring and made Conan Doyle, in his sensible but well-worn tweeds, feel positively shabby.

Wilde leaned close to his friend and whispered, "I admire his tailoring although—Ach!" He made a face. "A black suit with brown boots and white spats? Something's amiss with that!"

To Conan Doyle, everything about the man screamed "aristocrat," and then he opened his mouth and nailed the assumption in place: "You must excuse my late arrival," Lord Webb said in a deep, mellifluous voice. "I arrived rather late, or rather, very early this morning." His blue-eyed gaze, grossly swollen behind the pince-nez lenses, swept the room until he finally noticed the diminutive Frank Podmore. "Ah, it seems I'm interrupting." He drew out a chair and lowered his elegant form into it, casually crossing one long leg over the other. Then, with great deliberation, he took out a silver cigarette case from his inside jacket pocket, removed a cigarette, and fitted it to a black ebony cigarette holder. Reaching into his left pocket, he took out a matchbox and shook it to ensure it still contained matches. He removed a single match. Struck it. Puffed his cigarette to life. Then fastidiously returned the burned match to its box.

It was a mundane performance, but one that held the entire room's attention captive and only relinquished it when he was finished. As he drew on the cigarette holder clamped between his teeth, Lord Webb looked up distractedly and acknowledged Podmore with a dismissive wave, saying, "Please . . . do go on."

Podmore bristled. Cleared his throat. Pulled his shoulders back. He stood as tall as he was able in an attempt to recapture the audience, but most eyes, especially those of the women, were riveted to the svelte form of Lord Webb. Conan Doyle noted that even Mrs. Sidgwick had lost interest in Daniel Dunglas Hume and was staring at the suave newcomer.

Frank Podmore chewed his lip and stood looking around the room for several moments before speaking. "In any investigation of so-called psychic phenomena, one must approach with cautious skepticism, for we are in a field tainted by superstition, delusion, and sheer knavery."

A murmur ran through the membership.

"This fellow begins every speech with an insult," Wilde muttered. Conan Doyle nodded agreement, although he could not tell if Podmore was trying to be offensive or if the man was simply devoid of the tiniest scintilla of tact.

"Such is the case with hypnosis, which began with the fabrications of Franz Mesmer. Despite such tarnished beginnings, hypnosis has achieved a loyal following among those who usually exhibit better judgment, and the pseudoscience has finally left the music halls and entered the hallowed halls of academia."

Podmore went on for another ten minutes citing, with excruciating pedantry, a number of studies undertaken at various universities. He had committed a great deal to memory, and now lavished his audience with the most uninteresting minutiae. Podmore's nasal voice managed at once to be both irritating and monotonous. Conan Doyle had enjoyed only a few hours of sleep and soon found his eyelids sagging as he battled to stay awake.

Wilde, too, must have been suffering the same effect. He leaned close to Conan Doyle's ear and murmured, "I see now that Mister Podmore is a master of hypnosis: the entire room is about to lapse into unconsciousness."

Wilde's comment tickled Conan Doyle. All eyes in the room turned his way as he choked off a laugh.

Lord Webb finished his cigarette, removed it from the black holder, and tossed it in the fire, and then interrupted Podmore midstream. "And are we to have a practical demonstration of hypnosis?" he asked.

Podmore stopped mid-sentence and fixed the aristocrat with his ratting terrier stare. "I am lecturing on the advances in the study of the mind made possible by the newest applications of hypnosis."

Lord Webb rose to his full height. "But surely a practical demonstration would be much more efficacious. After all, the members can read your paper at their leisure when the meeting is long over. While we are all gathered here, it would seem more germane to have a practical demonstration."

"I assume, Lord Webb, that you are an expert in hypnosis?"

The aristocrat nodded modestly. "As a matter of fact, I am. Advanced education was discouraged in my family—my father deemed it unseemly for one of an elevated social class. Quite against his wishes, I attended the University of Leipzig where I studied under the great Doctor Johan Friedrich Blumenthal. You are no doubt familiar with his paper: *Die Phisoligicae und Mesmer?*"

Podmore's mouth opened. His lips twitched as he strained for a response, but then he dropped his head, shamefaced—intellectually outgunned.

Without invitation, Lord Webb strode to the center of the room and stood beside Podmore as if to make the differences in their heights more pronounced. The younger man squirmed a moment and then silently capitulated, returning to his seat where he glowered beneath his ginger brows, radiating hatred.

"The first thing a hypnotist must ascertain," Lord Webb began, "is whether a patient is a suitable subject for hypnosis—not everyone is. So, I propose an experiment and ask now for several volunteers." He looked around the room as if tossing down a gauntlet. His gaze swept over Frank Podmore, who looked away, refusing to make eye contact. When no one immediately volunteered, Conan Doyle raised his hand and said aloud, "I wish to volunteer."

Webb's pince-nez caught the light from the window and his eyes vanished behind two glowing disks. "Excellent." He looked around. "Any others?"

Several more members rose to their feet: Oscar Wilde first, and then Sir William Crookes, and finally Eleanor Sidgwick sprang to her feet, taking her husband by surprise.

"Oh, I don't think he meant ladies," Henry Sidgwick said quickly.

"Nonsense, Henry," Lord Webb corrected. "Women make excellent subjects. Their egos are far less obstructive than the male ego, and so they are far more suggestible." He beckoned the volunteers forward with a wave and assembled them in the middle of the room. Then he walked along the line, a general reviewing his troops. He stopped when he came across Conan Doyle and Wilde. "I don't think I've had the pleasure of meeting you two gentlemen."

"I am Doctor Conan Doyle, and this is my friend, Oscar Wilde."

Webb looked impressed. "Indeed! I thought I recognized you both. Two very notable gentlemen. We are honored, indeed." He shook their hands and moved on to Eleanor Sidgwick. She offered her hand; he took it and kissed it. "Eleanor and I are already acquainted, although I have never hypnotized her."

"Oh Lord Webb, if you place me under your thrall, you must

promise not to ravish me!" She trilled her girlish laugh and asked, "*Have* you ever hypnotized a lady and then ravished her?"

Webb smiled indulgently. "Never, I assure you, Eleanor. I am bound by a code of ethics."

"Oh," she said in a rather disappointed voice.

"He could not do so, either way," Podmore spoke up. "One cannot be impelled to commit an act against one's basic moral beliefs—even under hypnosis."

Lord Webb lavished Podmore with the ingratiating smile one awards to a precocious but stupid child. "Once again, you are quite wrong, Frank. A master hypnotist, a true charismatic, can make a hypnotic subject do anything he bids him to do. Yourself, for example. If I were to hypnotize you, I could order you to climb to the highest rooftop of this house and throw yourself off. And you would do so"—he added with an unmistakable tone of malice—"*willingly.*"

Podmore's jaw clenched at the threat. He dropped his eyes to the rug and crossed his arms over his chest.

"Now then," Webb said pleasantly. "Let us begin our little experiment." He turned to the four volunteers. "I would like you all to close your eyes." When they had complied, he continued, "Please imagine that you stand with your heels at the very edge of a tall cliff. Behind you, a precipitous drop of thousands of feet. Now, feel the wind on your face." He pursed his lips and walked along the line blowing in the faces of the volunteers. All began to waver, fighting to remain upright—all except Conan Doyle, who stood immovable as an iron streetlamp.

"You fight, you seek to resist, but the wind is too strong." Webb once again walked the line of volunteers, blowing harder in their faces. Sir William Crookes wavered and then took a staggering step backward. Eleanor Sidgwick also lost her balance and stepped back. When he reached Wilde, the tall Irishman practically toppled over. Conan Doyle, however, did not so much as waver.

"Have you ever been hypnotized, Doctor Doyle?"

"No," Conan Doyle admitted. "I have used hypnosis in my own practice, but I have never myself been successfully hypnotized."

The aristocrat paused thoughtfully, as if weighing his words, before saying, "It is clear that your ego is afraid of losing control." He shared a knowing smirk with the room. "Some minds resist— especially those that are afraid to lose their grip. The best subjects are creative people. Risk-takers. Those open to new sensations. Those who are comfortable giving up control." He slapped a patronizing hand on Conan Doyle's shoulder. "That hardly describes you, does it, old boy? But I'm grateful you brought your friend along. Mister Wilde here shows every sign of being a first-rate subject."

"I am not in the least surprised," Wilde said. "I am seldom described as anything other than first-rate."

The room laughed and applauded politely.

"Thank you for your indulgence," Webb said, dismissing the others, who returned to their places. Feeling an unease he could not account for, Conan Doyle reluctantly left his friend and resumed his seat.

"Now, Mister Wilde." Lord Webb grabbed an empty, hard-backed chair, spun it around, and placed it in front of Wilde. "Please sit and we'll begin."

The dapper Lord took out his pocket watch, set the watch to spinning on its fob, and dangled it by the chain in front of Wilde's face. "Mister Wilde, focus on the watch and think of nothing else." Webb's voice, operatic to begin with, became deeper and more resonant. "You are feeling very drowsy . . . and with every second that passes, with every breath you take, so you will become drowsier and drowsier . . ."

The watch twirled. Oscar Wilde's eyelids trembled and grew heavy-lidded.

"And now, you cannot keep your eyes open, so let them close."

Wilde's eyes drooped shut. His large frame sagged in the chair. His breathing became deep and sonorous.

"Now, Mister Wilde, even though you are asleep, you will hear every word I say. And obey every command I give you. Is that clear?"

"Yes," Wilde mumbled.

Conan Doyle bit his lip; his stomach clenched. Was Oscar shamming? Or was he really under Lord Webb's influence? He shot a look at Dunglas Hume, who met his gaze and shook his head as if to say: *This is not a good thing.*

"Mister Wilde. Please stand."

Wilde surged to his feet, arms hanging slack, head lolling.

"Hold out your right hand."

Wilde robotically obeyed. Lord Webb reached into a jacket pocket and drew out a slender metallic object—a large needle. Conan Doyle saw it and blanched inwardly: he knew what was coming next. Webb flourished the needle for all to see. "This is a needle of the type commonly used to sew sails. One of the miracles of hypnosis is its ability to stop pain. I believe that, some day, drugs such as morphine will be considered crude and dangerous. Instead, surgery, childbirth, wounds received in battle, will all be relieved by the power of suggestion alone." He turned his attention back to his subject. "Mister Wilde, your right hand is becoming numb . . . completely numb." And with that he drove the needle straight through the back of Wilde's hand, completely piercing through to the other side. Hope Thraxton gave a little shriek, as did Eleanor Sidgwick. Several of the men shouted in surprise. Conan Doyle leapt to his feet, angry.

"Now see here, sir—"

Webb silenced them all with a gesture. "Please remain calm. The only danger in hypnosis is if the bond between the hypnotist and his subject is arbitrarily broken."

The room fell silent. Conan Doyle did not believe such was the case, but with his friend under Webb's thrall, he was not about to risk matters. He sank back into his chair.

"Mister Wilde. Do you feel any pain?"

"No."

Webb smiled as he drew the needle out slowly . . . slowly . . . slowly . . . an inch at a time, clearly relishing the discomfort he was causing his audience. "No need for squeamishness," he said in a calm voice. "Mister Wilde feels nothing, nor will he remember any of this afterward." He pocketed the needle. "Mister Wilde, when I say the word . . ." He looked around the room for inspiration, and finally his gaze alighted upon Conan Doyle. "When I say the words *Sherlock Holmes* you will sleep. And when I say the word . . . *Watson*"—he smiled, apparently amused by his own joke—"then you shall awaken. Do you understand?"

Wilde mumbled agreement.

"Now, I will demonstrate how a suggestion, once implanted deep in the mind, can be summoned again. He turned to his subject. "Mister Wilde, I want you to stand on the piano stool."

Oscar Wilde stepped up onto the piano stool. Conan Doyle fought to remain sitting: a fall from such a height could easily cause injury.

"Mister Wilde, are you listening, sir?"

"Yes."

Webb's face turned earnest. He snapped his fingers beneath Wilde's nose and said, "Watson!"

Oscar Wilde blinked open his eyes and looked around, dumbfounded at the faces staring at him. "Oh my! How much champagne have I had?"

"Thank you, Mister Wilde," Lord Webb said, giving him a hand as he stepped down. Wilde threw a puzzled look at Conan Doyle as he retook his seat.

"Whatever happened, Arthur?"

"I shall tell you later."

The SPR members applauded, except for Daniel Dunglas Hume, and Sir William Crookes who spoke up in a loud voice, "Yes, very droll, Lord Webb. But it was transparently clear that Mister Wilde was simply playing along."

Lord Webb stiffened and turned to look at the scientist. "Exactly what are you insinuating?"

"Mister Wilde was just being a good sport," Sir William said, smiling slackly. It was clear to all that he'd started drinking earlier than usual that day. "I don't believe for a second that he was truly hypnotized. In fact, I have long been of the opinion that hypnosis is a complete sham."

Sir William's words were like an open-handed slap. Philipp Webb clenched his jaw, not uttering a word. Then he turned to look at Wilde and said quietly: "Sherlock Holmes."

Oscar Wilde immediately sagged in his chair, eyes closed.

"Stand, Mister Wilde."

Wilde jerked to his feet.

Webb pulled the piano stool closer to the piano. "Come forward."

In a deep trance, Wilde shuffled closer.

"Mister Wilde. You are trekking in the Himalaya. First you must climb the foothills. Step up, sir."

Wilde remounted the piano stool.

"Very well, Philipp," Sir William said. "You've made your point. No need to take it farther."

But Webb ignored him. "And now you are about to summit the mountain. Climb again."

Wilde stepped from the piano stool onto the closed lid of the piano.

"Face this way, sir."

Wilde turned until he was facing the group.

"Take a step backward."

He complied, his heels overhanging the very edge of the piano lid.

"Mister Wilde you stand on a mountain ledge, a cold hard wind is blowing in your face. Behind you . . . the abyss."

Wilde's face contorted as if from the cold. He teetered, fighting for balance.

Conan Doyle rose to his feet. He was about to call for the demonstration to be ended, but the Count beat him to the punch. "Zat is quite enough, Lord Vebb. I demand you stop zis reckless display before it results in injury—"

"Yes," Conan Doyle added loudly. "Cease at once!"

But the aristocrat was not in the least affected by their protests. "Sir William thinks our friend here is shamming," he argued. "He has as good as called me a fraud!"

The room fell deathly silent as Conan Doyle and everyone else realized just how dangerous the titled gentleman could be.

"Very well, Lord Webb," Sir William wavered to his feet, the urgency of the situation finally burning through the haze of alcohol. "I retract my words and apologize. Please have Mister Wilde step down from there."

But Webb now didn't seem to care about his audience. He was clearly enjoying himself. "Mister Wilde, you stand upon the edge of a precipice. All it would take to make you fall is the slightest breeze." He stood at the side of the piano, pursed his lips, and began to blow air at Wilde's face. "Feel that? That is the wind. Resist!"

Wilde's knees jellied as he strained to keep his balance. Conan Doyle and everyone in the room watched helpless, transfixed by a sense of powerlessness. If Wilde fell backward, he would break his neck.

"Lord Webb!" Conan Doyle spoke in a low growl, "Stop this now!"

Ignoring the request, Webb pursed his lips once again and blew harder.

Wilde's large body began to topple.

Screams and shouts of alarm.

At the last moment, Webb clapped his hands together and cried: "*Watson!*"

Wilde's eyes sprang open. His body jackknifed as he fought to catch his balance. Finally, he wobbled upright and stood at his full height, looking around. He suddenly noticed where he was—clearly baffled. "Ah, how very odd. I appear to be standing atop a piano. Am I about to give a recital?"

Conan Doyle rushed forward. "Oscar, are you all right?"

"Why, yes," Wilde said, tugging his waistcoat down and adjusting his cuffs. "When is the display of hypnosis to take place?" Conan Doyle went toe-to-toe with Lord Webb, his large fists clenched into hammer heads. "That was reckless, sir!" For a moment, it seemed certain that Conan Doyle would fling himself upon the aristocrat, but then he swept him aside with his arm and helped Wilde step down from the piano.

Lord Webb sank back into his chair and crossed his legs. He calmly inserted a fresh cigarette into the ebony holder before striking a match and lighting it. "Hypnosis is a rudimentary skill a child could manage." He tossed a careless glance at Podmore. "But as I said, to become a true master one must possess charisma."

Frank Podmore leaped up from his seat and marched to the door. He flung it wide, revealing Mrs. Kragan, who had been peering through the crack. Podmore shouldered past, nearly knocking her over. She looked startled for a moment, but then composed her face and stepped into the room.

"Milady," she announced in a shaky voice. "Luncheon is served in the dining room."

Members of the SPR began to file out, many jabbering excitedly. Henry Sidgwick crept up to the two writers, wringing his hands in obvious embarrassment. "I really must apologize most profoundly. I should have stopped Lord Webb. I'm ashamed for what happened and I deeply regret it. I hope you can forgive us."

Wilde showed not the least concern. "I will be full of forgiveness as soon as I'm full of lunch." He patted his ample stomach. "Apparently, hypnosis makes one quite ravenous."

Conan Doyle looked around for Lady Thraxton, but she had already left. The Count lingered, and it was clear he had watched the fiery interchange with great interest.

Fortunately, Lord Webb chose not to attend the luncheon.

❦

CHAPTER 15

NAMING THE SUSPECTS

The first séance is set for this evening," Conan Doyle said, eyeing the paper program. "And yet we are no nearer to determining a potential suspect."

The two had retired to Conan Doyle's room, where Wilde was staring out the window at black rags of cloud dropping sheets of rain on the sheep scattered across the fields. Finally, he turned away from the window and gave his full attention to Conan Doyle, who was sitting at the small writing desk, drumming his fingers atop its leather surface.

"Arthur, have you considered the possibility that there might not be a murderer to find? After all, we are here on the pretext of a vision related to you in a darkened room by a woman who claims to talk to the dead. And as yet, we have not even spoken directly to the young lady."

Conan Doyle's guilty face gave him away.

"Ah, you *have* spoken to the young lady," Wilde surmised. "Last night? The note you were so eager to conceal?"

"I am sorry to have hidden it from you. You are correct. I did meet with the young lady. But I did not tell you . . ." Conan Doyle flustered. "I did not tell you in case you thought something inappropriate took place between us."

"In that case, you had better tell me all of the *appropriate* things that took place."

For the next fifteen minutes, Conan Doyle narrated the events of the previous evening, including the visit to the crumbling west wing and the mirror maze in the turret room. He left out details about the shockingly scanty fashion in which the young lady was dressed and the way she had stirred his ardor. Wilde said nothing as Conan Doyle spoke, but puffed away at a Turkish cigarette, his eyes narrowing now and then as he absorbed a fresh detail. When Conan Doyle finished, Wilde tossed his cigarette butt in the unlit fireplace and breathed out a lungful of smoke. "Very illuminating," he said. "The young lady has lived the life of a virginal heroine in a *penny dreadful*."

"The Scottish author felt an uncharacteristic flare of anger against his friend. "What precisely are you inferring, Oscar? Are you calling Lady Thraxton a liar?"

Wilde recoiled with surprise. "I am sorry, Arthur. It is just that, this place, this ghastly house, seems to be nothing but an aggregation of gloom and tragedy. I am sure every word the young lady spoke was the truth."

Conan Doyle went into a sulk. Ignoring Wilde, he rose from his chair, rifled through his suitcase, and produced his leather-bound Casebook. He returned to his place at the writing table, pulled free the shiny key secured by a ribbon around his neck, and unlocked it.

"A journal, Arthur? I did not know you kept one."

"Not a journal. A Casebook. We must begin by identifying all possible suspects, and then determine which of them has a motive for murdering Lady Thraxton. We cannot be on guard against everyone. Therefore, we must attempt to narrow our list of suspects."

"Spoken like your hero, Sherlock Holmes."

Conan Doyle took out his fountain pen and drew a number of columns running down the page. At the top of the first column he wrote: *Suspect,* in the next he wrote *Motive,* and in the next he wrote *Means.* He pondered a moment and then added a final column: *Likelihood.*

He paused and lifted the Casebook to show his diagram to Wilde. "What do you think of this, Oscar? As a beginning?"

The Irish playwright squinted at the diagram with a doubtful frown on his long face. "This doesn't involve maths, does it? I was a student of the Classics. You know maths was never my strong suit."

"It's not about maths. It's about probabilities. We cannot work backward as in a normal murder case where we have a body, a murder scene, a weapon, and suspects. We have to solve a murder in the future tense. So we must begin with suspects, which includes everyone in this house—the entire membership of the Society. We must sieve through them, separating the least likely from the most likely."

"And the domestics."

"What?"

"And the domestics," Wilde repeated. "Really, Arthur, you must attend the theater more often. In the majority of murder mysteries performed on the boards, the culprit is invariably the butler."

"Why the butler?"

Wilde smiled toothily. "Because butlers, maids—in fact all domestics—are invisible. They are free to roam the entire house without raising suspicion. Free to lurk on a landing . . . or to linger in a drawing room on the pretense of dusting the china hutch . . . or lighting the samovar . . . or whatever. They have access to every room. They know where the good silver is kept and behind which portrait the wall safe is hidden. If a house is a giant brain, they are its nerves."

Conan Doyle nodded, his face thoughtful. "That's very good, Oscar. Excellent, in fact. I know we've scarcely arrived, but we haven't much time. We have met all the players. If you had to pick one, who do you think is capable of murder?"

"I think the most likely suspect is our American cousin: Mister Daniel Dunglas Hume."

"Hume?" Conan Doyle repeated skeptically. "What reason would Hume have for murdering Lady Thraxton?"

"She is a rival psychic. Mister Hume is a large man with a large talent and a large ego. As the libidinous Mrs. Sidgwick said, he is the polestar of our little get-together. A star I'll wager who does not wish to be occluded. And never forget we are speaking of murder in the future tense. Hume is a notorious womanizer. He will likely make advances to the fetching young Lady Thraxton. If she spurns his advances . . . well, that alone may be enough."

Conan Doyle replayed every interchange between Hume and Lady Thraxton he had witnessed: Hume kissing her lace-gloved hand, standing too close to her, and the immodest way Hume ravished the young lady with his gaze from across the room. It all suddenly seemed much more plausible—especially given Eleanor Sidgwick's gossip that Hume was both a libertine and a penniless adventurer who lived off the wealth of others. He wrote *Daniel Dunglas Hume* on the line below. In the column *Motive*, he placed a check mark. In the column *Means*, he placed another check. A man who could levitate and had other powers could easily murder a young, defenseless woman.

Conan Doyle looked at his notes. "I also think that the Count, whomever or whatever he truly is, bears close watching."

"The Count?" Puzzlement lined Wilde's long face. "Why the Count?"

"He is the only guest parading around with a pistol strapped to his waist. He is always hovering close to Lady Thraxton. And he is a foreigner."

"We are in England, Arthur. Both you and I are foreigners."

Conan Doyle bristled. "Oh, that's hardly the case and you know it, Oscar."

Wilde pondered a moment and then said, "Arthur, there is a name you must add to your list."

Conan Doyle looked at him expectantly.

"Yours," Wilde said calmly.

"Mine? You cannot be serious, Oscar. I am here to save the young lady."

"Yours was the only face she recognized in her vision."

Conan Doyle flinched as if from a blow. "Yes . . . but we know that I would never—"

"Arthur," Wilde interrupted. "We have been friends for some years now. You are the most decent man I have ever known. Honest and true. Faithful and trustworthy. Sober and rational—to a fault. But since the moment we entered this house, you are quite changed."

"I—I don't know what you mean," Conan Doyle spluttered. "H-how so?"

"You are passionate and fiery. Quite the opposite of your usual solid, dependable, and—please do not take umbrage at this—predictable self. The only thing I know for certain is that you lack the means to carry out the murder. That is, you do not have a firearm in your possession."

At the words, Conan Doyle dropped his head. His shoulders slumped. Without a word he stood up and stamped a foot upon the seat of the chair he had just been sitting in. Then he dramatically snatched up his pants leg to reveal the revolver strapped to his ankle with a necktie his wife had given to him just the previous Christmas. "Behold, Oscar, I am more prepared than you think."

To his credit, Oscar Wilde failed to bat an eyelid. After several moments of reflection, he drily observed: "For once, Arthur, you are innovative in your fashion sense. But I fear it is a look that shall never catch on."

Conan Doyle chuckled at the remark as he drew out the revolver. "Unconventional, I admit, but at least I shall not enter the fray unarmed."

"Or unlegged," Wilde said, goggling at the large revolver cradled in Arthur's hands.

"You are shocked, I'm sure."

"I am shocked you had room for that artillery piece in your tiny suitcase. Really, Arthur, someday you must reveal to me the secrets of your packing technique."

Conan Doyle sagged into his chair and gazed morosely into space. "You are right, Oscar."

"Thank you," Wilde said, looking pleased, and then added, "About what?"

"Right in all respects. A loaded pistol? A darkened séance room? I could very easily shoot the wrong person. And you are justified in saying that I have not been myself since the day we arrived." Conan Doyle frowned at the revolver hefted in his hand. "We are here on the basis of a premonition. Enmeshed in a struggle against Fate. Perhaps I have unwittingly brought the murder weapon to the scene of the crime." His lip curled in disgust. "I should throw the blasted thing into the river. That way I cannot possibly—"

A loud rap at the door interrupted him. Both men looked at one another. Conan Doyle was seized with a momentary terror that their conversation had been eavesdropped on. He snatched the loose tie from his leg, wrapped it around the pistol, and slipped them both into a desk drawer. "Come!" he called.

The door creaked open and Mister Greaves creaked into the room. He stood leaning on the door handle for several long moments, wheezing, his lungs pumping like cracked leather bellows. Conan Doyle realized the poor fellow had just slogged up three flights of stairs. When the old retainer had caught his breath, he announced, "Sirs . . . the next session will commence . . ." he wheezed but had insufficient breath to continue. His legs quivered, his knees threatening to buckle. Conan Doyle leapt from his chair and insisted that the old butler sit down and rest.

"Thank . . . thank you, sir . . . most kind," Greaves said. After several wheezing breaths his pallor deepened from white to gray and he finished his announcement. "The next session will commence in half an hour. Sherry will be served in the parlor any time you gentlemen are ready to come down."

His errand completed, Mister Greaves shuffled out the door. When the door had closed on his back, Conan Doyle looked at Wilde and tut-tutted. "It's ridiculous that a man of such advanced age is still working. I would have thought the family would make him retire and provide for him."

"Yes," Wilde agreed. "But this is Thraxton Hall. I have no doubt that when the poor chap passes they will have him stuffed and stand him in a corner. I doubt anyone would notice the difference."

* * *

As they descended from the third floor, the two friends found that they were following several other guests en route to the parlor, including the Sidgwicks and Daniel Dunglas Hume, who was locked in conversation with the enigmatic Count. As they reached the first floor landing, Conan Doyle spotted the head housekeeper, Mrs. Kragan, exiting the portrait gallery. Like all good servants in the presence of guests, she froze in place and lowered her head respectfully—the better to be invisible. But as the chattering guests left the entrance hall, she glared after them, her lined face stony with bitterness. But then she looked up, noticed Conan Doyle and

Wilde observing her, and fled down the small staircase that led below stairs to the kitchens and servants' quarters.

"There goes the delightful Mrs. Kragan."

"Ach!" Wilde said, making a face. "There's a banshee from the bog if ever I saw one. Give her a pair of knitting needles and a freshly sharpened guillotine and she would happily cackle the day away. The woman seems to lurk everywhere. My wife would put her in her place in a trice."

Conan Doyle pondered the remark. "At first I thought she was merely protective of her mistress, ensuring she is seldom left unaccompanied in a room with a gentleman. However, I am beginning to think there is something sinister in the relationship."

Wilde raised an eyebrow. "Sinister?"

"She shadows Lady Thraxton at all times. As if she is spying on her. After the incident in the mirror maze, her son was forever banished from the house. I've no doubt that Mrs. Kragan harbors a long-festering enmity toward her mistress."

Oscar Wilde's long fleshy face puddled into contemplation as he mulled Conan Doyle's words. He drew his silver cigarette case from his inside breast pocket, sparked a lucifer with his thumbnail, and puffed one of his aromatic cigarettes into life. "Enough for murder?" he breathed in smoke words, then shook his head dismissively. "If so, I imagine she would have poisoned her Ladyship's tea many years ago."

Conan Doyle grunted and said, "Poisoners are amongst the most commonly hanged murderers. It is typically a woman's crime and hard to explain away as an accident—especially when someone young and in good health dies unexpectedly. Mrs. Kragan may be many things, but she is no fool. Still, she is the only suspect with a known grievance against Lady Thraxton."

Conan Doyle stood drumming his fingers on the milled oak banister rail as he thought, and then said, "Some murderers are impulsive. Some opportunistic. Others are patient plotters: shadow-lurking vipers content to bide their time and allow the venom to accumulate, drop by drop, before they strike." He shook his head as if to clear away the image, and added in a voice swollen with enthusiasm, "Oscar, as a fellow Irishman, you are just the person to speak with her."

Wilde's face fell. "You have just described her as a pit-dwelling viper and you wish me to confront her? Oh God, no, Arthur! You know that I would do absolutely anything to help you—anything that isn't difficult . . . or unpleasant . . . or dangerous. And speaking to Mrs. Kragan is all three. The woman is a gorgon. I shall be turned to stone."

"You're the man for the job," Conan Doyle insisted. "You're both Irish. Speak to her about the old country."

Doubt blossomed on Wilde's face. "What about the 'old country'? Neither of us has lived there in twenty years."

"Start with that. Then ask her about the Thraxton family. Her years of service. Specifically, Lady Thraxton. Try to discern her feelings toward her employer. Sound her out."

Wilde extinguished his partially smoked cigarette on the inside of the silver case and replaced it in one of the holders. He looked far from happy. "I shall regret this, Arthur," he moaned. "I know I shall."

"In the meantime, I shall examine the portrait of Mariah Thraxton that graces the entrance hall. I barely glanced at it when we first entered the house, but it contains a number of references I find most enigmatic."

* * *

Even though he had no idea of the below-stairs layout of Thraxton Hall, Wilde was able to navigate his way through the narrow, gloomy corridors with the aid of a sense of smell honed by years of gourmandizing. At last he stepped into a bright, warm, steamy room refulgent with the smell of baking bread and large pots simmering on the hob, bubbling with soups and stews.

His stomach growled—a lion awakened.

A long, scrubbed pine table was set at one side of the kitchen—the table at which the domestics would take their meals. Wilde was surprised to find two rather rough-looking characters seated one on either side, both tucking into the leftovers of breakfast. One was a small, dark man with black hair and protuberant dark eyes. He held a piece of toast in both small hands, nibbling at it so that he resembled a vole discovered lurking in the pantry. The other man was a hulking, raw-boned minotaur with a fiery thatch of red hair bristling atop his large skull. His huge, prognathic jaws bore similar topiary in the form of side-whiskers the size of hedgerows. As Wilde entered, his large hands were tearing a loaf in two. The Irish poet watched with distaste as the redhead crammed a huge chunk of bread in his mouth, chewing slack-jawed and openmouthed, masticated food rolling around on his tongue. Both men failed to notice Wilde's presence, as they were ogling the scullery maid's bottom as she stooped to remove a smoking joint from the oven.

"You have lost your way, sir," an Irish voice said. It was not a question.

Wilde spun around to find himself face-to-face with Mrs. Kragan.

"*Dia dhuit*," Wilde said, bowing slightly as he used the traditional Gaelic greeting. He smiled a warmth he did not feel. "It is always a pleasure to converse with someone from the old country."

The greeting had no effect. Mrs. Kragan confronted him with a face flung shut like an iron gate. "I find very little of Ireland left in you, sir. You are more English than the English."

"Yes, I do regret that I have lost my Irish brogue."

"But none of the blarney."

Wilde laughed, attempting gaiety. He was suddenly sweating and dabbed at his face with a handkerchief. The kitchen was humid, but Mrs. Kragan's stare was a pot boiling over.

"What have you come poking around for, sir?"

"Ah, yes. I merely wished to inquire whether the waters of the ford had receded. Therefore, I might plan my escape."

The iron gate cracked open slightly, though mistrust lurked in the crow's feet. "The river is still too high." She nodded at the rough characters slouched at the table. "Hence we are forced to accommodate the two fellows you see there."

"How terribly inconvenient," Wilde said, and then added casually, "I have to say, they do not look much like undertakers."

"They are not."

"And yet they arrived by hearse? An unusual form of transport."

"You are not in the city now, Mister Wilde. The wagon is used as a hearse for funerals. The rest of the time, it is used for removals. These fellows fetched Lord Webb and his baggage from the station."

"And a coffin, too, I understand?"

For the first time the iron countenance cracked, the eyes widening slightly. But then the gates banged shut again. "You are confused, sir. They fetched only Lord Webb and his luggage. His baggage did include a large steamer trunk." Her black eyes glittered. "Any more questions, Mr. Wilde?"

"No . . . no I don't believe so." He smiled toothily and added in a pleasant voice: "Please do give my regards to Mr. Kragan."

She flinched at the remark, but quickly recovered. "I am a widow."

"Ah, I see. My condolences." Wilde's eyes dropped to her left hand. "But you do not wear a wedding ring in remembrance?"

"My husband died many years ago. I am not a sentimental woman."

Wilde allowed himself a smile. "Thank you, Mrs. Kragan. Your warmth and courtesy are well appreciated." And with that, he bowed, said, *"Slán agat,"* the traditional Gaelic farewell, and quit the kitchen, leaving the gray-haired housekeeper glaring after him.

* * *

Conan Doyle's footsteps echoed as he crossed the marble entrance hall. A great candelabrum hung from the ceiling. Every candle was lit, and their combined glow filled the giant portrait of Mariah Thraxton with a warm yellow light so that it appeared less like a painted canvas and more like a window into another room, another reality. He stood gazing up at it. Now that he studied it closer, he found that the resemblance to the current Lady of the Manor was more than familial, it was blood close, like two sisters. Mariah Thraxton was older in the painting, perhaps in her early thirties, while Hope's features were still those of a girl barely out of her teens. But where there was kindness in Hope's eyes, there was craftiness in Mariah's. Where Hope's smile was shy and guileless, the corners of Mariah's sensuous lips curled up in a sly challenge and mockery danced in her eyes.

Conan Doyle scrutinized the rest of the portrait and suddenly realized that he recognized the room: it was the mirror maze, the disheveled turret in the west wing before the vandal hand of Time had torn it to ruin. And then more realizations showered down upon him. On first glance, he had taken the painting to be of a lady at her dressing table, primping before her hand mirror. But Mariah sat at an octagonal table inscribed with strange occult symbols. The mirror she held was small and circular. It was turned just far enough to show her face reflected in it, and the large mirror hanging on the far wall reflected that reflection. The view through the window at her shoulder showed that the valley had changed little, except that the coppice had not been planted and the stone circle showed plain. And then he noticed another detail that chilled him: in the open window behind her, a ragged-tailed crow perched upon the sill.

"Does she look like a witch to you?" a querulous voice asked.

Conan Doyle started. He looked down to see Madame Zhozhovsky standing at his side, staring up at the painting. He had been so preoccupied he had failed to hear her stumping gait cross the marble hall.

Madame Zhozhovsky turned from the painting and fixed him with her uncanny gray gaze. "Of course, women of power are often accused of being witches. It is the male way of coping with threats to their dominance."

"I don't feel threatened at all by women who possess power," Conan Doyle said.

"Really?" The old lady smiled. "Then you support universal suffrage? You believe women should be given the vote?"

Conan Doyle's mouth fell open. He strained for a response. He had reasons for opposing women's right to vote, but they were complicated, like many of his opinions on matters of sex and politics.

Madame Zhozhovsky turned her attention back to the portrait, an infuriating smile on her face. "I thought not. Mariah was a woman very much out of her time. She had ideas and aspirations that were not considered fit for a woman two hundred years ago. Not considered fit even today. She had a brilliant mind and spent a large part of her husband's fortune on books. Alfred Thraxton was overly fond of hunting, drinking, and whoring. Had Mariah been content to keep to her books, she would have outlived him by a score of decades. But the silly girl wanted to go beyond mere reading. She wanted to experience things forbidden to men . . . and especially to women. As a woman, as a wife, she was not free to travel, so she traveled in the only way she could—on the spiritual planes."

Conan Doyle looked down at the diminutive figure at his side. "So do you believe she was a witch?"

"Witch?" Madame Zhozhovsky smiled ironically, without meeting his gaze. "A once-revered term now turned pejorative. There are many ways to travel for those who have the gift, and she was a woman of power. Her presence in this house resonates still." She raised her crooked walking stick and pointed to the painting. "Notice the beauty mark on the left cheek, just level with her mouth."

Conan Doyle peered up at the portrait. Even with his acute vision, he could just barely make it out from this distance. "Er . . . yes, I believe I can see it."

"It is in the shape of the crescent moon—an ancient occult symbol. Young Lady Thraxton bears the same mark."

Conan Doyle cleared his throat and asked casually, "Do you believe that Lady Mariah was practicing black magic?"

Madame Zhozhovsky turned slowly, painfully. "Do you see the circular mirror she holds?"

Conan Doyle's eyes flickered back to the painting. "Yes."

"It is not a mirror in which a lady adjusts her makeup. It is a scrying mirror. Do you know what scrying is, Doctor Doyle?"

"It is a type of crystal gazing, is it not?"

"Scrying is a form of divination practiced by seers using crystals, bowls of water, smoke, and often a black mirror such as the one you see in the painting."

"But the mirror in the painting is not black. It holds her reflection."

"Look closer, Doctor Doyle. The scrying mirror holds a reflection, which in turn is reflected in the mirror at her side. The tales told about her death say that, as Mariah lay dying, she called for her maidservant to fetch the scrying mirror. It caught her reflection as she uttered a curse."

"A curse?"

"That the house of Thraxton would never know a moment of happiness . . . and that one day she would return from the grave."

Conan Doyle craned forward, straining to make out the tiny image in both mirrors. "Extraordinary! But why would she call for a mirror?"

"Because a reflection never dies," Madame Zhozhovsky said, a note of triumph in her voice. "Mariah Thraxton delved into things no woman should delve into. Her knowledge of the occult terrorized the servants. In the end, when her husband finally became sober enough to notice, it terrified him. And so he murdered her. And as you have already heard, a man can murder his wife if she is a witch and be absolved of all blame."

"She sounds like quite a character. I should like to have met the woman."

Madame Zhozhovsky turned and began to stump away, back toward the parlor. "Oh you shall, Doctor Doyle," she called over her shoulder. "Mariah is Hope Thraxton's spirit guide. You will be able to talk to her at the séance tonight. I, too, shall attend . . . if my arthritis permits."

* * *

When Oscar Wilde emerged from below stairs and stepped into the entrance hall, Conan Doyle was nowhere to be seen. The tall Irishman threw a quick look around, and was turning toward the parlor, when he heard a voice calling his name from a way off.

"Oscar, down here."

Wilde followed the voice into the portrait gallery, where he found his friend studying one of the portraits.

"Look at this, Oscar."

Wilde studied the painting of a distinguished gentleman in his forties. His eyes traced down to the brass nameplate. "Lord Edmund Thraxton. Isn't he the chap who—?"

"Disappeared while walking on the moors," Conan Doyle said, finishing the thought. "Yes, but I find this particularly interesting." He pointed to the red rose tucked into a crevice in the gilt frame.

"A rose? A token of remembrance. I do not see why that is so remarkable. It is a common enough practice. Apart from his unnatural abhorrence of mirrors, I am sure that the current Lady Thraxton has many fond memories of her grandfather. After all, she was raised by him after her father abandoned her."

"I examined this very portrait just the other night. Someone had tucked a red rose into the frame, but the flower was withered, the petals brittle and dry. This is a fresh rose."

Wilde shook his head, nonplussed. "And your point is?"

"As we came down the stairs, I noticed Mrs. Kragan just leaving the gallery."

"Mrs. Kragan?" Wilde said, his tone incredulous.

"Yes, and she does not strike me as the type of servant who would be sentimental about her former employer."

"Indeed not. The woman is as sweet as a spoonful of cyanide. But one does not become a harridan overnight. Perhaps in her younger years she was—" Wilde stopped short, his eyes widening as if struck by a sudden thought.

"What?"

"Arthur, you told me the story of Seamus Kragan, the housekeeper's son, who locked young Lady Thraxton in a room in the west wing where she nearly died."

"Yes?"

"I thought at the time it was quite remarkable that the young man was not bounced off to jail and the housekeeper sacked on the spot."

"Hope told me that she begged her grandfather not to sack Mrs. Kragan."

Wilde fixed his friend with a meaningful look. "And if you were Lord Thraxton, would you be persuaded by a young girl's tears after an attempt to murder the only surviving heir?"

Conan Doyle thought for a moment, agitatedly brushing his walrus moustache with his fingertips. "Now that you mention it, it does seem odd, but then why—?"

"Think, Arthur. This would have been more than twenty years ago, before Mrs. Kragan had time to turn gray and shrivel up. If you look beneath the wrinkles and the scowl, you'll find she was once a handsome woman."

"What are you suggesting?"

Wilde smirked. "Something quite scurrilous."

Conan Doyle looked both ways to ensure no one was eavesdropping and then muttered in a low voice, "That Seamus Kragan was fathered by Lord Thraxton?"

"It happens in the best of houses. Perhaps we have opened a cupboard door and the first skeleton has tumbled out."

"But she is referred to as *Mrs.* Kragan?"

"But wears no wedding ring."

"This is all wild conjecture!"

The Irishman smiled. "Was that a pun, Arthur? *Wilde* conjecture? Am I at last a bad influence on you?"

They both chuckled. "Well," Conan Doyle said, "we'd better cut along. The next session is about to begin."

"Yes, very well."

But as they took a step toward the parlor, Conan Doyle abruptly stopped and grabbed his friend by the sleeve. "I've just had another thought. Florence Thraxton was found at the bottom of the grand staircase, her neck broken. Perhaps she did not fall. Perhaps . . . she was pushed." He mulled the idea a second longer and added, "But, of course, this is all speculation."

"Of course," Wilde agreed. "A love triangle that involves an illegitimate child and a murder? How delightfully sordid!"

CHAPTER 16

CATCHING THE BULLET

Teleportation," Hume began, "is the ability to move physical objects from one point to another, instantaneously."

The Society for Psychical Research had reconvened in the parlor and the Yankee psychic held the floor.

"Could you teleport yourself back to America?" Frank Podmore asked sarcastically, lounging in his chair, his short legs crossed at the ankles.

Hume bristled at the insult. From his expression, it was clear to all that his dislike for Podmore was like an itch crawling beneath his skin. "Mister Podmore has a most peculiar sense of humor. In truth, I typically demonstrate the ability using a small object, such as a coin."

Wilde stood up from his seat. "That is true." He pulled the Berkeley Gold Medal for Greek from his inside pocket and held it aloft for all to see. "Mister Hume successfully teleported my medal in front of a full audience at Gatti's-Under-the-Arches."

The members of the SPR murmured excitedly to each other.

"A music-hall trick such as might be performed by a moderately skilled conjurer," Podmore scoffed. An uncomfortable silence descended upon the room. Only Lord Webb, sitting in an armchair near the fire, seemed to be enjoying the spectacle, his smirk clenched around the ebony cigarette holder.

The American smiled ironically. "Mister Podmore, you are coming dangerously close to insulting me."

Podmore jumped to his feet. "Several years ago, you claimed to have caught a bullet in flight—purely using your so-called powers of teleportation. Is that correct?"

Hume's eyes grew guarded. Clearly, Podmore was laying a trap for him. "Yes," he nodded, "I accomplished that feat."

Podmore smiled. He walked up to Wilde, snatched the medal from his hand, tossing it in the air and catching it. "So why do something so mundane as a tossed coin? I think we'd all like to see the bullet catch." He lobbed the medal back to Wilde, who caught it with an aggrieved look on his face. "Or is that a feat too difficult to reproduce without a *friendly* audience?"

Hume's eyes flashed death, but he swallowed his anger and said mildly, "I could certainly reproduce the feat, but unfortunately—or perhaps fortunately for you—I did not bring a gun with me."

Podmore smiled and stalked over to where the Count was sitting. "Count, for the purposes of this demonstration, might I borrow your pistol?"

The Count dallied, clearly conflicted. The masked face looked to Wilde, who shook his head and silently mouthed *no*.

Henry Sidgwick jumped to his feet and attempted to lead Podmore back to his seat. "Come now, Frank, this has gone far enough."

"Count!" Hume said in a loud voice that froze the action. "Please oblige Mister Podmore and lend him your pistol. I release you from any culpability."

Then, with clear reluctance, the Count unsnapped the black leather holster, drew out his weapon (a Webley Mark I revolver), and gingerly handed it over. As Podmore gripped the pistol, a look of sick triumph washed over his face. He turned and brandished the weapon for all to see. "Excellent!" Podmore said. "Make yourself ready, Mister Hume."

"Frank!" Sidgwick shouted. "Stop this madness now!"

"I have a solution," Conan Doyle said calmly. All eyes focused on him. "There's no need to risk death here." He looked at Podmore. "Aim the gun at that suit of armor. If Mister Hume fails, your point will be proven and no one need die."

Podmore looked visibly disappointed, but nodded and said, "Very well, Doctor Doyle. You are quite correct—I only need to prove the fraud."

Daniel Dunglas Hume's eyes roved the room abstractedly. For once he had lost his strutting rooster look. The lines under his eyes seemed to have darkened and deepened. "Allow me a moment. I shall need to prepare my mind." He dropped his head, gripping the bridge of his nose with two fingers as though deep in contemplation. His shoulders rose and sagged as he sucked in a long breath and let it out. Without looking up he reached out with his right hand, fingers spread. "I am ready!" he called in a taut voice.

Conan Doyle became increasingly concerned as Podmore settled into his stance, the gun aimed at the chest of the suit of armor, his free hand in his pocket—it was clear he had received training and was no stranger to pistol shooting. Conan Doyle had not expected such proficiency from a man who was a civil servant employed by the Post Office. He shared an anxious look with Wilde.

The room fell deathly silent. The Count took an involuntary step closer. Eleanor Sidgwick dropped heavily onto a couch and covered her eyes with her hand. Lord Webb shifted forward in his chair, relishing the conflict. Conan Doyle feared that Podmore would shift his aim to Hume at the last moment. He watched Podmore's finger tighten on the trigger.

"Stop!" a voice cried. Everyone froze. Madame Zhozhovsky had risen from her chair and stood with a hand thrown out, her gray eyes uncanny. "You tempt Fate in a place ill-favored. The earth-bound spirits hunger for the taste of fresh blood. Do not allow them to slake their thirst."

Podmore had dropped his aim at the interruption. He threw a questioning look at Hume. The American paused a moment, then nodded quickly to Podmore. "Continue, sir. You have besmirched my honor and I would be vindicated." Hume stabbed a finger to his chest. "Forget the armor. Aim here!"

"No!" Sidgwick shouted.

"This is insanity," Conan Doyle chimed in.

Podmore's face tightened with resolve. Madame Zhozhovsky muttered a baleful prophecy, "This will end in death," as she sank into a chair, her gaze fixed resolutely out the window.

Podmore raised the gun once more. The muzzle wavered as his finger tightened on the trigger. Hume's brows knotted in concentration, beads of sweat glistening in the creases of his forehead. The hammer of the revolver rose . . . and fell.

KA-BANG!

In the confined space, the shot was deafening. At the instant the pistol fired, Hume snatched his hand back, balled into a fist. A sinuous wisp of smoke curled from the barrel of the revolver. The bitter tang of cordite spooled in the air. For a heart-stopping moment, Conan Doyle was sure Hume had managed it. But when the dapper Yankee opened his hand, it was empty. At the same instant, the suit of armor toppled to the ground with a pots-and-pans clang, where it lay on its side, rocking. The bullet had failed to penetrate the thick breastplate, but left a deep round dent.

"Hah!" Podmore cried, a look of triumphant glee on his face.

Hume seemed to visibly deflate. He stared around the room with a look of terrifying vacancy, his eyes hollow and defeated. Then he sucked in a shuddering breath, stumbled forward, and collapsed face-first to the floor.

THE GENIE

Conan Doyle stood over Daniel Dunglas Hume, who lay sprawled on the bed in his room, having been carried there by Oscar Wilde and himself.

"How are you?" Conan Doyle asked.

"A little winded," Wilde answered. He patted his jacket pockets, searching. "Perhaps a cigarette will help—"

A pained expression washed across Conan Doyle's face. "Not you, Oscar. I was referring to Mister Hume."

"Ah," said Wilde in a disappointed voice, looking rather put out.

Hume smiled weakly, waved a weary hand in a casual gesture, and let it fall heavily to the bed. "I am much obliged, gentlemen. I assure you I shall recover shortly."

The American was going to say more, but Conan Doyle was wearing his doctor hat and shushed Hume as he checked the pulse at his wrist—rapid and shallow. Next he moved his thick fingers to Hume's neck, feeling at lymph nodes that were swollen to the size of walnuts. He stood back and after several minutes' contemplation, exhaled loudly through his nostrils, looking at his patient with gloomy concern. "How long have you had the consumption?"

Hume's dry lips peeled back from his teeth in a mortician's

smile. "Years . . . perhaps five." The face that had seemed so youth-ful and vibrant that morning looked a hundred years old.

A dark cloud swept behind Conan Doyle's eyes. Hume's condi-tion was disturbingly reminiscent of his beloved Touie's. "I thought as much the first time I saw you. But then on the next occasion, you seemed completely well. Vigorous, in fact."

"The mind," Hume explained. "The mind can accomplish any-thing. Through an act of will I convince my body that it is still a young man's, and most of the time it believes me. But the levitation, the teleportation, with each feat I am like a genie, using up my life force."

The words sank deep. Finally Conan Doyle asked the question he knew he must ask: "How much time?"

"According to my doctor, I should have died six years ago." The American chuckled darkly and flashed a broken smile.

"But you are still very much with us."

Hume nodded and urged, "Up! Help me sit up."

Conan Doyle slid an arm behind Hume's bony shoulders and eased him upright. He was shocked at the American's frailty. The body beneath the dandy's clothes was thin and wasted.

Meanwhile, Oscar Wilde, who was terrified of sickness and disease, remained plastered against the wall beside the door, hold-ing his cigarette level with his mouth, sucking air through it as if to burn up any lurking contagion before it reached his lungs.

The movement dislodged something in Hume's chest and he launched into a coughing fit that lasted several minutes. It ended when he was simply too exhausted to cough anymore. When he took the silk handkerchief from his mouth, it was stained arte-rial red.

"The Lord gave me great powers," Hume said in an under-water, phlegmy voice. "But I have squandered them." The noble head shook with regret. "For fame. For the ladies. For the comfort of high society." He looked up at Conan Doyle with empty, ravaged eyes. "I wanted to be known as the greatest psychic of all time, but I frittered it all away . . . because I am a damned fool."

Wilde took the cigarette from between his lips and muttered sagely, "We are all fools for our vices, Daniel. And the man who believes he has no vices is the biggest fool of all."

Hume's eyes swiveled to take in Wilde's large frame holding up the wall. "Yes, but you gentlemen have already written your names large across the firmament. A hundred years from now—nay, a thousand years from now—men will know who Oscar Wilde and Arthur Conan Doyle were." He laughed bitterly and stared at the blank wall, as if seeing his future projected there. "A year after my death, no one will remember the name of Daniel Dunglas Hume."

* * *

"Do you know, Arthur," Wilde said as they navigated the stygian hallways back to the parlor, "I've been thinking about what Mister Hume said to us, and I believe him."

Conan Doyle stopped and looked at his friend expectantly. "You mean you *don't* think he is plotting Lady Thraxton's death?"

Wilde furrowed his brow. "No, I believe Mister Hume is correct about my name appearing in the history books a thousand years from now. In fact, I shouldn't at all be surprised if *Lady Windermere's Fan* is still packing the playhouses."

Conan Doyle grimaced.

"Oh, and your writings, too, old chap," Wilde quickly added. "I'm certain Sherlock Holmes will keep the name of Conan Doyle alive for a hundred years, nay two hundred."

A look of profound injury flashed across Conan Doyle's face.

They walked the rest of the way in stony silence.

* * *

When Conan Doyle and Oscar Wilde reached the parlor, they found it empty, apart from Mister Greaves and the willowy maid, Agnes, who looked a handsome-enough woman until one tried to meet her eyes and found that each pupil focused on widely diverging points. The two domestics were tidying the room, straightening cushions and gathering up abandoned sherry glasses. Even though his back was to the pair, Mister Greaves immediately sensed their presence and turned his opaque gaze to meet them. "The guests are taking advantage of the cessation of the rain with a stroll in the gardens. You gentlemen may reach them through a door just before the conservatory."

The English country garden was laid out with geometrical paths and still-dormant flower beds. Beyond was a large hedge maze. Conan Doyle and Wilde caught brief glimpses of the SPR members as they appeared and then disappeared behind the tall hedges.

"What now, Arthur?"

"I'd like to speak to the enigmatic Lord Webb."

"You think he has something to hide?"

"A man who travels with a coffin must have something buried, if only a secret."

"Look," Wilde said, indicating with a nod. "There he is, just entering the hedge maze."

The two friends strode over to its entrance. "This is a large maze," Wilde noted. "Finding him could take some time."

"Perhaps we should split up. You take one entrance; I'll take the other. One of us should come across him."

"Very well," Wilde said. "I feel rather like Theseus. Let us hope Lord Webb does not transmogrify into a minotaur."

Wilde plunged into the far entrance and vanished from view. Conan Doyle stepped into the maze by the other entrance and immediately touched a hand to the left wall. He knew that keeping one hand to the wall of a labyrinth was a surefire way of navigating through to the other end, though not necessarily the quickest, as it entailed navigating every blind passage and dead end along the way. The labyrinth turned right and opened onto a long avenue. Coming toward him from the other direction was Sir William Crookes, strolling side by side with Henry Sidgwick.

"Gentlemen," Conan Doyle said in greeting. The men nodded as they passed. The maze turned left, and then left again, followed by a sharp right. In the center of the avenue, a bust of the Greek goddess Athena stood on a marble plinth. Conan Doyle noted its position as an aid in navigation. He carried on and reached a spot where the maze opened on either side. He stopped and pondered a moment, then kept to his original plan and turned left. At another left he turned the corner to find a dead end with a lone figure lurking in it—the Count.

The masked face swiveled up to face him, silent and enigmatic.

"I appear to be lost." Conan Doyle laughed with false joviality and hastily backed away. He hurried along the next avenue. As he passed another opening, he looked left in time to glimpse Lord Webb before he disappeared behind another hedge wall. Conan Doyle immediately abandoned his maze-navigating strategy and hurried off in pursuit. He raced around a corner and almost collided with a very startled Frank Podmore. Excusing himself, he brushed past the younger man and, when he reached the next turn of the maze, took off at a run. But after several minutes of running blindly along the avenues, he slowed to a walk and finally stopped.

By now he was breathing hard and sweating through his tweeds. Hopelessly lost. And then he heard the plash of running water. Ears perked, he stumbled after the sound until he stepped into an octagon of open space with a fountain at its center bordered on either side by a stone bench.

Seated on one of the stone benches was his quarry, poised like a scorpion in its den, pincers up, stinger raised and ready to strike.

"Doctor Doyle," Lord Webb said. "You appear out of breath. Perhaps you should rest a while?"

"Yes, I think I shall," Conan Doyle answered, dropping heavily onto the stone bench opposite.

After several moments of silence, Webb smiled and said, "I do hope our American friend is quite well. I'm afraid these psychic manifestations seem to tax the life from him."

"He is resting comfortably. Although I have strongly urged him to curtail such activities until he is feeling better."

"I could help him," Lord Webb said, peering at Conan Doyle through the pince-nez perched on his large nose. Magnified by the convex lenses, his blue eyes loomed like bloated goldfish bumping up against the inside of twin fish bowls. "Hypnosis is all about control of the mind, and through control of the mind comes control of the body. Ordinary medicine is so limited."

Conan Doyle swallowed the clear insult to his profession and parried with a question addressed directly to his attacker. "So, Lord Webb, how is it that you became associated with the Society?"

"I attended a séance at Lady Thraxton's London residence where I first met Mr. Sidgwick and his wife." He paused and added: "And, of course, our dear little Frank."

"How lucky for them."

"Yes," Webb agreed.

"So, have you attended many séances conducted by the Society?"

"Indeed, I am a regular. It was there that Henry conceived of the notion of forming the Society for Psychical Research and of this first seminar." He smiled with false modesty. "With my full encouragement, I hasten to add."

During their conversation, dusk had darkened the sky. By now it was difficult to make out faces in the gloom. "The bats are emerging," Webb said, looking up at the black shapes flitting overhead. "I think it's time we go indoors. I must prepare Lady Thraxton for the first séance."

"Prepare?"

"During the séance, Lady Thraxton's soul leaves her body and hovers overhead while her spirit guide takes possession of her corporeal form. Before the séance, I induce a light trance in her Ladyship. It softens the rift."

Conan Doyle's mouth dried up.

Webb stood up from the bench. The audience was apparently at an end. "Mister Doyle, let us leave aside the niceties and for one moment ignore the difference in our social standings. You obviously sought me out to ask a question. You need not feel inhibited because I am a Lord and you are a commoner. I give you permission to ask me anything."

Feeling at a disadvantage sitting down, Conan Doyle also rose to his feet. "Very well, then, I shall be blunt. I need to know if you came to Thraxton Hall with the intention of doing harm to Lady Thraxton."

A look of amusement formed on Webb's face. He very nearly laughed, but clearly read the earnestness on the other man's face. "I should hardly think so, old fellow." He clapped a hand on the young doctor's shoulder with more than friendly force. "After all . . . I fully intend to marry her."

* * *

Conan Doyle found Oscar Wilde sitting on the damp grass, leaning with his back against the pedestal bearing the bust of Athena. Apart from the fact that he was smoking one of his Turkish cigarettes, he looked like a lost and abandoned child.

"At last," Wilde said wearily, "you have found me. I have been wandering in ever-diminishing circles for the best part of an hour. I confess I am footsore, fatigued, and famished. I tried communing with the Hellenic goddess of wisdom"—he indicated the bust above with a nod of his head—"but apparently she is not fond of the Irish."

When Conan Doyle did not answer immediately, Wilde regarded his friend with an inquisitive tilt to his head and asked, "What is it, Arthur? You look all out of sorts."

"I am out of sorts. I received a piece of news that I find rather disturbing." He reached out a hand and pulled Wilde to his feet. "I bearded the lion in his den."

"By lion I presume you are referring to Lord Webb?"

Conan Doyle nodded, his lips compressed to a grim line. "He casually informed me that he intends to marry Lady Thraxton."

Wilde reacted first with surprise, and then with skepticism. "I wonder if he has yet to inform Lady Thraxton of his intentions?"

"An apt point, Oscar. I had not considered that."

After a pause, Wilde said, "But why are you so concerned about Lady Thraxton? You are a married man."

Conan Doyle dropped his head and exhaled loudly. "Yes, I realize that. It's just that, I had entertained notions—" He wrestled to find the appropriate words. "That is, at some time in the future, after . . ." He trailed off, leaving the thought unfinished, but it was clear Wilde knew he was referring to the imminent death of his wife, Louise.

"Tread carefully, Arthur."

"You think I have ideas above my station?"

Wilde smiled ironically. "You and I are both men of some means. But our greatest fortune lies in our fame—we are not of the aristocracy. Hope Thraxton is a Lady and Philipp Webb is a Peer of the Realm. You and I are fortunate to have incarnated in the nineteenth century. Two hundred years earlier our status would have been little better than that of troubadours and jesters. No place would be laid for us at the table. We would be allowed to dine on the leftovers of supper only after the hounds had finished licking the plates clean."

Conan Doyle bit his lip. "Yes, perhaps you're right. I'm being ridiculous. It's this house—I'm not thinking rationally." He shivered as the chill of dusk bit deep. "Come, Oscar, let us quit this blasted maze before it's too dark to fathom our way out."

The two friends finally escaped the hedge maze and traipsed back toward the looming edifice, stepping on the feet of their own lengthening shadows. The skies above had deepened to a purple gloaming and Thraxton Hall had drawn a cloak of shadow about its stony shoulders, its glowing yellow windows watching like luminous eyes.

A moment later, branches rustled in the hedge maze as the Count emerged. Concealed in a pool of darkness, he watched as the two men entered the Hall by the conservatory door. The Count's hand rested on the grip of his Webley pistol—half drawn from its holster. Now he let the pistol slide from his fingers, back into its leather holster, flipped the cover shut, cinched tight the short strap, and followed after.

꧁꧂

THE FIRST SÉANCE

The séance was not scheduled to take place until 10:00 P.M., but Conan Doyle and Wilde had deliberately arrived thirty minutes early to reconnoiter the location.

The séance was to be held in the eastern turret room. The windows of the octagonal shaped room had been bricked up and plastered over. The walls were covered in dark green leather and devoid of paintings. The room was lit by a single naked gas jet that had left a shadow of greasy soot stretching to the ceiling. The only furniture was a large round mahogany table circled by eleven empty chairs.

"Not much space to hold a party," Wilde noted as the two men entered.

"Nor to commit murder," Conan Doyle said. "Especially if one expected to escape afterward." He nodded to the door. "No windows and only one way in or out."

"Maybe the murderer does not plan to stop at one victim?" Wilde speculated.

Conan Doyle ruffled his moustache agitatedly as the gravity of Wilde's words sank in. "That is a dire possibility I had not contemplated."

"Do not take this the wrong way, Arthur. I know you have the greatest esteem for Lady Thraxton, but I have read of devices being used by bogus mediums: trapdoors, hidden panels, and the like."

"Yes, Oscar, you are quite right. I agree and think we should begin with a thorough examination of the room."

The two spent the next thirty minutes on an inch-by-inch inspection of the walls, rapping with their knuckles for hollow sounds that would betray a hidden panel, stamping upon the floor searching for trapdoors. The final step involved a hands-and-knees search under the table, checking the carpentry for hidden pedals, secret compartments, or any place a weapon could be stashed.

"How droll," Wilde exclaimed. "I have not crawled about beneath a table since I was five years old. I confess it has lost much of its fascination and my knees are no longer up to it."

"Nothing!" Conan Doyle exclaimed, staggering up from the floor and flopping into a chair. Wilde dragged himself into a chair opposite. "If there's a weapon involved, it must be brought in by one of the sitters."

At that moment, the door opened and Henry Sidgwick entered followed by the remaining members of the Society. "Ah!" Sidgwick said. "Our two new members are eager to attend their first séance. I assure you, gentlemen, you will not be disappointed. I have never met a medium the equal of Lady Thraxton."

The members filed in and began selecting their seats. Conan Doyle was not surprised to find that Daniel Dunglas Hume was absent. His chair, the eleventh, was dragged into a corner.

"Please note," Sidgwick continued, "the head of the table is reserved for Lady Thraxton."

Frank Podmore was first to sit. The Sidgwicks took two seats side by side. Sir William Crookes dropped heavily into the empty seat between Conan Doyle and Wilde. Madame Zhozhovsky waddled in and Wilde gave up his seat to her, as it was closest to the door.

The Count marched into the room, clicked his heels, bowed, and dropped into the empty chair next to Wilde. Conan Doyle noticed with rising anxiety that the Count was wearing his pistol holster. His mind churned with reasons to ask the Count to switch places, but he could think of none.

As soon as everyone was seated, a pregnant silence descended. People coughed, shifted in their seats, avoided eye contact. Conan Doyle suddenly realized that he was the only one not wearing gloves. He reached inside his jacket, drew out a pair of white cotton gloves, and pulled them on. Two chairs remained unoccupied: the head of the table and the seat on its left. The silence thickened, tightening around the group until it squeezed an apology out of Henry Sidgwick. "Lady Thraxton is preparing herself. Hopefully, she will only be a moment longer."

The "moment longer" turned out to be a very long moment.

Conan Doyle's spine was a spring ratcheting tighter with every second. As discreetly as possible, he reached down and touched the revolver strapped to his ankle, and then drew his pant leg up, so that the hem of his trousers hung upon the pistol grip. He exchanged a worried glance across the table with Wilde.

There was a click as the door handle rotated, and Lord Webb entered, guiding Lady Thraxton to the table by the lightest touch of their interlaced fingertips. He pulled out her chair, and she slid silently into it, resting her hands on the tabletop. Throughout, her expression remained blank, her eyes wide and staring. She seemed oblivious to her surroundings.

At the first sight of her, Conan Doyle felt something warm burst in his chest. Sensing the ardor of his own gaze, he had to look away momentarily.

"I have placed Lady Thraxton in a light trance," Lord Webb explained, "to ease the rift as her mind tears free of its corporeal shell."

Conan Doyle's pulse quickened at his words. Hope Thraxton was staring straight at him, but her gaze was empty and void.

Henry Sidgwick addressed the circle in hushed tones: "For those who have never attended a séance, let me explain. Each sitter must take the hand of his neighbor to form an unbroken circle. During the séance, Lady Thraxton's soul will leave her body and her spirit guide shall take possession, so that it may speak through her. It is imperative for the medium's safety that, during the time she is out of her body, the circle remain unbroken—no matter what. Do we all understand?"

There was a murmur of assent from around the table.

"Lady Thraxton's spirit guide is named Mariah. Once again, I repeat, it is imperative that the circle be unbroken."

Conan Doyle thought of the Mariah Thraxton brutally murdered by her thug of a husband and then buried at the crossroads as a witch.

Hope slowly bowed her head and spoke in a stretched-thin whisper: "Dim the lights so that the spirits may draw close."

Mister Greaves hovered at the back of the room, and now he fumbled for the petcock and slowly turned down the flow of gas. The room dimmed until the gas flame fluttered and went out. Conan Doyle heard Mister Greaves brush the wall and the door creak open and closed. A moment later, the key turned in the lock, locking them all inside.

A familiar sense of vertigo gripped Conan Doyle as he found himself, once again, in the darkness with Hope Thraxton. The only light came from a small candle in a brass holder, flickering at the center of the séance table, rendering the sitters as little more than jittery shadows. The main glow illumined the face of Hope Thraxton who, as if gathering herself, lowered her head as she drew in a shuddering breath and let it out.

"Mariah. My friend. My spirit guide. I seek your help. Hear me. I yield my body as a vessel for you to speak."

Long seconds passed, punctuated only by the sitters' anxious breathing.

"Mariah, I seek your counsel. My body is open, ready for you to possess . . ." Moments passed. She spoke again. "Mariah—"

The medium's body convulsed, struck through by a sudden tremor. She sucked in a dreadful gasp. Her shoulders slumped, and then vertebrae cracked as her head lashed back, her mouth straining wide. A scream came from somewhere deep within, beyond the range of human lungs. Beyond flesh and bone. It was the scream of spirit cleaving from the void and entering consciousness. The piercing wail sent a frisson of terror skittering up the spines of the members seated around the table. It peaked in a nerve-shattering screech, and then died in her throat. Hope seemed to empty out, and slumped in her chair, head lolling.

Conan Doyle's eyes darted around the group. Most had rapt expressions. Even Podmore's skepticism seemed to have given way to a look of intense focus. For dreadful seconds, Hope Thraxton lay still as death. But by degrees, her shallow breathing became discernible.

An icy breeze tickled the back of Conan Doyle's neck, chilling the sweat. Shocked gasps resounded from around the table as the temperature of the room plummeted. For a moment, the air cloyed with the dank smell of earth tinged with a hint of corruption.

The candle on the table guttered, the flame dimming almost to darkness. And then the wick crackled and flared bright, flinging the sitters' elongated shadows across the walls.

The young medium's head raised slowly. She drew back the veil as her eyes fluttered open. Her lips twitched into a fey smile. When she spoke, an archaic, accented voice came out: "I am here."

It was no longer Hope Thraxton's face. It was no longer Hope Thraxton's voice. The nape of Conan Doyle's neck prickled with gooseflesh as he realized that he was looking upon the face of Mariah Thraxton, murdered some two hundred years ago.

"Why have you dragged me from the darkness of purgatory? What is it you seek?"

Henry Sidgwick, his face bursting and earnest, leaned forward and spoke. "We have assembled to speak with the spirits. We have questions we would put to them."

The medium's head tilted, a pout formed upon her lips. "And what of me? Am I so uninteresting? I am a lady of great beauty . . ." The frown dissolved into a provocative smirk. ". . . and of great appetites." She looked around the table, lavishing the men with her sensuous gaze.

"Such pretty, pretty men. The men were not so fair in my time. They were rough and coarse and lost interest in a maid as soon as they'd spent their fetch in her." The medium's eyes shone liquid, her voice husky. "I would feign have had you all as my lovers." She focused on Conan Doyle. "Especially gents with moustaches, for it would tickle my cunny when you kissed it."

The sitters squirmed to hear such coarse pronouncements issue from a young lady's lips. Eleanor Sidgwick dropped her face in shame. Madame Zhozhovsky glared, disapproving as Queen Victoria herself. As a doctor, Conan Doyle had dealt with mad women and women of the street, but still he felt his face blush hot and was glad of the darkness.

To prevent her saying more, Henry Sidgwick interrupted with a question: "Lady Mariah, we, the living, have questions for those who have passed to the other side."

The medium eyed him with disdain. "You remind me of my husband—a tiresome man." She let out a vexed sigh. "Very well. Ask what you would know."

Sidgwick looked around the table. "Who has a question for the spirits?"

No one spoke for a moment, and then Conan Doyle cleared his throat and said, "I do, Lady Mariah." The young medium's transformed face fixed upon his and Mariah Thraxton's wanton smile returned.

"Those spirits who have passed over," he began, "can they foresee the future?"

The medium arched an eyebrow. Beguilement crouched in the corners of her smile. "From the spirit world we see the past clearly. But the future is glimpsed only vaguely, as through a glass swept with clouds and darkness."

Conan Doyle felt the question coiled upon his tongue, and could not help releasing it. "Is there anyone present who wishes harm upon another member of the Society?"

The question evoked a surprised gasp from the rest of the sitters. And then Mariah Thraxton's laugh ripped out. "Death is already here." The medium's eyes slowly trailed to the single chair that sat unoccupied in a corner of the room. "Death sits there, patiently waiting."

All eyes turned to look. A tall, willowy darkness seemed to recline in the empty chair, whether supplied by the sitters' overheated imaginations, or a chance collision of shadows; regardless, a wave of fear swept the room.

"Now see here, Doctor Doyle," Sidgwick began to say. "I don't think this is precisely what we came here to—"

"For whom has death come?" Conan Doyle interrupted.

Mariah's smile turned malicious. "There are things the spirits are forbidden from revealing. Truths that would confound all beliefs, all human understanding. You must look to Death for the answer."

A surge of icy air swirled about the table, fluttering the ladies skirts and mussing the men's hair. Several shouted aloud in surprise. The candle at the center of the table guttered . . . and went out.

Darkness, sudden and absolute. No one spoke for several moments. Then Henry Sidgwick's strangled voice called out, "Mister

Greaves! Mister Greaves, please come in and light the gas. The séance is adjourned."

* * *

When Wilde and Conan Doyle stepped back into the parlor, the other SPR members huddled in knots, speaking in subdued voices. Mr. Greaves moved among the members, offering up a silver tray of brandies to salve frazzled nerves.

Both Wilde and Conan Doyle snagged a glass as he shuffled past.

"Bit of a shocker," Wilde remarked.

"Yes," Conan Doyle agreed. "Far from what I had expected." His eyes scanned the parlor for Lady Thraxton, but she had retired to her rooms, as had Sidgwick's wife.

"I hadn't expected anything quite so foreboding," Wilde added. "It seems our worst fears have been confirmed."

"I would not be so quick to believe the spirit guide." It was Madame Zhozhovsky, whose short, rotund form sat ensconced in a chair near Wilde's elbow. She had overheard their conversation and spoke without bothering to turn her face toward the two men, all the while feeding nuts to the monkey in her lap from a leather purse that hung around her neck. "The dead can be just as full of deception as the living. They can be vain. They can be wicked."

As usual, Frank Podmore was lurking within eavesdropping range and leaped forward to launch into an animated defense. "I can assure you, Lady Thraxton is no hoaxer and her spirit guide is entirely reliable."

Madame Zhozhovsky paused in feeding Mephistopheles and swiveled her gray eyes up at the irascible postal clerk. Her expression showed she was not the least impressed by his earnestness. "Young man, when you have spent a lifetime studying the occult as I have, when you have trod the mountain passes of Tibet and walked with the Ascended Masters, maybe then you would know the tricks and deceits of the dead, as I do."

Podmore, who was the only one in the room not clutching a brandy glass, sniffed contemptuously. "*Ascended Masters*, indeed!"

"Mister Podmore, you know nothing of my abilities and would be well served to curb your tongue. I have no doubt you think I am nothing but an old crone, but there is a reason crones have been feared and revered for millennia."

A muscle in Podmore's jaw tremored at the implied threat. "And you, madam, have no regard for the skills of an investigator using modern, scientific methods of detection. I have single-handedly exposed dozens of fraudulent mediums and psychics. I have also attended many séances conducted by Lady Thraxton, and I can personally attest to their veracity. Lady Thraxton's gift is real. Her abilities unequaled."

But Madame Zhozhovsky had evidently heard enough. Oofing, she levered her bulk up from the armchair using her twisted walking stick and lumbered from the room, muttering: "Pearls before swine . . . Pearls before swine . . ." As if in a final riposte, the monkey trailing behind her on its leash squatted and shat on the rug before the leash pulled tight and yanked it away.

Conan Doyle was struck by a sudden realization. "F. Podmore? I read your article in *The Strand Magazine* about Lady Thraxton."

"Really?" Podmore moved forward, clearly flattered. "I did author such a piece."

"Yes," it was most enlightening . . . and surprising. I had formed the opinion that you were a skeptic in these matters."

"A *discerning* skeptic," Podmore corrected. "I have had many encounters with frauds and charlatans. Lady Thraxton is the only genuine medium I have ever met."

"And she assisted you with your bereavement?"

Podmore's face grew guarded. "What?"

"You have lost someone close to you. Recently."

The young man's mouth dropped open. "How? Who told you? Was it Zhozhovsky? I detest that old hag."

Conan Doyle shook his head. "No one told me. When Madame Zhozhovsky was reading your palm, I noticed that you wear a woman's engagement ring on your little finger. In remembrance?"

Podmore dropped his gaze. "My late fiancée," he said quickly.

"A noble gesture, sir. I am sorry for your loss." The Scottish author nodded sympathetically. "What better reason to consult a medium?"

"You also have lost someone?" Podmore asked, closely watching Conan Doyle's face.

"My beloved wife is dying of consumption. It will not be long now. I am preparing myself."

For once, something approaching empathy burned in Podmore's eyes.

"Through Lady Thraxton, you have communicated with your loved one?" Wilde asked.

Podmore nodded. His jaw quivered. He looked away, his brown eyes gleaming. "After I lost Mary, I visited many mediums." His face grew thunderous with scorn. "They were all charlatans. Lady Thraxton is the only true medium. She is a revelation."

It was an unusual surge of enthusiasm for the acerbic young man. For the first time, Conan Doyle comprehended that Podmore's sneering cynicism was nothing more than a healing scab protecting a deep and still-weeping wound. "And these séances, were they conducted at Number 42 _____ Crescent in Mayfair?"

Podmore did not need to answer the question; the change in his expression gave the answer away. "Who told you?"

"I have visited the house myself . . . recently."

"Although I am sworn to secrecy," Podmore began, glancing around to make sure no one was close enough to overhear, "the

séances were attended by some of the best in London society. Including several people of rank, very high in the peerage."

"How many other members of the Society attended?"

"The Sidgwicks. Sir William—in his cups as usual—and, of
course, our illustrious Lord of the Manor."

"Lord Webb?" Conan Doyle said. "Indeed?"

"Yes, always at her side."

"Doctor Doyle—" Henry Sidgwick's voice interrupted. "A
word, sir."

Conan Doyle hesitated. The two men stepped away from Podmore and moved close enough to the fire that Conan Doyle felt
and smelled the heat singeing his trousers.

Sidgwick's face was grave. "About the séance today—"

"Yes?"

"Are you trying to disrupt our efforts? Is it your intention to in-
still fear in our members?"

"No, nothing of the sort." Conan Doyle strained to find a way out.
"I merely have questions about Fate, the future . . ." He trailed off.

"And you think one of our members wishes to do harm to another? Why? Where did you come upon this information?"

"No, not at all. It's just that . . . it's just that my mind has been
preoccupied lately with such questions." Sidgwick stared disbeliev-
ingly. Conan Doyle sought to throw him off the scent by disclosing
his wife Touie's condition. It took him another ten minutes before
he could pry himself away from Sidgwick and return to Wilde, who
was valiantly guarding the drinks tray.

"That looked like an intense conversation," Wilde noted as he
helped himself to another brandy.

"Yes, it rather was. I think I may have given the game away with
my questions at the séance."

Wilde noticed his friend's empty glass and waved the cut glass
decanter at him. "Might I recharge your glass, Arthur?"

"Absolutely." Conan Doyle held out his glass. "And be generous. I'd like to sleep tonight."

Wilde gurgled brandy into Conan Doyle's glass and said, "What do you make of Mister Podmore's revelations?"

"I found them somewhat discomfiting," he admitted, pausing to take a sip. "Our little group is proving to be far more incestuous than I at first thought."

"Something has occurred to me about our Mister Podmore," Wilde said, throwing a quick glance around to ensure their conversation was not being overheard.

The other SPR members were saying their good nights and drifting out of the room. Podmore alone remained, slumped in an immense armchair, his eyes closed, head fallen forward, bearded chin resting on his chest.

"Apparently the man who never sleeps snores whilst he is awake," Wilde noted.

Conan Doyle put a finger to his lips and made a shushing sound. "He may be shamming so as to listen in on our conversation."

"In which case he is a very convincing snorer."

Conan Doyle grasped Wilde by the elbow and chivvied him farther away from Podmore's armchair. They took up a new spot by the suit of armor, which had been repaired and reassembled, but still bore a huge dent in its breastplate.

"What about Podmore?" Conan Doyle asked.

"It occurred to me—one moment . . ." Wilde lifted the visor of the knight's armor and peeked inside. "No one lurking in there," he said, "just wanted to make sure." He leaned toward Conan Doyle and spoke in hushed tones. "Consider this, Arthur. Our Mister Podmore is a man of great passions. He initially was a zealous supporter and ally of Daniel Dunglas Hume. But when his hero disappointed him, he became Hume's bitterest enemy. We have both heard him gush about Lady Thraxton. What if he were to discover something about her? Something that shattered his belief in her mediumistic powers?"

Conan Doyle frowned.

"Do not forget, Lady Thraxton is the medium who has brought him messages from his beloved lost fiancée. What if he discovered—or even suspected—that she was a charlatan?"

Conan Doyle chewed his moustache as he considered Wilde's theory. "His hatred would be a thousand times greater."

"Enough to consider murder?"

"I think not," Conan Doyle said mildly.

"How can you say that? He rails constantly against the other psychics, calls them charlatans and baldly accuses them of fakery. He has a positive mania when it comes to Mister Hume. What if he felt himself betrayed yet again, but this time by Lady Thraxton?"

Conan Doyle rocked back and forth on the balls of his feet. "I agree with all you say, Oscar. Still, I do not think him capable of murder."

"And why not? He is a weasel of a man, condescending and spiteful."

"But murder is a gross act. The greatest transgression of our culture. Mister Podmore is small in both stature and in character."

"So was Napoleon, and look at the damage he did."

Conan Doyle fountained with laughter. "No, I still do not see it."

The two sipped their brandies in silence for several moments, before Conan Doyle asked, "What did you make of the séance, Oscar?"

The large Irishman swallowed his mouthful of brandy and allowed an indolent smile to float to the surface of his large face. "I am a man of the theater," he reminded Conan Doyle. "I think what we witnessed tonight was pure theater."

The Scottish doctor fidgeted at his words. "Whatever do you mean, Oscar? Do you include what we witnessed at the séance?"

"I'm sorry, Arthur, but yes."

Arthur felt the heat rise in his cheeks. "And what of the scene between Madame Zhozhovsky and Podmore?"

Wilde waved the question away with an insouciant gesture. "Tell me, Arthur, do you believe Madame Zhozhovsky is really Russian?" He went on without giving Conan Doyle time to respond. "Do you really think she is a mystic who has trekked the lofty peaks of Tibet where she received her teachings from an immaterial cadre of 'Ascended Masters'?"

"Well . . . frankly . . . no . . . no I don't believe a word of it."

Wilde leaned forward and laid a consoling hand on his friend's arm. "And neither do I. Rather, I am convinced that Madame Zhozhovsky is an elderly spinster from Barnsley in Yorkshire who likely worked in a pie shop for most of her life. I imagine she dog-eared a few tomes on esoteric beliefs before concocting the outrageous character of *Madame Zhozhovsky* and her clairvoyant claptrap. I believe everyone at this retreat is an actor playing a part and delivering a bravura performance—even the delightful Lady Thraxton."

The remark raised Conan Doyle's hackles. "Well, I respectfully disagree."

Wilde drained his glass and stood up. "It is far too late to argue. Come, let us retire also. It has been a momentous day. Our minds will be clearer after a few hours' sleep."

Conan Doyle swirled the last dregs of brandy in his snifter and tossed them back. "Yes, I think you are right about that."

The two walked quietly to the door, but as they passed the sleeping Podmore, Wilde dropped silently to his knees and began to fiddle with Podmore's shoes.

"Oscar!" Conan Doyle hissed in an alarmed whisper. Wilde turned, put a finger to his lips to shush him, and continued what he was doing. A moment later he rose to his feet, gripped Conan Doyle by the arm, and propelled him rapidly from the room.

"What on earth were you up to?" Conan Doyle demanded.

"Tying Podmore's shoelaces together," Wilde said, grinning like a fool. "It was my signature prank at school—I was famous for it."

"What? Oscar, are you mad? But whatever for?"

"I believe you are right. I think the diminutive Mister Podmore was shamming sleep to eavesdrop on our conversation. If so, this will serve him jolly well right."

Conan Doyle gasped at his friend's audacity, but could not suppress a chuckle. As they were ascending the grand staircase they heard a startled cry from the parlor, the crash of toppling furniture, and the thump of a body hitting the floor.

At the sound, both men burst out laughing and hurried up the staircase, chortling like naughty schoolboys.

CHAPTER 19

THE CRYPT OF THE THRAXTONS

Conan Doyle lay in his bed for an hour, but sleep would not come. Finally, he gave up and lit the lamp on his bedside table, then propped the Casebook open on his knees and let his eyes wander over the chart he had drawn. The word Sherlock Holmes had said to him in the dream repeated in his head: *Motive . . . Motive . . . Motive. . . .* But as his eyes traced the names of the SPR members, he failed to find a single name he could point to as having a compelling reason to kill Hope Thraxton.

The room was close and airless, so he slid out of bed and went to crack a window. But as he flung up the casement, he looked out and glimpsed a heart-stopping sight. The third storey looked down on the rooftops of the east wing and the windows of the other guests' rooms. Now he watched as the casement of one of the windows raised, a vague human figure appeared in the dark opening . . . and then floated out into space.

The moon had yet to rise. Through the darkness, he could just make out the murky image of a man in a long frock coat gliding along the line of windows. The silhouette reached a room where the top window had been left cracked open. The figure hovered in place for a second, and then floated onto its back and slid in through the open window. Conan Doyle blinked away afterimages. He wasn't entirely certain of what he had seen, but if his eyes hadn't been playing tricks, the shadowy figure could only be one person: *Daniel Dunglas Hume.*

Conan Doyle tore off his nightshirt and began to throw his clothes on. He was hurriedly snatching up the laces of his shoes when he heard a floorboard creak and looked up in time to see a note slide beneath his door. He rushed to the door and flung it open.

No one.

He leaped into the hallway and looked about, releasing an astonished gasp when he found it empty. The hallway was forty feet long. He puzzled how someone could have slipped the note under his door and run away in time not to be seen. And then he sniffed the air. The unmistakeable musk of Hope Thraxton's perfume spiraled in the air. He stepped back inside and plucked up the note.

The portrait gallery.
I will be waiting.
H.

* * *

Conan Doyle crept down the stairs and crossed the entrance hall. Here and there he paused, flattening himself against a wall or ducking into a shadowy alcove, listening to hear if anyone was lurking somewhere, watching. When he had convinced himself no one was about, he slipped inside the portrait gallery. He had not brought a lamp, so he fumbled in his pockets, took out a match, and scratched it along the edge of the box. It fizzed and burned. The tang of sulfur caught in his throat. Then he liberated a candle from its wall sconce and kindled the wick. Cupping his hand around the flame, he crept along the gallery, eyes straining to catch sight of Hope. But he reached the end of the gallery and she was not there. He looked around him, raising the candle to cast a halo of light. The quivering candle flame animated the faces of the Thraxtons watching from the walls and gave them the illusion of life. The luminous eyes of the portrait to his right snared his attention. The painting was of a man in modern dress, posed stiffly, one hand gripping the back of a chair, his cold gaze fixed upon the viewer. This portrait had an engraved brass plaque at its base that read: "Lord Edmund Thraxton III." Beside the portrait of Edmund was a bare space where the ghost of a rectangular dust print revealed where a smaller portrait had once hung.

An intriguing absence.

And then a disembodied giggle raised the hackles on the back of his neck. The laughter seemed to come from thin air, somewhere overhead.

"Hope?" he hissed, "Are you there?"

He crept forward and heard stifled laughter again. It appeared to come from a marble statue of a woman posed in a wall niche. Then the statue came to life as Hope Thraxton stepped down.

"Did I surprise you?" she asked in a playful voice.

"Much as a heart attack surprises its victim."

She giggled at that. "I'm sorry I alarmed you, Doctor Doyle."

"Please, call me Arthur. Doctor Doyle is what my patients call me."

"Does your friend, Mister Wilde, call you Arthur?"

"Yes."

"And your wife? Does she call you Arthur?"

"Yes."

A fey smile played upon her face. "Then I shall call you Conan. For I am not your patient and I am not yet your friend."

Her words dismayed him. "But I rather think we may become friends."

"Do you really think so? Isn't that somewhat presumptuous? I am, after all, a Lady."

"I . . . I . . . I'm terribly sorry. I did not mean—

She laughed a musical laugh and touched a hand to his chest. "I am teasing you."

"Ah, oh . . . I see. But then, what should I call you?"

She did not answer for a moment, her smile turning coy. "You must call me Milady—until we know each other better."

Conan Doyle struggled to find a response. In the darkness, the young woman seemed transformed: bold, and playful—so different from the shy creature lurking behind the dark veil.

"We must compare notes," he said. "The third séance is but a day away."

"Yes," she replied, a tremor in her voice.

"Have you had the dream again?"

She answered with a quick nod, her eyes evading his by looking away into the shadows.

"And what faces do you see?"

She turned back to him, her eyes lambent. "Only your handsome face."

At her words he lost the power of speech.

"Come," she said and linked his arm in a familiar way that would have shocked and scandalized Conan Doyle had he seen such behavior in two other strangers so recently introduced—and one a married man, at that. They walked toward the ballroom.

"No," she said, in answer to a question he had only thought and not voiced. "It is not a happy house. Not for me. Not for my father. Not for my grandfather. Not for any generation going back to the day the first brick was laid. The locals whisper that it was built in a bad place—upon a fairy fort or a site sacred to the blood-hungry gods of the ancient Britons. It has seen many tragedies: suicides, murders, stillborn children. There are regions in the house where I cannot bear to tread—rooms that scream, walls that weep, staircases that groan. The very stones of this place are suffused with decades of silence and despair." Her face quivered with emotion. "But mostly loneliness . . . terrible, terrible loneliness. . . ."

She looked away from him, her face masked by shadows. Then just as quickly she turned to him with her eyes sparkling and filled with mischief. "Would you like to meet my family?" she asked gaily.

"Family? I don't understand, I thought—"

She laughed again and pulled him to a narrow door. She took down a large key from its hook and unlocked it. A stone staircase spiraled down into blinding darkness.

"We'll need a lamp," Conan Doyle said. He found one set beside the door and lit it with his candle, then trimmed the wick to a soft glow.

The steps were steep and precipitous, with no handhold or railing. Conan Doyle dragged one hand along the cinderous wall in an effort to keep his balance. After a dizzying spiral of counterclockwise revolutions, they corkscrewed to the bottom and stumbled onto a flagged stone floor.

From the deep chill, he could sense they were belowground. The smell told him they had descended into a crypt, dank and reeking of corruption. The halo of light thrown by his raised lamp revealed ranks of coffins.

"This is my family," she said. "The Thraxtons, reaching back generations." Her face loomed and he felt her breath warm upon his cheek—a closeness that stirred him. "Come, I will show you what no one else has ever seen."

She led, and Conan Doyle followed. The crypt floor took on a downward slope as they descended farther, passing through rooms of coffins crossed by galleries running off to either side. And as they walked, they also journeyed back in time. The coffins became simpler, cruder. More dilapidated. Their echoing footsteps finally brought them to a place where the coffins, soaked in centuries of rot, had disintegrated, spilling bones upon the floor. Here and there, skulls leered from gaping holes in coffins riddled to splinters by the voracious appetites of boring wood lice.

The journey continued on until their feet swept stone flags untrodden in decades, raising gritty clouds. Bitterness filmed Conan Doyle's mouth. An incipient cough tickled the back of his throat and he knew he was breathing the dust of Hope Thraxton's ancestors.

She stopped at a place where the crypt seemed to end. The vaulted ceiling ran jagged with cracks and inky water dripped from above. Hope stood gazing at it. "This used to be a way out. Seamus and I would sneak down to the river through here—there is a door at the end. But then this appeared after my grandfather was lost on the moor."

Conan Doyle took a step forward, raised the lamp high, and saw something quite inexplicable.

From this point onward, a viscous pool of black liquid flooded the crypt. It appeared to be seeping up from the foundations. As he watched, it burped up several large bubbles with a glugging sound and surged sluggishly forward.

"The level is higher than the last time I came," she said. "By several yards."

"What is it?" Conan Doyle asked in a stunned whisper.

"The black lake that will finally engulf this house and drown all its ghosts." She turned and looked at him, her face tragic. "Including me."

He tore his eyes from hers with difficulty. There had to be a rational explanation for this weird phenomenon. He looked around for a stick to probe the black liquid, but there was none to be found. He walked back to the splintery ruins of the nearest coffin and retrieved the yellowing femur bone of some ancient Thraxton from where it lay on the stone flags.

Up close, a bituminous smell rose from the lake, and when he probed the end of the femur bone into the pool it came up glossy black and dripping slime.

"It could be pitch or tar," he speculated, "something naturally occurring. Perhaps the hall was built on an ancient peat bog."

He looked to Hope, but she had turned her back and was already gliding away, past the ranks of crumbling coffins. Back the way they had come.

He hurried to catch up and they returned in silence to the first chamber.

"Shall I show you something more?" she asked.

Conan Doyle was afraid of what she might show him next. "We have been gone for some time. We should go back."

But instead, she grabbed his hand and rested it on one of the newer coffins.

"Whose coffin is this?" he asked.

She flashed him a mischievous smile and lifted the lid. It took a moment for Conan Doyle to gather his nerve and look down. Thankfully, the coffin was empty.

"I don't understand—" He started to say, but then the young woman sat on the edge of the coffin, swung her legs up, and lay down inside. "It is mine," she said gaily. "I often come down here to lie in it—to see what it will feel like."

"Young lady, no! You must not!"

He reached into the coffin, slipped his arms around her waist, and began to lift her out. She put a hand on his chest as if to stop him, but then her hand grasped the lapel of his jacket and pulled him close until their faces were inches apart. He could feel her breath on his face and the warmth of her skin beneath the silken nightgown, the quickened pulsing of her heart. He saw up close, for the first time, the tiny crescent moon birthmark in the corner of her lips. He succumbed to the gravitational pull, and their lips brushed. But then—at the very last moment—Conan Doyle realized what was happening and pulled away.

"I—I . . ." he stammered. "We must get back."

His words struck like an open-handed slap. A flash of shock and resentment swept her eyes. She sprang from the coffin without his aid and hurried from the crypt, never once looking back.

*　*　*

Even though it was close to two o'clock in the morning, a crack of light showed beneath the door of Oscar Wilde's room. When Conan Doyle lightly rapped on the door, his friend's voice immediately called, "Come."

Conan Doyle shambled in to find the Irishman propped up on a mountain of pillows. He was wearing black silk pajamas and a magnificent gold brocaded dressing gown embroidered with Chinese dragons. Once again the red fez perched atop his head, tilted at a raffish angle. He had a hookah cradled in his lap, and now he placed the mouthpiece between his full lips and drew at it. Water burbled as he sucked in a lungful and then jetted silver smoke from both nostrils.

Conan Doyle looked skeptically at the water pipe. "What's in that thing?"

"Do not ask," Wilde answered, "or I shall be forced to lie and tell you it is tobacco."

Whatever was in the pipe was evidently potent, for Wilde's features were melting into a fleshy puddle of contentment.

Conan Doyle sniffed the air, nostrils flaring. "Smells like hashish. I wanted you sharp, Oscar. I'm counting on your quick mind."

"I am salving my mind."

"Embalming it, more like!"

"As a doctor you should know, Arthur, that one man's poison is another man's medicine." A silly grin smeared across Wilde's long face. "And your fellow, Sherlock *Whatshisname*, was a free user of cocaine."

"Yes, *between cases*, not during one!" Conan Doyle harrumphed with irritation, but then his own guilt softened him. He sank onto the end of Wilde's bed, and dropped his head into his hands. "Forgive me," he said in a voice of utter defeat. "I apologize. I . . . have something to confess. . . ."

Wilde laughed gently. "I'm afraid I am quite the opposite of a priest."

"Yes, but you are a man of the world. I don't think I could tell another living soul."

"Oh," Wilde breathed, "my poor, dear Arthur. You are a doctor, a man of medicine, and yet you are powerless to save your own wife. No one could. And now . . . now there is this young woman who has come to you to save her. She is fresh and beautiful and has awakened feelings that even your strict Jesuit upbringing is unable to quash."

Conan Doyle nodded, his eyes gleaming. "I have no excuses for my behavior."

"Tush!" Wilde said. "Stay silent for a moment, Arthur, while I play doctor to your soul."

The Scotsman said nothing, and acquiesced with a nod.

"Arthur Conan Doyle, you are the very best man I have ever known." Wilde chuckled. "And likely ever will. Your beloved Touie has been an invalid for years. Any lesser man—no, strike that—*any* other man would have sought solace in the arms of a mistress, a paramour, a prostitute . . . or a close friend's wife. You and I both have a code we live by. Two very different codes, admittedly—and I would add that my code is a good deal more elastic than yours—but codes, nonetheless. That is why I have admired you since the day we first met."

"Yes, but I made a vow—"

"And what is a vow but a promise we make to our own vanity?" Wilde put a hand on Conan Doyle's shoulder. "Touie is dying, Arthur, and that is precisely why you must live. You are still a young man. Do not squander life, when I know you understand how very precious it is."

Conan Doyle shook his head with resignation. "We may fail. I realize that now, Oscar. We may be powerless."

"Nonsense," Wilde said. "You and I are two of the finest minds in England—nay, I'll be immodest; after all, I have much to be immodest about. We are two of the finest minds *in the world*. Together, we shall prevent this murder. We shall save Hope Thraxton."

Wilde's words were encouraging, but as Conan Doyle trudged back to his bedroom, he thought about Hope Thraxton's erratic behavior and relived the moment when Hope had shown him the coffin that she would lie in, imagining her imminent death. As these thoughts percolated in his mind, an unpleasant reality loomed, one that he had been unable to broach with Wilde—the possibility that Hope Thraxton's porphyria had driven her into madness.

DEATH COMES TO THRAXTON HALL

The sound of weeping dredged Conan Doyle up from a suffocating tangle of dreams. He lay still a moment, ears straining, uncertain whether the sound was real, or merely the residue of a dream evaporating from his mind.

And then he heard it again: a child's sobbing, the faint scratching of nails on wood, and a small voice whispering a barely audible string of sibilants.

Beware.

Heart thumping, he sat up in bed. Holding his breath. Listening.

Beware.

He slipped quietly from bed and crept barefoot across the cold rug to the door, where he hovered motionless.

Nails scratched on the far side of the door.

Beware.

His hand tightened on the knob, slowly turning. When he felt the latch ease open, he tensed himself and snatched the door wide.

Shadows. Emptiness. Nothing.

He stepped out into the dark hallway and peered along its length. At the corridor's end he could dimly perceive the shadowy silhouette of a small girl. As he moved toward her, she took a step backward into the light. The glow of a paraffin lamp left burning at the top of the staircase fell across her face. It was a young girl in a grubby blue dress: the ghostly figure he had seen in the coppice. But she was real, of that he was certain, for she was solid, and the lamplight gleamed in her eye.

"Who are you, little girl?" he called in a hoarse whisper.

She took a step backward. *Beware.*

"Beware of what?" He took a step toward her, holding a hand out, beckoning. "I have children of my own. A little girl almost your age. Won't you let me help you?"

Beware of the mirror.

"What mirror?" He eased a step forward. "Please tell me what you mean."

It was the same girl in the blue dress he first spotted in the coppice. He was certain of it.

Find the mirror and you will find her.

He took another step, but the child turned and bolted, running down the hallway that led to the grand staircase. Without thinking, Conan Doyle gave chase. As he thundered around the corner, she was thirty feet ahead. And she was definitely real: he could hear her small feet drumming as she ran away. She turned right down another corner and he followed, gaining ground until he was mere feet behind. This hallway ended in a blank wall and he knew he had her cornered. But the little girl continued running until she reached the end of the corridor . . .

. . . and went straight through the wall.

Conan Doyle slid to a halt, breathless and amazed.

* * *

The next morning, as he descended the grand staircase, still groggy from lack of sleep, Conan Doyle reached the fateful step that made the entire staircase shake like jelly. Unprepared, he missed his footing and barely avoided a breakneck tumble by seizing a banister. The shock was enough to jolt him fully awake. As he regained his footing, he looked down at the entrance hall and found it was not empty. Lord Philipp Webb stood beneath the extinguished candelabrum, staring up at the portrait of Mariah Thraxton. Although he was some distance away, Conan Doyle thought he could detect a look of sensual longing on the patrician face.

Just then, Mister Greaves shuffled into the entrance hall, startling Lord Webb. He straightened his posture, his face regaining its usual haughty expression as he hastily replaced the black pince-nez on his nose.

"You there—servant," he snarled. "Where is breakfast being served?"

Mister Greaves paused. "In the conservatory, sir. If you like I could lead you—"

"That won't be necessary," said Lord Webb, cutting him off in mid-sentence. He turned on his heel and strode off down the hallway. Conan Doyle paused a moment and then followed at a distance. Webb was a fast walker, and Conan Doyle had a job to keep up as the aristocrat strode along the hallways, devouring the distance with his long legs, and swept into the conservatory. Conan Doyle lingered a moment outside and then entered. Once again, he was late arriving and most everyone else had already breakfasted, as evidenced by the wreckage of plates the domestics were clearing away. Lord Webb was already seated at a small table, giving his breakfast order to the maid, while a lone figure sat at a small wrought-iron table next to the windows: Oscar Wilde, who was scribbling in a notebook as the Scottish doctor flopped heavily into the chair beside him.

"What are you writing, Oscar?"

"A poem," Wilde said. "Like the Romantic Poets, I am inspired by ruins, especially when I am residing in one." He finished a line and looked up at his friend. "Good Lord, Arthur. You've been in a fight. Tell me, did you win?"

Conan Doyle shook a head spun full of cobwebs. "Once again I slept poorly. Keep having the most beastly nightmares."

"Ask them to move you."

Conan Doyle massaged his eyes with the palms of his hands until flocks of black crows swarmed his vision. "Oddly enough, I don't want to. The dreams are quite fascinating. Much dross for future stories."

Wilde responded with a baffled shake of his head. "Arthur, only you would find something good in nightmares."

Conan Doyle glanced down at Wilde's plate. A large fish, skeletal from the gills down, stared up reproachfully. "What are, or rather were, you breakfasting on, Oscar?"

"Trout," Wilde replied. "Caught from the very stream that is currently holding me hostage." He dabbed a linen napkin to the corner of his smirk. "I consider that a form of revenge."

The only fish Conan Doyle ever ate at breakfast was kippers. He looked up as the head housekeeper, Mrs. Kragan, entered with Mr. Greaves at her shoulder. She scanned the tables, spotted him, and walked swiftly over.

"I'll have porridge followed by bacon and—"

"Doctor Doyle," she interrupted, "you are a medical doctor, are you not, sir?"

The question took him by surprise. "Uh, why yes. That is correct."

A look of discomfort swept her haggard features. "Then we may have need of your services."

Conan Doyle thought of the blue girl he had seen or dreamed of the night before—the spectral girl whose appearance presaged death—and felt a cold current of dread flood through him.

* * *

"It is Madame Zhozhovsky," Mrs. Kragan explained as they hurried along the second floor hallway. "She asked to be awakened at seven A.M. each morning. I've knocked repeatedly and so has Mister Greaves, but there's no answer."

When they reached the room, Toby the gardener, a rustic chap in a stained smock, was holding a pickaxe, apparently ready to break the door down.

Conan Doyle had been present at a number of police investigations and immediately took command. "I take it the door is locked and you have no second key?"

"Alas," Mr. Greaves said, "the second key to this room was lost forty years ago."

"What's more, the door is locked from the inside," Mrs. Kragan interjected. "We have no choice but to break it down."

Conan Doyle knelt and peered in through the keyhole. Fortunately, the key had not been left in the lock. He thought a moment and then addressed the head housekeeper: "Mrs. Kragan, I shall need two hairpins, the longest and stoutest you have."

The matron blinked at the request, but after a moment's hesitation pulled two such pins from her enormous pile of hair, releasing two long gray strands.

"Thank you," Conan Doyle said, receiving them. "I will need to recompense you for these pins, as I'm about to destroy them."

With practiced, deft moves, Conan Doyle inserted the ends of the hairpins into the lock and, with his strong hands and some grimacing, bent the ends. He then reinserted them into the keyhole, twisting one and vibrating the other in the lock. A moment later the lock snapped open to the surprise of everyone watching, earning him a round of applause and a clap on the shoulder and a "good show!" from Oscar Wilde.

He blushed at the response. "Research for my detective fiction," he explained to all. "I swear I have never used this knowledge for untoward purposes."

Conan Doyle turned the door handle, cracked the door six inches, and called inside: "Madame Zhozhovsky, are you decent?"

When he received no reply, he lingered a moment and then slipped inside the room, drawing the door shut behind him. Several minutes passed.

"I hate suspense, don't you?" Wilde asked of no one in particular. "The only suspense I enjoy comes between the popping of the cork and the first sip of champagne."

No one laughed. He cleared his throat and fidgeted, for once at a loss for what to say. Finally, the door opened slightly and Conan Doyle's head popped out.

"Will you come inside, please, Oscar?"

"Me? Whatever for?"

"I require your assistance."

"Are you quite certain?" Wilde looked around. "I'm sure there must be a multitude of people, far more qualified than I—"

"*Now*, if you please, Oscar," Conan Doyle said, seizing his friend roughly by the sleeve and dragging him inside.

As soon as Conan Doyle had Wilde inside the room, he thrust the door shut. "I'm sorry, Oscar, if the taint of death disturbs you, but I need a second of pair eyes to see what I don't see. And I need your keen mind."

"It's not dead people I'm afraid of," Wilde said. "After all, I was born and raised in Ireland. I have seen my share of dead siblings and deceased uncles, of *layings' out* and *wakes*. It is that peculiar *old lady smell* I recoil from."

The room did, indeed, hold the reek of stale sweat, mothballs, and cheap perfume along with the kind of funk one often associates with the aged. Madame Zhozhovsky lay atop her bed, fully clothed.

Her small feet dangled over the end of the mattress. Her head was tilted back, mouth agape, eyes wide open. But instead of her uncanny gaze, the pupils were clouded with the opaque stare of death. Wilde took one look and recoiled.

"Ugh!" he exclaimed. "My life is a constant struggle to fill my mind with the beautiful and the sublime and now you make me look upon this. I shall never eat monkfish again."

"Come now, Oscar. Look not only at her. Look around the room. I'm counting on your artist's perception to catch what I might have overlooked."

Wilde snatched a lavender-scented handkerchief from his breast pocket and clamped it over his nose and mouth as he bent over the corpse, scrutinizing it.

"Looks like she died of fear," he said in a muffled voice. "She wears an expression of consuming horror upon her face—as if she perished mid-scream."

"Yes," Conan Doyle agreed. "Exactly how I would have described it."

"Whatever could have caused it?" Wilde looked at the door, which had been locked from within, and then around at the room. It was small and sparsely furnished with a few hardback chairs, a small dressing table, and an ancient chestnut wardrobe against one wall. Then he noticed the windows, one of which had been opened at the very top, allowing a two-foot gap. His eyes returned to meet Conan Doyle's.

"Yes," Conan Doyle said. "I noticed the very same thing."

"Do you think?"

"It seems an uncanny coincidence."

Conan Doyle cleared his throat and said, "There is something I must tell you of, Oscar. Something I observed from my bedroom window last night."

Wilde's bushy eyebrows rose, his large lips pursed in a lascivious expression. "*Observed from your bedroom window?* A promisingly naughty beginning. I hope your story has an equally ribald ending."

Conan Doyle shook his head. "Sorry to disappoint, Oscar, but no." He shifted his feet uneasily. "In truth, it may be of no consequence at all, because I am still not certain of what I saw."

"Please do not keep me in suspense any longer, Arthur, or I may strain a muscle."

Conan Doyle related the story of seeing what he took to be the shadowy form of Daniel Dunglas Hume levitating from his window. "But it was so dark I could scarcely make out any particular detail and besides . . ." He looked rather embarrassed. "The room I occupy is conducive to the most vivid dreams and hallucinations. "I might very well have imagined the whole event."

He threw an exasperated look at his friend and returned to examining the corpse.

"Something is missing," Wilde said, looking around.

"What?"

"Not entirely certain. Something that should be here."

Wilde prowled the room, nosing into cupboards and opening and closing drawers, prying open the giant wardrobe only to find little more than a sacklike dress and Madame Zhozhovsky's nether garments dangling amid the cobwebs.

"Oscar," Conan Doyle said quietly. "I am now certain our elderly lady did not die of natural causes or because of a fright. Come here."

Wilde reluctantly returned to the bedside. "Look at this," Conan Doyle said. He lifted the enormous double chins of Madame Zhozhovsky to reveal a narrow leather strap wound tightly around her throat.

"Strangled!" He looked up at Conan Doyle in astonishment. "But by whom?"

"Precisely," Conan Doyle replied. His fingers traced the strap until he came to a frazzled end. "The leather looks like it's been chewed through." He unraveled the strap and traced its other end to a loop around Madame Zhozhovsky's left wrist. "It is a leash, not a garrote!"

The realization hit them in synchrony and they both spoke aloud at the same moment:

"The monkey!"

He and Wilde stepped away from the body and looked around the room with fresh urgency. "Her death could be a complete fluke, an accident," Conan Doyle said. "She sits on the edge of the bed to begin undressing and the monkey, which was often perched on one shoulder, could have entangled her neck with its leash. She struggles and the monkey panics, inadvertently choking her to death. Finding itself trapped, the monkey eventually chews through the leash and escapes."

"Escapes where?" Wilde asked. It was an apt question and for the next few minutes they probed under the bed and into every drawer, nook, and cupboard that could possibly harbor a small primate. But found nothing.

"The open window," Wilde concluded. "It must have gone out the window."

The two friends moved to the window where they stood looking out, eyeing the façade skeptically. "There's not a ledge nor a handhold in sight—even for a monkey." Conan Doyle's eyes scoured the ground below the window. "And no monkey sprawled dead on the ground below." He turned his back on the window and swept the room with a furious gaze. "Well, he must be somewhere!"

"That's what Stanley said about Livingstone," Wilde quipped, "and look how long it took him to track the fellow down."

"Oscar," the Scots writer said after several moments pondering, "have you read Poe's 'Murders in the Rue Morgue'?"

"Yes." A light went on in Wilde's eyes. "The chimney!"

But a quick perusal of the fireplace revealed not the slightest speck of dislodged soot on the cream-colored hearth tiles. Conan Doyle crouched down and peered up the chimney. "The flue is shut tight. So there's no possible way the monkey went up the chimney."

He clambered to his feet and the two friends exchanged a mystified look.

"So where is our monkey, then?" Wilde asked.

The words he had famously put into the mouth of Sherlock Holmes echoed in his mind: *Once you have eliminated the impossible, whatever remains, however improbable, must be the truth.* Accepting it, he turned and eyed the open window with resignation. "The monkey is not in this room—therefore it must have gone out the window. It either fell to its death and was carried off by wild animals, or it successfully clambered down the walls somehow and may never be recovered."

"So what do we tell the others?"

Conan Doyle stroked his moustache, lower lip thrust out. "The truth. We have a murder suspect who has escaped."

"Or a possible witness who cannot speak."

The two men fell into a thoughtful silence, contemplating the conundrum set before them. And then, at the same moment, both raised their eyes and gazed once again at the open window.

"It does seem a coincidence, does it not?"

"Yes," Conan Doyle agreed. "I think we should speak to our levitating American cousin."

* * *

They found Daniel Dunglas Hume perched on a damp park bench in the formal garden. The Yankee psychic watched them approach with a guarded smile. "I take it you gents are not here to enjoy the soft English air between rain squalls?"

Conan Doyle answered with a question. "You heard about the death of Madame Zhozhovsky?"

The handsome head nodded. "I did, sir, and was greatly aggrieved to hear of it."

"And yet you never came to her room this morning? Everyone else was there. Your absence was noted."

Hume would not meet Conan Doyle's gaze. "I understand the old lady died of natural causes."

"It is possible that Nature played a role," Wilde said. "But there was nothing natural about her death."

"Then I was misinformed," Hume said.

"But why did you not come?"

Hume looked peeved. "I was . . . indisposed. I have been under considerable strain recently. I was resting—"

"Resting?" Conan Doyle's face hardened. "And yet I saw you levitate from your window last night and float back in at another. It must have been one o'clock in the morning."

Hume attempted to laugh it off. "One in the morning, you say? I believe Mister Doyle, you must have been dreaming—"

"*Doctor* Doyle, if you please, sir. I know what I saw and I saw you levitate from room to room. Do you deny it?"

"It never happened." The American got up from the bench and made to leave.

Conan Doyle arrested him with a hand on his sleeve. "I have a few more questions, Mister Hume."

Hume's friendly demeanor dissolved. He snatched loose his sleeve. "As I said, *sir*, it never happened."

"The window of Madame Zhozhovsky's room was lowered." Wilde said. "A two-foot gap at the top."

"Just the same as you levitated through," Conan Doyle added.

Hume's expression never wavered. It was obvious the American was a formidable card player. "I heard the old lady's death had something to do with the monkey—its leash wound around her throat. Sounds like a tragic accident to me."

"Except there are some vexing anomalies," Conan Doyle said. "For one, the room was locked from the inside. Therefore, the only way in and out was through the open window."

"And yet the monkey has vanished," Wilde added.

"Surely it climbed out the open window. Isn't that what monkeys do?"

"Except there are no handholds outside the window—even for a monkey. Just a sheer drop of forty feet—and we found no dead monkey on the ground below."

"*Doctor* Doyle, are you now also an expert on monkeys and their climbing techniques?"

Conan Doyle bit his lip. It was different writing the dialogue for his Sherlock Holmes stories, where Holmes was always cleverer than those he interrogated.

"Forget the monkey. Here is a fact known only to Mister Wilde and myself. Last night, around one in the morning, I looked out my bedroom window and saw you clearly. You levitated out your window, floated toward where the other guests were sleeping, and went in through another open window. If not Madame Zhozhovsky's, then whose room did you enter?"

Hume's gaze clashed with Conan Doyle's. "You are mistaken. I had nothing to do with Madame Zhozhovsky's death. I believe she was a fraud, but I held no enmity toward her. How could I? She was just a silly old woman who wanted the same thing I have sought all my life—fame. Now you *gentlemen* must excuse me."

He pushed past Conan Doyle, who halted him with a final

question. "Very well, I am not accusing you of murder. Just tell me I did not witness you levitate from your window."

Hume's back stiffened with anger. When he turned there were storm clouds gathering in his eyes. "Perhaps you did or did not see me. About that I will say nothing more. Do not ask again. I would sooner take the truth to my grave, or . . . if you insist upon it . . . yours."

CHAPTER 21

THE SECOND SÉANCE

You're saying she was murdered by a monkey?" Frank Podmore scoffed. He was leaning forward in his chair, eyeing Conan Doyle skeptically. The members of the Society for Psychical Research had reassembled in the parlor, where Conan Doyle and Oscar Wilde were conducting an inquest of sorts.

"And where is this murderous monkey now?" added Lord Webb, his voice choked with barely concealed contempt.

"I'm afraid only the monkey knows," Wilde answered. "Which, come to think of it, sounds like the ending to an off-color joke I once heard." He was leaning against the mantelpiece, warming his legs as he smoked one of his Turkish cigarettes.

Conan Doyle threw Wilde a cutting look, cleared his throat, and continued. "We assume the beast climbed out the window."

"I saw the window," Frank Podmore interrupted. "It was cracked open at the top. A two-foot gap." He directed his gaze toward Daniel Dunglas Hume, who was lounging on a divan. "The same size opening that Mister Hume demonstrated his ability to levitate through."

Hume stiffened in his seat. "Are you insinuating that I had something to do with Madame Zhozhovsky's death?"

Podmore smiled ingenuously. "Not at all, Mister Hume. Merely pointing out the coincidence. I find coincidences fascinating, don't you?"

"Please, gentlemen!" Conan Doyle said, stepping between them. "Baseless accusations are not going to help us here. As a practicing physician, I've had the responsibility of sitting on a number of boards of inquest. I promise you, given the lack of an eyewitness, the available evidence warrants a verdict of death by misadventure."

"But surely there is one witness you're forgetting about."

All heads turned. It was Sir William Crookes who spoke, and now he rose unsteadily to his feet, an earnest expression on his face.

"Yes," agreed Wilde, "but as we've just said, the monkey has run away. And anyway, even if we managed to catch the beast, none of us speak monkey."

Sir William fixed Wilde with a withering look. "Not the monkey, you oaf! The only other witness was the victim: Madame Zhozhovsky."

Conan Doyle looked at the scientist quizzically. "But she is dead. I don't understand—"

"Lady Thraxton is a medium," Sir William interrupted. "The best in the world. We must conduct a séance. Lady Hope can contact the spirit of Madame Zhozhovsky so we might hear firsthand the manner of her death."

All eyes in the room turned to look at Lady Thraxton. She reposed in an armchair, her veiled head bowed. Seeming to sense their stares, her head rose slightly as she said in a timid voice: "If you say so. Yes, I suppose . . . yes."

Sir William spoke again. "It might not be acceptable evidence in a court of law, but it is imperative that we find out if there is a murderer amongst us." He sank back into his chair. "As rational people, we must use every means available to us to resolve this mystery. A woman is found dead in a locked room. She has been

strangled. Her companion, a pet monkey, is missing. A vexing puzzle, but we possess a most unique means to unravel this enigma."

"Yes!" Podmore agreed. "Quite brilliant, Sir William! A séance
is just the thing." The ratting-terrier eyes gleamed with ardor, chal-
lenging Conan Doyle to object.

Conan Doyle swallowed but remained silent. He glanced at
Wilde, who shook his head helplessly, and then finally at Lady
Thraxton, who was staring blankly at the rug. "Lady Thraxton," he
said in a gentle voice. "Are you certain you are ready to go through
with this?"

There was a prolonged silence. Then the Lady, who seemed to
have forgotten she was being addressed, looked up and said distractedly, "Yes . . . oh yes. Quite prepared."

Sidgwick leapt to his feet. "Excellent! Then we should have our
séance in say two hours, after preparations can be made."

The meeting broke up and members began to drift from the
room. Conan Doyle waited until Hope Thraxton got up from her
seat and made to intercept her on the way to the door, but she was
too far ahead and he watched as she disappeared down the hall
and around the corner.

Wilde appeared at Conan Doyle's shoulder. "Well, well, Arthur.
What do we do now? Fate has stepped in and changed the plans."

Conan Doyle chewed his moustache and waited until the
stragglers left the room. "We have to prepare for any eventuality."

"What if a member enters carrying a concealed weapon? What
about the Count with a pistol in his shiny holster?"

"We must insist that he leaves his pistol outside the room."

"And what about your revolver?"

"It will be strapped to my ankle," Conan Doyle said. "And I
shall not hesitate to draw it at the first sign of mischief."

* * *

"Mariah," I seek your counsel. "My body is open, ready for you to possess. . . ."

The members of the SPR were once again assembled around the séance table. This time Conan Doyle sat immediately to Lady Thraxton's left hand, Wilde beside him. Lord Webb sat to the young medium's right hand, and the two men eyed each other.

Hope Thraxton, her face a captive shadow behind the veil, stared into the flickering candlelight, flamelight reflecting in her eyes. "Mariah, my body is open as a vessel for you."

And then, once again, Hope convulsed and shrieked as her spirit guide possessed her. It struck Conan Doyle that he was witnessing a Delphic oracle writhing in a transport of ecstasy.

When the medium drew back her veil, her face was once again the face of Mariah Thraxton. "Why have you dragged me from the darkness of purgatory?"

Conan Doyle took the initiative, leaning forward. "We wish to contact a friend recently passed over to the other side."

The medium's head tilted; a cruel laugh burst from her mouth. "I know the one you speak of. She is with me now. She has many questions and will not stop jabbering."

"Yes . . . please, let us speak with Madame Zhozhovsky," Henry Sidgwick added.

The medium let out a vexed sigh. "Oh, if you wish it, very well."

Hope's head slumped. A tremor rippled across her face. An explosive gasp pushed past her lips. When her head lifted again, it had acquired a crooked tilt. Her eyes had rolled back into her head, showing nothing but milky marbles.

Conan Doyle's skin crawled. The beautiful young woman had transformed into a crone.

"Hello?" The voice that came from her lips was old, querulous. "Where am I? What's happening?"

Eleanor Sidgwick drew in a sharp breath. The voice was unmistakably that of Madame Zhozhovsky.

"Madame," Conan Doyle said. "We are seeking the cause of your death."

"*My? My* death?" The face narrowed with suspicion. "Who says I am dead? It is a lie," she snapped crossly. "Do not believe them!"

"The other night, Madame," Wilde said. "What happened? You were in your room. What happened in your room?"

The medium's brow furrowed, the lips pursed petulantly. "My foot was sore. I sat down on the bed to remove my shoe. And then . . . someone . . . in my boudoir. How did you get in? The door is . . . Wait . . . . I know what you are. You cannot hurt me. You are a ghost. You are dead. No! Stop! Something around my throat. Tightening. *Tightening!* Can't breathe! Help me! *Help!*"

The medium's head thrashed. She began to make horrible choking sounds; the veil fell over her face, sucking in and out as she fought for breath. Conan Doyle looked to the other sitters, but everyone was frozen with fear.

"The Lady is clearly distressed," Wilde said. "Surely we must do something."

"Do not break the circle," Henry Sidgwick urged, "lest we cause irreparable harm!"

Hope Thraxton began to thrash in her chair as she fought for breath. Her choking was dreadful to hear.

"Dammit! She's asphyxiating!" Conan Doyle urged.

"Do not break the circle," Lord Webb repeated. "We must do nothing until Hope is back in her own body. Madame Zhozhovsky, relinquish your hold," he commanded the thrashing figure. "Allow Lady Thraxton to repossess her body."

The choking reached a strangled pitch. Hope's body shuddered as if in its death throes.

"Do something!" Eleanor Sidgwick urged.

"No!" her husband shouted.

Webb's face showed panic. "Hope, awaken! Awaken, I say!"

She continued to gag for air.

"Break the circle!" Conan Doyle said, trying to loose his hands from the grip of his neighbors. "She's strangulating! Break the circle."

"No!"

"Yes!"

"I can't let go!"

"Neither can I!"

"Let go of me!" Podmore yelled in a girlish shriek. "Both of you, let go of me."

Cries of shock and alarm grew as the sitters struggled. Conan Doyle realized he was gripping both his neighbors' hands with all his might and could not fathom how to relax and let go.

A last death rattle squeezed from the medium's throat and she collapsed in the chair.

Conan Doyle rocked his chair back on two legs, put both his feet against the edge of the table and drove with all his might. His sweating hands slipped free of the cotton gloves and he shot backward onto the floor with a thump.

"I'm free!" Wilde shouted, suddenly able to let go.

Conan Doyle leaped to his feet. "The circle's broken!" He ran to where he thought the door was, but in the darkness banged his knee into a chair. Ignoring the pain, he limped to the door and began hammering with his fist. "Light. We need some light in here. Mister Greaves, open the door. Open the door!"

A moment later, Mister Greaves entered, bearing a burning taper. Conan Doyle snatched it from his hands, fumbled for the gas petcock, and lit it. Amber light, intense and dazzling, washed the darkness from the room.

Hope Thraxton lay slumped in her chair. Conan Doyle flew to her side, feeling at her neck for a pulse.

"Do not touch her!" Lord Webb shouted. "Her soul may still be hovering, inchoate. She must be allowed to revive naturally."

Conan Doyle ignored him, feeling at her neck for a pulse. "She has no heartbeat! She's stopped breathing!" He swept her up in his arms. "Oscar!" he shouted. "Follow me."

They barged from the séance room and ran down the corridor to Lady Thraxton's rooms. Fortunately, the door to her bedchamber was not locked, and they burst inside. Conan Doyle crossed quickly to the bed and laid Hope's limp form upon it.

Conan Doyle put his head to her chest, listening. "She is still not breathing!" He took hold of her by both arms and began the resuscitation procedure he'd been taught in medical school, pressing both her forearms against her diaphragm and then lifting them high above her head.

But after a few minutes, her lips were still blue. "It's not working, Oscar!"

And then with a cough, Hope Thraxton drew in a choking breath. Gagging, spluttering, she breathed again as Conan Doyle pumped her arms back and forth.

"Thank the stars!" Wilde said.

"Is she?" Henry Sidgwick asked from the open door behind them, where the anxious faces of the other sitters crowded around him.

"She is alive." Conan Doyle shouted. He looked at Wilde. "Oscar, in my room you will find a small medical kit in my baggage—"

Wilde's eyes widened. "That's on the third floor!"

"Yes," Conan Doyle agreed, "so you need to hurry."

Wilde's large face fell, but then he acquiesced with a bow. "Of course."

He left the chamber, squeezing through the huddle of SPR members crowded at the door.

Conan Doyle felt for a pulse at Hope Thraxton's throat. It was fast and thin, but slowed perceptibly under his touch. When he was satisfied, he stood up and turned to address the other Society members. "It has been a near thing, but I believe Lady Thraxton will make a full recovery. For now I must stay by her side to observe her vital signs. Thank you for your concern. I will send Oscar to report on her condition once she fully revives."

"Wait!" Lord Webb said. "She is still in a trance. I must—" he began to say; Conan Doyle closed the door firmly in his face.

The young Scottish doctor returned to the bed and sank down beside the fitfully breathing form of Hope Thraxton. Her face was still covered by the dark veil, which sucked in and out with every breath. He hesitated a moment. *I am a physician*, he told himself. *This is entirely professional. It is medically necessary.* And then he lifted the veil.

It was the first time he had seen her face, unveiled, in the full light of day. She was stunningly beautiful. He hovered over her, studying her face intently. A flush of pink climbed into her cheeks. Her lips twitched and parted slightly, releasing a breathy sigh.

He leaned over her and pressed an ear to the downy curve of her throat, listening. The pulse was steady now, pounding . . . *or was that his own pulse?* His nostrils pooled with her perfume—the same perfume he had smelled in the darkened room of her Mayfair home. Her skin was warm and flushed pink. He caressed a cheekbone with his fingertips. She murmured softly and leaned into his touch. He saw then the small birthmark on her left cheek and crouched closer to examine it. As Madame Zhozhovsky had said, it was in the shape of a waning crescent moon. And then an impulse seized him that he could not resist. An impulse that quickly became a compulsion, and quickly grew bestial. He knew what he was about to do was wrong. Unforgivable. He was possessed by an impulse that broke his vows as a doctor and as a husband, but which he could no longer fight. He pressed his lips to the tiny birthmark, to the perfect skin of her downy cheek . . . and kissed her.

Hope Thraxton made a little cry and began to stir. And then her eyes fluttered open. She looked up abstractly at his face and murmured in a breathy voice, "I . . . who . . . who . . . ?"

Conan Doyle quickly drew back. "You fainted during the séance."

She blinked, her senses slowly returning.

"We may not have much time. I believe now more than ever that your prophetic dream is real."

"Dream?" she asked in a voice dopey and distant. "What dream?"

Conan Doyle chafed her wrists between his large hands to warm her blood, trying to bring her back to her senses. "The dream we discussed in your Mayfair home, when we first met."

"Mayfair home?" Her brow furrowed. "I have no home in Mayfair. I have never left this house."

Conan Doyle's throat knotted. "What? But you must remember. You summoned me there. Two weeks ago. You told me of the vision in which you are murdered."

"Murdered!" Her eyes grew wild as she began to struggle in his grip. "I scarcely know you, sir. We never met until the other day."

"No, you must remember! You showed me the crypt."

"My murder? The crypt!" Her struggle became frenzied, and then her eyes rolled up and she swooned away, limp in his arms.

Just then the door banged open and Wilde rushed into the room, panting and breathless, Conan Doyle's small medical bag clutched in his hand. Mrs. Kragan rushed in behind him.

"I found—" Wilde started to say but then stopped mid-sentence, eyes wide, mouth open. It was a compromising position to be discovered in. Even to Wilde it must have looked as though Conan Doyle was ravishing her.

Mrs. Kragan shrieked and ran over to the bedside.

"The Lady has merely swooned," Conan Doyle explained, trying to keep his voice level.

The housekeeper hurled a murderous, doubting scowl at Conan Doyle. "Swooned, is it?" She shoved the much larger Conan Doyle out of the way and began to massage Lady Thraxton's wrists.

"You are aware, madam, that I am a doctor?" Conan Doyle insisted, but his voice sounded weak and unconvincing even to his own ears.

"Yes, and I can see exactly what kind of doctor . . ." the head housekeeper said, then added in a voice dripping with scorn, ". . . and a perfect gentleman."

Conan Doyle's face flushed crimson. He snatched the medical bag from Wilde's grip. A moment's rummaging produced a bottle of smelling salts. He uncorked the bottle and waved it under Lady Thraxton's nose. She recoiled, violet eyes startling open.

"Ah! See, she revives," Wilde said reassuringly, but he could not help throwing a probing look at his friend. He swept over to the tea service on the bedside table and hoisted the silver teapot. "Perhaps a spot of tea would be reviving—"

Mrs. Kragan snatched the pot from his hand. "The tea is this morning's and is quite stewed. I will fetch a fresh pot. And now if you *gentlemen* would kindly remove yourself from her Ladyship's bedchamber!"

The Scottish doctor said nothing further. He nodded to Wilde that they should quit the room and the two men proceeded to leave. But as he was walking to the door, a small portrait hanging above a secretary desk caught his eye and riveted Conan Doyle to the spot.

It was a painting of a young girl in a blue dress, clutching a rag doll to her chest.

* * *

Hours later, Conan Doyle entered Wilde's room, his leather Case-book tucked under one arm. The Irishman was sitting in the beside chair, legs crossed, a book of erotic engravings open on his lap, a glass of red wine in his hand. The open bottle on the bedside table revealed that he had just pulled the cork on his first glass. He looked up, but said nothing as Conan Doyle crossed the room to join him.

"Oscar, about what happened earlier. I—I need to explain."

Wilde said nothing. His head acquired an inquisitive tilt, his right eyebrow a question mark poised at the end of a sentence.

"After our initial meeting in the darkened room in Mayfair, I did have some concerns. The young lady's condition, her morbid sensitivity to the light, is caused by a disease called *porphyria*."

"Yes, you have told me. Hence the shutters? The darkened rooms? The veil?"

"Precisely. The day after our first meeting, I took the liberty of writing to a fellow physician who is an expert in the subject."

"And?"

Conan Doyle keyed open the Casebook and took out the small envelope. He handed it to Wilde, who took it from him and un-folded the letter. Conan Doyle bit his lip, watching silently as Wilde's eyes scanned the page. As the Irish playwright read the short missive, a series of expressions blurred seamlessly one into the other: surprise, befuddlement, irritation, disbelief, and finally resignation. When he had finished, he silently refolded the letter and looked up at his friend with a smile like a cracked teacup. For once, Wilde's famous garrulousness had quite deserted him.

"You're not saying anything," Conan Doyle finally prompted.

Wilde sighed. "Really, what is there to say?"

"I trust you will not place too great an emphasis on the reference to mania."

"How much emphasis should I not place upon it? If the woman suffers from mania. If she is an hysteric. Then our journey here. This entire enterprise. The fact that I have left my wife, my beloved children, and the comfort of my domicile, has been a complete—"

"As I said, Oscar, not in all cases is madness concurrent with the disease."

Wilde fixed his friend with a decidedly unfriendly look. "So this young woman, who interviews you in total darkness and vanishes the next day, leaving an empty household. Who claims to be a medium that speaks to the dead. Who sees visions of her own murder. Who has a premonitory dream of you lying dead in a coffin. This is the young lady whose sanity you do not question? Yes," he continued, his voice leaden with irony, "she sounds perfectly sound of mind."

"I'm sorry, Oscar . . . but . . . but you're right. I fear I may have dragged you along on a snipe hunt."

"I would not use the expression 'may have,' Arthur." Wilde tossed off his glass of red wine, threw himself out of the chair, and stepped over to an open suitcase that seemed to contain nothing but bottles. He pulled out a smoky brown bottle of absinthe and a small glass.

While Doyle watched, Wilde returned to the bedside table where he laid the absinthe spoon across the glass, set a sugar cube atop it, then poured out three fingers of the potent, anise-flavored spirit. "And how long have you known this?" he asked.

"A week before we left London." Conan Doyle flushed with shame. "I'm sorry, Oscar. I feel a fool now."

Wilde struck a match and set light to the absinthe-soaked sugar cube, which burned with a weird blue flame, bubbling brown and hissing as it melted into the spirit. He tipped the spoon into the glass, gave it a vigorous stir, then topped it off with a splash of water from a stone jug.

"Perhaps you could leave now, Arthur," Wilde said, falling back into his chair and raising the absinthe glass to his full lips. "I have a busy evening of excessive drinking ahead of me."

CHAPTER 22

THE LIBRARY

With Oscar Wilde embarked upon a voyage toward inebriation, Conan Doyle decided to seek company with the other guests.

The parlor was empty when he reached it, but he followed the sound of voices along the hallway and into a high-ceilinged room that proved to be a capacious library with floor-to-ceiling bookcases complete with ladders to ascend to the highest shelves. As he stepped inside, the aroma of must and that slightly vanilla scent that lingers in used bookstores washed over him.

The members of the SPR were all gathered in a seating area in the middle of the expansive space, reclining upon a collection of enormous wing-backed armchairs and sofas arranged on a threadbare Persian rug. Conan Doyle scanned the group. The Sidgwicks were seated side by side on the long sofa. Sir William Crookes sprawled in one of four large armchairs, his waistcoat misbuttoned. Podmore lurked nearby, pretending to be perusing the tall shelves, but no doubt eavesdropping with his ears pricked like a greyhound's. To the author's dismay, Lady Thraxton was nowhere to be seen.

"Ah, Doctor Doyle," Henry Sidgwick's voice called out. "We are so glad you chose to join us."

Trapped.

Conan Doyle really did not wish to join them if Lady Thraxton was absent, but it was too late. To leave now would seem boorish. He plastered on a fake smile and wandered over to join the others. The library floor was warped, buckling, and off-kilter by several degrees. Conan Doyle crossed the groaning floorboards with the rolling gait of a sailor traipsing the deck of a four-master.

"I really should check in on her Ladyship," he announced brightly, already plotting his escape.

"No need, Mister Doyle," said a smarmy voice. Lord Webb's pince-nez'd face appeared around the wing of one of the voluminous armchairs. "I visited her a moment ago. She has quite recovered and is resting comfortably. Best not to disturb her, old man."

Conan Doyle bit the inside of his cheek. He did not appreciate being ordered about by the likes of Lord Webb.

"But where is Mister Wilde?" Eleanor Sidgwick asked.

"I'm afraid he is . . . indisposed . . . " Conan Doyle said, and then added, beneath his breath, ". . . if not already paralytic."

"Lord Webb has very cleverly discovered the wine cellar," Sir William chortled. "He managed to wrangle a key from old Greavesie."

"Fully stocked and hasn't been touched in years," Webb added. "Seems a waste to let it turn to vinegar."

"You must sample this most delicious port," Sir William Crookes said, lofting a freshly dusted bottle. He paused to refill his empty glass. "It is a '63 and quite unequalled."

"Come along, Doctor Doyle, join us," Henry Sidgwick urged. "Do take a seat."

Conan Doyle relented with a nod—the only alternative was to return to his gloomy bedchamber. When he dropped onto the sofa next to Eleanor Sidgwick, he noticed for the first time that the Count sat ensconced in the tall wingback chair next to Lord Webb. The masked foreigner made eye contact briefly, but Conan Doyle quickly looked away.

"To your health," Sir William said, handing him a glass goblet filled nearly to the brim with port.

Conan Doyle took a sip and savored the port's comforting glow as it trickled down his throat like hot silk, warming his belly— perhaps not everything at Thraxton Hall was beyond redemption. He licked his lips and said, "I wanted to bring up the matter of what transpired at the séance today. It was a very near thing. I really think we ought to cancel tomorrow's séance."

"I could have told you of the dangers, had I been consulted."

All looked up at the sound of an American accent. Daniel Dunglas Hume stood a few feet away. Somehow he had managed to walk the length of the library without causing a single floorboard to squeak. Conan Doyle eyed him critically. Once again, Hume looked hale and hearty: no trace remained of the consumptive wreck he had attended to earlier.

"There are dangers involved in contacting the recently deceased," Hume continued. "Especially when death comes sudden and unexpected."

"She said she was murdered by a ghost!" Sidgwick said. "Strangled!" He looked around at the others. "Is that possible? Could something as immaterial as a spirit wreak physical harm upon a living person?" He looked up at the Yankee psychic. "What do you think, Mister Hume?"

"I have heard of physical attacks by malevolent entities. But strangulation by wrapping a leash around the victim's throat seems more likely the work of a living nemesis who bore ill will toward the old lady." Hume made a point of glaring at Frank Podmore as he said it.

Although he was facing away, ostensibly perusing the books, Podmore's back visibly stiffened at the implied accusation.

Lord Webb took a sip of his port and casually remarked, "I rather think the *evil monkey* theory advanced by Mister Doyle is far more credible." In his pompous, plumby accent, Webb managed to make the theory and, by inference, its author, seem laughably ridiculous.

Conan Doyle bristled and was about to retaliate when Mister Greaves limped into the room clutching an armful of bottles and looking like the Ghost of Christmas Past, his black butler livery streaked with dust, rags of gray cobwebs snagged in his hair and trailing from his ears and shoulders like ectoplasm. He tottered to the table and thumped down a collection of bottles silky with decades of dust. It was obvious he had spent hours rooting around in the wine cellar.

"I managed to find a '56, a '57, and a very nice amontillado," Greaves said.

Conan Doyle was intrigued and asked, "How on earth did you manage to find a specific vintage, Mister Greaves, when you cannot read the labels?"

Greaves set down the last bottle and turned to face Conan Doyle. "I managed the cellar for the third Lord Edmund. I placed every bottle in its rack, arranged by vineyard, year, and expense. Even though that was thirty years ago, I have an excellent memory, sir."

At that moment, Eleanor Sidgwick let out a stifled cry and touched her fingers to her forehead, wincing with pain.

Henry Sidgwick lunged forward and grasped his wife's hand. "Are you quite well, my dear?"

She squinted at him. "Just one of my migraines coming on." She rose to her feet and the men rose, too. "Please, excuse me, I think I shall retire."

"Take your medication, dear," Sidgwick nagged. "I'll be up in an hour or so."

"I doubt that." Lord Webb laughed, hefting one of the new bottles that Greaves had just fetched. "I rather think we shall be making a night of it!"

Mrs. Sidgwick said her good nights and turned to leave. As she passed Hume, the backs of their hands brushed and their eyes met in a look heavy with meaning. Conan Doyle happened to catch the exchange and was shocked. In an instant, he was forced to reconsider just whose room Hume was likely visiting the previous night.

Mrs. Sidgwick accompanied the ancient butler as they crossed the creaking floor to the door.

"Will you not join us in a drink, Mister Hume?" Sir William asked.

The Yankee shook his handsome head. "I thank ya for the kind offer, but I am a teetotaler."

"Then you have *something* in common with Frank," Lord Webb said, throwing a sardonic look at Frank Podmore, who was still pretending to browse the bookshelves. Podmore answered with nothing more than a furious look and then marched out of the library.

"I have a book to read," Hume said. "Which is why I came here in the first place. I was looking for Doctor Doyle."

Conan Doyle looked up, surprised.

"It is a book of your Sherlock Holmes stories, sir. I would be most gratified if you would sign it for me."

Hume held out the small leather-bound volume. Conan Doyle eyed the book warily—as if it were a loaded bear trap. It seemed impossible to escape Holmes, who was able to materialize in one form or another. "By all means," he said with forced good humor, taking the book from the American's hand. He searched the inside pocket of his tweed jacket and took out his fountain pen, flipped to the title page, and scrawled, *Best wishes to my American cousin,* and signed, *Arthur Conan Doyle.*

Hume thanked Conan Doyle and bowed to the assembled group. "Ya'll must excuse me now, I plan to read a few of Doctor Doyle's most edifying stories before retiring."

He raised the slim volume of Sherlock Holmes stories in salute.

"Thank you, once again, Doctor Doyle." He bowed his head and headed for the door. Conan Doyle watched him go and was struck by the fact that, as the Yankee psychic crossed the library, not a single floorboard creaked, almost as if Daniel Dunglas Hume were a being conjured from nothing more than light and shadow.

It seemed as good a time as any to make an escape. Conan Doyle rose from the sofa, announcing that he, too, was retiring for the night. He bowed to the group, then turned and left. Although he trod carefully, the floorboards squealed and groaned with every step.

He left the library and climbed the rickety grand staircase to the second floor. As he passed a dark alcove, a hand shot out from the shadows and seized his arm. By reflex, his free hand balled into a fist and he was about to throw a punch, when a face advanced into the light.

Frank Podmore.

"The deuce! I very nearly dropped you with a roundhouse right!"

Podmore's terrier eyes took in the large fist, cocked and trembling, which Conan Doyle relaxed and dropped.

"If this is about the shoelace prank—"

Podmore sniffed. "Forget that. I am used to being an object of ridicule. I wanted to warn you—"

At first Conan Doyle assumed that Podmore was threatening him. "Warn me of what?"

"The high and mighty Lord Webb."

The look of concern on Podmore's face told Conan Doyle that the young man was in deadly earnest. "You fear he intends to harm Lady Thraxton?"

"I fear he has designs on her Ladyship." Podmore's face tightened. "I believe he is trying to inveigle himself into a position of favor—the man is precisely the type of cad who would exploit a vulnerable young woman."

"To what end?"

Podmore snorted and glared at Conan Doyle as if he were stupid. "Lady Thraxton inherited the title, but she is only twenty years old. Once she reaches her majority she will own the house. More importantly, the Thraxton family fortune, which has been held in trust since the death of Lord Edmund Thraxton . . . will be hers."

"But Lord Thraxton did not die—officially. I understood that he vanished . . . simply disappeared into thin air."

"It is the *same* thing," Podmore remarked in a tone of pedantic impatience. "He has been declared legally dead by a court of inquest."

"If the Thraxton family fortune is being held in trust, then who is Hope's legal guardian?"

"The head housekeeper, Mrs. Kragan," the younger man answered, apparently amused at the stunned look on Conan Doyle's face. "You may well look surprised, Doctor Doyle, but I assure you it's true."

While Podmore had dropped his guard, Conan Doyle sought to press forward his advantage. "One final question: did you come to Thraxton Hall with a firearm? A small pistol easy to conceal on your person?"

Podmore's eyes widened. But after his initial surprise, he regained himself. "I believe I've answered enough of your questions, Doctor Doyle." And with that, the younger man turned and stalked off into the darkness.

* * *

The whole night Conan Doyle tossed restlessly, clinging to a narrow ledge of sleep. The events of the previous days repeated themselves in a revolving carousel. At one point, as his mind floated up from sleep, he heard a child weeping and was awakened by the ear-ringing crash of a door being slammed shut.

His eyes snapped open. He was awake, yet the reverberations of the slamming door seemed to carry on and on and on until they died down to a repetitive *tap-tap . . . tap-tap . . . tap-tap . . .*

A familiar hawk-nosed figure sat in the armchair facing the bed. He had rolled up his shirtsleeve and was tapping a forefinger on the barrel of a syringe, the needle of which was plunged into a bulging blue vein in his forearm.

Sherlock Holmes.

"You really are lost, aren't you, Arthur?" Holmes mumbled around the leather tourniquet clenched between his teeth.

"What? You again?"

Holmes spat out the tourniquet. "Yes, me again. Your *creation*," Holmes said sneeringly, the tortoise eyes levered up to meet Conan Doyle's. "You'll pardon me if I take a moment to indulge in the only human vice you permitted me. But then I suppose you had your reasons. I would scarcely have been able to solve every impossible murder in England had I spent my time mooning around after young girls as you do."

Conan Doyle sputtered with rage at the insult. "M-mooning about? I'm here to save a woman's life!"

As the hypodermic's plunger began its slow descent, opiate clouds billowed behind Holmes' heavy-lidded gaze. He withdrew the syringe and set it down on the writing desk, then unraveled the leather tourniquet lashed tight around his bicep, massaging a veiny forearm tracked with needle scars. "So what progress have you made thus far?" He mocked Conan Doyle with a tight smile. "The final séance is tomorrow night—the final séance, at which Hope Thraxton will be murdered—shot twice in the chest."

"How do you know it will be the final séance?" Conan Doyle asked.

"Because murderers possess a keen sense of theater and always save the best for last." The narrow face pursed its lips in disapproval. "Have you determined who will be the trigger man . . . or woman? What made me such a formidable detective?"

Conan Doyle flustered. "A keen mind? Solving problems through logic and deduction—"

"Great powers of observation," Holmes interrupted. "Recall how I was able to astonish my good friend John Watson on our first encounter by deducing that he was a doctor. He had been a military man in Afghanistan, where he was wounded in the right, or was it the left leg? (You were a little slipshod on that detail.) All through the powers of observation."

"Is there a point to all this? If so, cut to it, and spare me the drama."

"You have been to the Thraxton crypt. You very nearly kissed Lady Thraxton in her coffin, but your coward heart failed you. Something was quite peculiar about one of those coffins. Something you should have noticed—had you been aware . . . had you been paying attention to anything other than the downy curve of her cheek with its crescent moon birthmark poised, so tantalizingly, at the corner of her mouth."

Conan Doyle blustered. "Peculiar? What do you mean, peculiar? Peculiar in what way?"

"I'm afraid you'll have to find that out for yourself." Holmes unleashed a vulpine smile. "After all, I am merely the puppet. You are the puppet master."

Having his own words flung back in his face silenced Conan Doyle.

Holmes drew a languid breath in through his hawkish nose, his nostrils flaring as he exhaled. "I have a joke for you, Arthur." He fixed his creator with a dreamy gaze as the 7-percent solution worked its alchemy. "When is a door not a door?" He arched a questioning eyebrow. "When it's ajar." A clumsy laugh bubbled from Holmes' lips. "Sorry. A dreadful pun, I know. You gave me a mind like an adding machine but forgot to include a sense of humor." He slumped back in the armchair. His eyelids fluttered and closed. His head lolled. The image of Holmes grew blurry at the edges, its color drained into monochrome, and then became shiveringly translucent, until nothing remained but a tenuous outline that burst like a soap bubble and vanished.

Conan Doyle's eyes opened a second time, springing his mind from the dream-within-a-dream. He lurched up in bed, his heart flailing, the words of his fictional creation resounding in his head. "A door that is not a door . . ." He heaved aside the heavy woolen bedclothes and flung himself from the bed. He dressed quickly and slipped from his room, mindful that the rest of the house would not stir for another hour.

* * *

The room Madame Zhozhovsky died in was unlocked. A trunk containing her clothes sat on the bed. The aroma that so offended Wilde's sensibilities still hovered. Her body had been placed in one of the empty coffins in the Thraxton family crypt, preparatory to being shipped back to her family (in Barnsley, Yorkshire, as coincidence had it) as soon as the ford became passable.

Conan Doyle wandered the gloomy room, probing. The wardrobe had a sticky door that required a firm yank to open. It was empty, apart from cobwebs clinging in the corners and a dead spider twirling at the end of its silken thread. He shouldered the wardrobe door shut and looked around the room. As he had found in many years as a physician, the residue of death still lingered—a palpable presence.

And then he heard it: the sound of claws scratching against stone and an inhuman gibbering that raised gooseflesh. He tilted his head and strained to listen. The sound of something scrabbling in the walls began again. He followed its progress until it passed behind the wardrobe. Silence followed and then the insistent scratching started again. He wrenched open the wardrobe door and peered into its shadows. Nothing. But then he heard the scrabbling again.

It was coming from *behind* the wall.

When is a door not a door? The words of the apparition of Sherlock Holmes rose to the surface of his mind.

Conan Doyle struck a lucifer and lit the bedside lamp. He returned to the wardrobe and lofted it high, washing the inside with light. The wardrobe seemed solid enough, but as his fingers felt along the top of the lintel, there was a loud click as something spring-loaded depressed beneath his touch. The back of the wardrobe popped inward with an audible gasp, revealing an inky black void: a secret passage hidden in the walls smelling of dust and dead air.

Slowly, cautiously, he raised the lamp and peered in.

A demonic face lunged from the darkness, blood-red eyes burning with hatred, fangs bared. Conan Doyle shouted in surprise as a small and furry devil latched onto his face, nails clawing his scalp as it clambered over his head and leaped off, scampering out the open door, shrieking.

The monkey.

It had been trapped inside the walls all this time. Conan Doyle dabbed at his scalp with a white handkerchief; it came away flecked with crimson. The monkey's claws had drawn blood. And yet, ever the pragmatist, he considered the pain a minor price to pay for having discovered the means by which Madame Zhozhovsky's murderer had accessed her room.

He paused for several moments, staring into the black opening. *I should go back to fetch Oscar,* he thought. *Going it alone would be foolish.* But he felt the thrill of an Egyptologist to whom a hidden chamber in the Great Pyramid has just opened. The pull was irresistible. *Perhaps I'll just explore a little way to ensure that this really does lead somewhere.* Ignoring his own good advice, he plunged inside and crept along a stony passageway so narrow that his shoulders brushed the walls.

The passageway was longer than he expected. Forty feet on, it intersected another passageway running at ninety degrees. *Which way to go?* He lofted the lamp and scanned the floor. The passage to his left, which led toward the western wing, was furred with dust, but the passageway to his right was tracked with blurred footprints. He turned right and followed another twenty feet until he came upon a set of stone steps that plunged downward. At the stair's end, a short passageway zigged hard right, and zagged left. And then he stepped out into a dark, echoing space he recognized.

The crypt of the Thraxtons.

He had descended to the first level of the crypt. He could see that a number of skylights were set into the vaulted stone ceiling and the morning sunlight, filtered through layers of moss and scum, created a sickly greenish, underwater twilight. And then he noticed the sharp glimmer of a candle in the distance. Conan Doyle crept toward it as quietly as he could. As he passed the first rank of coffins, he saw where the light came from: a fat tallow candle burning atop a coffin lid. He set down his lamp, picked up the candle in its heavy silver candleholder, and lifted the coffin lid. A quick glimpse confirmed that its occupant was Madame Zhozhovsky, whose eyes he himself had closed, and around whose head he had wrapped a gauze bandage to hold her mouth shut. He lowered the lid and advanced to the next coffin.

Most of the coffins were recent, their shiny black lacquer gleaming in the lamplight. However, this one was of an antique design, weathered and rotted from years spent buried in the ground. When he lifted the lid he found nothing but the stench of corrupted flesh and a complete skeleton, still clad here and there in tattered rags of leathery gray flesh. A closer look at the pelvic structure confirmed his initial suspicions about gender—a woman's skeleton. The coffin was otherwise empty, apart from a few scattered trinkets. He picked them up and scrutinized them by the lamplight—two ancient copper bands. And then he noticed that the skeleton's ankle and wrist bones had been drilled with corresponding holes. Conan Doyle knew enough about folklore and ancient customs to recognize what he was dealing with: the copper bands had been used to bind the limbs of the corpse together; it was a custom commonly practiced with suicides and witches to prevent them from rising from the grave.

This was a witch's corpse, he thought.

As he dropped the copper bands back into the coffin, his hand brushed fabric. What he had at first taken to be a piece of the disintegrating coffin lining proved to be a black fabric bag. He held the candle closer and saw the flaked and faded remains of hierophantic symbols. He reached inside the bag and drew out a cold, smooth, round object. At first he thought it was a polished disk of onyx and then recognized it for what it really was: a scrying mirror. He now had no doubt as to whose skeletal remains these were:

Mariah Thraxton.

His mind vaulted back to the dark, rainy evening of Lord Webb's arrival, when he had watched a coffin being unloaded from the hearse.

His eyes were drawn up to the candle flame as it faltered in a sudden draft where no draft should have been. The skin at the back of his neck prickled. He had only a moment to realize the draft could only come from someone looming up behind him. In the same instant, he was struck a stunning blow across the back of the head. A flash of light burst behind both eyes. His knees went slack, and his forehead smacked the cold stones as he crumpled to the ground. Somewhere, a man was moaning most horribly, and then he realized it was his own voice. He distantly felt the sensation of being lifted and then falling into blackness. As he slipped from consciousness, he realized he had been dumped inside the coffin. He tried to cry out, but could not find his voice. He tried to raise his arms but he was a puppet with its strings cut. He heard the cackle of a cruel laugh, and then his ears resounded with the boom of a coffin lid being slammed shut.

Darkness pooled in his mind, and he slipped silently beneath its surface.

* * *

"I'm afraid these scones will be the death of me," Oscar Wilde said as he sank his mossy incisors into his third scone—or was it his fourth? He was sharing a breakfast table with the Count who, improbably, was dressed in full military regalia for toast and tea. The choice of breakfast partner had been forced upon Wilde, as Conan Doyle was tardier than usual.

"I do not zink zat you vill die from eating a scone," the Count said. "But eeze likely you vill get fat."

Clotted cream and gooseberry jam squirted from the corner of Wilde's mouth as he bit down, his eyes rolling back into his head as he chewed in an ecstasy of sugar and double cream. He wiped his full lips on a napkin and mumbled around a mouthful of scone, "Diplomatic of you to say so, Count, but I am already fat. However, if I continue eating like this I run the risk of becoming positively porcine."

Mrs. Kragan and the maids scuttled the tables, clearing away the breakfast things. Wilde picked up the tiny silver bell and tinkled it to gain her attention. "I say," he called. "Might I have a fresh pot of tea, Mrs. Kragan?"

The Irish housekeeper flung a scowl his way without interrupting her ministrations. "Breakfast is long over, Mister Wilde. Kitchen's busy making lunch."

"Ah," Wilde said in a despairing tone, setting the silver bell down. "Shall I take that as a *no?*"

Mrs. Kragan did not even bother to answer. But as she bustled past carrying a tray laden with breakfast dishes, Wilde arrested her by grasping her elbow. "I say, you haven't seen Doctor Doyle this morning, have you?"

The dour face glared down at him. "I'm sure I have little knowledge of the wanderings of all our houseguests. Have you checked the doctor's room?"

"Yes, I have. He obviously rose early. I could see by the basin that he hadn't washed or shaved."

"Well then, you know more than me, sir." And with that, she clattered away with her tray full of breakfast dishes.

"How very odd," Wilde mused.

"Vat is zat?" the Count asked.

"My friend Arthur does not miss much, and he rarely misses a meal."

"Perhaps he went for his morning, how do you English say it, confrontational?"

Wilde allowed himself a smile and a chuckle. "Constitutional, Count. The word is constitutional, but you're very close, and 'confrontational' is probably quite accurate in Arthur's case." He rose from the table and tossed his napkin down. "Please excuse me, I must seek out my friend."

The Count also stood, clicked his heels, and snapped a low bow to Wilde. "I am a trained military commander. Might I assist in zis search?"

"No, that's quite unnecessary. I'm sure Arthur's safely ensconced in some little nook."

* * *

Conan Doyle awoke from a hideous sleep, images torn from a nightmare still uncoiling in his mind.

Bewildered, he tried to stretch out a hand in the darkness, only to collide with an unseen surface. Blind, frantic gropings soon proved his worst fears as he realized, with soaring dread, where he was.

A coffin.

Fear surged through him, throbbing like a raw nerve torn loose of the flesh. His breathing quickened to gasps and then erupted into deafening screams. The sound, resonating in the cramped space, fed upon itself, cascading his terror ever higher. Barely able to lift his arms, he pounded his fists against the unyielding darkness, flailing blindly, nails raking the inside of the coffin lid. His anguished howls rose to a piercing shriek before his voice cracked and his arms fell slack and leaden.

Lying in the darkness. Panting. Heart banging. His body rilled with sweat. His situation seemed impossible. *Regain yourself, Arthur,* Conan Doyle told himself. *You must control your fear, or you are a dead man.* He forced himself to take a number of slow, deep breaths, but the air in the coffin seemed used up and spent. He felt another surge of terror and only choked it down by sheer force of will.

Matches, he thought. *In my jacket pocket.* With difficulty, and only after shifting and twisting in the narrow coffin, was he able to snake a hand into his pocket and retrieve his box of lucifers. Given the dread nature of his situation, it was a small triumph. One-handed, he managed to draw a single match from the box and strike it against the rough wood of the coffin lid.

The match sputtered and flared, filling the coffin with light and a choking whiff of sulfur. He was lying on the bones of Mariah Thraxton, the teeth of her skull pressed into his cheek in an obscene kiss. However, seeing the tight confines of his prison was even more terrifying than the darkness. The light quickly dimmed as the match burned low. Conan Doyle inched his fingers to the very end of the matchstick, until the flame burned his thick fingers. He dropped the match with a pained howl, and the darkness fell upon him.

He closed his eyes, unwilling to fill his mind with the utter blackness of the coffin. Instead, he conjured the image of his beloved Touie, and of a pleasant summer's day idling together in their garden, watching the children play croquet. But then the image slipped away, and instead he saw the black lake slowly creeping toward him, surging up the crypt's stony throat, and drowning the side galleries, sweeping the coffins before it like buoyant boats. Something about the black lake held a terror beyond death. He realized what it truly was: nothingness passing forever from existence, and that he occupied just one of a fleet of coffins sailing through eternal night on a dark voyage toward a final destination: Oblivion.

* * *

When Oscar Wilde reached the parlor, the door had been left open. The morning lectures had begun, and Henry Sidgwick was on his feet, addressing the Society in his soporific drone. Wilde scanned the surprisingly attentive faces long enough to assert that only the Count and Conan Doyle were not present, and then quietly withdrew before he could be seen and inveigled to stay. He climbed the stairs to the second floor, where he caught a thief in the act of stealing: a small, furry shape skittered up the stairs, an apple clutched in its hands.

The monkey aptly named *Mephistopheles*.

Wilde thundered up the stairs after it. The monkey scampered along the second floor landing and dodged through an open bedroom door. It was a room he recognized: Madame Zhozhovsky's.

Wilde quickly guessed that Conan Doyle had returned to study the crime scene a second time. Before he entered, he took the precaution of covering his nose and mouth with a lavender-scented handkerchief.

"Arthur, are you in here?" he called, stepping inside. A quick glance disappointed him. But then he noticed that the monkey was also nowhere to be seen. The wardrobe door was slightly cracked. It swung open to his push and his jaw dropped when he saw the obsidian rectangle of the secret passage. There was no question now of where Arthur had gone. Wilde couldn't see far into the passage, but he knew that secret passageways were seldom dusted. He was wearing a black velvet jacket and black trousers—the worst possible choice. And then he looked down at his feet. He was wearing his two-guinea shoes. Exploring the passage was out of the question—he was simply not dressed for it. But then he reviewed the wardrobe he had fetched, and realized he was in a bit of a pickle. Wilde had picked out a selection of outfits based on style, color, and texture—he had not packed for the possibility of crawling through secret passages. Arthur, he reasoned, was a strong and resourceful man, excellently equipped for self-preservation. But still he dithered at the threshold, torn between fashion and friend-preservation. Yes, Conan Doyle was perhaps his best friend. But Wilde was wearing perhaps his best jacket.

He faced a vexing dilemma.

And so he stood, peering into the darkness, unmoving, his mind reefed in an inextricable knot. Finally, he shook himself, liberated a lamp from the hallway table, and plunged into the secret passage. He reasoned that, should Conan Doyle perish because he dallied, he would never feel comfortable wearing the clothes again.

Thus it was a moot point.

He paused when the secret passageway reached a junction, with one shaft leading off to his left and one to his right. With a lifelong preference for the sinister, he turned left. Within twenty feet he stumbled upon a flight of stone steps ascending steeply upward. At this point he contemplated turning back. He was a big man in a narrow space and claustrophobia was tightening a knot at the base of his skull. Nevertheless, he steeled himself, muttered, "*ad astra*," and began the long climb.

He was puffing hard, his thighs burning by the time he reached the top step, coughing on the dust his feet were raising. "This jacket and trousers will never come clean," he mourned aloud.

But then he saw that the way ahead was barred not by stone, but by a wooden door. Set in the top was a brass spy-hole cover. It was stuck fast, glued in place with the dust of decades, but cracked loose when he put his weight behind it. A cone of daylight streamed out, splashing across Wilde's face.

He contemplated a moment. *Who could stand before a spy hole and not peer through? Certainly not Oscar Wilde.* He pressed his face close to the spy hole and gazed into a dimly lit space filled with mirrors. As his hand pressed against the door, it rested upon a handle mechanism, which unlatched with a metallic *ka-chunk*. The secret panel broke loose with a *crack* and swung inward, stone dust grating beneath its sill.

Feeling rather like Lewis Carroll's Alice, Oscar Wilde stepped from the darkness into the mirror maze.

CHAPTER 23

THE FAR SIDE OF THE MIRROR

The smell of formaldehyde was sharp and pungent. The room he was in had the cave-like feel of a chamber deep beneath the ground. Around him were tables covered in sheets draped over familiar shapes—corpses. Suddenly, one of the corpses sat bolt upright, and the sheet whispered to the floor. The dead man's eyes were glassy and staring. Rictus had drawn the lips back so that he flashed the rotten stumps of a ruined smile; a knife wound across his face gaped like a second livid, red mouth.

Conan Doyle knew he was in the very worst place to be. Terror swarmed and prickled beneath his skin.

A swinging door at the far end of the room whuffed open and a small form stumped forward, tapping the way with a cane.

"Wh-who is that?" he called out.

The diminutive figure tap-tapped forward into a pool of lamp-light.

Madame Zhozhovsky.

"What's going on?" he cried, terror surging in his throat. "What's happening? Where am I?"

The old lady put a crooked finger to her lips and shushed him. "You are in, what the Buddhists call, the Bardo."

"Am . . . am I dead?"

She shook her head. "Consciousness has withdrawn from your body. You linger on the threshold. But beware—this is the realm of nightmares. Your greatest fears. A place between life and death, where the soul is tested and triumphs . . . or is destroyed, absorbed and imprisoned for eternity."

More of the corpses sat upright. Sheets slid to the floor. And then tables groaned and squeaked as, one by one, the dead climbed down. Conan Doyle saw faces eaten away by syphilis and cancer, missing noses, empty sockets lonely for an eye.

"Who are these people? What is this place?"

"An illusion. An hallucination. What you fear the most, torn from a memory. Part of what you never resolved in life."

"Yes," Conan Doyle gasped. "I recognize parts of it: the morgue at Edinburgh hospital. I worked the night shift as a student of medicine. I was alone, and I was terrified."

The corpses shuffled toward him, encircling him.

"This is not real," Zhozhovsky said, "but the terror is real. You must let go of it."

The figures crowded closer until he could taste the cloying reek of rotting meat and decay. They began to paw him with bloody stumps, hands shedding sheets of gray skin.

"Look away," she urged. "You must look away. Paradise is there, you just have to turn your gaze a fraction."

A ruined face gibbered inches away, rotten corpse breath washing over him.

"I can't . . . can't look away. . . ."

Hands began to paw at him, trying to pull him to the floor. He knew that if he lost his footing and fell he would never stand again.

"Resist!"

"I cannot! Help me!"

"You must resist. Put your mind somewhere else."

He retched, gagging. The stench of rotting flesh was over-whelming, triggering waves of fear and revulsion. A scream coiled in his chest, gathering, and he knew if he opened his mouth, if he unleashed it, the scream would annihilate him.

"Look away!"

He pushed through the shadows in his mind, and grasped onto a memory, like a drowning man clinging to a chunk of flotsam.

Instantly, he was out of the dark place. He looked around. He was standing on the windy battlements of Edinburgh Castle, look-ing out over the gray city toward Arthur's Seat, the hills to the east. A tall man towered beside him: it was his father, and he was a small boy. He recognized it as a moment from his youth, before his fa-ther's drinking robbed him of his mind. The familiar bearded face looked down at him and smiled. "Have you come to stay with your old dad, young Arthur?"

A small woman stumped toward them. She lowered her hood: Madame Zhozhovsky.

"This, too, is an illusion. You still hover on the boundary be-tween life and death. You must go back. Your mission on Earth is far from over."

Conan Doyle looked at his father. He could not remember him looking so young. Joy tightened his chest. It was a happy moment. One of the happiest moments in his life. Why should he leave it?

"None of this is real. You must leave."

"But why?"

"If you die in Thraxton Hall, your soul will be bound to it for eternity—as mine is."

"I want to stay. I don't want to leave—"

"Steel yourself and turn away!"

With a supreme effort, Conan Doyle tore his eyes from his father's.

Instantly, the castle, the battlements, his father, vanished.

He was back in the crypt of Thraxton Hall. He looked down to see a coffin. At the same instant, he could see himself lying inside, eyes shut, head lolling slack, a handful of burned matches in his soot-smudged fingers.

Madame Zhozhovsky had disappeared, but he felt a presence close by. A small figure appeared at the end of the crypt: it was the little girl in the blue dress. She stood watching him mutely, tears falling as she sucked a finger, and then turned and fled.

He hesitated. She could be a trickster, a revenant. Despite his misgivings, he left the coffin and followed. He rounded a corner into another passageway of the crypt. The girl sat on the stony ground, her filthy bare legs folded under her. She looked up at him with despair on a face streaked with tears.

"Who are you, little girl? Are you Annalette Thraxton?"

Without answering, she sprang to her feet and hurried away. But at the entrance to another passage she stopped and looked back shyly, waiting for him to follow.

The girl is a portent of death, he thought, *she could be luring my soul to destruction.* He resigned not to follow her. But then she held out a hand. It was a gesture that took him back to his own children. Something broke inside him. He stepped forward and took her hand. It was cold, tiny, and frail. She fixed his face with an importuning look and tugged. Meekly, he allowed himself to be led. She pulled him into a narrow, stony passage, and he found himself climbing a stone staircase that ascended through darkness. As they reached the top of the stairs, he saw a shining window. Light flooded in from the other side. As he reached the window, he saw that it was, in truth, the back side of a mirror. He looked through it and saw the interior of the mirror maze. And then, to his surprise, a hidden door juddered open and a dusty figure stumbled in. Oscar Wilde! He strode into the room, brushing dust from the shoulders of his jacket, and looked around.

Conan Doyle hammered on the glass with his fists and cried out, "Oscar! I'm here. Behind the glass. Oscar!"

But the Irishman showed no signs of hearing him. Instead, he poked around the room and finally strode straight up to the mirror and peered into it.

He must see me, Conan Doyle thought. He emptied his mind, pressed both hands flat against the mirror, and concentrated with everything he had, trying to transmit a mental cry for help to his friend.

Oscar, it's me. I'm dying, trapped in a coffin in the crypt. You must find me before it's too late.

Wilde's face took on a serious look. He leaned closer, peering deeper into the glass. But then he merely brushed the dust from his large eyebrows and combed the cobwebs from his hair.

Oscar! Conan Doyle screamed. It was his last chance. His only chance.

Wilde abruptly turned from the mirror and strode to the far window. He looked out and must have seen something, because he suddenly bolted from the room.

Conan Doyle realized, with despair, that his friend had been oblivious to the mental signal. He looked around for the young girl, but she, too, had vanished. And then he felt a tidal surge drawing him back from the mirror. Back down the staircase. Back along the passageway. Back into the crypt. The coffin that imprisoned him loomed and drew him irresistibly back inside. With rising horror, he knew that he had failed, and that death and the unrelenting darkness would swallow him . . . forever.

A TERRIBLE SACRIFICE

Opening the secret door had loosened decades of dust, which sifted down upon the shoulders of Wilde's black velvet jacket. Gingerly, he attempted to brush the dust from his shoulders without getting any on his trousers, but he was certain his entire ensemble was ruined. He stepped forward to the cheval dressing mirror and peered in. The mirror's silvering was disintegrating, but Wilde could see enough in the tattered reflection to spring an expression of despair to his face. He resembled a mummy disinterred from a dusty alcove of the British Museum. His large eyebrows were giant caterpillars limned with gray fuzz; his rich chestnut curls were matted with clingy cobwebs. The black velvet suit—now fuzzy as a giant lint ball—would have to be burned. Wilde would have to soak in a hot tub filled with his best bath salts to freshen his skin and scour away the grime of eons.

He glanced around the room. Conan Doyle was obviously not there, and the room held nothing of note except for a collection of the most inordinately ugly mirrors he had ever seen gathered into one place. He paused again to check his reflection in the mirror, brushing dust from his eyebrows as he leaned close.

Then, quite remarkably, he received a strong mental image of

Conan Doyle interred in a coffin. The effect was shockingly disconcerting, and he drew back from the mirror. Suddenly from behind he heard a cry and the crack of a whip. He abandoned the mirror and moved to the window. When he looked out, he was just in time to see the black hearse draw away, the two ruffians he had spied in the kitchen, sitting at the reins. A sudden flash of inspiration struck him and he fled from the room as fast as he could.

* * *

Colors swam in his eyes, and Conan Doyle knew it was a sign that his brain, starved of oxygen, was dying. He sucked in a labored breath, but the air in the coffin was used up. He realized the end was near and focused his mind, determined that his final thought would be of the ones he loved. He thought of his wife, Louise, on their wedding day, her face still young and flushed with youth. He thought of cradling his son, a babe in arms, and singing him to sleep. He tried to think of his daughters, the sweetness of their faces as they fed the ducks at the village pond, but the darkness was starting to leak into his mind. Their images dissolved as his mind drowned in shadow.

* * *

To the great surprise of Mister Greaves and one of the maids, Oscar Wilde, dusted gray as a ghost, rushed past them in the hallway, galloped into the entrance hall, then flung open the front door and leaped down the steps. As he ran onto the gravel drive, Wilde looked to see the hearse trundling away in the distance. Toby, the gardener, was just leading an immense brown stallion and looked up in surprise as the large houseguest accosted him. "The horse!" Wilde shouted breathlessly, snatching the reins. "I must have it!"

"I'm sorry, sir," Toby said. "But you can't ride this 'orse."

"Emergency!" Wilde shouted. "Need the horse."

"But you can't ride him."

"No time to argue. Time is crucial. Give me a leg up."

Reluctantly, Toby cupped his hands; Wilde stepped into them and clambered on the back of the horse. It was a huge brown shire horse, bred for plowing and hauling. Wilde considered himself a passable horseman, but the mount lacked a saddle. Still, he just had to catch the hearse. He dug the heels of his two-guinea shoes into the horse's flanks. The beast whinnied, tossed its huge head, and plunged forward. The horse galloped a dozen strides, then slid to a halt and dropped its head, catapulting Wilde over the top. He performed an arm-flailing somersault and landed flat on his back with a spleen-rupturing "OOF!"—the wind knocked out of him.

The Irishman looked up to see Toby standing over him.

"Told you ya couldn't ride him, sir. There's only me what can ride Fury."

Toby assisted Wilde as he staggered, wincing, to his feet. When the playwright could finally draw breath, he said in a tight voice, "Then you must carry me pillion."

Moments later, Fury thundered off with Toby at the reins and Wilde bouncing wildly behind, oofing with every lunge. They cantered out of the courtyard, down the stony lane, and galloped through the gates of the grounds.

Finally the road descended to where the hearse was pulling clear of the ford, water dripping from its wheels.

"Stop! Stop!" Wilde called out. The driver of the hearse, the short man Wilde had seen in the kitchen, shared a look with the large man at his side. For a moment, it looked as if they would ignore his cries and carry on, but then the hearse pulled up just a few yards clear of the ford.

Toby drew Fury up and Wilde slid off the back of the horse, walking stiff-legged.

"Thank you," he said breathlessly, and then added, "It is a fortunate thing I already have two strapping children. After that ride, I believe my days of fatherhood are forever behind me." After he caught his breath, he turned his attention to the hearse and its two drivers on the far side of the ford. "You there," he shouted, "fetch that hearse back over here."

The small man wiped a runny nose on his sleeve and shouted back. "We can't, sir. There ain't no room to turn the hearse about."

Wilde threw a questioning glance at Toby atop the horse. "He's right," the gardener agreed. "You'll have to wade across."

Wilde looked down at his two-guinea shoes, now scuffed at the toes and gray with dust. He looked back at the two ruffians. He was convinced that Conan Doyle lay in a coffin in the back of the hearse. Every second he delayed could be critical. He took a deep breath in through his nose, pulled his shoulders back, and waded into the ford. With the first step, frigid water flooded his shoes, snatching the breath from his lungs. The bottom of the ford was covered in river-rounded rocks, slippery with moss and green slime. Midway across, the press of water was strong. One foot shot out from under him. He stumbled, splashing water, arms windmilling, and nearly fell, but managed to catch himself and wobble upright. Finally he splashed from the water onto muddy ground, his silk socks squelching with each step. He marched up to the hearse, summoning every ounce of gravitas he possessed. "The coffin," he said in his most imperious tone. "I demand to see inside it."

The two men looked at one another uncertainly. Wilde was tall and broad, but the redheaded ruffian was the size of a draught ox—and almost as intelligent. He scratched his fiery muttonchops with a sandpaper sound. When he answered, his tone spoke of clenched fists and broken noses. "Wot you wanna look in the box for?"

Wilde cleared his throat, feigning impatience. "I believe you have a friend of mine in there." He turned to shout over his shoulder to Toby. "If these ruffians refuse to comply, you are to ride to Slattenmere and fetch the appropriate authorities."

Toby's face registered puzzlement. It was clear he had no idea who the "authorities" might be, or why their compliance was necessary. Still, Wilde's bluff worked. A look of fear flashed between the two men. Slowly, reluctantly, the small man opened the double doors. Inside the hearse was a coffin and several leather trunks.

"The lid," Wilde commanded, nodding at the coffin. "Open it."

With a final reluctant grunt, the two men set about unfastening the coffin screws, which were in the shape of silver doves. He watched as they undid the final screw.

"Stand aside." Wilde slid his fingertips under the coffin lid and snatched it open, fully expecting to see Conan Doyle, blinking but grateful to be rescued.

"Oh gawd!" Wilde lamented, recoiling from the scene. "Not again." Inside the coffin, her eyes wide open and the bandage holding her mouth shut fallen away from the jostling ride, was the corpse of Madame Zhozhovsky. Wilde shut tight his eyes, fumbling in his jacket pocket for a scented handkerchief, and clamped it over his nose and mouth before opening them again.

"What was you looking for, sir?" Toby asked a downcast Wilde after he slogged back across the ford. The Irishman stared down at his ruined shoes, his lower lip thrust out petulantly.

"I thought I had received a telepathic message from a friend who was in dire straits. I now realize that all this exposure to psychic mumbo jumbo is serving to turn my brains to mush. I have no doubt that I will return to the hall to find Conan Doyle taking his ease in a comfy armchair, smoking a fine cigar and mulling a snifter of brandy."

* * *

By now it was stifling hot inside the coffin, and Conan Doyle drifted in and out of oxygen-starved delirium. Distantly, he heard something . . . a squealing . . . and knew what it was: voracious rats chewing into the coffin, hungry for fresh meat. But the squealing went on, and dimly he recognized it as the sound of coffin screws being unscrewed.

A glimmering crack formed in the darkness, and then split wide as the coffin lid was flung open. Fresh, cool air swept his body. He squinted up into the light, where a luminous angel hovered over him. The angel floated closer. Cool hands cupped his face and raised his head. The angel had a face lifted from the stained-glass window of a Renaissance cathedral: a being lit from within—short, Joan of Arc hair, a graceful swan neck, features noble, and androgynously beautiful.

I am dead, he thought. *And this is the body's resurrection.*

The angel placed a loving hand upon his cheek and bent low over him. His lips met the angel's in a kiss as it breathed life back into him. As his lungs filled once again with air, a terrific pressure roared into his head. The sutures of his skull creaked as the pressure built and built. Hammer blows pounded against the back of his eyeballs as his brain, a balloon blown past bursting, exploded in a shower of fiery sparks.

CHAPTER 25

RESURRECTION

When Conan Doyle opened his eyes again, he found himself back in his bed in the gloomy bedroom. *Had it all been a particularly vivid and nasty nightmare?* But then he noticed Oscar Wilde sitting at his bedside, smoking one of his Turkish cigarettes.

"Oscar? What on earth?" He pawed the sheets, gripped the bedside table to assure himself that what he was now experiencing was real. "I was on the precipice of death. I saw an angel. But it was you who rescued me!"

Wilde jetted smoke from both nostrils, shaking his large head. "I'm sorry to say, Arthur, you're quite wrong. After I discovered the secret passage in the Madame's former room, I became convinced— quite irrationally—that you had been locked inside a coffin."

"But I was! Struck from behind. Knocked senseless. Then thrown into a coffin. You saved my life!"

Wilde smiled uneasily. "I would love to take credit for the deed. But I must confess it was not I who saved you."

"What? Then who?"

"I unfortunately opened the wrong box and received a most unwelcome surprise. And it was no angel you saw, my friend. But I have worse news."

"What?"

Sorrow flashed across Wilde's large face. His eyes grew misty. "My beautiful two-guinea shoes. They are quite ruined." As proof, he propped his feet on the bed to display them.

"Surely you can't be serious!"

"I am. They are quite ruined, Arthur. No amount of polish and soft brushes will restore them."

"But I saw an angel. I was resurrected."

Wilde shook his head, extinguishing his cigarette on the sole of his shoe. "No, I'm afraid the credit goes to the Count. I breakfasted with him and mentioned that you were missing. He offered his military experience in tracking you down. Foolishly, I declined. Fortunately, the Count is a huge fan of your Sherlock Holmes stories, and when neither you nor I appeared by the second session of the SPR meeting, the Count decided to do some of his own sleuthing."

"The Count?" Conan Doyle looked crushed. "The Count rescued me?"

Wilde nodded. "And apparently with little time to spare."

"But I saw a celestial light. An angel kissed me back to life."

"Ah," Wilde made a guilty face. "I'm afraid I may have had a hand in that. You see, when the Count and Mister Greaves carried you to bed, you were moaning and complaining of the most beastly headache. And so when I arrived I gave you a tincture of laudanum, dissolved in a glass of gin. I think that might have been the source of your celestial vision."

"Laudanum?" Conan Doyle blinked dumbly. "Where on earth did you get laudanum?"

Wilde dropped his eyes, picking at an imaginary bit of fluff on his trousers. "I do carry my own supply. Strictly for medical emergencies. I deemed this was one."

Conan Doyle struggled to pull himself up in the bed. "How many hours have I been asleep?"

"Day," Wilde corrected.

"What?"

A day," Wilde said mildly. "You have slept the clock around. Oh, and I should mention that the Count has agreed to say nothing and I've managed to keep this whole affair hushed up—so as not to alert the murderer who, as we now know, is very real. I told the other members of the SPR that you had retired to your room due to a particularly severe migraine."

Conan Doyle sat rubbing his temples. His head still throbbed. Then suddenly he fixed Wilde with a look of dread. "You say I've slept a day away? Then that means that séance is . . . tonight!"

Conan Doyle began to fight his way out of the bedclothes, although his head pounded with every movement. As he wobbled to his feet, Wilde jumped up from the chair, his face a mask of concern.

"Arthur, you must stay in bed. I insist."

Conan Doyle held his throbbing head with both hands, trying to still the room's slow revolution. "No, Oscar. I've rested enough. We are now certain there is a murderer in our midst. And we have only a few hours to discover who the killer is."

* * *

As the pair descended the stairs, they could see Lord Webb speaking with the surly head housekeeper, Mrs. Kragan. Conan Doyle gripped Wilde's arm as they reached the second floor landing and pulled him back, so he could observe their interaction. Whatever words were exchanged between them, Mrs. Kragan turned away as if struck across the face. She turned and scurried below stairs and Philipp Webb sauntered away.

Wilde and Conan Doyle shared a look.

"What do you make of the esteemed Lord Webb?" Conan Doyle asked. "From his manner and deportment he is clearly from an aristocratic family, but there is something about the man. Something . . . well, I don't like the fellow."

Wilde pondered the comment a moment. "I share your misgivings," he admitted, his eyelids lowering with suspicion. "Lord Webb is not all that he appears to be, of that I am certain."

Conan Doyle shot his friend a quizzical look. "Precisely what do you mean by that?"

Wilde paused to pick a fleck of tobacco from the tip of his tongue before answering. "I mean that the Count is not the only one wearing a mask. I'm ashamed to say it took me a while—we never really conversed face-to-face—but now I am convinced that Lord Webb is as Irish as I am."

Conan Doyle's mouth dropped open. "What? Are you certain? No! Surely not. The man does not have the slightest trace of an Irish accent."

Wilde flashed an indulgent smile. "Arthur, the first thing I forgot at Oxford was my Irish accent. Lord Webb has buried his well, but every now and again there surfaces a telltale inflection, a turn of phrase most un-English. I admit I cannot decipher rustic dialect, but I have an infallible ear for Irish accents. I hear the streets of Dublin in his long vowels and the quickness of his speech. An accent is a habit unlearned only by great effort and diligent practice—as I clearly demonstrate."

To his shame, Conan Doyle had been completely taken in by Lord Webb's polish and panache. "You astound me, Oscar. I feel a positive clod. You are more Holmesian than Holmes."

"I know the Irish," Wilde said. "And I know how they hide their Irishness when amongst the English. After all, I am one of the tribe."

"But why would he change his accent?"

Wilde smiled. "Much as it discomfits me to quote Shaw, 'It is *impossible for an Englishman to open his mouth without making some other Englishman hate or despise him.*'"

"But he is not English. He is an Irishman."

"Even worse. As an Irishman, he is beneath contempt. Come now, Arthur. You yourself are a Scotsman who went to boarding school in England. Tell me that you did not mollify your accent to avoid the attention of the other lads, not to mention their knuckles?"

Conan Doyle absorbed Wilde's observation and said nothing more as they descended to the entrance hall, where Mister Greaves was just opening the front door to a red-faced Frank Carter. The young man was holding a letter and breathing hard. As they turned and walked toward the parlor, Mister Greaves shouted after them, "Doctor Doyle. A moment, sir."

Surprised to hear his name called, Conan Doyle turned and waited as Mister Greaves shuffled toward them.

"A telegram, sir," Mister Greaves said. "For you, sir. Young Frank just fetched it from the village."

Stunned, Conan Doyle took the white envelope from the silver tray Mister Greaves proffered. Telegrams rarely brought good news. With trembling hands, he tore off the end of the envelope, drew out a sheet of stationery, and unfolded the paper. Dread flooded his chest as he read the terse message:

RETURN AT ONCE. LOUISE DOYLE ON FINAL JOURNEY. DR. F. BARNES.

He blinked several times, his eyes scouring the page a second time.

"Who is it from, Arthur?"

Conan Doyle strangled on the lump in his throat. His eyes suddenly lost all focus. "From . . . from, an old colleague of mine who looks in on Touie while I'm away. I'm afraid the news is—" He lost his way and then found it again. "I'm afraid—"

Unable to speak, Conan Doyle handed Wilde the telegram. The tall Irishman's muddy complexion turned ashen as he read the brief message. He handed the telegram back and said in hushed tones, "My dearest Arthur. I'm so very sorry. What now?"

Conan Doyle folded the telegram carefully and placed it back in its envelope. For several long moments he stared blindly at nothing. Finally, he shook his head numbly and muttered, "I—I don't know. I don't know." He looked at his friend. "How can I possibly leave?"

Wilde gripped Conan Doyle's shoulder and shook his head sadly. "No, Arthur. The question is: how can you possibly stay?"

* * *

"I *do* hope your migraine is better, Doctor Doyle," Eleanor Sidgwick said, smiling as Conan Doyle and Oscar Wilde entered the parlor. "As a fellow sufferer, I can fully empathize."

The Scottish doctor did not answer but merely acknowledged her with a nod of his head. His stunned expression and grave demeanor was immediately noted by all present and conversation fell away.

"I have to announce that . . . due to a tragedy of a personal nature . . . I . . . must leave."

Lady Thraxton was standing by the Sidgwicks, and clutched at her throat, her eyes wide.

Henry Sidgwick noticed the short envelope in Conan Doyle's trembling hand. Everyone in the room recognized it as a telegram. Everyone had received such a telegram at one time or another and could easily guess at its contents.

"I have just received news that my wife, Louise, is gravely ill. In fact, I pray that I can return to her side before . . . before she departs this life."

The room gasped at his news. Hope Thraxton's knees buckled and she sat down heavily in a chair.

"Lady Thraxton," Conan Doyle said.

She raised her head, shock spilling across her face.

"Lady Thraxton, my good friend Oscar shall be staying on and . . . and you may count on his assistance—in any circumstance."

Despite his words, Lady Thraxton's eyes dimmed and filled with tears. At the sight of her despairing face, an iron fist seized Conan Doyle's heart and squeezed. He acknowledged all assembled with a curt bow and quickly stepped from the room.

✳   ✳   ✳

Wilde sat on the bed, his legs crossed, as he watched Conan Doyle hastily repack his suitcase. Conan Doyle cinched the leather belt holding his cricket bat *Thunderer* to his bag, and then moved to the writing desk. He eased open the drawer, took out the revolver, and unwrapped it. The black gun gleamed with fatal potential. "I'm leaving the revolver for you," Conan Doyle said.

Wilde blanched. "Heavens, Arthur. You will do no such thing. I could not possibly carry a pistol."

"It could save your life, Oscar."

"No, it's out of the question. Revolvers are bulky. Heavy. All my jackets are immaculately tailored. A gun would completely ruin the line of my suit."

Conan Doyle fixed his friend with a firm look. "It could save the life of Lady Thraxton."

Wilde dropped his head in acquiescence. "Ah, yes . . . very well, then."

Conan Doyle held out the revolver to Wilde, who eyed it uncertainly, and then reluctantly took it from his hands.

✳   ✳   ✳

On the ride back to Slattenmere, Conan Doyle jostled alongside the young Frank Carter on the seat of the pony and trap. Sickened with worry, he had no energy for idle conversation.

Am I doing right? He tortured himself for the hundredth time. *Am I leaving a young woman to her fate only to rush to the side of another whose death is inescapable?* And then in the same moment he thought, *But how can I not be at the side of my beloved Touie in her final hours?*

All details of the journey to the train station failed to register in Conan Doyle's troubled mind. He finally came to himself when he was standing on the platform of the Slattenmere station, his newly printed ticket in one hand, his small leather suitcase clutched in the other.

At the whistle of the approaching train, Conan Doyle's stomach churned with queasy dread. Moments later, the engine chuffed alongside the platform and shuddered to a halt in a shriek of brakes. Carriage doors flung open, waiting. Several passengers got off. Two got on. Conan Doyle did not move, staring numbly at the waiting train.

A young conductor drowning in a uniform two sizes too large stepped down and threw a glance up and down the platform. He raised the whistle to his lips but paused when he noticed Conan Doyle. "Are you bound for London, sir?"

By pure reflex, Conan Doyle's legs carried him toward the waiting train. He handed his ticket to the conductor and asked, "What time we will arrive in London?"

"Around four P.M., sir. All trains are running on time." The conductor punched the ticket and handed it back. "First-class carriages are up at the front."

The conductor walked farther up the platform, waved his red flag to the driver, and gave an ear-piercing blast on his whistle. Conan Doyle stepped aboard the train, wandered up the corridor to the first-class carriages, and slid into the first unoccupied compartment. He was just settling into his seat as the train whistle blew, the brakes released with a thunk, and the train began rolling. As he looked out of the window, Conan Doyle knew he had taken an irrevocable step he might well regret for the rest of his life.

* * *

Oscar Wilde was strolling past the music room when a tuneless tinkle of notes played on the piano drew his gaze inside. Lord Philipp Webb stood at the keyboard, his long fingers idly stroking the ivories. He must have felt Wilde's gaze because he looked up at that moment. "Ah, Mister Wilde. I wonder if I might trouble you for a few minutes of your time?"

Wilde dallied a moment. He had never shared a private conversation with the titled gentleman, but could think of no excuse not to. "Certainly," he said, and stepped into the room.

"Do close the door behind you. The house is full of eavesdroppers. I believe you know to whom I am referring."

It was an obvious stab at Frank Podmore. Wilde dallied a moment, visibly uneasy, but complied, drawing the heavy door shut behind him.

"Wonderful," Lord Webb said. "Now we may speak confidentially." He patted the pockets of his immaculately tailored suit, apparently searching for something. "I say. I seem to have forgotten my cigarettes. Could I cadge one off you, old boy?"

Wilde reached into his inside pocket and pulled out his silver cigarette case. He flipped it open and offered it up.

"These are Turkish, aren't they?" Webb asked, helping himself to a cigarette.

"Yes. I have them specially imported by my favorite tobacconist on the Old Kent road."

Philipp Webb drew the cigarette under his large nose, savoring the spicy aroma of the tobacco, and then inserted it into his ebony cigarette holder. "A light?"

"Of course," Wilde said, scratching a match and lighting first his own and then Webb's cigarette.

"That's a wonderful cloak you're wearing. One could conceal all manner of things in something so voluminous."

"Yes, but luckily, not so large as to hide my genius."

Philipp Webb laughed and drew on his cigarette holder, exhaling a smoke ring, which rose to the ceiling of the music room and burst.

"South of the Liffey?" Wilde asked casually. "Aungier Street? Or Chapelizod?"

Webb froze. His face visibly paled. The corner of one eye twitched. It took him a moment to regain himself. "Very good, Mister Wilde. You have a discerning ear."

"When it comes to detecting the Irish masquerading as the English, I do. After all, I consider myself the foremost exemplar."

"A remarkable ear." Lord Webb's eyes took on a steely glint. "In addition to being a remarkable subject for hypnosis. In fact, I don't think I've met a person more susceptible to the influence."

"Thank you."

"No, that's not a good thing."

Wilde raised an eyebrow. "It isn't?"

"No, it is not, because I have already implanted a hypnotic trigger word in your mind. Now all I have to do is fix your gaze and utter the words *Sherlock Holmes,* and you will instantly fall into a trance."

Wilde went rigid, his eyes glassy and staring.

Webb removed the burning cigarette from between Wilde's thick fingers and tossed it in the fireplace. "Now Mister Wilde. Are you carrying a weapon in that voluminous cloak?"

"Yes," Wilde spoke robotically.

"I would very much like to see it. Please show me."

Wilde reached into an inner pocket and drew out Conan Doyle's service revolver.

"An impressive weapon. Is it loaded?"

"Yes."

"Excellent. Mister Wilde, you will be at the séance tonight?"

"I have promised Arthur."

"Yes, that's right. He had to leave, quite unexpectedly." Lord Webb could not conceal a smirk. "I'm afraid the telegram was a cheap ploy, a distraction to remove him from the house so I could enjoy a private moment with you. Fortunately, Mister Doyle lacks the deductive powers of his fictional detective. He will be back in South Norwood before he discovers the deception. Not that it would matter if he were still here. Lady Thraxton's Fate is to die. It appears that she will perish by your hand. Tonight, at the séance, when I say the words *Sherlock Holmes*, you will produce the revolver and shoot her twice in the chest. Do you understand?"

"Yes."

"And then, quite naturally, as a gentleman you will feel tremendous remorse at your murderous act, so you will place the gun to your temple and blow your brains out. Do you understand?"

"Yes."

"Good. Now put the gun away. When I say the word *Watson* you will awaken. The only part of this conversation you will remember is that I asked you for a cigarette and we smoked together. Is that clear?"

"Yes."

"Very good." Webb snapped his fingers in Wilde's face and said "*Watson*."

Oscar Wilde blinked as he came out of the trance. He went to puff the cigarette held between his fingers but found that it had inexplicably vanished.

"Thank you for the cigarette and the conversation, Mister Wilde. I will see you at the séance tonight."

"Yes," Wilde replied, feeling strangely bewildered. "See you tonight."

Lord Webb bowed and strolled from the room. Wilde stood

looking around, unable to shake a sense of confusion. He remembered smoking a cigarette, but did not remember entering the music room. He checked the pocket of his cape. The revolver was still there. Reassured, he strolled out of the music room and headed for the parlor. He had three hours before the final séance began.

* * *

Conan Doyle was sweating through his tweeds by the time he slogged into the main street of Slattenmere.

At the very last second, he had bolted from his first-class compartment, thrown open the train door, tossed his suitcase onto the platform, and leapt from the moving train after it.

The Scottish author had no grand plan. He had not diagramed where this plot was heading. He was operating purely on instinct, making things up as he went along. After leaping from the train, he had snatched up his suitcase, dusted himself off (he had taken a bit of a tumble jumping onto the platform), and then marched at a brisk, military pace the one and a half miles from the station to Slattenmere.

Despite its rather ugly name, Slattenmere was a pretty village with a picturesque square—complete with a sleek black horse grazing on the village green. There was a corner shop with a POST OFFICE sign and a thatched-roof public house: the SAILOR'S RETURN, according to the wooden sign swinging above its door.

Cool air smelling of spilled beer and pipe smoke swirled about him as he stepped into the gloomy saloon bar. He ambled to the bar and set down his suitcase. The pub landlord, a stout, ruddy-cheeked man with bristly sideburns and the tattoo of an anchor on his meaty forearm, was polishing a pint mug with a bar towel.

"Good day," Conan Doyle said. "I am looking for Frank Carter. Would you know his whereabouts?"

The landlord made a sour face. "Arr, if you be looking for young Frank, you just missed 'im."

"Will he be back soon?"

The landlord shook his grizzled head, slinging the towel over one shoulder as he hung the pewter pint pot on a hook above the bar. "'Fraid not, sir. He just left on a run to Baxchester, the next town over. Won't be back 'till late."

Conan Doyle agitatedly brushed his moustache as he pondered his next course of action.

"Do I know you, sir?" the landlord asked, peering at him queerly.

"Pardon?"

"I'm a good one with faces," the landlord said, grinning to show a wide set of yellowing, peg-like teeth. "I know I seen you somewhere."

"I'm sorry but you are mistaken. I've never been to Slattenmere before." Conan Doyle watched as the landlord began polishing another tankard and was reminded of his thirst. "I'll have a pint of your best ale, barkeep," he said, climbing onto a bar stool. The landlord pulled him a pint, still shooting him quizzical looks from beneath his bushy brows. He scraped the foaming head level and slid the tankard across the bar. Conan Doyle slapped down a crown and the landlord scooped it up. The beer still held the chill of the cellar and he quaffed deeply, brushing foam from his walrus moustache with the back of his hand. "Perhaps you could help me with something else."

The landlord looked at him quizzically. "We can do you a pie or sandwiches if you're hungry, sir, only you'll have to wait until Elsie arrives. She'll be here in a tick."

"Actually, if you could tell me where I can send a telegram, I'd be indebted."

The landlord's brows concertinaed in puzzlement. "I'm sorry, sir. We don't have no telegraph office."

Conan Doyle gaped in surprise, then rummaged in his pocket and drew out the telegram, unfolding it on the bar. "Look here," he said, pointing. "It says it was sent from the Slattenmere telegraph office."

The landlord chuckled. "I think someone's having a bit of a joke on you, sir. The nearest telegraph office is fifty miles away. There ain't never been no telegraph office in Slattenmere. We ain't big enough to warrant. Now if you'll excuse me, I gotta go change the barrel."

The landlord walked away, chuckling. Conan Doyle examined the crumpled telegram in his hand, completely stymied. Then he looked up, catching his own stunned reflection in the bar mirror— the reflection of a man who had been made a fool of by a simple ruse. But who could have done it?

"The murderer, obviously," said a familiar voice. He looked to the stool at his side, and found it empty. But when he looked back at the mirror he saw the image of Sherlock Holmes sitting next to him.

"You've been bamboozled, Arthur," Holmes said, a cigarette burning in the hand he casually rested on the bar. "The murderer wanted you gone and you took the bait. You've left your friend Wilde in the lurch. He is a clever man, but I doubt he will be able to prevent Lady Thraxton's murder at the séance, which will take place in just a few hours."

Conan Doyle banged down the pewter mug and dropped from his stool. As he turned to leave he heard a raucous laugh, which drew his eyes to two figures seated in the shadows in the back of the pub. One was a large ginger man. The other, a short, vole-eyed creature. He recognized them instantly as the drivers of the hearse and suddenly realized: these were the owners of the black horse grazing on the village green.

"Are you going to confront them, Arthur?" Holmes called from behind. "They'll just deny it. You have no evidence of any wrong-doing. Perhaps you should first obtain some proof. It's one of the elementary techniques of detection, as you should know."

Conan Doyle spun to fire a riposte back at Holmes, but the bar stool was empty and the only reflection the mirror held was his own.

He left his suitcase nestled next to the bar stool and ducked outside. The small village square was empty, apart from a man watering a hanging petunia basket in front of the post office. The black horse had its head down and was contentedly nibbling the bright green grass. And then Conan Doyle noticed the hearse drawn up in a small alleyway between houses. The back of the hearse was not locked, and when he opened the doors, the familiar stench of death wafted over him. A half dozen flies, the color of green glass, buzzed his face. The hearse still contained the coffin. The men were obviously not real undertakers, who would never have dallied in a pub while in possession of a recent corpse. No doubt they meant to dump it in a river or a field once they had quit Slattenmere.

Conan Doyle looked around and quickly clambered inside. In addition to the coffin, the hearse contained a number of leather trunks. The first trunk was not locked and sprang open to his touch. It was stuffed full of clothing. A moment's rooting and the first thing he pulled out was a rubber mask, ghostly and skeletal, the kind of prop commonly used in sham séances. A sheet of wood was laid up against the inside of the hearse, and when he slid it loose he saw that it was a music hall sign that read: MESMERO: MASTER OF HYPNOSIS, complete with a painted depiction of a man in a shiny black suit fixing the viewer with a hypnotic gaze.

Mesmero was unmistakably the same man who was passing himself off as Lord Webb. Now, he had no doubt who had been wearing the rubber mask when a ghostly figure entered Madame Zhozhovsky's room and strangled her.

* * *

The red-haired behemoth guzzled the last of his beer, banged his pint pot down, and belched extravagantly. "Wot say ya, Billie? It's yer round, mate."

Both men startled as a rubber ghost mask landed in the middle of their table. They looked up to see Conan Doyle standing over them, the cricket bat held discreetly at his side. "I understand you two are part of this charade," he said. "Now I'd like some answers, if you don't mind."

The two cronies recovered quickly from their initial shock, as men of the criminal class usually do. Conan Doyle never saw the redheaded brute slip the fish knife from his jacket sleeve until he burst up from his chair, bellowing like an ox, his face contorted with hatred. He swung a huge arm, slashing at the doctor's face. Unfortunately for him, he also brought his large head into the exact space where Conan Doyle was swinging his cricket bat with all his might. *Thunderer* connected with the redhead's skull with a resounding *crack* and the behemoth crashed down upon the table, crushing it beneath him, and pinning his small confederate to the floor.

It was a blow that would have knocked a normal human senseless. But amazingly, the bone-crushing minotaur groaned, shook his head, and staggered to his feet, his huge fists clenched into cannonballs.

A tremendous battle ensued, but several minutes of cacophonous struggle ended with Conan Doyle standing victorious, the two cronies unconscious and groaning on a floor littered with broken chairs and overturned tables.

The small man feigned unconsciousness, but yelped when Conan Doyle prodded him in the kidney with the business end of *Thunderer*. "The coffin you brought to the hall, where did you get it from?"

"We dug it up."

"Dug it up from where?"

"Gallows Field."

Conan Doyle sifted that information.

"The man you work for. What's his name?"

"I dunno. The guvnor."

Conan Doyle prodded again with the cricket bat. "His name."

"Oww, give off, will yer? His name's Seamus. I dunno his last name."

Seamus? A sickening realization tattooed needlepoints across Conan Doyle's face. Wilde's astute observation about Lord Webb's concealed Irish accent suddenly made sense. The faux aristocrat was, in reality, Seamus Kragan, the son of the Irish housekeeper. Packed off to live with relatives in Ireland, he had returned in disguise after years of banishment. But what could he hope to accomplish by murdering Lady Thraxton? What was his motive? But then Conan Doyle remembered what Podmore had spoken of: Hope Thraxton was the only surviving heir to the Thraxton fortune. If she died, the fortune would pass to a recipient chosen by the executor: Mrs. Kragan.

"Here what's your game? You've wrecked me pub!" It was the landlord. He bellied around the bar, clutching a stout wooden rod in his large hand, his ruddy face like a clenched fist.

"I see you're a man who served in her majesty's navy," Conan Doyle quickly observed.

The words stopped the large man in his tracks. "What? How'd ya know that?"

"By the belaying pin in your hand, which you undoubtedly took as a souvenir of your service, and by the anchor tattoo on your forearm, which I'd warrant you had done in a Chinese opium den in Portsmouth upon your return from a voyage to the West Indies."

The landlord's mouth sagged open. And then recognition

flooded his eyes. "I knows who you are now. I reckon I seen your picture in *The Strand Magazine*."

Despite himself, Conan Doyle couldn't help but preen.

"You're that Sherlock Holmes fellow, what solves all them crimes."

Though it pained him not to correct the landlord, circumstances obliged Conan Doyle to go along with the charade. "Yes, you are quite correct, I . . . I am . . . Sherlock Holmes. And I need you to hold these dangerous felons until the local constabulary can be summoned."

"You can rely on me, Mister Holmes," the landlord said, slapping the belaying pin into his open palm. "I'll make sure these bastards don't go nowhere."

Conan Doyle strode out of the Sailor's Return a few minutes later, his cricket bat once again strapped to his suitcase. He knew young Frank would not return for hours and time was against him. He was desperate to find a ride . . . and then he saw the black horse still grazing peacefully on the village green and instantly knew what means of transport he would be using to return to Thraxton Hall.

THE DEATH OF A GREAT PSYCHIC

Bedraggled peacocks parading in the gathering twilight screamed in a mixture of terror and outrage as the black hearse thundered up to the phoenix steps of Thraxton Hall, wheels churning gravel. Dusk was quickly falling. Toby the gardener was wheeling a barrow of shovels and rakes toward the potting sheds, cleaning up at the end of a day's labor. Seeing the hearse, he dropped the barrow handles and rushed forward to catch the reins tossed to him as Conan Doyle jumped down from the driver's seat.

"Hide the hearse around the back of the house," he said. "Somewhere out of sight."

"We thought you wuz on a train for London by now, sir."

"There has been a change of plans."

"How did you hear, sir?"

Conan Doyle's feet were already ringing up the stone steps, his suitcase swinging at his side, when Toby's words froze him on the spot.

"Hear what?"

"Your friend. He's near death. I doubt he's gonna last the night."

Conan Doyle's mouth bittered with the taste of copper pennies. If something had happened to Oscar, he would never forgive himself. Dreading the answer, he forced himself to ask: "Who is near death?"

Toby tugged at his cap. "The Yank: Mister Daniel Dunglas Hume."

Conan Doyle relaxed a little, thanking the stars it was not Oscar, but the news still perturbed him. "Has a doctor been sent for?"

Toby shook his head. "Mr. Hume said it was too late for what ailed him. He did predict you would return. He's asked to see you afore he passes."

* * *

Conan Doyle burst into Daniel Dunglas Hume's bedroom to find the American slumped upon his bed, his head floating on a cloud of pillows.

"I just received the news," Conan Doyle said.

The American's ravaged gaze followed Conan Doyle's journey across the room to his bedside. Hume had the look of a creature fished from the bottom of the sea, and when he spoke, the words came out in an underwater gurgle. "I am on the final journey, sir." He had to pause to suck in a labored breath before he could continue. "The Genie is just about used up."

Hume's face was veiled in shadow. Conan Doyle slid the lamp forward on the bedside table, but to his puzzlement, the shadow remained.

"It is death," Hume explained. "A shadow no amount of light can chase away. I have kept it at arm's length for many years. But I can restrain it no longer."

Conan Doyle nodded sadly as he checked the pulse at Hume's throat and then pressed an ear to his chest, listening. The American's congested lungs made a sound like the ocean sucking in and out of a sea cave. When Conan Doyle stood upright, his expression was grave.

Hume smiled up at him, which had a rather ghastly effect. He had lost his good looks and seemed to have aged forty years. His features were sunken, the cheeks gaunt, the eyes peering out from dark hollows like death-row prisoners skulking behind bars. "I'm dying, Doctor Doyle. I can no longer hold back the shadowy tide."

Conan Doyle nodded.

"So at least I'm no longer a suspect?"

Conan Doyle smiled gently. "No. You were only briefly a suspect."

"Believe in Fate, Mister Doyle. It controls our destinies, despite our best efforts to elude its influence. Years ago, I foolishly used my powers to foresee my own death. The knowledge was a poison kiss to my soul. I knew I was fated to die here, in this place. I tried to avoid it. I traveled around the world. I have freely spent the money of the rich. I used my powers like a fool. But I was too busy running from death to live the life I had. Sadly, in the final throes, it ends for me as it ends for all men . . . in a deathbed."

Conan Doyle contemplated the American's words for several moments before speaking. "You are a man whose vision penetrates the veil," he said quietly. "Is there nothing we can do to prevent the murder of Hope Thraxton?"

Daniel Dunglas Hume was about to speak, when his voice cracked and a wicked coughing spasm shook his frame until it seemed it would tear him apart. Conan Doyle held him up with a hand beneath his shoulders as Hume hacked and gagged into the lace handkerchief clamped to his mouth. The coughing spasm finally petered out, not because Hume had successfully cleared his lungs, but because he was simply too exhausted to continue.

"Fate is a slippery path," Hume gurgled. "We can seek to hide from it. We can dodge it momentarily, but we cannot escape its grasp. For a moment it seemed as though you would not be here for the final seance, but something has drawn you back. Fate is difficult to thwart . . . although . . ." He flashed a final, memento-mori smile.

". . . although I have learned that seeing the future and truly understanding what the vision means are not always the same thing."

Conan Doyle leaned over Hume and laid a hand on his clammy
brow. "If you need anything to make you comfortable . . . please
summon me."

He went to turn away, but Hume seized his wrist with a bruis-
ing grip surprisingly powerful for a man lingering on the verge of
death. "Before I kick loose of this earth, I will summon the final
glimmerings of everything I am to assist you. I may not be there
with you in body, but if I can hold back the hand of death a while
longer, trust that I shall endeavor to be there in spirit." His grip
slackened. The hand fell limp. His eyes grew heavy-lidded. Exhaus-
tion dimmed his face. "But now I have a long way to go, and must
prepare myself for the journey."

CHAPTER 27

THE FINAL SÉANCE

Once again the darkened room and the circle of sitters, each holding the hand of a neighbor. A restless sense of unease gripped the members of the Society for Psychical Research. Hope Thraxton lowered her head and said in a shaky voice, "Let the light be dimmed so that the spirits might draw near."

Mister Greaves turned down the gaslight and the room submerged in twilight—the solitary candle flickering in the center of the table the only illumination.

Everyone jumped at a sharp knock. The door flung open, framing a male silhouette in the doorway. Mister Greaves fumbled to reignite the gas jet, and the amber light revealed the features of Arthur Conan Doyle, his jaw squared, his eyes fierce.

"Doctor Doyle!" Sidgwick blurted in surprise.

"Arthur?" Wilde rose from his seat, his eyes questioning and astonished. "You've returned. Whatever happened?"

Conan Doyle held up a hand to quiet them. "Please, everyone, be seated. I journeyed all the way to Slattenmere only to find that the telegram I received was nothing more than a sick and malicious prank." He eyed the man who had been masquerading as Lord Webb with disdain. "Obviously the work of a degenerate mind."

The dapper figure met his gaze coolly. Conan Doyle looked to Lady Thraxton, whose face flooded with relief. "And so I have hurried back and appear to be just in time."

The table had been arranged for only eight sitters. The Scottish doctor walked over to grab the spare chair—the chair that, during the first séance, Mariah Thraxton had identified as "Death's chair." He dragged it to a place next to the faux lord, and the other sitters moved to make space for him.

Wilde was seated on Lady Thraxton's right hand. He threw a questioning glance at Conan Doyle, who indicated Lord Webb with a slight jerk of his head. Wilde nodded that he understood.

Conan Doyle had no exact plan, but determined that he would wait for the false lord—Seamus Kragan—to make his move, and then pounce.

Hope Thraxton once again dropped her head and whispered, "Let the gaslight be lowered so that the spirits might draw near."

The room dimmed to darkness and Mister Greaves quietly slipped out. They heard the key turn in the lock and the rasp of tumblers snapping shut, locking them in.

"Remember," Sidgwick chided, "for the safety of Lady Thraxton, let no one break the circle."

"One need not have the mind of a *Sherlock Holmes* to remember that," Lord Webb remarked.

Conan Doyle eyed the imposter sitting next to him. In the dim light, Seamus Kragan returned the cold stare, the dark brown eyes glinting with flecks of candlelight. It was an odd thing to say, and Conan Doyle assumed it was a thinly veiled jibe against himself. He did not see how, across the séance table, the words "Sherlock Holmes" made Oscar Wilde go rigid, his face turn waxen, and his keen-eyed gaze dissolve into a glassy stare.

Conan Doyle coiled himself, ready to spring.

Hope Thraxton sucked in a deep breath and let it out in a shuddering sigh as she relinquished her body. "Mariah. My friend. My spirit guide. I seek your help. Hear me. I yield my body as a vessel for you to speak."

A cold draft surged through the séance chamber, drowning the pleasant aroma of beeswax beneath the gagging reek of the grave. The candle guttered in the breeze.

Conan Doyle tensed as a shadowy figure at the far side of the table rose from his seat. In the stuttering candlelight he saw to his surprise that it was Oscar Wilde.

And then he glimpsed the service revolver in his hand.

Aimed at Hope Thraxton.

"Oscar, no!" Conan Doyle shouted, surging up from his seat. His thighs slammed into the edge of the table, jostling the candle in its dish so that melted wax sloshed over the burning wick, extinguishing its flame and plunging the room in darkness.

Two deafening gunshots rang out. BOOM! BOOM! Conan Doyle saw Oscar Wilde's blank, impassive face briefly lit by muzzle flashes.

A woman screamed. The men shouted out. In the chaotic darkness, bodies collided. A chair toppled and crashed to the floor with a heavy thud.

"Mr. Greaves!" Sidgwick cried out. "Mister Greaves, unlock the door. We need light. We must have light!"

A key scrabbled in the lock and the door swung open, throwing in a slab of illumination. The members were out of their seats, milling in confusion. Mister Greaves lit the gas jet and warm yellow light washed the shadows from the room.

Beside the toppled chair, Lady Hope Thraxton lay slumped on the rug.

The Scottish author gaped in horrified disbelief. Oscar Wilde stood, staring blankly, the service revolver gripped in his hand, smoke purling from the barrel.

"Oscar!" Conan Doyle blurted. "My God! What?"

For a moment the room fell silent. No one moved. And then Wilde robotically raised the pistol and pressed the muzzle to his temple.

"Oscar! No!"

His finger was tightening on the trigger when Frank Podmore lunged forward, wrenched the gun from his hand, and threw it down on the table. Wilde staggered a moment, as if confused, and then raised his empty hand to his head, pulling the trigger of an imaginary pistol over and over.

"Seize him!" Lord Webb shouted. "The man's a murderer!"

Podmore waved a hand in front of Wilde's fixated face, who did not so much as blink. "Mister Wilde is in a deep trance," he said. "He's been hypnotized"—Podmore threw an accusatory look at Lord Webb—"and I can guess by whom."

Ignoring all else, Conan Doyle dropped to his knees and tended to Hope Thraxton. The front of her black dress bore two scorched bullet holes—without the slightest fleck of blood. His fingers snatched loose several buttons. Inexplicably, the skin of her chest was smooth and untouched. At that moment, she sighed loudly. Her eyelashes fluttered and then her violet eyes opened. "Wha—?" she began to say, but Conan Doyle put two fingers to her lips and bent low, whispering into her ear. "Lie still. This is not over yet."

She closed her eyes, and did not move.

"Is she . . . ?" Eleanor Sidgwick asked, breathlessly.

Conan Doyle rose from the body, his face grave. He fixed Lord Webb with a steely gaze. "I'm afraid, Lady Thraxton is dead . . ." He pointed a finger at Webb and said, ". . . murdered by this man."

Webb laughed at the accusation. "Don't be absurd. We all witnessed what happened. Your friend Wilde is a cold-blooded killer. Caught red-handed. And you blame me?"

Conan Doyle fixed the false lord with a hateful stare. "Mister Podmore is correct. The so-called Lord Webb is a fraud, a music-hall mesmerist. He has used his powers to murder Lady Thraxton by using my friend Oscar as his assassin."

Webb sneered. "What possible motive would I have for such an act?"

"I have discovered that Lord Webb's real name is Seamus Kragan. He is the illegitimate child of a union between the head housekeeper and the late Lord Thraxton. After his first attempt at murdering Lady Thraxton, Seamus was banished to Ireland. He has, no doubt, with the aid of his mother, been planning his return and the theft of the Thraxton inheritance. Lady Thraxton was about to reach her majority and inherit the Thraxton family fortune. The executor is the head housekeeper, Mrs. Kragan. If there are no surviving heirs—even though he is illegitimate—Seamus Kragan stands to inherit the family fortune and the house along with it."

The man that all had previously known as Lord Webb merely snickered, a bemused smile on his face. "That is quite the most outlandish poppycock I have ever heard. I believe, Mister Doyle, that your puerile detective scribblings have deprived you of the ability to discern fact from fiction." He removed the pince-nez, set them down on the table, and smiled handsomely. "You are delusional. I am not who you claim me to be, nor do I have anything to gain by murder."

Frank Podmore stood gazing into Oscar Wilde's blank, unseeing eyes. He snapped his fingers in front of Wilde's face and said in a commanding voice, "Mister Wilde, at the count of three, you shall awaken. One . . . two . . . three. Awaken!"

Wilde did not flinch. Podmore took a step back, perplexed.

"The bumblings of an amateur," Lord Webb murmured, grinning.

Podmore heard the comment and turned his attention back to Wilde. Struck by a sudden inspiration, he clapped his hands in Wilde's face and barked the word: "*Watson!*"

Wilde started, blinking furiously, looking around in puzzlement. "Where am I?" He seemed to notice Conan Doyle for the first time. "Arthur, you have returned! What's happening?" And then the realization struck him. "Ah, it's happened again, hasn't it? I've been hypnotized." He noticed the others' stares. "I feel as though I've awakened from a particularly nasty dream. I hope I haven't done anything untoward. Will we all laugh about this episode in the morning?"

"What happened to you, Oscar?" Conan Doyle demanded. "What is the last thing you remember?"

Wilde looked around dazedly at the scene of mayhem—the shocked faces of the SPR members, the toppled chairs, the inert form of Hope Thraxton—quite incapable of taking it all in. "I was walking past the music room when Lord Webb invited me in. We smoked a cigarette together. Or at least, that's the last thing I remember—"

All eyes turned to look at the dapper man in the handsome suit. When it became clear he had been unmasked, Seamus Kragan lunged forward and snatched up the pistol on the table. The face of the prissy English aristocrat tightened and grew vulpine as he abandoned the pretense. "It seems Fate is on my side, after all," he said in a broad Irish accent. He pointed the revolver at Conan Doyle's chest. "Shot with your own pistol, how ironic." He unleashed a sick laugh.

Conan Doyle stepped forward until the muzzle of the pistol pressed hard into his chest, fearlessly protecting the others with his body.

"Very gallant, Doctor Doyle. Are you so eager to die?"

"You have used two bullets already. I'll take the third. That leaves you only four bullets left and there are many of us."

"Three shots are all I need: One for you, one for Oscar Fingal

O'Flahertie Wilde, and one for the irritating little weasel, Podmore! I'll reserve one bullet for my escape. I doubt if anyone else will be so anxious to receive it." The hammer of the revolver rose as his finger tightened on the trigger.

He could not possibly miss.

Mister Greaves surged forward and blindly wrapped his arms around Kragan, crashing them both into the wall. The two struggled briefly, and then the younger man wrenched an arm free and viciously pistol-whipped the old retainer. It was a wicked blow, and the heavy revolver opened a deep gash in the butler's scalp. He let out a moan and slumped to the floor.

"Fools!" Seamus Kragan bellowed as he backed away, brandishing the gun. "I am always one step ahead of you." He was backing toward the door when:

BOOM!

Blood sprayed the wall. Seamus screamed and grabbed his arm. His knees buckled and he barely managed to stay on his feet. But as he staggered out the door, he raised the Webley and fired a wild parting shot into the room.

BOOM!

And vanished.

Conan Doyle looked around; The Count had remained seated during the whole exchange, which allowed him to quietly draw his weapon, screened from view by the table. Now he rose from his chair, the pistol gripped in his gloved hand, a tendril of silver smoke curling up from the muzzle.

"Good shooting, Count!" Wilde said, clapping a hand on his shoulder.

Luckily, Seamus's wild shot harmlessly struck the edge of the séance table.

"We must go after him!" Sir William Crookes urged.

"No!" Henry Sidgwick yelled. "It's far too dangerous."

"What about poor Lady Thraxton?" Eleanor Sidgwick added. "Whatever are we to do—?"

A gasp of deep shock rippled through the room as Conan Doyle dropped to his knees and helped Hope Thraxton sit up. "She lives," he announced. "Both shots did not so much as break the skin!"

"It's a miracle!"

"It's the spirits," Eleanor Sidgwick insisted. "The spirits have protected her."

Hope suddenly noticed the figure lying slumped on the floor. "Oh, Mister Greaves!" She reached over and gently pulled Mister Greaves' head into her lap. The scalp wound was deep. Blood ran down the side of his face and puddled on the rug.

"I'm sorry, milady," he said in a faltering voice, "but I was unable to stop the bounder. I blame myself. I should have recognized Seamus—even without my sight—I should've!"

A long, shuddering groan tore from Mister Greaves' lips. Hope Thraxton looked up at Conan Doyle with an expression of utter despair. "Please save him," she said, her voice torn to rags, "I fear he is dying."

Conan Doyle nodded and turned to his friend. "Your silk scarf, please, Oscar." Wilde handed it over, and Conan Doyle tightly bandaged the old butler's head. "It will slow the bleeding." But then he fixed her with a look that confirmed her worse fears. Her eyes pooled and she looked down, biting her lip.

"I fired twice?" Wilde asked in a shattered voice. "How did the Lady survive?"

"The gun was obviously loaded with blanks," Podmore said.

"No," Conan Doyle countered. "I loaded it myself. There are two bullet holes in Lady Thraxton's dress, but not a mark upon her skin. It is as if the bullets vanished in midair." He looked around at the others, equally mystified.

"Gentlemen," Sir William Crookes interrupted, "we have a murderer running loose in the house. We must form a hunting party and run the blaggard to ground."

"No," Conan Doyle said, taking command. "He is still armed and most of us are not." He glanced at Wilde. "Oscar and I will go after him."

"Might I not go, too?" It was the Count. "I am military trained and, as you saw, an excellent shot."

"No, Count," Conan Doyle argued. "You have a pistol. We need you to stay here and protect the others."

Enigmatic as ever, the figure behind the white mask said nothing for several moments, but finally acquiesced with a click of his heels and a bow of his head.

"Come along, Oscar," Conan Doyle said, "the game is afoot."

"Ugh!" Wilde gasped, rolling his eyes. "I feared you were going to say that."

* * *

"The bullet has severed a major artery," Conan Doyle noted as the two men followed a spatter of crimson drops along the hallway. "He won't get very far."

Conan Doyle had expected Seamus Kragan to bolt out the front doors, but the blood trail weaved across the marble tiles of the entrance hall and plunged into the portrait gallery. The two friends paused. "He's gone into the west wing—a place that is perfect for ambushes."

"At the risk of damaging morale, Arthur, I have to question your strategy. He has the gun and we do not. Shouldn't we be running away from him?"

"He's bleeding out. And a wounded animal is always the most dangerous. We need to know where he is."

The two men dashed through the portrait gallery. Conan Doyle flung open the heavy double doors and they eased cautiously into the ballroom, senses alert, eyes scanning.

"He's moved on," Conan Doyle said. The two crossed the ruined ballroom, following the steady drip of blood.

"Where's he going?" Wilde asked in a whisper.

"He grew up in this house and knows it intimately. I'm sure he's got an escape route planned."

They emerged through the doors at the far end of the ballroom into the entropic ruin of the west wing. Both men froze on the spot, listening. The light outside was fading fast and the rooms and hallways seethed with a conspiracy of shadows.

"This is dangerous," Conan Doyle whispered. "He could be lying in wait for us."

"You're right as always, Arthur. Let us go back. I feel a headache coming on."

They heard the crash of a slamming door.

"That's him," Conan Doyle said. "Not far ahead."

The two men crept along the hallway as quietly as possible, but stealth was impossible with a blizzard of fallen plaster crunching underfoot.

And then they saw her: the luminous figure of a young girl in a blue dress.

"What on earth?" Wilde gasped.

The blue girl stared at them and pointed a finger at a closed door. Her image dimmed and faded from view.

Wilde looked at his friend. "Tell me you saw the same thing?"

"I've seen her before," Conan Doyle said, his voice a ragged whisper. "She's giving us a sign. Seamus has gone down to the crypt."

* * *

The other members of the Society for Psychical Research kept a respectful distance as Lady Thraxton knelt upon the rug, cradling Mister Greaves' head in her lap.

"Please, your Ladyship," the old man croaked. "I'm getting blood all over your fine dress."

"Shush," she said. "Mister Greaves, you have looked after me all my life. Now I must look after you."

"I'm sorry I let him get away, ma'am. I shoulda known it was young Seamus come back. That boy always had the devil in him."

"Hush," she said, stroking his wild mane of gray hair, now clotting with blood from the gaping wound.

The Count took a discreet step back from the group. And then another.

"I reckon you'll be needing a new butler soon," Mister Greaves said. A melancholy smile creased his lined face.

Lady Thraxton choked out a loud sob. "Please don't leave me, Mister Greaves. What ever will I do without you?"

The Count took a step to his left. The open doorway was one stride away.

The butler's glaucous eyes widened. "I feel young again. I feel young. And there's my Annie. My wife. My lovely Annie."

"He's crossing over," Eleanor Sidgwick said in a choked voice.

"My lovely girl. I'm young again. I'm young again. I'm young . . ." The smile froze and faded as the last breath slipped from his lungs.

"Oh, Mister Greaves!" Lady Thraxton cried, hugging his neck as she began a keening wail.

The Count used the distraction to step from the room. As he strode rapidly down the hallway toward the west wing, he drew the pistol from its leather holster.

CHAPTER 28

THE BLACK LAKE

They stumbled from the bottom of the spiral stairs into the crypt. Wilde bowled into Conan Doyle and the two men nearly fell.

"Ugh," Wilde complained. "First I am covered in dust, flailed alive with cobwebs, and now I must endure the stench of corruption. A crypt indeed? What a ghastly tradition. When I die I shall have them bury me in a conservatory of sweet-smelling flowers. My adoring public will water them with their tears."

"Quiet!" Conan Doyle urged.

The two men scanned the shadows, eyes straining to pierce the darkness, nerves stretched taut. From somewhere, far off, they heard the crash of a coffin lid being ripped off and flung to the ground. Conan Doyle nodded the direction. He snatched up the lamp, and the two men crept in the direction of the sound. As they drew near, they saw a shadowy form crouched over an open coffin.

Seamus Kragan.

A lamp turned low had been set atop a nearby coffin. Seamus had tucked his wounded arm into his waistcoat and was reaching into the coffin with his good arm, rummaging for something.

"This must end now, Seamus," Conan Doyle called. "Give yourself up."

Seamus leapt up and wheeled around, revolver leveled. He had something tucked under his injured arm—the scrying mirror.

"No," Seamus called. "Not after all these years. Not when I'm so close."

"Close to what? Ruin?"

"I have the mirror. Mariah will help me."

"Mariah?"

Seamus Kragan stood crookedly, listing to one side. "Hope was not the only one that Mariah spoke to." He choked out a humorless laugh. "She also spoke to me. It was she who told me to lock Hope in the mirror room. I was nothing but a servant's child. Mariah promised that if I killed the last remaining heir of Thraxton her curse would be fulfilled. She would be restored, and I would rule at her side as Lord of Thraxton Manor."

"Lord of the Manor?" Wilde said. "Shared with a dead harpy?"

"If I might drink from crystal goblets and dine on golden plates, I care not whether my bride is an angel from heaven or a demon from hell."

Conan Doyle stepped forward into the light. "It's too late for that, Seamus. You're bleeding to death. I am a doctor. I can still save you."

He scowled at the offer. "Save me for what? For the gallows?"

Seamus whipped up the pistol and squeezed off a shot that ricocheted off the stone flags in front of them. Stone chips sprayed, peppering their faces.

Seamus Kragan turned and ran, deeper into the crypt.

"Come on, Oscar," Conan Doyle urged. "He's bleeding out. In shock. Confused. He won't be on his feet much longer. And the crypt has changed since he was a boy. He doesn't realize he's running toward a dead end."

The two men hurried along, following the bobbing glow of Seamus Kragan's lamp in the distance, their pounding footsteps ringing against the stone walls, kicking aside bones as they descended into the oldest and darkest recesses of the crypt. Finally they came upon Seamus standing at the edge of the black lake, staring into its heaving surface.

"So, I'm cornered," he said in a choked voice. "Like a rat."

"Surrender peacefully," Conan Doyle said in a gentle voice. "You may yet escape the gallows."

Seamus Kragan turned and it soon became obvious he was laughing, not sobbing. He held the revolver loosely at his side and now he raised it and aimed at the two friends. "I won't be giving myself up to the likes of you two fools. I'm gonna be the Lord of the Manor. It is my Fate. Mariah has looked into the future."

"You're deluded, Seamus. You won't be on your feet much—"

"No! You're *deluded, Mister Conan clever Doyle!*" Seamus's bellowing voice echoed on for seconds. A tremor rippled through his body—shock setting in. "I was twenty-two when I left Ireland and returned to London—a young man with no money, no education, and no trade. I fell in with a traveling hypnotist and became his assistant. He thought I was nothing more than another dumb Mick—a dogsbody. But I was young and crafty and I watched. Soon I learned his ways, stole his act, and went my own way. From there it was an easy move to spiritualism and false séances. The grieving are gullible victims, eager to surrender their life's savings to speak one last word with the dead. To be comforted. To believe that life doesn't end at the cemetery gate." He cackled a laugh and Conan Doyle recognized who had struck him from behind and tossed him into Mariah Thraxton's coffin.

"You are everything despicable," Wilde said.

Seamus spat at Wilde's feet. "We don't all come from fine, high-born families like you, Mister Wilde. We may both hail from Dublin, but I grew up south of the Liffey, as you so correctly guessed. And aren't we both pretending to be something we're not? So don't you judge me!"

The black lake at Seamus's back gurgled and heaved, as if growing agitated.

"So I made a good living as a medium. And then one day, as I pretended to summon my spirit guide, damned if Mariah Thraxton didn't answer the call. She reminded me of our talks in the mirror maze and promised that I would rule at her side as the Lord of Thraxton Hall. First I had to search Gallow's Hill, find her coffin, exhume it, and release the bands binding her. Once I had removed the last living heir of Thraxton, Mariah's curse would be fulfilled and she could return in physical form, as a revenant."

Seamus released a laugh fraying at the edges into hysteria. The muzzle of the revolver lowered a half foot as his arm drooped beneath its weight. He was weakening by the moment, growing wobbly on his feet.

Conan Doyle shot a quick sideways glance at Wilde that asked: *Should we rush him?* But Wilde urged caution with a slight shake of his head.

"But I needed to kill Hope Thraxton in a very public way that would not cast suspicion on myself—or my mother. And then I chanced to read a story in *The Strand Magazine*. A story about a brilliant consulting detective named Sherlock Holmes. The author was a clever man of great cunning. And so I thought—who better to serve as murderer? How ironic! Obviously, I was disappointed when you proved a poor subject for hypnosis. But then Fate intervened again. You not only brought the murder weapon, but also conveniently supplied the murderer—your friend Oscar Wilde, a most suggestible subject. How can a jury convict me of murder? It was your friend who pulled the trigger. Two bullets in the chest at point-blank range. Before a roomful of witnesses."

"And yet she lives," Conan Doyle said calmly.

Seamus Kragan flinched as if struck across the face, but then cold cynicism oozed back into his features. "You lie. I saw two bullet holes, still smoking—"

"Which burned the outer fabric of her dress, but did not so much as break the skin."

"That's impossible!"

"I would agree. Impossible . . . unless some supernatural force intervened."

Seamus's eyes lost focus, grew wildly distracted. "Mariah?" The name grunted out of him as if driven by a punch in the guts.

"She betrayed you, Seamus. Lied to you. Just as she lied to Hope. She is a revenant, a thing animated by wickedness and malice to deceive and do harm to the living. When you dug up her coffin and released the copper bands binding her, you sealed your own Fate."

Behind Seamus, the black lake retreated, sucking back into itself, and then released an eructation of gas that sneezed a fine mist of black slime high into the air, spattering the clothes and faces of the three men.

A shaky laugh tore from Seamus's lips. "Another fiction, Doctor Doyle? Another story? Too late, I'm afraid." He wiped the bituminous spray from his face with the back of his gun hand. "I have three bullets left. And there are only two of you." He raised the revolver and aimed at Conan Doyle with a wildly tremoring hand. "Mariah's premonition will yet come true."

Just then the black lake belched up a huge bubble of gas and heaved forward, a tarry black wave surging around Seamus Kragan's feet. He staggered, fighting to keep his balance, and then his feet shot out from under him. The revolver slipped from his grip and clattered to the ground, He lost hold of the scrying mirror, which hit the stone floor and rolled away. Arms windmilling, Seamus toppled backward into the black lake, slapping the surface with a splash. He plunged beneath the surface for a dozen seconds and then suddenly surged upward again, spitting and choking, his arms trailing glutinous tendrils of black slime. Around him the treacly waters heaved and roiled—the queasy stomach of a giant stone beast vomiting up an indigestible meal.

Conan Doyle and Wilde rushed to the edge, but Seamus was beyond their reach and they could do nothing but watch as he flailed and struggled before the lake sucked him under, headfirst. A turmoil of choking bubbles burst upon the surface, Seamus Kragan's feet obscenely kicking the air for a few seconds before the lake sucked him under for a final time.

A diminishing trickle of bubbles broke upon the surface. And then, nothing.

"Good Lord," Conan Doyle said. "That was horrible."

"Yes," Wilde agreed. "Brown boots with white spats. A cad to the end."

* * *

The two friends were trudging back up the sloping floor of the crypt, Oscar Wilde carrying the lamp, the revolver in Conan Doyle's right hand, the scrying mirror clutched in his left hand.

Both men froze at the metallic *ka-chunk* of a shotgun being snapped shut.

When Wilde raised the lamp, the light fell upon the formidable, gray-haired figure of Mrs. Kragan. An extinguished lamp stood at her feet. She cradled the cocked and loaded shotgun under one arm. She had been waiting patiently in the darkness.

"So. My Seamus is dead? You have killed him?"

Conan Doyle and Wilde exchanged a glance. And then Wilde spoke: "We tried to reason with him, but he fell into the lake."

Her eyes gleamed with tears. Her mouth twisted in a broken scowl. "This cursed house has taken everything from me: my youth, my love, my hope, and now my only child."

"And what have you taken from it?" Conan Doyle asked in a voice sucked dry of sympathy. "I believe it was your hand that pushed Lady Thraxton down the stairs to her death."

The matron's eyes flashed with hatred. "She didn't love him. Not like I did. And I bore him a son."

A sudden revelation struck Conan Doyle. "Lady Thraxton was with child at the time, wasn't she?"

Mrs. Kragan's eyes widened, her lips compressed to a furious line.

The tissue of lies and murder was at last teasing apart in Conan Doyle's mind. "And Edmund Thraxton. He didn't disappear on the moors, did he?"

"You . . . you . . . filthy English . . . You've said enough. . . ."

"And you also conspired to murder the true heir, Hope Thraxton," Wilde added. "I have little doubt that you were the true mastermind behind this entire plot, not Seamus."

"They say confession is good for the soul. Here is my confession—both barrels." She hoisted the heavy shotgun and pointed it at the men. "I will burn in hell, but you two will get there before me."

"Oscar! Down!" Conan Doyle shouted. He and Wilde flung themselves to the stony floor as she squeezed the trigger and the first barrel fired with a thunderous roar. The shotgun blast hit an antique coffin and tore the rotten side off. A rain of yellowing bones and leathery corpse flesh pattered down upon their heads.

The kick of the shotgun staggered Mrs. Kragan backward. She regained her balance and strode toward them. Conan Doyle had dropped the service revolver as he hit the ground and it skittered away. As he reached for the gun, Mrs. Kragan's foot pinned it to the flags. He looked up into the twin black maws of a shotgun hovering inches from his upturned face.

She would not miss this time.

"You will join my Seamus in the black lake!" she hissed.

A deafening shot rang out.

Mrs. Kragan's head jerked violently. Her eyes grew wide. A trickle of blood ran from both her nostrils, and soon became a gush. Her eyes dimmed and went vacant. She toppled forward and pancaked facedown on the stone floor. When Conan Doyle and Wilde clambered to their feet, they saw that the back of her head had been blown away.

Their ears still ringing from the gunshot, the two friends watched as a shadowy figure glided toward them. As the lamplight fell upon it, the figure gained color and substance, but lacked a human face.

Or rather, it possessed a face concealed behind a mask.

THE SHADOW OF DEATH

The Count strode into view, his pistol raised. Smoke tendriled from the muzzle.

Conan Doyle felt a stab of fear. He had never trusted the Count from the beginning and had no doubt that he and Oscar would be shot next. But then the Count slid his pistol back into its shiny leather holster and cinched the closing strap. He clicked his heels and threw them a curt bow.

"I take it ze pretend Lord Webb. He iz dead?"

Wilde rushed forward and threw his arms around the Count in a bear hug. "Well done, Count. You have saved us once again!"

Conan Doyle hesitated and then stepped forward and shook the Count's hand. "Yes, thank you. We are twice-over in your debt, sir."

The mask looked from one to the other. "It eeze over zen?"

"Yes, thank goodness," Wilde said. He turned to Conan Doyle. "It is over, isn't it Arthur—?" But Conan Doyle had returned to the edge of the black lake. He stooped and picked up the scrying mirror and stood gazing into its depths. For a moment, he thought he saw his own muted reflection. When he returned to join the others, his face was grave.

"I regret to say: No, I believe the danger is far from over."

* * *

Conan Doyle knocked quietly at Daniel Dunglas Hume's door. "It is Doctor Doyle," he called out. He listened for a moment and heard no reply. When he entered the room, the Yankee psychic was lying atop his bed, fully dressed, looking straight at him.

"I thought I'd let you know what transpired," Conan Doyle said.

Hume did not say anything, nor did he move the slightest, and then Conan Doyle noticed the glassy stare and the handkerchief clutched in one hand, stained a deep vibrant red. A rope of bloody saliva dangled from the corner of his mouth. Conan Doyle moved to the bedside and felt for a pulse in Hume's throat. Nothing. His skin was gelid and plastic to the touch. The Scottish doctor placed a hand on Hume's face and gently closed his eyes.

Wilde stepped in through the open door and witnessed the tableau. "What? Is he—?"

Conan Doyle nodded sadly. "He has passed."

"How long?"

"An hour, maybe longer."

Although not as tall as Conan Doyle, in life Daniel Dunglas Hume had been a physically imposing presence, filled with gravitas. Now, heavy with the inertia of death, he seemed like a stone colossus toppled by an earthquake.

Wilde joined Conan Doyle at the bedside and laid a hand on his friend's shoulder. "He was truly a marvel."

"Yes."

Wilde sniffed the air and made a face. "What *is* that strange smell? Like something burning?"

Conan Doyle tilted his head to one side, sniffing. Suddenly his eyes widened in recognition. "Cordite."

"Ahhhhh, cordite," Wilde repeated, then threw a baffled look at Conan Doyle. "What on earth is cordite?"

"Gunpowder, of the kind used in bullets." On a sudden impulse, Conan Doyle reached down and lifted Hume's arm. The cold hand was closed about something and rigor was beginning to set in. Conan Doyle had to prise open the tight fist. There, sitting in Hume's palm, were the lead slugs from two bullets. Conan Doyle and Wilde exchanged an astonished look.

"Two bullets," Wilde gasped. "So that's where the shots went!"

"His final miracle was to save Lady Thraxton's life. He truly was the greatest psychic of all time."

CHAPTER 30

A REFLECTION NEVER DIES

I'm afraid Mister Greaves has passed," Henry Sidgwick said.

"How is Lady Thraxton?" Wilde asked.

"Understandably traumatized. She is resting in her rooms. My wife Eleanor is at her bedside." Sidgwick's bloodshot eyes turned to Conan Doyle. "Perhaps you would be kind enough to look in on her, Doctor Doyle."

"Yes. I would be most happy to do so."

When he entered Lady Thraxton's rooms, the young medium was lying atop her bed, still dressed in her black séance robes. Eleanor Sidgwick sat in a chair pulled close to the bedside, holding the younger woman's hand.

Conan Doyle strode over to the bed and looked down on her.

Her eyes roved his face questioningly.

"What has become of Seamus?" she asked in a ruined voice.

Conan Doyle rocked on his feet, reluctant to add more distress to the young woman. "He has come to justice . . . by his own actions."

She thought a moment and then asked, "And Mrs. Kragan?"

Conan Doyle cleared his throat. "I'm afraid she, too, has come to grief."

Hope Thraxton covered her mouth with a hand, eyes welling with tears.

She turned her head, and lay staring in distracted silence at the far wall.

Conan Doyle paused a moment, looking down at that lovely face, his eyes tracing the slender line of her jaw to the crescent-moon-shaped birthmark at the corner of her full lips. Then he tore his gaze away, breathed a sigh, and turned to leave. As he walked to the door, the portrait of the young girl in the blue dress once again captured his eye. As he examined it at close range, his spine stiffened. He drew out a fountain pen from the inside pocket of his jacket and looked about the desk for a piece of writing paper. He flipped open a red leather stationery box. It held a neat stack of the distinctive notepaper that bore the phoenix watermark. He took a sheet and sketched the crescent moon birthmark on it:

Then he returned to the bedside again, and briefly examined Hope's face, comparing it to his sketch. She bore the identical birthmark. He left the lady's chambers a moment later, his face calm and composed, while in his brain, a lightning storm raged.

* * *

Ah, there you are, Arthur."

Wilde strode across the polished marble of the entrance hall to where Conan Doyle was staring up at the portrait of Mariah Thraxton. "Arthur," he repeated, touching his friend's elbow, "are you quite well?"

Conan Doyle turned a grave face to his friend. "When first

we arrived at Thraxton Hall, I was immediately struck by this portrait."

"I concede that it is well executed. Especially for its time."

"More than that: it has a strange quality to it, almost as if it were alive. When I scrutinized it a second time, in the company of Madame Zhozhovsky, she pointed out a detail that now seems strangely anomalous."

"Strange? In what way?"

"Look closely at the birthmark on Mariah's Thraxton's cheek. It is in the shape of a crescent moon. The scrying mirror she holds in her hand reflects her face, and the crescent moon birthmark. Do you see that?"

Wilde's brown eyes narrowed as he scoured the portrait. "Yes, yes I believe I see what you're referring to."

"How much do you remember from your geometry lessons?"

"I told you I was never much for mathematics."

"Axes of symmetry?"

Frown lines wrinkled Wilde's brow. "The term vaguely rings a bell. I'm sorry if I'm being a bit lead-witted, Arthur, but what exactly does all this mean?"

"It means I now understand why Lord Edmund Thraxton feared mirrors."

Conan Doyle turned abruptly on his heel and set off toward the parlor. "Come, Oscar."

Wilde hurried to catch up and fell in step. "Where are we going?"

"To arm ourselves with something capable of breaking glass."

Wilde grabbed his friend's sleeve and snatched him to a halt. "I don't understand. Whatever for?"

Conan Doyle's face clouded over with intent. "We must find every last mirror in the house . . . and destroy it."

* * *

A few minutes later, Arthur Conan Doyle and Oscar Wilde stepped inside the mirror maze, both armed with brass pokers. Faced with a multiplicity of reflections, it was hard not to flinch at a sudden movement. The reflected glow of their lamps, bounced from mirror to mirror, transformed the room into a vault of light.

Wilde said, "Now what?"

Conan Doyle pulled a piece of notepaper from his pocket and unfolded it. He held it up to show Wilde. "This is a sketch of Lady Thraxton's birthmark. It is in the shape of a crescent moon. Notice that the 'horns' of the moon are pointing to the left, indicating a waxing moon."

He turned to face the large cheval mirror and held up the note before it. "Now look at the sketch reflected in the mirror."

Wilde's eyes flickered over the image in the glass. At first he seemed nonplussed, but then a spark flashed in his eyes and his full mouth tightened. "In the mirror, the image is reversed: the waning moon becomes a waxing moon!"

"When Mariah Thraxton lay dying, shot twice by her husband, she called for a servant to fetch her the scrying mirror. It captured her reflection and, as Madame Zhozhovsky remarked: *a reflection never dies.*"

"Which explains Lord Thraxton's abhorrence of mirrors?"

"The birthmark is hereditary; all the Thraxton women have it. Strangely, in the entrance hall portrait, the birthmark on Mariah's face is of a waning crescent moon, while the image reflected in the scrying mirror is of a waxing crescent moon."

"That's odd."

"More than odd, unnatural. When I examined the portrait closer, I realized that the entire thing is mirror-reversed. Something happened to that portrait when Mariah died. Transformed it. I believe that, through her dark magic, Mariah has endured as a spectral entity, moving from mirror to mirror."

"That is quite fantastical."

"Yes, and that is why we must destroy every last mirror in the house."

"Oh, dear! Must we? Smashing a mirror brings seven years bad luck."

"I'm afraid we have many more than one to break."

"I shall regret this," Wilde said. "I know I shall." He backed off several paces and nodded to the large cheval mirror. "You're the luckiest, old fellow. You go first."

Conan Doyle raised the brass poker and swung it full force into the cheval mirror, shattering it into jagged daggers. The two of them moved about the room swinging left and right, so that the crash of glass was deafening.

"Seven years bad luck," Wilde moaned as he smashed a mirror. "Fourteen years bad luck," he added as Conan Doyle smashed another. Wilde smashed a third. "Twenty-one years bad luck." The orgy of smashing continued until their feet slipped and skidded on ankle-deep shards of broken glass. Suddenly Wilde cried out, "Stop! Stop!"

Conan Doyle froze, his arm raised. "What is it, Oscar?"

"My mathematics cannot keep up. I make it two hundred and forty-five years of bad luck. Surely we can stop now?"

Conan Doyle scanned the room. Not a single mirror remained intact, save for one, which he now reached into the hip pocket of his tweed jacket and drew out: the scrying mirror. For a moment, he studied the obsidian disk, seeing his own inverted reflection bowled in its concave surface. As he gazed, the glass fogged with swirling clouds that coalesced into an image—the scowling face of Mariah Thraxton. He dropped the mirror as if it were red hot, raised the poker above his head, and brought it crashing down into the middle of the glass: *Wa-chunk*. Mariah's image vanished as the onyx surface starred over in a spiderweb of opaque white cracks— an eye for gazing through time forever blinded. Then he scattered its fragments across the room with a vicious kick.

"Two hundred and fifty-one years bad luck," Wilde moaned. "I may never leave the house again."

"I'm afraid we're not done," Conan Doyle said.

"Good Lord, no!" Wilde moaned, wiping his sweating brow with a lace handkerchief. "Surely not a single mirror can remain in this wretched house!"

"Not a mirror, but one remaining image of Mariah Thraxton: the portrait in the entrance hall. I believe it holds a strange power. And as long as it exists, I fear the house will forever be under her curse."

CHAPTER 31

A STEP INTO THE LIGHT

Come along," Conan Doyle coaxed. "You'll be quite all right, I promise."

He and Wilde stood on either side of the phoenix steps that climbed to the front doors of Thraxton Hall. It was early on a gray morning. Dawn had yet to break. The rest of the SPR members stood assembled at the base of the steps. All attention was fixed on the shadowy threshold, where Lady Hope Thraxton lingered.

"I-I'm frightened," she said in a tremorous voice.

Conan Doyle climbed a step toward her and held out his hand encouragingly. "Take my hand. The sun has yet to rise. I promise as a doctor that you will suffer no ill effects from the light."

Several of the waiting Society members now called out encouragement. Agnes the maid was standing behind her mistress, hands pressed to her mouth, tears shining in her eyes. Hope Thraxton took a tentative step over the threshold and Conan Doyle guided her down to the next. A ripple of applause greeted her.

Hope shielded her eyes with one hand as she peered around uncertainly. "The world is so bright."

"Yes," Conan Doyle agreed. "And you make it brighter still."

"And you have the rest of your life to explore it," Wilde added.

Taking both their hands she stepped down until she stood between the two friends. "I can never thank you enough. You have both done so much."

"There is one task that remains to be done your ladyship. A task that only you can perform." Conan Doyle indicated the center of the circular drive where the gardener had stacked a bundle of branches and wooden faggots: a bonfire waiting to be lit. The three descended the steps to the fire. Something tall was set in the middle of the kindling, draped with a tarpaulin. Conan Doyle snatched it away, revealing the portrait of Lady Mariah that had hung in the entrance hall.

Conan Doyle beckoned forward Toby, the gardener, who handed him a lit taper. He, in turn, placed it in the hand of Hope Thraxton. She looked at the taper and then at the portrait, her wide violet eyes brimming with reluctance. "Oh, no! Must I really burn it? Surely not!"

He nodded. "We have destroyed the scrying mirror and every mirror in the house. There is no place left for the malevolent spirit of Mariah Thraxton to hide—no place except for the portrait. It is the last remnant of her malign presence, and I fear this house will forever be under her curse until it is destroyed."

Oscar Wilde studied the portrait discriminatingly, tilting his large head this way and that. "I don't know," he mused. "I'd quite like it for my parlor. It would go well with the French sofa—" Conan Doyle silenced him with an elbow in the ribs before he could say more.

Doubt and uncertainly swept the young woman's face. She dropped the burning taper on the ground. "No. I cannot burn it. We are of the same blood. If she was wicked, then she was driven to it by the brutality of the age. I cannot judge her."

"What about Madame Zhozhovsky," Conan Doyle asked, "murdered at her behest? What of Mrs. Kragan and Seamus? Both their deaths can be laid at her feet, for Mariah's evil poisoned their minds." He stooped, picked up the still-burning taper, and held it out to Lady Thraxton. "It is a malevolence that must be destroyed. You must burn the portrait. Only then will you lift Mariah's curse from the house of Thraxton."

Lady Thraxton took the taper with a trembling hand. But as she leaned closer and extended the burning candle, a burst of foul-smelling air gusted, snuffing the flame. She gasped and looked up at Conan Doyle in fear. He snatched the taper from her hands, quickly relit it, and handed it back. But the second time she tried to light the wood, the wind gusted again and the flame went out.

"Allow me," said Wilde. He scratched a match to life on the sole of one of his ruined two guinea shoes, paused to light a Turkish cigarette, then casually tossed the burning match into the pile of wooden faggots. The kindling had been drizzled with turpentine and lit with a dull *whumph*. The portrait caught fire immediately and tongues of luminous blue flame licked up the canvas.

A piercing scream shattered the morning quiet. They shrank back from the fire, hands clamped over their ears. Within moments, the bonfire was a roaring blaze, spitting and crackling. The screaming pitched to an agonized howl as the canvas blackened and buckled in its frame and the painted eyes of Mariah Thraxton burned through, releasing gouts of orange flame. A sudden whirlwind lashed the treetops of the nearby coppice, filling the air with leaves and small branches. It swept across the courtyard and centered on the fire, where it sucked the burning canvas from its frame and tumbled it in spindizzy circles above their heads. The flames greedily devoured the image of Mariah Thraxton until the last canvas tatters disintegrated in a swarm of fiery embers. The screaming abruptly ceased, and then the whirlwind moved on, snaking across the gravel drive before it whirled away across the fields.

Calm returned, just as the sun kissed the horizon, and the first rays of dawn illuminated the limestone façade of Thraxton Hall and the stunned faces of Arthur Conan Doyle, Oscar Wilde, and the members of the Society for Psychical Research.

* * *

An hour later, several carts, traps, and a single enclosed carriage arrived to conduct the SPR members back to the Slattenmere train station. As they were loading baggage onto the carts, workmen from the village arrived toting tall ladders and began to screw tight the shutters at every window.

After a brief period of awakening, Thraxton Hall was returning to its gloomy somnolence.

"Reet, then," Young Frank said, sliding onto the wooden seat next to Conan Doyle and Wilde. This time he had loaded the cart with Wilde's extravagant surfeit of baggage without a single word of complaint. "Are we ready for the off?"

"One moment," Conan Doyle said, jumping down from the cart. "I must say a final good-bye."

He vaulted up the stone steps and plunged through the shadowy maw of the doorway. In the echoing marble entrance hall, Hope Thraxton stood waiting beneath the place where Mariah Thraxton's portrait had once hung, the space around her visibly darkening as window shutters were banged shut, and the once-banished shadows crawled back into their old familiar places.

Conan Doyle approached her hesitantly, finding himself struck speechless: a man with too much to say and no time in which to say it. But she spoke first. "I must thank you again. You have saved me."

"I am happy to hear you say that." His face lost composure as he grappled with his emotions. "I . . . you know I am not free. I am a married man. But my wife is . . . one day . . . in the near future . . ."

She touched two fingers to his lips to shush him. "I know what is in your heart. But you must live your life as it happens; do not yearn for a tomorrow that even a medium cannot predict."

At her words, all his pent-up feelings released. He dropped his head in a nod of surrender. When he had gained control of himself again, he quietly asked, "After you come into your inheritance, will you remain at Thraxton Hall?"

Hope's eyelashes fluttered. A tear fell to the marble floor. "Where else can I go?"

"You could close the house. Move to London."

She wiped away another tear and laughed bitterly. "Why? You know of my condition. It matters little where I reside. One darkness is much the same as another."

"But in London you could have friends. Receive guests. Perhaps . . . perhaps I could visit—"

She interrupted before he could finish. "I have looked into your future, Arthur. You *shall* find love . . . but not with me."

"Can you be so sure? As you once said, even to a medium the future is a glass swept by clouds and darkness."

She flashed a smile of broken melancholy. "Then let us believe that we shall meet again someday."

He swallowed the knot tightening in his throat. When he spoke again, his voice was ragged. "You *must* come to London. You *must*. I despair to think of you living alone in this place that has known so much unhappiness."

"No." She shook her head resignedly. "I must remain in Thraxton Hall and keep company with its ghosts . . . until I become one."

"I will not say good-bye. Just farewell."

She took his hand. "You *will* fare well, Arthur Conan Doyle. You are a good man, brave and kind and deserving of love. You will."

He clasped her small hand between both of his, not willing to let go. And then, with a wrench that tore him all the way to his soul, Conan Doyle drew his hands from hers and turned to walk away. As he stepped through the door of Thraxton Hall into a dazzle of morning light, he turned to look back a final time. Hope Thraxton remained in the shadowy entrance hall, but now there was a small figure standing beside her, holding her hand—a young girl in a bright blue dress.

* * *

Before they set off, Henry Sidgwick insisted they all take a vow of secrecy, promising to never reveal the events that had transpired to protect the name of a great English family. Conan Doyle thought of his Casebook and the astonishing revelations he would never be able to share with the world—at least, during his lifetime.

The two friends rode side by side on the front seat of Frank Carter's wagon. Lost in his own thoughts, Conan Doyle said little during the journey. Even Oscar Wilde was uncharacteristically quiet.

As the wagon reached the gnarled hanging tree at Gallows Hill, they found a ragged-tailed crow lying dead in the road in a sprawl of wings, its black claws curled around nothing.

At the sight, both friends exchanged a wordless look that spoke volumes.

THE GRAND REVEAL

White clouds billowed and swirled. The railway engine's brakes released with a metallic clunk and the train lurched forward as the small Slattenmere station reversed away. Arthur Conan Doyle and Oscar Wilde were once more ensconced in a first-class carriage—this time the 10:45 train bound for London. The Scottish author stared blindly out the window, oblivious to the Lancashire countryside as the station fell behind and the green monotony of fields whizzed past.

"You're still back there, aren't you, Arthur? Back at Thraxton Hall?"

It took a moment for Conan Doyle to recognize he was being addressed. He started, sitting up straight before glancing over at his friend. "What? Oh. Oh, no," Conan Doyle hurried to reply. It was a lie. His mind contained nothing but the almond curve of Hope Thraxton's eyes, the soft crimson pillows of her lips.

"Still," Wilde said, rising from his seat, "not to worry." He opened one of his suitcases and began to sort through clothes. He paused and smiled toothily at his friend. "Soon you will be home with your beloved Touie."

"Yes," Conan Doyle agreed, offering up a sad grin. But Wilde had conjured visions of his wife. Having her in his mind after only a moment ago thinking of Hope scalded him with his own infidelity—albeit infidelity only in thought.

Wilde held up a pomegranite red shirt for appraisal. "What do you think, Arthur? This with a black jacket, a white cravat, and an opera cloak thrown about my shoulders? Oscar Wilde has been on a supernatural adventure. I wish to exude a sense of mystery when I alight from the train in London."

Conan Doyle frowned skeptically. "Oh, I hardly think anyone will be waiting for us, Oscar."

Wilde chuckled. "Au contraire, Arthur, I have little doubt there will be throngs. After all, I had young Frank ride fifty miles to the nearest village with a telegraph apparatus to wire the newspapers and a dozen friends of mine. They have been told to spread word of our arrival. If crowds do not choke Waterloo Station, I shall be eternally miffed."

Ten minutes later, Wilde had finished dressing. "I shall go and perambulate the corridor to gauge the effect of this wardrobe choice on the second-class passengers." He slid open the door, pausing a moment to draw on a slouch hat and tug it down at a dramatic angle over one eye. "Whilst I am gone, Arthur, try not to get into any trouble."

Conan Doyle grunted a response. Wilde flashed a devious grin and disappeared.

But as soon as his friend left, Hope Thraxton swam up in the Scottish author's mind. He imagined her, a solitary figure pacing the long, gloomy corridors of Thraxton Hall, dressed in a black silk gown, drawing behind her a train sewn of shadows. He thought of his dead father, his dying wife, and of the terrible uncertainty of life. And though he tried not to, he could not help it when his thoughts veered into the future.

I have made a vow to Touie, but she will not live much longer. . . .

It was a horrible, shameful thought, and he lacerated himself for it.

The carriage door opened. Conan Doyle pulled his eyes from the window, expecting his friend. But it was not Oscar Wilde, and it took a few moments for his mind to register. The figure was wearing a white military uniform and a peaked cap. The face beneath the cap was hidden behind a white leather mask.

The Count.

The figure paused to lock the carriage door, and then, inexplicably, drew down the blinds over the corridor windows. When the Count turned around, Conan Doyle saw that he was clutching the black Webley and now he took a seat opposite Conan Doyle, the pistol leveled at his face.

"What the devil?"

"I zink zat you like me not very much," the Count said in his thick Eastern European accent.

Conan Doyle's mind was racing. His service revolver was packed with his belongings; he doubted whether the Count would mind waiting while he rummaged his suitcase for it. "I suppose this means you were in league with Seamus Kragan all along?"

The Count slowly shook his head. "I zink you misunderstand me in all ways, Doctor Doyle."

The masked face turned slightly at a sharp knock on the carriage door. The Count rose, keeping the pistol trained on Conan Doyle, and flipped off the lock. Wilde entered, glancing only momentarily at the Count. "Ah, I see you two have met." To Conan Doyle's astonishment, Wilde sat down on the seat next to the Count, crossed his legs nonchalantly, and began to light up a cigarette.

"What? So . . . so you . . . Oscar . . . How? . . . I—"

"You may write about Sherlock Holmes," Wilde said coldly, "but it's obvious that you fall far short of your fictional hero's legendary skills at sleuthing."

Conan Doyle could only gape, befuddled.

Wilde fixed Conan Doyle with a mirthless and deadly stare. But after a few long seconds, his shoulders began to shake and finally he could hold it in no more, throwing back his head and laughing uproariously. "Your face, Arthur—" he choked between laughs. "Oh, if only you could see your face. . . ."

Wilde chortled for several minutes, and when the gales of hilarity finally died down, he reached across and patted his friend on the knee. "I am sorry, old stick, perhaps I took that joke a bit too far." He glanced at the Count. "I don't think we need that pistol anymore." Without a word, the Count slipped the Webley back into its shiny leather holster.

"And now, I think it is time for the grand reveal."

The Count rose to his feet and drew off the military cap. The hair beneath was coppery red like the beard, combed back and stiffened with pomade. But then the Count slipped his fingers beneath the hairline, peeled it up, and drew off a wig. Next came the beard and moustache, and finally the white leather mask, and Conan Doyle gasped to find that the Count was not a *he* after all, but an androgynous beauty with the face of a Raphaelite angel.

"You have already met George," Wilde said.

Conan Doyle gaped with astonishment. "All this while. You never said! You never let on! How did you do it?"

"When you told me of the Society," Wilde explained, "I wrote to them as the Count of Borovania, an Eastern European country which does not exist—I confess I stole the idea of the watermarked paper and used a Prussian double eagle. The SPR were delighted to entertain a guest of Eastern nobility. I kitted out George with military togs from one of Bram Stoker's theatrical productions and, *voila*, the Count was born. I know you think I am indolent and self-indulgent—and while that is true—I was actually keeping watch on you all the time. George here was my eyes and ears." The Irishman placed a hand to his chest and bowed his head theatrically.

As George fluffed up her short blond hair, and complained about the itchiness of the wig, Wilde turned to her and said, "George has served us admirably well, but it is time to put him away. I believe Arthur will be more comfortable if Georgina accompanies us the rest of the way home."

The young woman laughed gaily and sprang to her feet. She threw open one of Wilde's suitcases and drew out a long dress. When she began to unbutton her shirt, Conan Doyle quickly turned his back to preserve modesty, although once or twice he caught a reflection in the carriage window that snatched the breath from his lungs.

"You may turn around, Arthur," Wilde said finally.

When Conan Doyle turned to look, George had utterly vanished. In his place stood a ravishing beauty: Georgina.

"It is a pleasure to meet you again, Doctor Doyle." The actress spoke in the cut-glass accent she affected in Wilde's drawing room comedies. She curtsied and batted her long lashes coquettishly. "I do hope you will like me better than the horrid old Count."

The transformation was stunning. Arched eyebrows framed a pretty face with powdered peach cheekbones; her lips were a succulent kiss of cherry rouge. She wore, once again, the ash blond wig that sent ringlets tumbling down about her shoulders. Her willowy frame was draped in a white silk gown that revealed narrow hips and a modest but surprising bosom.

"Yes," Wilde said, catching the direction and intent of Conan Doyle's baffled gaze. "Where *did* she hide that?" He had a long linen bandage tossed about his neck like a scarf and now he drew it off and dangled it under his friend's nose. "An old theatrical trick," Wilde explained. "From the time when women actors were proscribed from treading the boards and had to bind their, ah . . . *feminine* attributes."

"I—I—I see," Conan Doyle stuttered, cheeks reddening. "I mean . . . yes . . . of course." And all the while he spoke, he thought of the vision of the angel that had freed him from the coffin and kissed him back to life. Georgina was *that* angel.

The remaining hours of the train journey passed easily. The three friends formed an intimate troika, comfortable in their silence. Conan Doyle sat scribbling the denoument of their adventure in his Casebook, his pen raising the ghosts of Thraxton Hall and once again laying them. At last, he jotted the final postscript, signed *Arthur Conan Doyle* and the date, *April 14, 1894*, across the bottom of the page. Then he closed the Casebook, folded over the leather strap, and snapped the lock shut. He glanced at the seat opposite where Wilde and Georgina now conversed in bantering tones as they played cards—Wilde finally had the chance to play that game of cribbage he had so longed for.

As Conan Doyle replaced the Casebook in his portfolio, another leather-bound volume spilled out—the exact twin of the first. He could not remember why he had thought to fetch two, but now he eased out the book of blank pages. Then, for some reason he could not fully fathom, he drew out his pen and carefully inscribed upon the cover, *Book 2*, adding a colon, which hovered like a question spoken aloud, begging to be answered.

The carriage jolted and swayed, drawing Conan Doyle's gaze out the window. The train leaned into a curving sweep of track, rewarding the passengers with their first glimpse of London in the distance. Vast and imposing, the Capital City brooded beneath a troubled sky. As if in some Blakean vision, shafts of golden light slanted down from holes rent in the leaden clouds, limning the dome of St. Paul's and the tallest church spires rising from the huddle of soot-blackened buildings and factory chimneys.

They had been gone for less than a week, but in that time the travelers had journeyed to a dominion where the rational world dissolved into the irrational. There, they had looked out upon the abyss and returned forever changed by their ordeal. Now London, a place once familiar, seemed strange and alien.

Conan Doyle thought of the struggling mass of humanity trampling its streets, thriving in its great houses, starving in its cold, stone alleyways, and suddenly realized the truth of his father's madhouse vision—all around them lurked an invisible realm of weird and uncanny presences and . . . occasionally . . . those worlds intersected.

Conan Doyle gripped the leather Casebook in his hands. "The game is afoot, Arthur," he muttered quietly to no one. And he knew that—for Wilde and himself—the adventure was just beginning.

AUTHOR'S NOTE

While I have aimed for historical accuracy wherever possible, this is very much a work of fiction and, like the master storyteller himself, Conan Doyle, I never let facts get in the way of a good story. As such, I have taken certain liberties for dramatic purposes. It is no fiction, however, that Conan Doyle and Wilde really were friends and admirers of one another's work. They belonged to an elite social circle of dazzling artistic talent, which included J.M. Barrie (author of *Peter Pan*) and *Dracula* author, Bram Stoker, as well as many famous painters and actors of the day, such as James McNeill Whistler and Sarah Bernhardt, to name-drop but a few.

The time frame of this novel was indeed one of the most turbulent periods in Conan Doyle's life. His beloved wife, Louise, was diagnosed with consumption (tuberculosis), and his father, Charles Altamount Doyle, an esteemed painter and illustrator in his day, died in an insane asylum after years of battling alcoholism. It was also the year Conan Doyle chose to kill off Sherlock Holmes, a move that sparked public outrage and caused readers of *The Strand Magazine* to cancel their subscriptions en masse. Many Londoners donned black armbands as a visual protest and sign of mourning.

Although the correct spelling is Daniel Dunglas *Home*, his

322 ᐸ AUTHOR'S NOTE

name is pronounced *Hume*. The spelling was changed to make things easier for the reader. While Conan Doyle actually met the "Yankee psychic" (and attended a number of séances conducted by him), Home died from tuberculosis in 1886, eight years prior to the action of the novel. Although his psychic abilities (including mediumship, telekenesis, and levitation) were tested by respected scientists of the time, Home was never caught faking.

Founded in 1882, The Society for Psychical Research boasted many prominent Victorian scientists and philosophers among its members and thrives to this day (http://www.spr.ac.uk/).

Some characters in this novel (such as Madame Zhozhovsky) are composites of actual historical figures. I must also point out that Sir William Crookes was one of the most brilliant scientists of his day and may or may not have had a penchant for top-drawer scotch. Lastly, although he was reputedly an excellent swimmer, Frank Podmore really did die from drowning as Madame Zhozhovksy foretold.

* * *

Thank you for purchasing this book. Arthur Conan Doyle and Oscar Wilde will return for the second book in the series, *The Dead Assassin.*

More information about this and other works can be found on the author's Web site: www.vaughnentwistle.com.